By Christine Feehan

Dark Prince • Dark Desire • Dark Gold
Dark Magic • Dark Challenge
Dark Fire • Dark Legend • Dark Guardian
Dark Symphony • Dark Melody • Dark Destiny
Dark Secret • Dark Demon • Dark Celebration
Dark Possession • Dark Hunger • Dark Curse
Dark Slayer • Dark Peril

Wild Rain • Burning Wild • Wild Fire

Magic in the Wind • The Twilight Before Christmas
Oceans of Fire • Dangerous Tides
Safe Harbor • Turbulent Sea
Hidden Currents

Waterbound

Shadow Game • Mind Game • Night Game
Conspiracy Game • Deadly Game
Predatory Game • Murder Game • Street Game

Lair of the Lion • The Scarletti Curse

CHRISTINE FEEHAN

DARK DESTINY

A CARPATHIAN NOVEL

AVONBOOKS

An Imprint of HarperCollins*Publishers*

DARK DESTINY. Copyright © 2004 by Christine Feehan. All rights reserved. Printed in the United States of America. No part of this book may be used or reproduced in any manner whatsoever without written permission except in the case of brief quotations embodied in critical articles and reviews. For information, address HarperCollins Publishers, 195 Broadway, New York, NY 10007.

First Avon Books mass market printing: July 2010

Print Edition ISBN: 978-0-06-316142-9
Digital Edition ISBN: 978-0-06-201647-8

MIX
Paper from
responsible sources
FSC
www.fsc.org   FSC® C021394

Cover design by Amy Halperin
Cover art by Patrick Kang
Cover photographs © Shutterstock

Printed in Lithuania

21 22 23 24 25 SB 10 9 8 7 6 5 4 3 2 1

*This book was written for so many people.
First of all, two men who have dedicated themselves
to a way of life. George Chadwick, sixth Dan Black,
Korean Tang Soo Do; and Roberto Macias,
fourth Dan Black, Korean Tang Soo Do.*

*For Gayle Fillman, fifth Go Dan, World Aikido Federation,
and her unfailing dedication to providing
a safe training area and a refuge for women in need.*

*These wonderful, dedicated people have always
reached out to women in difficult circumstances.
Without their guidance and continual support
I would not have learned the things necessary to
help the women whose lives I touched.
Thank you for your generosity and caring
on behalf of so many you helped and
probably were never even aware that you did.*

*For Anita, Billie Jo and all the others who rose out
of the ashes to become someone special,
giving your time to so many in need.*

*A special acknowledgment to Judy Albert and
my sister Ruth Powell, for sitting up until all hours of the
morning, talking shop with me and working out the kinks.*

Thank you all.

DARK
DESTINY

Chapter One

She woke to the knowledge that she was a murderess and that she would kill again. It was the only reason she continued her existence. It was what she lived for. To kill. Pain and hunger crawled through her body endlessly, relentlessly. She lay very still with the earth surrounding her, staring up at the star-studded night sky. It was bitterly cold. She was bitterly cold, the blood flowing in her veins like ice water, like acid that burned it was so cold.

Call me to you. I will warm you.

She closed her eyes as the voice slipped into her head. He called to her on every rising now. The voice of an angel. The heart of the demon. Her savior. Her mortal enemy. Very slowly she allowed breath to seep into her lungs, her heart to take up its steady beating. Another endless night. There had been so many, and all she wanted was rest.

She floated out of the ground, clothing herself with the ease of long practice, her body clean, where her soul was damned. The sounds and smells of the night were all around her, whispers and scents that flooded her senses with information. She was hungry. She needed to go into the city. As hard as she tried, she could not overcome the need for rich, hot blood. It beckoned and called to her as nothing else could.

Destiny found herself in a familiar part of the city. Her body traveled the accustomed path before she had even thought where she was going. The small church tucked among the rising buildings and maze of narrow streets and alleyways beckoned to her. She knew this neighborhood, this small city within the larger city. The buildings were stacked on top of each other, some touching, others with narrow pathways between them. She was familiar with each and every apartment and office building. She knew the occupants and she knew their secrets. She watched over them, watched over their lives, yet she was always alone, always apart.

Reluctantly Destiny climbed the steps to the church and stood at the entrance as she had so many times in the past. With her acute hearing, she knew the building was occupied, that the priest was finishing his duties and would soon be leaving. He was much later than usual.

She heard the rustle of the priest's robes as he moved through the church to the double doors. He would lock them—he always locked them before he left—but it wouldn't matter, Destiny could open them easily enough. She waited in the darkness, deep in the shadows where she belonged, watching the priest in silence, nearly holding her breath. There was an urgency inside her, a desperation. She returned again and again to the beauty of the small church. Something drew her, called to her, nearly as strongly as the call for blood. Sometimes she believed this was where she was supposed to die; other times she thought repentance might be enough. She always went to the church when she knew she had no choice but to feed.

The priest stood for a moment just outside the doors, looking around him, his eyes adjusting to the darkness. He actually looked right at her, but she knew she was invisible to him. He started to speak, hesitated, and made the sign of the cross in her direction. Destiny held her breath, waited for a lightning bolt to strike her. "Find peace, my child," the priest murmured softly and made his way down the stairs with his slow, measured tread. She remained in the shadows, as still as the mountains rising above the city. How had he sensed her presence? She waited until long after he had gone down the block and turned into the narrow alley leading to the garden behind his rectory. Only then did she dare to let her breath out slowly, to breathe again.

Destiny went to the ornate double doors, but this time they weren't locked. She looked back to the street where the priest had disappeared around the corner. He knew, then. He knew she needed his church, and he had silently given his permission for her to enter the sacred, hallowed place. He didn't know what she was, but he was a good man and he believed all souls could be saved. She pushed open the doors with a trembling hand.

Destiny stood in the doorway of the empty church, wrapped in darkness, her only ally. She shivered, not from the cold air surrounding her, but from the ice deep within her soul. Despite the pitch-black interior, Destiny could easily see every detail of the church's beauty. She stared at the crucifix over the altar for a long time, her mind in turmoil. Pain crawled through her as it did every moment of her existence. Hunger was sharp and ravenous. Shame was her constant companion. Destiny had come to this sacred place to confess her sins. She was a murderess, and she would kill again and again. It would be her way of life until she found the courage to destroy the evil thing that she had become. She dared not enter, dared not ask for sanctuary.

She stood for a long moment in silence with a terrible unfamiliar burning behind her eyes. It took her a few moments to realize the sensation was tears. She wanted to weep, but what was the use of it? She had learned that tears brought the echo of ugly, demonic laughter, and she had taught herself not to cry. Never to cry.

Why do you insist on suffering? The voice was deceptively beautiful. Male. Gentle. A soothing blend of masculine exasperation and charm. *I feel your pain; it is sharp and terrible and pierces my heart like an arrow. Call me to your side. I will come to you at once. You know I can do no other. Call out to me.* There was an underlying whisper of power, of compulsion. *You know me. You have always known me.*

The voice brushed at the walls of her mind like the flutter of butterfly wings. It whispered over her skin, seeped into her pores and wrapped itself around her heart. She breathed the voice into her lungs until she needed to answer, to hear it again. To call out. To obey. She needed that voice. It had kept her alive. It had kept her sane. It had also taught her things—hideous, murderous things, but necessary.

I feel your need. Why do you insist on silence? You hear me, just as I feel you when your pain becomes too much to be borne.

Destiny shook her head, a firm denial against the

temptation of that voice. The movement sent her thick mane of rich dark hair flying in all directions. She wanted to rid her mind of the deceptive purity of that voice. Nothing could induce her to answer. She would not ever be trapped by a beguiling voice again. She had learned that lesson the hard way, sentenced to a living hell she dared not think about.

Destiny forced air into her lungs, controlling her emotions, knowing that there was a chance the hunter could trace her through the sharpness of her despair. A movement in the nearby shadows had her whirling around, crouching low, a dangerous predator ready to attack.

There was a silence, and then once again movement. A woman moved up the steps of the church slowly, coming into Destiny's line of vision. She was tall and elegant with flawless coffee-cream skin and hair the color of bittersweet chocolate. Her hair curled in every direction, a riot of shiny spirals spilling down to her neck, framing her oval face. Her large brown eyes probed the darker shadows, searching for signs that she was not alone.

Destiny used preternatural speed, slipping deep into the recesses of the corner alcove, back away from the church doors, using stillness to her advantage. She froze in place, hardly daring to breathe.

The woman walked to the double doors, stood for a moment, one hand resting on the edge of the open door. She sighed softly. "I came here looking for you. My name is MaryAnn Delaney. I know you know who I am. I know you come here sometimes—I've seen you. I saw you tonight and I know you're here." She waited a heartbeat. Two. "Somewhere," she whispered aloud, as if talking to herself.

Destiny pressed her body so tightly against the side of the church, her skin hurt. They were both in terrible danger, but only one of them was aware of it.

"I know you're here; please don't run away again," MaryAnn said softly. Despite her thick jacket, she rubbed her arms to ward off the cold. "Just talk with me. I have so much to say to you, so much to thank you for." Her voice was low, gentle, as if she were speaking to a wild thing, coaxing it to trust her.

There was a terrible tightness in Destiny's chest. She was choking, suffocating, hardly able to breathe. She waited a heartbeat. Two. Drew deeper into the shadows. She could hear the sound of her own heart beating. She could hear MaryAnn's heart following the rhythm of hers. She could hear the beckoning invitation of the ebb and flow of blood rushing through veins. Calling to her. Intensifying her terrible hunger. Her tongue felt the sharpness of her lengthening incisors. She trembled with the effort to control herself, to stop the inevitable.

This woman was everything that she was not. Mary-Ann Delaney. Destiny knew her well. She was compassionate and brave, her life dedicated to helping others. A light seemed to shine from her very soul. Destiny listened to her often—her lectures, her group discussions, even her one-on-one counseling sessions. Destiny had appointed herself MaryAnn's unofficial protector.

"You saved my life. A few weeks ago, when that man broke into my home and attacked me, you came in and saved me. I know you were hurt—there was blood on your clothes—but when the paramedics came, you were gone." MaryAnn closed her eyes for a moment, reliving the terror of waking up to find a furious man standing over her bed. He had dragged her out from under the covers by her hair, punching her so hard and so fast she had no time to defend herself. He was the husband of a woman she had helped escape into a sanctuary and he was determined to get the address from her. He had pounded her into a bloody heap on the floor, kicking her and then stabbing at her with a large knife. She had the raw scars on her arms where she had tried to protect herself. "I didn't tell anyone you were there. I didn't say a word about you to the police. They thought he must have tripped over the overturned furniture and fallen awkwardly and broken his neck. I didn't betray you. There's no need to worry; the police aren't looking for you. They don't know anything about you."

Destiny bit down hard on her lip and stubbornly remained silent. Fortunately, the incisors had receded. She had enough sins on her soul without adding Mary-Ann to the list of her victims.

"Please answer me." MaryAnn opened her arms wide. "I don't understand why you won't talk to me. What harm could there be in telling me if you were hurt that night? There was blood all over you, and it wasn't from me and it wasn't his blood."

Destiny felt tears burning in her eyes, clogging her throat. Her hands clenched into two tight fists. "It wasn't my blood. You don't owe me anything." The words were strangled, barely making it past the lump in her throat. It was partially the truth. MaryAnn's attacker had not put a scratch on her. "I'm just sorry I wasn't there earlier, before he hurt you."

"He would have killed me. We both know that. My life isn't the only thing I have you to thank for. You're the one who leaves me the money for our safe houses,

aren't you?" MaryAnn pursued. "And our women's recovery programs."

Destiny leaned against the wall, tired of pain, tired of
being so alone. There was something incredibly warming and soothing about MaryAnn. "It's no big deal, it's
just money. You do all the work. I'm happy to help in
some small way."

"Come home with me," MaryAnn said. "I'll make us
tea, and we can talk." When Destiny remained silent,
MaryAnn sighed softly. "At least tell me your name.
I feel your presence often and think of you as a friend.
What would it hurt to tell me your name?"

"I don't want the ugliness of my life to touch you,"
Destiny admitted softly. The night was enfolding her as
it always did, gently whispering to her so that she saw
its beauty despite her determination not to see anything
good in it.

"I'm not afraid of ugliness," MaryAnn persisted. "I've
seen ugliness before, I will again. No one is meant to be
alone in the world. We all need someone, even you."

"You aren't making this easy." The words were
wrenched from Destiny, almost a sob. "You don't know
how evil I am. There is no redemption for me. I should
never have allowed our lives to touch, not even for a
moment."

"I'm very grateful that you did. I wouldn't be here
otherwise, and I have much to live for."

Destiny pressed her palm to her mouth, ashamed that
her hand was trembling. "You're different from me.
You're good, you help so many people."

MaryAnn nodded her agreement. "Yes, I do, and without you, I would never have been able to help another

woman or child. You've done that, not me. I couldn't have saved myself; I'd be dead right now."

"That's twisted logic," Destiny pointed out, but she found a small smile hovering on her lips in spite of the pain knifing through her. She had heard MaryAnn talk with other women many times, her voice always gentle and understanding. MaryAnn always knew the right thing to say to set her clients at ease. She was using that same gift on Destiny. "My name is Destiny." Her name sounded strange to her own ears, it had been so long since she had heard it. Saying it aloud was almost frightening.

MaryAnn smiled, her teeth very pretty, her smile contagious. "I'm so pleased to meet you. I'm MaryAnn." She stepped forward and held out her hand.

Before she could stop herself, Destiny gripped the outstretched hand. It was the first time in a very long while that she had touched a human being. Her heart slammed painfully in her chest and she jerked away, sliding back into the shadows. "I can't do this," she whispered. It was too painful to look into those clear eyes, to feel MaryAnn's warmth. It was easier to be alone, to hide in the shadows, forever a night creature.

MaryAnn stood quietly, faintly shocked by the extraordinary beauty of the young woman hiding in the shadows. She was smaller than MaryAnn had first thought—not short, but not tall either. She had lush curves, but her body was sculpted by muscle. Her hair was thick, wild, a mass of dark silk. Her face was arresting, her eyes enormous, haunted, long-lashed and mesmerizing. They were a vivid, brilliant blue-green, holding shadows and secrets and unimaginable pain. Even her mouth was sculpted and inviting. But she had much more than physical beauty. There was a subtle allure that Mary-Ann had never seen before in a woman. The voice was musical, mysterious, compelling. Mystical. Everything about Destiny was different. Unexpected.

"Of course you can do this. We're only talking, Destiny. What's the harm in talking? I was feeling a little lonely tonight and I knew I had to see you." MaryAnn took a step toward the shadows that held Destiny, wanting to ease the terrible despair on that beautiful face. She had seen trauma many times, but those enormous aquamarine eyes were haunted beyond anything Mary-Ann had ever known. Those eyes had seen things that should never have been seen. Monstrous things.

Destiny allowed her breath to leave her lungs in a little rush. "Do you know how many times I've watched you wield your magic on a woman in need? You have a gift for giving hope to someone who has stopped believing there is hope. If you think you owe me, you don't. You've saved my life many times over; you just haven't been aware of it. I listen to you often, and your words are the only thing in this world that make sense to me anymore."

"I'm glad, then." MaryAnn pulled gloves from her jacket pocket and drew them over her delicate hands to protect them from the biting cold. "You know, at times everyone feels alone and hopeless. Even I do. We all need friends. If you are uncomfortable coming to my home, perhaps we could get a drink at the Midnight Marathon. It's always a bit noisy in there. Would it really be so terrible to come and have a cup of tea with me? It isn't as if you're committing to a long-term relationship." There was an edge of humor to her voice, an invitation to join her in shared amusement.

"Tea? I haven't had a cup of tea in years." Destiny pressed a hand to her stomach. Her entire being wanted to bask in MaryAnn's company, but her stomach rolled at the idea of forcing herself to appear normal. She could only imagine the disgust and horror in Mary-Ann's eyes if she learned the truth.

"Then I would say it's time. Come home with me," MaryAnn invited softly, obviously pleased.

The wind rushed over the steps toward the doors of the church, flinging up leaves and twigs. Above their heads the clouds began to spin dark threads. There was something more, something in the wind that tugged gently at their clothes and hair, while it rustled alarmingly in the trees and bushes. It was almost like a voice softly murmuring to them. Calling, whispering, just out of reach. MaryAnn strained to listen, turning her head this way and that to catch the sound.

Destiny leapt at her, her breath coming out in a slow hiss of warning. She caught MaryAnn's thick jacket by the lapel, at the same time jerking the doors of the church open wider. She thrust MaryAnn inside. "Listen to me." Destiny stared directly into the other woman's eyes. "You will not leave this church until morning. No matter what you hear or see, you will not leave this church." She spoke the command firmly, burying in the other woman's subconscious a compulsion to obey.

Destiny sensed the danger behind her and whirled, going low, attempting to jerk her shoulder out of harm's way. She had spent precious seconds ensuring that MaryAnn was safe, and despite her incredible speed, long, razor-sharp nails ripped her arm open from shoulder to elbow. She was already moving, sweeping with her leg as she did so, scoring a solid hit.

From far away came the soft familiar voice that so often summoned her in an ancient tongue. *Call me to you now!* It was a command, nothing less, as if he had felt her physical pain and knew she was in danger.

Destiny firmly closed off her mind to everything but the coming battle. She focused completely, watching the undead with an unblinking, predatory stare. She was still, balanced on the balls of her feet, her breath moving evenly in and out of her lungs. Vampire. Creature of the night. Hideous monster. Mortal enemy.

Her assailant was tall and slender with gray-white skin and black hair. His teeth gleamed at her as he faced her. "Call the other woman to us." The voice was low, musical, gentle, a subtle invitation.

Destiny rushed at him, straight as an arrow, whipping a dagger from a sheath between her shoulder blades, going straight for his heart. The move was totally unexpected. He thought his voice had enthralled her, that she would obey. And she was a woman. The last thing expected of a woman was for her to attack. It was usually the element of surprise that enabled Destiny to be victorious.

The blade sank into his chest, yet he managed to slam his talons into her injured shoulder, raking deep furrows into her flesh as he leapt backward. He dissolved instantly into a greenish vapor and streamed through the night away from the city. Droplets of red mixed with the green, leaving a toxic, venomous trail for Destiny to follow. Deliberately she inhaled the noxious scent so she would know him anywhere.

She heard the echo of that familiar male voice deep inside her mind, her soul, a cry of denial followed immediately by a strange warmth. The wounds in her shoulder burned, but she was used to pain and shut it out. The strange melodic chanting of words in an ancient tongue shimmered in her mind and provided her with some solace. Still, she couldn't ignore the blood streaming from her body. She had not fed in several days and needed sustenance. Mixing the rich soil from the priest's garden with her own healing saliva, she packed the gaping lacerations. Very carefully, deliberately, she braided her hair in preparation for battle. Before she followed the undead to his lair, she needed to feed. The city was filled with the homeless, with unfortunate creatures who would have no chance to escape her, even in her weakened condition.

Nicolae Von Shrieder hunkered down atop the massive cliff overlooking the city. He was closer this time than he had ever been. He was certain of it. She was out there somewhere, tired and hurt and vulnerable, fighting her war alone. He felt her pain every moment of his waking hours. When he closed his eyes on the rising sun, he felt gut-wrenching agony crawling through her body, through his body.

Patience. He had learned patience in a hard school. Centuries of living had taught him discipline and patience above all else. He was an ancient with powerful gifts, yet he could not bend her to his will. He could not summon her to him. He had taught her well. Too well.

Far off, he heard the cry of a raptor, a high keening alerting him, and he lifted his face toward the stars. Very slowly he straightened, rising to his full height. "I thank you, my brother," he murmured softly. The wind caught his voice and whipped it out, carrying the soft sound through the dense treetops and taking it further, over the city. "Our hunt begins, then."

He would never forget the shocking moment when she had first connected with him. A child in sheer terror. Her pain and agony had been so sharp, so acute and overwhelming, her young mind had reached across time and space to merge with him. Mind to mind. Even as a child, she had been a powerful psychic. The images he received from her had been so vivid, so detailed, he had lived the nightmare with her, through her. The brutal slaying of her parents, the monster draining their blood in front of the child.

He closed his eyes against the memories, but they flooded his mind as she so often had. He had been continents away, with no way of tracking her, finding her. Yet he lived with her through the repeated cruelties, the beatings, through the countless rapes and murders she had been forced to witness. She had crawled into her mind, seeking refuge, and found him there. He whispered to her, distracted her, shared his knowledge with her. A mere child taught to kill. He had no other gift to give her. No other way of saving her.

Those were hideous years, years of hopeless seeking. The world was a very large place when one was looking for one small child. He was an ancient, sworn to protect mortals and immortals alike. A powerful being, a hunter and destroyer of the vampire, sent out centuries earlier by his prince, sworn to rid the world of such evil. He had tried to tell her there was a difference between vampire and hunter, but in his mind, she saw his battles, his kills. She saw the darkness in him, spreading like a stain over his soul. And she was afraid to put her trust in him.

Nicolae stood completely still, raw power clinging to his muscular frame as he presented his leather-clad arm to his traveling companion. The large owl circled overhead once, a lazy spiral, then plummeted fast, talons outstretched. The raptor landed on Nicolae's forearm, and Nicolae bent his head toward its wicked beak. "You've picked up the scent of our prey."

The round, beady eyes that stared back at him were filled with intelligence. The bird flapped its wings, once, twice, as if in answer, then launched itself into the air. Nicolae stared after it, a faint smile in no way softening the hard edge of his mouth. She was hurt. She was chasing a vampire and she was injured.

There was no denying the connection between them, yet she refused to acknowledge him, to answer him. He had no idea how she could be so strong when she lived with such constant pain, but he could do no other than find her. He had never seen her, nor had she spoken to him, mind to mind or otherwise, yet he felt he would know her the moment he laid eyes on her.

He turned slowly, his body tall and muscular, a blend of elegance and sinew. The wind tugged at his long hair, black as a raven's wing, so that he drew it to the nape of his neck and secured it with a leather thong. There was a fluid, animal quality to his movements as he stretched, lifted his nose to scent the wind.

It had been many long centuries since Vladimer Dubrinsky, the Prince of Nicolae's people, had sent his warriors into the world to hunt the vampire. Nicolae, like so many others, had been sent far from his homeland without comfort of native soil or brethren. He had accepted that he would have no hope of finding a lifemate, but his duty to his people in those dire days had been clear. That bleak time had been filled with battles, with killing. The darkness had spread slowly, Nicolae fighting it every inch of the way. A new Prince had taken Vladimer's place and still Nicolae fought on. Alone. Enduring. Deep within him, the inevitable darkness had spread, consuming him until he knew he could wait no longer. He would have to seek the dawn, to end his own existence, or he would become the very thing he had hunted. And then she had entered his life. Back then, she had been a terrified child in desperate need. Now she was a lethal fighting machine.

Nicolae stood above the city and stared down at the lights twinkling like so many stars. "Where are you?" he murmured aloud. "I am close to you. I feel you near to me this time. Finally I am in the vicinity of your lair—I know I am."

She had entered his life so many long years ago. They had lived in each other's minds while a depraved monster had tortured a helpless little girl. Nicolae had forced himself to feel what she felt, refusing to leave her alone in her living hell. He had made the decision to train her when he could not find a way to get her to speak with him. And he had succeeded, all too well, in teaching her to kill. Where once violence had been his world, now his entire existence was dedicated to finding her. In a way, she had been his salvation.

Nicolae stepped off the edge of the cliff. Easily. Casually. Dissolving into mist as he did so. He streaked through the sky on the trail of the vampire, following the owl as it moved quickly through the night.

Nicolae had formulated a loose plan of action. When he found the young woman, he would take her to his homeland, take her before the Prince, Vladimer's son, Mikhail Dubrinsky. Surely the healers would find a way to help her. A vampire had converted her, made her a creature of the night, and the tainted blood flowing in her veins was an acid that burned her day and night. The young child had grown into a woman, honed in the fires of hell, filled with the battle experience of an ancient. Nicolae had imparted that knowledge to her, techniques only one of his kind should have. He had helped to create her; he needed to find a way to heal her.

The scent of the undead was a foul stench to Nicolae, even as the vampire tried desperately to mask his presence from the hunters. The trail led through the city itself, deep in its underbelly where there were no streetlights and no nice homes. Dogs barked as Nicolae passed overhead, but no one took notice. And then he caught the other scent. Drops of blood mingled with the vampire's spoor.

It was the woman, he was certain of it. His woman. He had come to think of her as belonging to him and he'd found, over the years, he was possessive of her. Like other males of his kind, he had long since become accustomed to feeling no emotion, yet at times he felt little flares of unexpected jealousy and fear on her behalf. He wondered if he was feeling her emotions as he shared her mind, but he had no answers. In truth, it didn't matter to him.

The only thing that mattered was finding her. He had no other choice. She had become his savior, even as he was attempting to save her.

He noticed where the huntress had broken away from the vampire's trail and veered off into the city. Nicolae knew immediately she was seeking blood. She had wounds, and she probably had not fed in several days.

He found her prey in an alley between two buildings. The man was young and muscular, half sitting against the wall, a small smile on his face. His head lolled slightly when Nicolae bent to examine him, but his lashes fluttered. The man was alive.

Nicolae knew he should be relieved to see she had not killed her prey, only taken what was necessary from him as he had so painstakingly drilled into her, but in truth, he wanted to throttle the man. Entering his mind, Nicolae learned she had lured him to her with a promise of paradise, with a sexy enticing smile, and her victim had willingly followed her.

The owl called to him impatiently from the roof of a building to his left. They were hunting, it reminded him. Nicolae was alarmed by his own lack of discipline. Initially he had wondered if the female child might be his lifemate when they had connected so strongly, but over the years, when she steadfastly refused to speak to him, he had decided it must not be so. Yet now, considering his odd reaction to her male prey, he wondered again.

Carpathian males lost all emotions and the ability to see in color by the time they turned two hundred, and so it had been for him. It was a bleak existence, relying on one's integrity to live honorably until a lifemate could be found. Only a true lifemate, the other half of each male's soul, could restore emotion and color to him. All the while the insidious temptation to feel for just one moment beckoned the males. If they succumbed and chose to kill while feeding, they became the very thing they hunted—the vampire.

Nicolae took to the air, streaking away from temptation. Away from the young man who had been close to her. The young man who had felt her body against his body. Felt the warmth of her breath on his throat. Her lips moving sensuously over his skin. The erotic, white-hot bite of pleasure/pain. A red haze, treacherous and blazing out of control, slipped into his head, making it nearly impossible to think clearly. Nicolae had the sudden urge to go back and rip out the man's throat. The desire burned hot and bright, his gut clenching and a strange roaring filling his ears, his mind. He turned in midair.

The owl changed direction, flying toward his face, preventing him from continuing in that direction, beak open wide and eyes staring directly into his.

You said it was forbidden to kill any but the vampire! The feminine voice was frightened, a soft denial, almost pleading. *You said never to kill when feeding and never to feed when killing.*

At the long-awaited sound of that voice, Nicolae's world turned upside down. He tumbled through the sky while the gray and dark of the night were replaced with shimmering, dazzling silver and brilliant colors. It was like a fireworks display, bursting all around him, robbing him of his ability to breathe, even to see. He closed his eyes against the assault on his senses, struggling to regain control.

The owl struck him hard just as she called to him a second time. *Pull up, you're falling. Pull up now!* There was terror in her voice.

Warmth spread, calmed him, and he righted himself. She had given him life again. Saved him from eternal darkness. His lifemate. The only woman capable of preventing him from turning vampire.

At long last she had spoken to him. Years of silence had conditioned him to believe she would never voluntarily speak to him, but when he was in danger from the raging beast within, she had leapt to save him in spite of her every resolve not to. She had filled the bleakness of his gray existence with colors and life.

Where are you? How badly are you hurt? he asked, praying she would continue to communicate with him.

Leave this place. I vowed if you ever came here, if you found me, I would not hunt you because you saved me. Go away from here. I don't want to have to kill you, but I will if you force me.

I am not vampire. I am Carpathian. There is a difference.

Her sigh was soft in his mind. *So you say, but I know nothing of Carpathians. I have only met the undead, with their voices so sweet and compelling. Voices such as yours.*

Why would I teach you not to kill your prey if I were vampire? He was patient. He could afford to be patient. She was his world now, the only thing that mattered to him. He had found her, and he would find a way to make her see the difference between a dangerous creature who had chosen to lose his soul, and a warrior fighting to maintain his honor.

I will give you no other warning. If you wish to live, leave this place and never come back.

Again he heard the soft, pleading note in her voice, felt it in his mind. She probably didn't even know it was there, but he heard and it filled him with elation. Nicolae believed that she would try to destroy him. She was strong and well disciplined. He had taught her well, and she was a fast, apt pupil.

They were connected, mind to mind, so Nicolae felt the sudden stillness in her. Instinctively he knew that she had reached the lair of the vampire. The undead was wounded, doubly dangerous, and in his own lair he would have numerous safeguards and traps.

Get out of there. I am close—I will destroy the vampire. It is unnecessary for you to take chances with your life.

This is my city, my home. My people, under my protection. I don't share with the undead. Leave. She closed herself off to him, slamming a mind block in place, a strong barrier he didn't bother attempting to penetrate.

Nicolae sped through the sky, the owl keeping pace with him, eyes searching for signs, senses flaring out to test the air for the noxious trail. He didn't bother to attempt to track Destiny; he had taught her too well. Her trail was nearly nonexistent. Without the wound, he would never have caught her scent, and she had already dealt with the laceration so that there was no more telltale spoor for him to follow.

Nicolae glanced at his traveling companion, the large owl flying so strongly beside him as it had done for years. They were traveling companions. Hunters. Brothers. Watching each other's backs. *I will go into the lair of the vampire and destroy him. It is not safe for you to do so, but should something happen to me, I ask that you take this woman to the Prince.* His brother could no longer battle the vampire. He was too close to the beast to resist the call of blood.

There was a heartbeat of silence. Two. Nicolae felt the wind rushing past them as they moved together through the sky. For a moment he thought the other would not speak. He so seldom did these days, preferring to remain in the form of an animal. *You give me a task I am uncertain I can fulfill.*

You can do no other than see to it she is safely returned to our homeland. She is my lifemate, although as yet unbound.

Again there was only the silence of the night. *Nicolae, I am older by several hundred years. My time is waning. You feel the crouching of the beast. I am the beast. How can you trust my word?*

For a moment Nicolae felt his heart jump. Vikirnoff had long battled the bleakness of a colorless existence. He had hunted the vampire for hundreds of years, destroying old friends. With each kill it became harder and harder to resist the need to feel something. If Vikirnoff made a kill while feeding, he would be lost for all time. Nicolae closed his mind to the possibility. Vikirnoff was strong and he would endure as long as there was need.

I trust you, Vikirnoff, because I know you. You are a warrior without equal and your honor is everything. You are my brother, the one who came to guard my back in my darkest days, as I have done for you. Give me your word you will do this if I should fail. You would never go back on your word. Not even the beast is stronger than your word. She is one of us, though converted by a vampire. A female capable of producing female children for our race. You must perform this one last task and then you can go to ground, only to awaken if you feel the call of your lifemate. Nicolae was firm, dealing warrior to warrior.

There was no other choice for either of them. They had stood for centuries against the vampire, alone in their territories until both were near the end. Until Nicolae had been connected with a child being physically and emotionally abused. His brother Vikirnoff, centuries older, had rushed to his side, to ensure that Nicolae would not succumb to despair when he couldn't prevent the continued assaults.

Chapter Two

Destiny looked around herself carefully at the cave to which she had followed the vampire. His lair was close. She had already encountered two of his traps and had slowly, meticulously unraveled them. Her chest was inexplicably tight, her lungs laboring to draw air. There was an anxiety in her that had never been there before when she was hunting. *He* was here at last. Nicolae. She whispered his name softly in her mind. He had told it to her often, the sound blending with his accent to form something beautiful, but she had never dared repeat it. Now the strange name tugged at her heartstrings. She had known the day would come when he would find her. He had been getting closer month by month, day by day. He was relentless in his pursuit of her, and all along, she had known she would have to face him one day. She thought she had been prepared, but in truth, she was terrified. She relied on him, on his concern for her, his companionship, strange though it might be.

Nicolae had come to her in her darkest hour, had

shared her torment, the depraved tortures of an evil mind. His voice had been sheer magic, transporting her to distant lands, and places where her captor had not been able to follow. She had left her body behind, but her heart and her very soul had soared free. Nicolae, so far away, had been her salvation. He had saved her life, saved her sanity.

But Destiny had learned the hard way not to trust an alluring voice. She had once responded to one, and that monster had killed her family. Since that time, so long ago, she had heard sweet voices over and over, and all those voices had belonged to liars, depraved monsters who thrived on the pain of others. She thought of Nicolae as her only family, yet she knew better than to trust him. He had saved her with his beautiful voice, but he had also taught her other things. He had taught her to kill her captors, taught her to kill the monsters preying on other families, other children. He had taught her to be as he was, a master killer.

Destiny ran her hand carefully along the rock wall, knowing there was an entrance, knowing the vampire had to be hiding somewhere behind what appeared to be a solid rock wall. Water was steadily dripping, the sound loud in the small confines of the cave. She tilted her head, examining the heavy rock above her head. It seemed solid enough, but there was a distinct uneasiness roiling in her stomach, a warning she had learned from vast experience to heed.

The cave felt like a trap. She took her time surveying the floor. It was uneven, damp in spots from water leaking continually from the walls. Lightly passing her hand over the rock, she nearly missed the subtle movement beneath her palm. Blinking to try to focus on what she couldn't see, Destiny pulled her hand quickly from the surface of the rock. Something lay there, waiting for an unsuspecting victim. Something microscopic, but deadly.

Destiny took a cautious step away from the rock wall. Immediately she felt the floor beneath her sink, as if she had stepped onto a sponge. Or a bog. She sank ankle deep into the strange mire. The mud clung to her ankle, sucked at her shoe. Tightened around her skin like a vise. Her heart jumped, her breath leaving her lungs in a small rush. She forced her mind to stillness, keeping panic at bay.

Rather than fight the black goo sucking at her foot, Destiny chose to dissolve. She shimmered for a moment in the darkness of the cave; then there was only a mist of colors glowing in the cavern, moving cautiously just above ground. The colors spun, bright droplets of water weaving together just over the largest damp spot where the water dripped steadily. Suddenly the mist bored into the heart of the spot, penetrating the wet soil and disappearing completely from the chamber.

Destiny found herself in a much larger cavern deep beneath the mountain. The smell of sulfur was nearly overpowering, the air thick and hot. Noxious gas seeped and swirled from the green pools that dotted the earth. Yellow vapor hung heavily in the air. She took great care to examine the ground before she took her true form, placing her feet on solid ground, her knees slightly bent, her body relaxed, ready to spring into action should there be need. Destiny had the feeling the need would be great and would come soon. Very soon.

She studied the chamber, not moving, hardly breathing, not wanting to disturb the flow of air, not wanting to trigger a dangerous trap. There were two openings leading deeper beneath the mountain; she could catch glimpses of subterranean passages which probably extended for miles. Sharp natural spears hung from the ceiling of the cave, great columns of mineral built up to form a legion of armaments, poised over her head. The stalactites made Destiny nervous. The enemy was close by, and in his lair he had the advantage.

Cautiously she scanned the chamber, using more than her physical vision. The stench of evil permeated the area, burning her eyes so that tears welled up. Destiny was careful not to rub her eyes. It was likely that the thick vapor filling the chamber was dangerous.

A hunter must presume that everything in the vampire's lair is a lethal trap. You cannot overlook the smallest detail, especially anything that appears to be natural. Nicolae had taught her that. Her savior. Her mortal enemy. He had prepared her with painstaking care for her battles with the undead. She lived because of him, yet she would be forced to face him in battle.

Impatient with her thoughts, Destiny shook her head. She couldn't afford to have her attention divided. Determinedly she pushed him out of her mind and turned her complete concentration to the problem at hand. She scanned the chamber, noting the position of each rock, of the dark, gleaming pools, of the vents of steam rising from them. She paid attention to the holes in the floor, the uneven ground, committing the layout to memory before she ever took a step.

Very cautiously she moved to her left, wishing she dared to be out in the open, away from the walls, but the risk was too great. Something moved just out of her line of vision. She felt the stir of air, the subtle difference in the swirl of vapor as it rose from the pool. A tendril of yellowish mist broke off from the vents of steam and floated idly toward her.

Something brushed her leg, tugged at the tightly woven material of her leggings. Destiny resisted looking. Instead she leapt upward, kicking out with the edge of her foot, shattering two stalactites and sending the remains plummeting into the bubbling pools. She landed lightly in a crouched position on the other side of the chamber. Her hands were up, ready for defense, as she surveyed the results of her handiwork.

The ceiling over her head was alive with movement for a moment, the natural-looking formations swaying slightly with the vibrations of violence. One cracked along its length, exposing briefly a dark interior and a whisper of movement before the crack faded into a seamless formation of minerals.

Without hesitation Destiny launched her attack, running along the walls of the chamber with long, light strides, her soles barely touching the wall's surface as she raced around the circumference, climbing higher with each step until she had reached the ceiling once again. There, she exploded into action, driving both feet into the one stalactite that had remained perfectly still. Dagger in hand, she attacked as the force of her blow broke open the cocoon, exposing the vampire. Her momentum carried her past the creature, but she whipped around in midair and plunged the sharp blade deep into the chest of the undead.

The vampire's scream was hideous, resonating throughout the chamber as he fell to earth. His cries were a command, and instantly the stalactites overhead rocked, then erupted with great winged predators. Miniature pteranodons burst from the cocoons, wings spread and flapping fiercely, great beaks opened wide. Vapor swirled and spread as the wings fanned the air.

The dinosaur-birds had bodies much the size of an eagle but their wingspans were shorter than either the eagle's or the extinct pteranodon's. Engineered by the vampire, the carnivores were designed to guard the chamber and keep out enemies. They flew at Destiny's face, snapping at her body with their fierce beaks.

She had landed near a bubbling pool. Carefully she stayed close to the walls of the chamber, knowing she would be easy prey for the screaming birds out in the open. The noise was an assault on her ears, yet she made no attempt to control the volume with her preternatural senses. She needed to hear the slightest whisper of sound in the cave. She punched one bird hard in the neck, knocking it from the sky as she leapt over the pool to reach the vampire, which was crawling away from her.

She landed on her feet, but something hit her left leg hard, knocking it out from under her so that she lurched sideways. In that instant, the vampire reversed directions and was on her, his face a vicious mask of hatred, his breath fetid, the bloody dagger he had pulled from his chest in his fist.

Destiny spun to face him, her hand going for his wrist. He was wounded, had suffered severe blood loss, so she was confident she was the stronger of the two. She trapped his wrist and wrenched his hand back toward him. Ducking to avoid talons coming at her face from above, she drove the knife into his chest a second time.

The vampire roared with hatred, tearing at the dagger. Destiny whirled to face a second attack from behind.

A monstrous lizard was climbing up out of the bubbling pool, saliva dripping from its formidable jaws. Its long tail, which had already scored a hit against her leg, knocking her aside earlier, was swinging ominously. The creature looked much like a Komodo dragon, with clawed feet and a peculiar swinging gait. Its speed was incredible as it rushed her. Destiny had no time to seize the heart from the vampire; she had to dissolve and scatter her molecules through the noxious vapor in order to save herself.

The vapor in the chamber was heavy and carried in it some kind of trap she had never encountered before. Immediately it seemed to latch on to the molecules of mist, soaking them up like a thirsty sponge. Panic flared in her, a sudden realization that she had been careless and was now caught in a trap.

Shape-shift into one of the birds. Nicolae's magical voice was calm, steadying. Close by.

Destiny did so instantly, taking the image from his mind rather than from her own, not realizing she had automatically reached for him, shared with him her peril, allowing him to "see" the trap and the chamber through her. She flapped and screeched right along with the rest of the strange creatures, all the while eyeing the vampire below her.

To her horror, the giant reptile shifted into human form, becoming a tall thin man with a beaked nose and graying hair. He reached out casually to the other vampire, helping him to his feet. In Destiny's mind, Nicolae went very still. Vampires traveled together at times, but they used one another, sacrificed one another. In all the long centuries of his battles, Nicolae had never witnessed one vampire helping another.

"Come, my dear, I grow tired of this little charade," the taller vampire said. He clapped his hands and the birds fell from the air, plummeting into the bubbling pools to scream impotently as they disappeared under the surface. "Vernon needs blood. I think you had best supply him, since you were the one to cause his distress."

Destiny settled to earth, shape-shifting to her true form as she did so. "Well, well, it's old-friend week, I see," she said, smiling coolly at the two vampires. She kept her eyes fixed on the taller one. He was strong and without a single wound and very, very dangerous. "I'm surprised a big bad vampire such as you would associate with a weakling like Vernon. He seems a bit out of your league. Three times I scored a hit on him—a bit much, don't you think?" There was taunting amusement in her voice. Her face was a pleasant mask, confident and serene, while inside, her brain was working out a way to escape. The hunter was now the hunted, but she would never, ever allow herself to be taken alive by such monsters.

Vernon snarled at her, exposing his long fangs. "You won't be smiling when I drain the blood from your veins." Spittle ran down the side of his mouth and he coughed, holding his hands over his wounds.

"Now, now, Vernon, she does have a point. A mere woman and she stuck you like a pig." The taller vampire smiled, exposing his sharp incisors. "No need to get nasty with her over your own incompetence."

Look for something more. Another perhaps. It seems unreasonable that they would be in the same lair, but he is drawing your attention for a reason. They are afraid of you. You have twice plunged a dagger into one of the undead and you are a woman, a puzzle to

them. *Look with more than your eyes but do not turn
away from him.* Destiny sensed Nicolae at the cave's
entrance, and her heart began to beat much faster.

*Do not show fear, even if it is of me. They will think
you weak, and you want them worried. They have never
encountered a female hunter before.*

She had to trust Nicolae; she had no choice. He had
hunted her for years, wanting her for himself or for
some plan she could not fathom. She couldn't imagine
him betraying her to other vampires at this late date.
And she knew from experience that he was right. Vampires did not share lairs. The situation was unusual and
highly dangerous. She scanned the chamber, utilizing
all her senses. She scented the third adversary immediately. She couldn't locate him, but she knew he was
there. She shared the information with Nicolae.

Destiny laughed softly, feigning unconcern while
Vernon snarled his hatred of her. She turned to the more
powerful vampire. "I don't understand. Usually when
one so powerful as yourself enters my home territory, I
hear rumors." Deliberately she flattered him, managing
to sound breathless and slightly flirtatious.

The tall vampire bowed low. "I am called Pater. And
you are?"

"Not fooled." Destiny whirled around, crouching low,
and extracted a dagger from her boot and drove it up
into the newest attacker's soft belly. As he shrieked, she
drove her fist hard through bone and muscle, straight to
the heart. Her fingers closed around it and she jerked
hard as she leapt backward to avoid as much of the
poisonous blood as possible.

Flinging the heart as far from the flopping vampire as
she could, she struck a spark off the rock wall, fanning

the embers as she raced up the wall, then tossing the flames at the pulsating blackened organ so that it incinerated immediately to a fine ash.

Vernon waved his arms recklessly, forgetting for a moment his terrible injuries. Destiny had destroyed the third vampire who had waited so patiently to attack her from behind while Pater distracted her. She dropped to the ground, ever conscious of the damp spots and the yellow vapor swirling thickly.

"I hope he wasn't a friend of yours, Pater," she said, smirking a little. Her leg, where the reptile's tail had struck her with such force, was beginning to throb and burn. "I certainly hope you aren't calling yourself Father. You're much too young, you know." She focused on the tall vampire, knowing Vernon posed little threat unless she was close to him. His strength was waning rapidly from loss of blood and the terrible wounds she had inflicted upon him.

The tall vampire merely smiled at her. He inhaled deeply, his eyes widening as he took in her scent. "You are one of us—the blood of our people flows in your veins." He looked slightly puzzled. "Haven't you heard the whispers of the movement? We are banding together, one by one, growing strong within our ranks. One piece of straw can blow away in the wind, but a bundle is solid. Too long our power has been hidden. We've been forced to fear while lesser creatures, beings no more than cattle to us, rule the earth. Why? Because we have never joined forces. Together we can defeat the hunters. They are few, and most are close to joining our ranks. We have eyes in the hunters' camps and we have been growing in our dominion over the cattle, infiltrating into positions of influence and power. Join with us."

A strange tingling had begun in her calf muscle, alarming because it radiated up her leg toward her thigh and also down to her foot. She tilted her chin, suddenly afraid of what he was going to say. Was this why Nicolae had hunted her for so long? To convince her to join the ranks of the undead in some new bid for power? The idea was chilling. Could she possibly stop such a movement on her own? Who would believe her? If she told anyone what she was, they would destroy her.

"You belong with us."

She winced at his words. She couldn't help the shudder that ran through her body, the sudden memories that sickened her. She slammed the door on them hard, terrified of what they would do to her.

Sensing her vulnerability, Pater took a gliding step toward her, barely skimming the ground. Destiny stepped to the side, not wanting to back into the wall of the chamber. She was certain there was something there. Unexpectedly, her leg went out from under her. She went down hard, a shocked look on her face. The strange tingling was a paralysis creeping up from the bruising on her calf muscle toward her thigh. Her foot was rigid, unable to move.

Snarling triumphantly, Vernon pushed past Pater, rushing her, greedy for blood. He stumbled in his haste, lunging forward. She saw his foot lashing out and she rolled awkwardly, the blow catching her on the temple, but without most of its original force. In retaliation, Destiny launched a rock straight at one of the wounds on his chest. She could see Pater gliding toward her with his unhurried stride, that same smile on his face.

The heavy rock smashed solidly into Vernon's mangled chest. He howled, spittle and blood spraying from his mouth as he nearly collapsed. "I'll kill her," he vowed, so incensed he could barely get the words out. His hatred manifested itself in the chamber. The yellow vapor swirled closer to Destiny, circling her as Vernon approached.

Destiny waited, watching his every move. Vernon was severely injured, his blood loss great. Despite her inability to move her leg, she was certain she was still the stronger of the two. She could take his heart if he was close enough. She would have to kill at least one of them—before she found a way to destroy herself. She was determined she would not be taken alive by either of them.

Something in her stillness made the vampire pause. Even Pater stopped moving to regard her uneasily. Vernon's hate-filled gaze narrowed, and he lunged at her.

The chamber exploded with fireworks, bursts of flame and a shower of sparks. A tall, powerfully built man landed solidly in the midst of the pyrotechnics. It was far too late for Vernon to retreat. The newcomer's hands caught his bullet-shaped head and wrenched hard, snapping bones. The attacker moved so fast he was a blurred image, his fist driving deep through the undead's chest cavity and extracting the heart from the screaming vampire. As Vernon fell, Destiny caught the glint of a dagger. It dropped from the vampire's nerveless fingers and landed a short distance from her.

Destiny stared up at the stranger. She knew him. She would know him anywhere. He was raw power and pure elegance with his long hair and strong face and piercing eyes. Eyes of death. Whirlwind of death. He took her breath away. She couldn't think of him as anything but her mortal enemy. A dangerous vampire who had killed again and again.

"How badly are you injured?" Nicolae demanded tersely, his brilliant gaze slashing through the heavy yellow vapor that was gathering around them. "This entire chamber is a death trap. We have to get out of here." He took a step toward her, leaned close, reaching for her to gather her into the safety of his arms. Pater had disappeared, and the feel of the chamber was alarming. The very air vibrated with tension and something far more sinister.

Destiny flung herself forward to meet him, a dagger concealed along her inner wrist. She would have only one chance to save herself. As Nicolae loomed over her, all muscle and sinew and flowing grace, her stomach lurched alarmingly, her resolve weakening for just a moment. Then she saw his eyes. Dark. Dangerous. Flames flickering in the depths. She thrust the knife at his heart.

Hands clamped around both of her wrists in a vise-like grip, pinning the flat of the blade against her skin. Someone caught her from behind, jerking her backward against a hard chest. Her captor was enormously strong, his grip unbreakable. Destiny threw her head back, attempting to make contact with her captor, hoping to smash his nose. The back of her head hit a chest so hard that pain exploded behind her eyes and in her temples. She could only watch helplessly as Nicolae bent ever closer toward her. Destiny brought up her one good leg, attempting to kick him.

"We have to get out of here," said a voice behind her. Low. Musical. Compelling. "You were careless, Nicolae. She nearly did you in." Her unseen captor twisted the dagger from her hand, and just that quickly slit her wrist.

The action was swift and unexpected, the cut deep and extremely painful. Blood poured from her wrist. Destiny scowled, unable to understand why they would do such a thing. Vampires craved blood and the power of *feeling* their prey die. They needed the rush of adrenaline in their victim's blood as much as the blood itself.

"Damn it, Vikirnoff, it wasn't necessary to hurt her." The low murmur of the voice registered even as she felt the combined power of the two men merge, thrust deep and hold her in their thrall.

Completely helpless, unable to move or to deny them anything, Destiny could only watch in horror as Nicolae gathered her to him, opening his chest with a single slash. He pressed her close, offering his ancient blood, blood she knew would bind them together for eternity. She struggled in her own mind, heard the scream of fear and panic wrenched from her soul, a scream that never made it past her throat. But she drank because she had no choice. They were far too powerful together.

It is necessary to remove the tainted blood from your system. Relax—we have to do this fast. We need to leave this place, and the vampire has poisoned your body with something new to us. Go inside yourself, analyze the compound, break it down and push it out of your body. As always, Nicolae's voice was gentle and steady.

She heard her captor chanting, words Nicolae had used in her mind before, a rhythm of soft, soothing music that somehow took the pain from her calf and her wrist. From her shoulder and arm where the vampire had managed to mark her. Strangely, as Nicolae's blood poured into her, the terrible burning that was with her day and night seemed to ease. She became aware of Nicolae's hand at the nape of her neck, cradling her head, massaging her neck. Gently.

Destiny closed her eyes to shut out what was happening to her, the helpless feeling of being utterly and completely vulnerable. The ground beneath them shivered, a forewarning. They couldn't dissolve into mist with the poisonous vapor surrounding them, and she couldn't run with the poison in her body paralyzing her. She had no idea why they were forcing her blood to run in a steady stream onto the ground and filling her with the powerful blood of an ancient, but it occurred to her that they were risking their lives by staying in the chamber with her.

A part of her brain was working furiously, considering her options, testing her strengths, determined to find a way to escape. Another part of her was relaxing into Nicolae's hold, sinking deeper into his compulsion, accepting his strange connection to her.

"You will have to do it for her, Nicolae." The voice floated up from behind her, sounding far away. "She is not capable. We will have to take her from this place ourselves. The trap is closing, and the one who escaped hopes to keep us locked here."

That pricked her pride. She could do anything they could do. She was strong and Nicolae had taught her well, perhaps far better than he realized. Destiny sought inside herself, past the pain and fear, past the knowledge of what and who she was. She simply dropped away, finding pure energy, finding a place of power and healing. Her blood was fascinating, and she could clearly see the difference between the blood pouring onto the ground and the blood being forced into her body. She could see the ancient blood at war with her own, driving it from her body, a battle fought in her veins for her heart and soul. There were thick dark spots spreading up from her calf, invading her muscles and multiplying at a rapid rate.

She turned her attention to those spots, the dark bacteria that had invaded her bloodstream to do the vampire's bidding.

Hurry. We must go now. I will carry you as close to the surface as possible, but you will have to be able to shape-shift in order to get out of here safely. As always, the melodic voice was unhurried and unconcerned. But Destiny was aware of the urgency of their situation. She knew the vampire Pater had escaped. His lair would be a dangerous trap designed to ensnare them. The shifts in the earth were all the warning she needed. Destiny concentrated on the spots of bacteria, breaking them down, pushing most of them out of her pores, pushing the threads that had rushed toward her heart back to the huge gash in her wrist.

The terrible paralysis was gone, along with the bacteria. Strength poured into her body with the ancient blood. Nicolae brought her wrist to the warmth of his mouth. Her heart stilled, skipped a beat, began to pound heavily. The fiery pain of the laceration eased, was replaced by a curious throbbing, a sudden heat creeping into her bloodstream. The two hunters loosened their mental hold on her, allowing her mind and body freedom from their compulsion. She snatched her hand out of Nicolae's possession, held it against her heart. She became aware she was cradled in Nicolae's arms as he rushed through the maze of subterranean chambers. Destiny swept her tongue across the gash in his chest, an automatic gesture to close the wound.

Deliberately she stayed limp in his arms, gathering her energy, waiting for her opportunity. She turned her attention to the grim-faced man running close to Nicolae's side. He was an inch or so taller than Nicolae, with the same flowing black hair and piercing eyes. He glanced at her, turning those flat, emotionless eyes in her direction, and a shiver went down her spine. She recognized death when she saw it.

The chamber they had fled boomed, and there was a loud crash that reverberated throughout the subterranean maze as the walls and ceiling collapsed in on the cave. They were moving with preternatural speed, yet the thick yellow vapor was only a pace behind them.

"I'm much stronger," Destiny pointed out. "Put me down, and we'll get out of here faster."

Nicolae shifted her in his arms without slowing his pace, allowing her feet to drop toward the floor until she was running with him. Nicolae immediately took up a position behind her, protecting her back while his brother set a grueling pace in front of them.

Destiny couldn't help admiring the flowing grace of her enemy as he ran, shifting shape as the opening loomed just ahead, a narrow crack none of them would be able to fit through. She had never imagined anyone could shift that fast, the large, elegant form compressing to that of a bat.

Now! Hurry, shift! It was the first time she'd detected urgency in Nicolae's voice. Destiny didn't waste time glancing behind her to see what was following them; the urgency in his command was enough of a warning.

She held the image of the bat uppermost in her mind, feeling the change take hold of her, move through her, consume her. Her bones wrenched and contracted, re-shaped and compressed. She skimmed through the narrow opening, nearly ripping the tip of one wing. She felt Nicolae crowding close behind her.

A wall of fire closed in behind them, reaching for them, moving nearly as quickly as they were, pushing the terrible yellow vapor before the greedy orange flames. This new chamber was smaller but held a chimney. Destiny followed the lead bat up through the narrow opening, her small body cringing from the blast of heat.

Faster. She whispered the word in her mind, anxious that Nicolae was going to get caught in the inferno. She didn't realize she had sent the word into his mind. That she had betrayed her anxiety to him. That behind her, even in the form of a bat, rushing in front of a firestorm, he smiled.

We will make it. He was calmly reassuring.

That annoyed her. She heard his soft, very irritating male amusement echo through her mind as she burst through the chimney and into the next chamber. It was small and dark and there was an eerie heaviness in the air. The heat was stifling. Nicolae swore under his breath, but the words were still a warning in her mind. At once she shifted back to her own shape, examining the thick walls of layered rock, the swirling patterns. This strange little cave had once been part of a lava flow but now was a lethal trap devised by a cunning monster. The yellow vapor poured into the small space, quickly filling every crevice.

Nicolae and his brother were also feeling along the

walls of the cave, judging the heat with their palms as they quickly covered as much surface as possible. "Over here, Vikirnoff."

Destiny watched as Nicolae stepped back to allow his brother to run his hands over the same spot. She moved closer, wondering what exactly they had found. Nicolae caught her arm and thrust her smaller body behind the protection of his just as Vikirnoff slammed the flat of his palm through the rock.

The ground shuddered, the walls wavered and began to crumble. Great chunks of rock fell in a shower above their heads. Nicolae turned, dragged her into the protection of his arms, bent his body over hers as he pushed her as close to the hole Vikirnoff had created as possible. Vikirnoff slammed his palm a second time to enlarge the hole. The yellow vapor, tangled around their necks like nooses, began to pull tight. The ground trembled again, then buckled, a hard jolt that threw them both against the red-hot rock. Destiny swallowed a scream of pain, fear choking her. She dared not open her mouth or breathe the terrible venomous fog ensnaring them.

Vikirnoff leapt through the jagged opening as the next tremor shook the earth. Nicolae caught Destiny around the waist and tossed her after his brother. She landed hard on the other side, automatically scanning her surroundings. Behind her, the wall collapsed in on itself, dust and debris mingling with the yellow vapor that had poured through the hole in an attempt to keep them in the smaller cave.

Destiny jumped back toward the wall, digging at the rocks, throwing them haphazardly out of the way. "He's trapped," she yelled, clawing at the rocks. They were hot and felt almost sticky. *Are you all right?* she called out to Nicolae, unable to stop herself, her heart nearly stopping. He couldn't be dead. Her one companion. Her savior. *Talk to me. Say something.*

Vikirnoff physically dragged her away from the wall. "Go," he ordered gruffly. "Do not take this poison into your body—go while you can. I will get him out."

Destiny hesitated, watched as Vikirnoff began to work at a ferocious pace, working against time while the earth bucked and caved in.

Go. The voice was as steady as ever. Unconcerned. Without worry. She spun around, leapt over an opening crevice and raced toward the upper chambers. Every step she took away from him added to the terrible weight pressing against her chest like a stone. She didn't understand it; she didn't want to understand it. She only knew that she could barely breathe, so strong was her need to turn back and go to his aid.

She raced away from the remaining tendrils of vapor, shape-shifting as she did so, streaking through the caves and chambers, climbing steadily toward the surface. She was a comet of mist, staying well ahead of the trailing poison, but something of her was left behind. Not blood this time, but something far more important. It was her soul that seemed to be left behind with him in that collapsed chamber.

She burst into the open, into the cool, refreshing air. Destiny shifted into the form of an owl, winging her way across the sky. Normally she enjoyed the sensation; the ability to take on this form was a benefit of what she had become. Now her mind was consumed with the need to know that Nicolae was alive and well. It was all she could think of, all that mattered.

Nice to know I matter to you. There was that inevitable male amusement, designed to set her teeth on edge, but this time she only felt relief. *We are clear of the chamber and fighting our way out of the vapor. We will join you soon.*

Destiny broke the connection abruptly. They would not be joining her. She needed the solace of the earth. Her wounds burned and throbbed, reminding her that she could feel pain when she wasn't making a continuous effort to block it out. Weary, she still made every effort to cover her trail. She could not take a chance of being found. She knew Nicolae, knew how skillful a hunter he was. He had given her access to his memories, and he had such a wide range of experiences, century after century of battles. She was in no shape to fight him, especially as he had a traveling companion with him.

Destiny deliberately doubled back several times, watching her back trail. She was determined to pick the time and place of her battle, to make certain the advantages were all on her side. She would never allow herself to be a captive again.

Bone-weary, she settled in a small grove of trees halfway up the mountainside in a national park. The wind was blowing hard, intensifying a biting cold that seeped into her body all the way to her bones. Shivering, she wove her safeguards, a maze of traps that would deter humans and slow vampires, as well as alerting her to their presence.

As she opened the earth, felt the rejuvenating soil beckoning to her, she thought about what Nicolae had done. He had saved her life, shoved her clear of the collapsing wall, acted the savior over and over again.

Was that the work of a true vampire? All that she had ever seen of vampires argued against his being one. True, their voices were fair and sweet and lured even the wary to them. They could appear handsome and sensual. But they couldn't mask their evil natures; they were selfish and spiteful and gloried in the pain of their victims. They would never willingly help anyone, or save anyone.

Yet there was Pater and his plan to unite vampires in a grand scheme to take over the world. No matter how far-fetched, the idea truly terrified her. Vampires had incredible powers, tremendous influence over humans, creating puppets to do their bidding, evil minions to carry out their orders even while their masters rested below the earth out of the sun.

Nicolae had never shown those traits, not even in his battles. During his fights, Destiny had felt the wildness in him rise, a demon crouched and poised ready to destroy, but it was always leashed, always under control. She sighed softly. She needed to find out much more about him before she destroyed him, her only companion.

She could admit to herself she would miss Nicolae if he never again merged his mind with hers. She counted on him. So many times while she was learning to kill the vampire who'd tormented her, she had drawn heavily on his memories. More than that, Destiny had relied on him for emotional support. Through even the most degrading, frightening times of her life, Nicolae had been with her. Sheltering her. Distracting her. Keeping her alive.

Destiny settled deeper into the soothing arms of the earth. Nicolae had often told her fairy stories of a race of beings. Carpathians. He had said he was one, that he hunted those of his kind who betrayed their race by becoming the most evil of all beings. In the beginning she'd thought he had made up the tales to distract her from the terror of her existence. Later she thought he was attempting to lure her to him, to make her believe he was something other than vampire. In all the time she hunted the undead, she had never run across any being such as he had described. As she closed her eyes and the soil poured in over her, as the breath left her body and her heart ceased to beat, her last thought was that she must find out more about this species. She prayed they truly existed.

Chapter Three

Destiny opened her eyes and waited for the terrible rush of pain to sweep through her body. Agony upon awakening had always robbed her of breath and all thought until she could find a way to simply breathe, to function. It was always then that Nicolae merged with her. Destiny's pain drew him to her, allowed him to find her in the broad expanse of the universe. This rising was different. The pain was there, in her blood and bones, a burning acid that pulsed and throbbed, but without the terrible torment that had been such torture over the last years. Nicolae had given her some relief with the infusion of his ancient blood.

Although it is less on this rising, I still feel your pain. Come to me. My blood runs in your veins, it will be easy for you to find me. Come to me and I will do my best to heal you. It was the softest of whispers, a sweet seduction.

Destiny stared up at the night sky, entranced by its natural beauty. Over her head tree branches swayed gently, the leaves glittering a strange silver. She was enthralled by Nicolae's beautiful, musical voice. It wasn't simply that she found herself wanting to just listen to it, she *needed* to hear him speaking to her. She couldn't count the times she had crawled into the refuge of her mind to avoid the atrocities of her life, and found him there waiting where she could just listen to the magic of his incredible voice. The strength of her need for him seemed to be growing, not diminishing, as she aged.

While you think to find reasons to fear me, you might remember I could have taken your blood, tied you to me for all time, but I did not. Why would I want a woman unwilling to come to me on her own? If I were attempting to ensnare you, I would have taken your blood, not given you mine. You have power over me now. You know I speak the truth.

Destiny lifted her chin in a kind of rebellion. She did not need him to state the obvious. *I will work things out for myself, Nicolae. I have no need or want of your unsolicited advice.*

He laughed softly, the notes joyous and pure, slipping into her mind to twine unexpectedly around her heart. Destiny sucked in her breath, her eyes widening with shock, with realization. A part of her *wanted* him close to her. She had awakened expectantly, eager for the sound of his voice, for the connection between them.

Crimson color crept up her neck and into her face as she floated from her resting place. She considered herself well disciplined, took a certain pride in it, yet she could feel butterfly wings brushing at her stomach and warmth spreading treacherously through her body at the mere sound of his voice. At the knowledge of his nearness.

I don't want you here. She said it with a certain fire. Shocked at herself. Shocked at the way she felt toward him.

His answering laughter was pure male amusement, sliding into her mind, under her skin, dissolving her bones. He had been too long in her mind not to recognize her confusion for what it was. Destiny hissed out a slow breath. *Emotions betray one, Nicolae—I learned that lesson from a master. It's a truth I accept.* Emotions had allowed Nicolae to find her. If Destiny hadn't heard MaryAnn speaking to one of her clients, if her words hadn't been the very thing Destiny had been starving to hear, she would have continued her nomad existence and Nicolae would not have found her.

I would have found you. There was complete confidence in his infuriating, beautiful voice. *You know I would have found you.*

Then there will be a battle between us.

Now there was a smoky edge to his laughter. *There has never been a war to fight between us, there never will be. We are two halves of the same whole.*

She winced at his words. To her, they were an accusation. She had seen his kills. She had touched that dark, crouching beast deep within him. As hard as she wished it otherwise, she was still what a monster had made her. For a moment she pressed her fingertips to her temples, closing her eyes, shutting out the beauty of the night, the beauty of his voice, the magic of the things she had become aware of.

Shape-shifting, soaring through the sky, running on four legs like a well-oiled machine, stars glittering like a shower of diamonds overhead—the sheer power of what she was. Destiny found it impossible to hate her existence. That realization only added to the weight of her guilt. She had always had choices, and she had chosen to live. Chosen to hunt and kill monsters. Chosen to stay close to MaryAnn Delaney. And she had chosen to listen to a depraved monster. He had murdered her family and turned her childhood into a living hell.

Stop it! Nicolae said sharply, a command from an ancient accustomed to instant obedience. *You were a child, a little girl, with no knowledge of such evil creatures. You could not possibly have prevented what that vampire did to your family, nor were you responsible. You have rare gifts. There are others in the world such as you, other young women, possibly young men, who inadvertently draw the monster through their incredible gifts. They are in no way responsible for what a vampire does. The vampire chose his way of life. At one time he walked in the light and had honor and respect. At some point in his life he knew he was risking his soul if he continued. He knew what to do but chose to become the undead. Look into my memories; I offer them freely to you. You cannot believe you are responsible.*

Destiny was silent a moment, wanting to believe him. Wanting to be absolved. Wanting the magic of his voice to wrap her up and take her away from all that had ever happened to her. *Your voice is a weapon.* She whispered the words to him aloud as well as in his mind. She needed the sound of her voice to believe it.

You are afraid. It is natural to fear what you do not understand, little one. His voice was so gentle she wanted to cry. She wanted to reach out to him and be held. Her reaction was so strong, so foreign to her nature, it shocked her. Frightened her even more. She felt off balance and indecisive, and she didn't like it. He hadn't called her "little one" in a long while. She tried to tell herself the endearment had thrown her, but she knew better.

She might be afraid, but she was no coward. She could at least be truthful with herself . . . with him. Her chin went up and she straightened her shoulders. *Yes, I am afraid. I don't know how to trust anyone. I don't know that I even trust myself. I trusted the beauty of a voice and I was deceived.*

You were a child. His very gentleness caught at her, turned her inside out.

Does that excuse me?

You did nothing wrong. And yet you blame yourself for surviving. You were meant to survive. Let me help you.

She raked her hand through her hair so that it fell in a dark cloud around her face. Hunger was burning through her body, gnawing and crawling. She tried to ignore it, tried to ignore the knowledge that feeding was no longer as repulsive to her as it should be. Just as she tried to ignore how easy it was to control her prey. She winced. *Prey. Did you hear me? I thought of them as prey, not people. That's what I've become. That's what he made me. How can you help me? How can I trust you? I know what you are. You helped me to kill him. You taught me to be what I am. I see the darkness in you. Do you deny it?*

Of course I do not deny it. The beast is a part of me. It is my strength as well as my weakness. But there is much more to me than a mindless beast bent on death and the torment and pain of others. Just as there is more to you than what he tried to make you.

There is darkness in me. She wouldn't lie. Not to him. Or to herself, not anymore.

My love. He said the two words softly, wrapped her up in his magic. *His blood flows in your veins, haunting you, tormenting and whispering, but it is* his *darkness you feel, not your own. Carpathians are great healers. The soil here is adequate, but the soil of our homeland is like no other. His tainted blood can be removed. His shadowing can be dealt with by our healers and the soil of our homeland.*

How can I trust anything you say to me? She repeated her question almost desperately, wanting something from him he could never give her. Reassurance. She wanted reassurance, yet she didn't dare believe ever again.

That is something only you can answer. There was no impatience in his voice, no anger, only a soft gentleness that threatened to fragment her heart. *You have to find that answer for yourself. If you truly cannot see a difference between me and that unholy monster who dragged you from the safety of your home and subjected you—subjected both of us—to his depraved tortures, then I have nothing with which to defend myself. And I never will. You have to see into my heart and soul. Look past the beast and see the man. See what you are to me. My heart and my soul. My everything. See me, all of me, not just fragments, and you will have your answers.*

She hated him for whispering the words in her mind. For tempting her. His touch was feather-light, brushing the words against her hideous memories with the caressing stroke of an artist's brush. He was luring her deeper into his web. She was mesmerized by him. By everything he said. Everything he promised. By what he left unsaid. The strength and power he possessed.

His knowledge. The way he had sheltered a helpless child. Even the way he had given her his blood and had not taken a single sip of hers. Blood was power. Connection. He had cradled her to him as no other ever had. Held her as if she mattered to him. He said things that pierced her armor like arrows. Beautiful things she needed, she craved. Beautiful things that terrified her.

Strangely, as she filled in the earth where she had rested, restoring it to its original state, a slight tremor in her legs caught her attention. Alarmed, Destiny lifted her hand in front of her face. It was shaking. *Damn you, I don't want you here.* What if she had to kill him? What if he gave her no choice? He was making her so weak, her body trembled. She couldn't afford him. She wouldn't have him in her territory.

You are worth the risk to my life; you always have been worth the risk. Nicolae spoke sincerely, as if he meant every word.

Destiny shook her head in denial. He wasn't going to leave, and as hard as she tried, she could not believe him evil. He wasn't going to make it simple for her by disappearing. Did she really want him to? The thought came unbidden. Sneaking in and tugging at her conscience.

"I'm fragmented." She said it aloud as she looked up at the sky. She wished she were truly friends with Mary-Ann and could talk to her about Nicolae. "A part of me would be disappointed in him if he didn't stay. If he didn't want me." There, she had admitted it to herself and she hadn't used the word *devastated*. The word might have floated for one second in her brain, but she hadn't acknowledged it aloud. Given it life.

How could she survive without him? She had lived

with him for years. Shared his mind on every rising. Listened to the magic of his voice. She didn't know, hadn't known when he had begun invading her heart. She had known she needed him for the continual battles with the undead. She hadn't realized she needed him to be alive.

Destiny could find him now, anytime, anywhere. There was a blood tie between them. She could monitor him at will, touch his mind to see what he was doing. It gave her an advantage over him. She would know when he was hunting her. And she would know if he made a kill.

Resolutely she turned toward the city teeming with life. She had left her business with MaryAnn for too long. She preferred to get it over with. Three running steps and she launched herself skyward, spreading her arms as feathers sprouted and the wind took her higher. The earth fell away, taking her fears with it. She blocked out all thoughts of Nicolae and Vikirnoff and allowed herself to indulge in the sheer joy of flight. She would never tire of taking on the form of an owl and used it often when she traveled.

The world was a thing of beauty when she soared through the sky, when the air washed her body clean and she felt whole and pure and alive. She cut through the clouds, not taking the time to play. She had business. She searched familiar places, looking for traces of MaryAnn. Her scent. The sound of her voice. Her soft laughter. She found what she was looking for in a small bar where the locals hung out to exchange the latest gossip.

Destiny sat on the roof of the deli across the street from the bar and surveyed the street. Despite the lateness of the hour, Velda Hantz and her sister Inez sat in their chairs on the sidewalk in front of their apartment building, watching the world go by. Both in their seventies, they were permanent fixtures on the street, greeting each passerby by name and yelling out friendly advice or motherly admonishment if the situation warranted. It was impossible to miss either of them, dressed as they were in their favorite colors of fluorescent pink and chartreuse green. Velda's pink-tipped gray hair was in its usual artsy windblown style, while Inez's rich purple do was swept up on top of her head. They both wore the latest running shoes, which they carefully scuffed as they sat in their chairs. Destiny found the sisters oddly endearing. More than once she had allowed them to see her, and always they called out friendly greetings and waved her over for a quick interrogation.

Knees drawn up, her chin propped in her hand, Destiny watched the two women, unaware of the smile on her face. She had moved often from city to city, state to state, always hunting the undead. Always staying ahead of Nicolae and his relentless pursuit of her. She knew the way his mind worked. He had given her access to his battles, his strategies, his very thought process. She had soaked up his knowledge, knowing her life depended on it, knowing other lives would depend on it. That had enabled her to stay ahead of him. Until she had heard MaryAnn Delaney speaking, counseling a young woman whose life was a shambles. That soft, clear voice, the things MaryAnn had said, kept Destiny chained to Seattle. To these streets. Eventually she had come to secretly think of all the people in the neighborhood as her responsibility.

Destiny sighed and straightened very slowly. She had

made a conscious choice to stop running and allow this city to become her home, to allow herself to care about its inhabitants. It gave her a semblance of normalcy she desperately needed, a purpose to continue her life when she knew she was evil.

Not evil. Carpathian. You carry the tainted blood of the vampire, but you are not vampire. I have explained this on more than one occasion. There was a patient note in Nicolae's velvet-soft voice. *What is troubling you?*

Destiny sighed softly, blew at a strand of hair that fell across her face. *Don't you have anything better to do than harass me? Are all men as annoying as you?*

There was a brief silence. She could feel him struggling not to laugh. No one ever spoke to him the way she did, and he was shocked as well as amused. It made her feel all the closer to him. Connected to him.

Good God. You are going to give me more trouble than I ever thought possible.

You have no idea. There was a certain feminine satisfaction in having the last word, delivering her line smartly and breaking the connection between them quickly and decisively. Just that brief communication between them had given her the courage necessary to do what had to be done. She forced herself to leave the safety of the rooftops.

The sounds of music and people talking seemed to burst from the walls of The Tavern. Destiny stood outside the bar, as she had so many times before. Her small teeth tugged nervously at her bottom lip. She never entered but perched instead on the roof, just listening to all the conversations. She always found it comforting, as if she were really a part of the neighborhood.

Tonight MaryAnn was inside the bar; Destiny was

certain of it. And MaryAnn would have questions. Lots of questions. Destiny would have to remove the woman's memories, something she was reluctant to do. She liked and respected MaryAnn, and the idea of deliberately removing her memories disturbed Destiny. She had avoided the issue for two risings, preferring to stay hidden in the solace of the earth, healing the wounds on her body and hiding from the ancient warrior hunting her. Hiding her dark soul from MaryAnn. Now she had no choice but to face her.

The door to the bar swung open and two men emerged, laughing, talking together as they walked past her without seeing her. She recognized them. Tim Salvadore and Martin Wright. She whispered their names under her breath, as if greeting them. They lived in a small apartment over the little grocery store on the corner. For business reasons, they tried to hide the fact that they were a couple, but everyone in the neighborhood knew they were more than roommates. No one cared; most liked the two men. Still, no one alluded to the relationship out of respect and courtesy.

Destiny bit her lip harder as she watched the two walk down the street. She enjoyed watching their lives unfold. They were nice, ordinary people who seemed genuinely devoted to one another. They were so much a part of the small community Destiny protected. Her gaze remained on the two men until they turned the corner and she lost sight of them. Then she looked back at The Tavern with a frown on her face.

She would have to go in and face MaryAnn. She was certain there would be revulsion and fear in MaryAnn's soft brown eyes after they spoke. Compassion and friendship would be replaced by the knowledge of what Destiny was. Destiny knew she could erase that knowledge from MaryAnn's mind, should she not be able to accept her as she was, but there would always be a barrier between them. Nothing would ever be the same again. Destiny would never be able to even pretend they were friends, and MaryAnn's friendship was important to her. She wanted MaryAnn's acceptance, but how could anyone accept her when she couldn't accept herself?

For a moment she stood outside The Tavern, her shoulders slumping, her heart heavy with dread. At once she felt him. Nicolae. He stirred in her mind, his touch gentle, inquiring, drawn by her deep sorrow. The ease of the connection surprised her. His gentleness warmed her. The way she craved his touch alarmed her. Destiny slammed her mind closed to him. She couldn't afford to risk his finding out about MaryAnn. It would be a certain death sentence for the woman. He would not allow the continued existence of a human who knew about vampires. Lifting her chin, she squared her shoulders and decisively pulled open the door.

At once the noise and smells assaulted her, jangling and jarring until she managed to turn down the volume in her mind. Nothing could stop the way her stomach knotted and twisted in protest of what she was about to do. Her gaze went unerringly to MaryAnn.

MaryAnn, sitting on a barstool, half turned toward the door. She was laughing at something the woman next to her was saying. Destiny knew MaryAnn so well, she could hear the forced notes of merriment. Destiny didn't look at the woman speaking with MaryAnn, or try to identify anyone else in the bar. She focused on

MaryAnn and willed her to look up, bracing herself for the horror and knowledge she would find in the depths of those soft brown eyes.

MaryAnn turned her head slowly until her dark gaze met Destiny's. Joy lit her face, banished the worry from her eyes. She jumped from the stool, leaving her companion in mid sentence, and rushed to Destiny. Time stood still while Destiny watched her hurtle across the room like a small rocket.

"You're alive! Thank God! I was so worried. I didn't have any idea whom to contact. I checked the hospitals, even the morgue." MaryAnn nearly flung her arms around Destiny but checked herself when she saw how uncomfortable the younger woman was.

Destiny stood staring at her, her mind numb, a perfect blank. Her carefully worded apology was wiped from her memory; she could only stare dumbly. Twice she cleared her throat.

"Come on, let's move away from the crowd," MaryAnn suggested gently, drawing Destiny a few steps out of the crush of people.

"You don't have a single ounce of self-preservation," Destiny accused. "Why don't you ever try to protect yourself?"

"I don't know. All I could hear was the sound of his voice. It was so melodic—hypnotizing almost. I couldn't see him clearly until you spoke to me. Then he sounded horrible and grating and he looked . . ." Her voice trailed off as she sought the right word. "A monster. His teeth, so jagged and sharp. His fingernails were something out of a horror film. But at first he looked handsome. I would have gone to him if you hadn't pushed me into the church. Thank you, Destiny."

Destiny could only stare at her in a kind of shock. "I'm not talking about him. You wouldn't have had a chance with him anyway. He was a vampire. They aren't easy to defeat, and you don't have the necessary knowledge or skills. I'm talking about *me*. You're happy to see me—"

"Of course I'm happy to see you!" MaryAnn interrupted. "I was so worried, Destiny. I looked for you every day, all the places you might go, but I couldn't find you anywhere. Don't ever scare me like that again. You should have come to my house. Didn't you think I'd be worried?"

"Yes, I thought you'd be worried that I might kill you by draining every drop of your blood," Destiny said. She could hardly endure the conversation. MaryAnn was telling the truth; Destiny could read her anxiety. It made no sense, and MaryAnn's lack of fear, lack of self-preservation, angered her.

"That's silly. I saw your injuries. I wanted to take care of you."

Destiny studied her hands. "How can you say that? You must know what I am."

"What is it you think you are?" MaryAnn asked softly, her voice as gentle as ever. There was no hint of condemnation. No hint of laughter. Just MaryAnn's quiet acceptance. Unconditional acceptance.

"You saw me. And you saw *it*. The vampire. You must know I'm one of them." Destiny couldn't look at her. She couldn't bear to see the revulsion looking back at her in those trusting eyes. "I'm sorry—I shouldn't have allowed our lives to touch. You won't remember, but I want you to know that I give you my word of honor I will never harm you."

There was a small silence, and her stomach churned and knotted. She felt MaryAnn's touch. Light. Her fingers settled on Destiny's forearm. "Why do you believe you are a vampire?"

Destiny stiffened as if she'd been struck. "He took my blood. He forced me to drink his. I think that's the accepted way of making a human into a vampire."

MaryAnn nodded. "Well, of course, from what I've seen in movies. Is that where you're getting your information, too? The movies?"

"You don't have to believe me," Destiny pulled her arm away from MaryAnn. She could hear hearts beating. She could hear the ebb and flow of blood. The whispers of private conversations. "I'm not crazy." She said it firmly, more for her own benefit than for Mary-Ann's.

"I know that. I couldn't leave the church, even though I knew you were in danger and I wanted to go help you. I sat there until morning, although I prayed for the strength to leave. But I couldn't. I saw him, Destiny. I saw and heard everything he said." MaryAnn shivered delicately. "He wanted you to call me out of the church."

Destiny nodded her head. "Yes—to share your blood." She said it bluntly, wanting to conclude this conversation. She had forgotten how emotions could tie one up in painful knots. She preferred physical pain.

"Let's go back to why you believe you're a monster. What makes you think so, Destiny? Because this maniac, this vampire, exchanged blood with you?" Mary-Ann asked. "I can only go by what I've read in books or seen in movies. I know little of vampires and didn't for a moment believe they existed until I witnessed that horrible man. Now I'm open to the possibility, but I still can't believe you are one. Garlic, for instance . . ."

Destiny shuddered. "I never go near the stuff. I don't know what it would do to me, but I don't dare try it." She pushed an unsteady hand through her hair. "I haven't looked in a mirror in years. I don't think I have a reflection, but I don't know for certain. I want so much to enter the church, but I can't take the chance."

"Sweetheart—" MaryAnn caught her firmly and turned her. "Your reflection is just as clear as mine in the mirror there. And you happen to be standing directly under a string of garlic. You haven't even noticed it."

Destiny's brilliant gaze found herself in the oversized mirror above the bar. She looked pale. Startled. Frightened. Did that face really belong to her? The last time she had seen herself she had been eight years old. How long ago had that been? She didn't know. She didn't recognize the woman staring back at her. Hanging above the bar where deli sandwiches were advertised were various food items, including strings of garlic in nets.

Afraid that if she took her eyes from her image it would disappear, Destiny watched herself shake her head. "I've never looked before. I was afraid of what I might see, or not see."

"Honey," MaryAnn continued with great gentleness, "when you pushed me into the church, you went inside with me. I was still struggling toward the man. I didn't have control of myself until you spoke."

There was a small silence while they both turned her words over in their minds. "I went into the church?"

"Then *you* had control of me," MaryAnn mused.

"Destiny, whatever you are, you're not evil. You're not anything like that monster." She shuddered, remembering the fangs, the jagged teeth stained with blood. She glanced around the bar, spotted a small empty table in a corner and steered Destiny toward it. She was beginning to understand why the young woman had such troubled eyes. How long had Destiny lived with the knowledge that such monsters inhabited the world?

"Sit down, Destiny." MaryAnn used an authoritative voice. Destiny was so pale, so shocked, she looked as if she might fall over. When Destiny seated herself, Mary-Ann took the chair across from her. "Did that man really take your blood and force you to take his?" It seemed a silly question to ask, something out of a Hollywood horror film, but MaryAnn had seen the creature, and she had known he was evil and that he was not human. She'd been a witness to the blurring speed Destiny had used in attacking the thing.

"Not him." Destiny's voice was so soft, MaryAnn strained to hear her. She sounded far away. "There was another. A long time ago. He . . ." Destiny trailed off, one hand going to her throat defensively. She covered her pulse, pressing her palm to her skin as if covering a ragged wound. For a moment she looked so vulnerable, so young and fragile, MaryAnn had to force herself to remain silent. "I can't think about it. I don't dare think about it."

"What do you think would happen if you did, Destiny?" Her voice was neutral. "Burying bad things only allows them to surface when least expected."

"Sometimes it's the only way to survive. Whom do I tell? The police? They'd lock me up in a mental institution." She met MaryAnn's gaze squarely. "How do you think I live now? You asked me to come home with you and have a cup of tea. For you that makes perfect sense. I'll never have a cup of tea again. Never." She pressed her fingertips to her temples. "My mother drank tea. I remember that now. I'd forgotten. Every morning she made tea in a little teapot and put a cozy over it to allow it to steep. She'd make mine with milk, more milk than tea really, but I felt so grown-up and close to her when we shared it." She closed her eyes, wanting to keep forever in her mind the memory of her mother's face, her scent and the way she smiled when she handed her the teacup.

She looked across the table at MaryAnn. "Thank you. I haven't thought of that in years. The last memories I had of my family were . . . bad. Frightening. I made myself forget everything so I could forget that. My mother was such a beautiful woman."

MaryAnn smiled. "I'm certain you must look a great deal like she did. What a wonderful memory. Do you have brothers or sisters?"

Destiny shook her head. "I was the only child."

"Other family?"

Nicolae popped into her head instantly when she should have said no. His voice, his presence. Destiny felt him strongly. What was he to her? Mortal enemy. No, never that. Destiny raked her hand through her hair, shaken by the depth of her attachment to him.

MaryAnn was waiting for her answer, seeming comfortable with the silence. Destiny's life was silence. She hadn't talked so much with anyone in years. Other than Nicolae.

"How do you know when you can trust someone?" Destiny asked softly. "How do you know they won't betray you?"

"I think sometimes it's instinctive," MaryAnn answered carefully, "although it is always possible to make a mistake. Usually you reserve judgment until you've been around someone, until you've seen their true character."

"Is that what you're doing now?" Destiny tilted her chin.

"With you?" MaryAnn's reply was mild. "You want something from me I can't give you. You want me to condemn you. You've saved my life at least twice. I like you as a person. I know you're troubled, but that doesn't make you the monster you want me to name you."

Destiny heard the swell of conversation in the bar, the blare of music. Laughter erupted from a table only a few feet away. She waved her hand. "This isn't real. You think you live in reality, but this isn't real."

"Of course it is. It's as real as your life has been, just completely different. You can't go back; I can't go back either, but we can go on."

"That's not true," Destiny said softly, raising her vivid eyes to meet MaryAnn's gaze. "It isn't true that you can't go back."

For the first time MaryAnn looked uncomfortable. She rubbed her fingertip along the tabletop as she composed her thoughts. Weighing her words. Thinking it through before she spoke. "I presume that means you can do something to my mind to alter my perception of reality."

Destiny nodded slowly, hearing the sudden increase in MaryAnn's heart rate. "I can take away your memories of me. Of everything you've learned about vampires. You won't remember and you won't ever have nightmares. You won't be in danger from . . . anyone."

"You can do that?"

Destiny smiled suddenly. There was no amusement in the depths of her eyes. "You would be shocked at what I can do. Yes, easily. I'm one of them, MaryAnn. I'm one of them, and I've become comfortable being one of them."

MaryAnn shook her head. "You're something different, Destiny. I don't know what, but you aren't anything like that creature who wanted my blood."

Destiny leaned across the table. "What do you think I exist on?" She placed her palms flat on the table, leaned closer still. Her voice was a soft hiss of warning. "I can hear your heart beating. I hear the blood rushing in your veins." She ran her tongue over her small, perfect teeth. "I have to fight to keep my incisors from lengthening. I haven't fed in two risings. I think about hunger every moment I'm awake. It crawls through me, an addiction I can't overcome. Don't make the mistake I did. Don't ignore the fact that something beautiful, something alluring, can be the most dangerous thing you will ever encounter."

MaryAnn's frown slowly disappeared. She leaned closer still. "It isn't going to work, you know. I know what you're doing. Of course the idea of vampires is frightening to me. I had no idea such things existed outside of movies and books, but I've had two days to think about that thing. He *felt* evil. I'm not scared of you, but you're deliberately trying to frighten me. You want to drive me away from you. I threaten you in some way, don't I? Why are you so afraid of me?"

Destiny pulled back as if MaryAnn had slapped her. She forced air through her lungs, forced the roaring in her head to a semblance of quiet. "I can't breathe in here. How do you breathe inside a place like this? I have to get out of here."

"Destiny, don't. I don't want you to remove my memories, and I don't want you to try to drive me away from you. I just want to be your friend. Is that really such a difficult thing? Do you have so many friends that you can't use another?"

"I can't breathe," Destiny repeated.

It was a measure of her discomfort that she didn't realize someone was approaching their table. He moved in silence, a stalking predator, and was upon them before she had a chance to scent him. Nicolae laid his hand on her shoulder, his fingers curling almost possessively around the nape of her neck. *Yes, you can, little one. I am here; just inhale and the air is there. If not, I will breathe for both of us. I will be your air.* The words whispered in her mind. Soft. Sensuous. Robbing her of her ability to speak.

Nicolae lifted his gaze from Destiny to the woman sitting across from her. His eyes were flat and cold as his gaze rested on MaryAnn. "What are you doing to her? I warn you, she is under my protection, and if you have done anything to hurt her, you will answer to me."

Chapter Four

Fear clawed at the pit of Destiny's stomach. Her first instinct was to turn and fight, but the pressure of his fingers at the nape of her neck was a clear warning, preventing her from moving. Without taking his censorious gaze from MaryAnn, Nicolae bent very close to Destiny, until his breath was warm against her ear and his lips skimmed her earlobe, a mere wisp of contact that set her heart pounding and sent heat rushing through her veins. "You cannot call attention to our kind in this place, Destiny. It is the last thing you want."

His hair brushed her skin like raw silk, and she felt a shiver all the way to her toes. His masculine scent enveloped her. Beckoned. Tempted. His arm, so casually draped over her shoulder, was hard with muscle and sinew, felt hot through her thin blouse. Destiny was so aware of Nicolae as a man, she couldn't think properly. Her world narrowed until it encompassed only the two of them. A strange roaring throbbed in her ears. Her body seemed heavy yet alive, every nerve ending shrieking at her, though whether in alarm or need, she wasn't certain. She didn't care.

Destiny had spent most of her life alone. Never touching another person unless she was feeding, rarely speaking to anyone. Yet now, here in this place, she was surrounded by people, overwhelmed by the smell of blood, the beating of hearts. Music pounded out a primitive rhythm. She was suffocated by perfume. Alcohol. The noise was deafening, the scents overpowering. This was too much. All of it. She never should have allowed the door to her past to crack open for even a moment. And here was Nicolae. Coming to her when she was lost in the midst . of hell. She wasn't prepared for her strange physical reaction to him.

"Why in the world would you think I'm doing something to hurt Destiny?" MaryAnn looked more shocked than intimidated. "I would never do such a thing. Destiny is upset and rightly so, but not at me. Are you a friend of hers?"

Destiny let her breath out slowly, forced herself to attempt to relax beneath those strong massaging fingers. MaryAnn's voice snapped her back to the reality of here and now. *Pretend.* She was a mistress of illusion when she had to be. The pad of his thumb lingered over the pulse beating so frantically in her throat, slid back and forth in a gentle, soothing caress. Nicolae could feel her body trembling—how could he not? He could hear her heart pounding loud and hard, and that telltale pulse told him much more than she wanted him to know. But she couldn't stop trembling. She, who was always so controlled, could not control her own pulse beneath his marauding thumb.

"Perhaps I misread the situation. I could feel Destiny's distress from across the room and I thought you were upsetting her." Nicolae smiled at the woman, a show of elegant charm. He bowed slightly, his white teeth perfect, his sensual face without guile. He looked like a lord of old, at home in a palace. He leaned lower to brush a lingering kiss across the top of Destiny's dark head. Strands of her hair caught for a moment in the stubble along his jaw, connecting them. "I cannot bear it when she is upset. Forgive me if I frightened you. I'm Nicolae Von Shrieder."

"MaryAnn Delaney." MaryAnn couldn't take her eyes from Destiny's pale face. For just a moment, she thought there were dots of blood on Destiny's forehead, but Nicolae leaned over the younger woman, his head and shoulders blocking MaryAnn's view, and with exquisite care seemed to press a small kiss on the spot. When he straightened, the tiny dots were no longer there, and MaryAnn was certain she had imagined them.

The swirl of Nicolae's tongue was too much for Destiny to endure. In another minute she would lose control completely. She had no idea what she'd be capable of if she became hysterical, but control was everything to her. She was determined not to lose it. Destiny pushed her palms against the table, sliding her chair deliberately into Nicolae, and surged to her feet, certain she would catch him by surprise.

As if he had choreographed her movement, Nicolae turned her neatly into his arms, drawing her body into the shelter of his. "Excuse us," he said to MaryAnn, and without missing a beat he whirled Destiny out onto the dance floor.

"What are you doing?" To her horror, her voice shook. Hunger was a craving now, a terrible, inevitable craving she couldn't ignore. Her face was pressed into the warmth of the hollow of his shoulder. She remembered the taste of him. With his blood on her tongue, the insatiable hunger had been appeased for once and the continual torment inside her had lessened. She had never felt so sated by anything.

"I'm dancing with you," he answered easily, pulling her closer to him.

Their bodies were pressed together, their clothing the only barrier between them. With each gliding step her breasts pushed into his chest, her nipples becoming sensitized from rubbing against his shirt. His muscles were taut and defined as he whisked her around the floor. More than anything, she was aware of the thick, hard part of him pressed against her stomach as they moved together. Floated together. It frightened her, yet fascinated her. Her own blood seemed to pool, low and thick, so that she throbbed and burned with an unfamiliar need.

Their feet barely touched the ground. She had never danced in her life, yet her body followed every movement of his flawlessly. As if she had been born to partner him.

"Close your eyes, give yourself up to the music." *To me.* He whispered the temptation in her ear, his hand moving over her back, tracing her spine. *You have not fed, Destiny. Why have you come to such a place hungry? Do you think to punish yourself?*

It was too close to the truth. She had come to remove MaryAnn's memories, to violate the trust of a woman who was inherently good.

You are not evil. He whispered the words against her skin, even as they brushed in her mind. His tongue swirled over her pulse. Tasted. Lingered. Her entire body clenched in reaction. *You are Carpathian, a race in harmony with nature. A protector of mankind. You do not kill wantonly or lightly.*

He was killing her. With hope. With dreams. With things she dared not reach for. Trust was something she could never give one of his kind. He made her feel things she didn't want to feel. Made her long for things impossible for her to have. Every ounce of self-preservation shrieked at her to wrench herself out of his arms and run for her life. Instead, almost helplessly she nuzzled closer, found his beckoning pulse with her mouth.

I could kill you, she breathed. *Drain the blood from your body right here.* She wanted him to know she was undecided. His fate was undecided. That her fingers curling in the silk of his shirt meant nothing. That her body molding itself to his didn't matter. That she had control. She had power. His voice was sheer magic. It washed over her, into her, wrapped itself around her heart and soul, but none of that mattered. It would never matter.

Yes, you could. The words purred in her mind, a blend of heat and smoke. *Take what you need, I offer freely.* He nuzzled her hair again, his breath warm against her cheek as he switched to speaking, his voice low and soft. "Each rising I wake with your pain crawling through my body. I wake with your sorrow in my mind." His hands found her hair, bunched silken strands in his fist. "It is my right to care for you, to be your solace. If you seek my death, little one, if that is what you need for your own survival, so be it. I would give my life for yours and never look back." *I am willing to give my life to you.* There was intimacy in his voice. There was tenderness. There was honesty.

Her eyes burned with her effort not to see him. Not to hear him. Not to trust him. Not to *need* him. Heat beckoned. Seduced. Her tongue lapped at his pulse. She felt his reaction. Not fear. Hunger. Sharp and terrible. Erotic hunger so strong his muscular body shuddered. Hardened. Grew hotter. His breath left his lungs in a rush of anticipation.

Nicolae whirled her into deeper shadows, away from prying eyes, blurring their images so that there seemed to be a veil of haze between the couple and the rest of the people in the place. She was in his arms at long last, fitting perfectly. Belonging. He willed her to feel it, feel their deep need of one another, even as he acknowledged her terrible struggle. She had survived the abomination of her childhood by choosing solitude. By never trusting. He knew what he was asking of her. Not even asking. Demanding.

Trust. Such an easy word. Such an impossible quality. How could he ask or demand such a thing of Destiny? She had been taught *never* to trust. Her life had depended upon it. Her very soul had depended upon it.

Nicolae allowed his lashes to drift down, his head to rest over hers. His heart fragmented. He knew his own power, his enormous strength. But he could not, *would* not force compliance from Destiny. If they came together it would be with her full consent. It couldn't be any other way. An evil monster had forced acts of humiliation and degradation upon her, along with years of unspeakable pain and horror. Nicolae could not force a relationship on her. How could he do anything that might resemble the actions of that depraved creature who had stolen her childhood, her family and her innocence?

Destiny moved restlessly in Nicolae's arms. *You shouldn't tempt me, Nicolae.* She hadn't meant to use his beautiful name. She wanted nothing intimate between them, and his name seemed musical to her. It came out sounding all wrong. Husky. Intimate. Aching. She breathed his name against his pulse while her body burned and pulsed and throbbed. While butterfly wings brushed at the pit of her stomach. Helplessly she touched her mouth to his skin. Tormenting herself. Torturing him.

"Destiny." There was an ache in his voice.

She made a sound of horror, wrenched her body away from his. Nicolae saw her eyes, the confusion and terror in their depths. "Get away from me right now," she demanded, backing away. Fearing him. Fearing *for* him.

Movement across the room caught his eye. MaryAnn had stood up, frowning. She took several steps toward Destiny but halted as Destiny lifted her hand in warning. Then Destiny was gone, moving so quickly she was a blur. Nicolae was left standing alone on the dance floor, his body as hard as a rock, his heart aching for his lost lifemate.

MaryAnn made her way to Nicolae's side. "Tell me what to do to help her." She touched his arm to draw his attention more fully to her. "I can see the sorrow in her eyes, and it breaks my heart. I know I can help her."

Nicolae stared down at the woman, seeing the compassion and determination written on her face. He had been slipping in and out of Destiny's mind for years even though he had never taken her blood to seal the bond between them. It had been Destiny's horrendous pain, coupled with her tremendous psychic abilities, that had allowed her to connect so completely with Nicolae. He had caught glimpses of the woman before him many times in Destiny's mind, although Destiny had tried to shield her from him. This woman knew more than any human should. She knew things that could get her killed.

"I'm no threat to you," MaryAnn said softly. Nicolae's face was a mask. Unreadable. Handsome and compelling. Dangerous. Instinctively she knew he was the same as Destiny, not quite human. "I want to help her. She saved my life twice."

"She has survived things so hideous you cannot even conceive of them. Why would you presume to think you can help her?"

Although his words were spoken in a low, beautiful timbre, something in that perfect tone made her shiver with apprehension. She was conversing with a powerful being, something she knew nothing of. Someone who made life-and-death decisions over others every day of his life. MaryAnn felt the impact of each of his words. She lifted her chin. "Because she chose me."

Nicolae studied her face for a long time. She had the feeling he was examining much more than her features. For one horrible moment she felt him moving in her mind. He didn't bother to hide it from her, deliberately showing her his power, a not-so-subtle threat. A warning. Whatever he found must have satisfied him, because he withdrew from her mind, leaving her memories still intact.

"Do you have any idea what you are asking?" Nicolae demanded in a low, compelling voice. "You must be very certain this is what you want. You know what I am. You know what she is. And you have an inkling of the demon we hunt. There is one in this city—at least one, maybe more. He is out there now, killing the innocent. Maybe hunting a small female child with the amazing gifts Destiny has. The knowledge of our existence that you have right now constitutes a danger to all immortals, whether they are vampire or hunter. It is allowed only in rare instances."

MaryAnn followed Nicolae across the room to a secluded table away from the crowds, knowing that whatever she said to him now would decide her fate. She thought of Destiny's eyes. Troubled. Filled with shadows and sorrows. "I can't leave her to suffer. She won't find her way back, Nicolae. I know she won't. You think you'll be able to reach her, and you might on some level, but it won't be enough. She's suffered a terrible trauma. That won't just go away because you will it to do so."

"You are risking your life." He wanted her to know the truth. "Destiny would not want you to risk your life for her." He pulled out a chair, stood courteously while MaryAnn slipped onto the seat. As he sat down across from her he waved off the waitress. "Think very carefully before you speak. I can remove your memories of all of this. Of Destiny. Of me. Of the creature that wanted to kill you. All of it. You will never worry about Destiny, because you will not remember that she exists."

"I don't want that." MaryAnn shook her head adamantly. "She's important to me, and I think I'm important to her." She leaned across the table toward him. "I can handle this. I really can. I'm afraid. I'd be silly not to be afraid, but you don't know what she did for me. Twice. She saved my life twice. She's given the sanctuary so much money, money we desperately needed to expand and to make sure the women had counseling and job opportunities. Destiny did that. She deserves a chance, too."

"MaryAnn—" His voice washed over her. Gentle. Compelling. "I will take care of Destiny. I give you my word of honor."

"I honestly don't think she will get better. I think she'll try, but you won't be able to help her overcome what's happened to her."

"I lived through it with her."

"I know," she said quietly. "I see the same things in your eyes that I see in hers."

"I understand her, understand what she needs. And we are meant to be together. Two halves of the same whole."

"She isn't whole, Nicolae; she's fragmented and lost. She can't go into a relationship that way and have it work. I think you know that or you wouldn't be talking with me. You would have already removed my memories."

"If I leave you with this knowledge, I will have to be able to monitor you at will. I am responsible for the safety of my people. I have to know that you are capable of keeping our secret at all times, and I will have to make sure that the undead cannot use you to get to Destiny."

MaryAnn swallowed her fear. "I think that's fair enough."

"It entails my taking your blood, MaryAnn. Not converting you, simply taking a small amount of your blood so that I can touch your mind at any time. It wouldn't hurt and you wouldn't be in danger, but the idea of it is uncomfortable to humans."

MaryAnn was silent, leaning her chin in her hand

while she studied his face. "Destiny wasn't given a choice, was she?"

Nicolae shook his head. "She was converted by the vilest of creatures. The undead. A vampire lives for the pain of others. He made her suffer for years. He subjected her to every humiliating degradation he could think of. He murdered men, women and children in front of her and forced her to drink their blood. He used her body for years in the most painful ways possible although she was an innocent child."

MaryAnn rubbed the heel of her hand over her face. "And you want me to desert her because I might be uncomfortable for a moment or two? I owe her more than that. Take my blood if you feel it is necessary, Nicolae, and let's find a way to help her."

Destiny rushed out into the night, dragging great gulps of air into her lungs. It was humiliating to be shaking like a child just because she was in such close proximity to so many people. She wouldn't admit her distress had been caused by anything else. How could she want to touch a man's skin? Be held in his arms? Breathe him into her body?

She knew about men, what they did, what they wanted from a woman . . . a girl . . . a child. A scream welled up from her soul, the terror of a child trapped with a monster. She pressed the scream back with her hand, as if to shove it back down her throat and bury the terror where she would never have to look at it. See it. Think of it.

The night is so beautiful, Destiny. Clear and cold and crisp. Look above you at the stars. His voice came like magic. Soothing. Gentle. Out of nowhere, simply there in her mind. Pushing away the memories of hard, hurting hands, rivers of blood, the faces of the damned. *There is nothing so beautiful as the night. Even the leaves are a shimmering silver. I did not remember that. Did you notice the color? Silver and gold tonight. The wind is whispering to us. Hear? Just listen to it, little one. It speaks to us of the secrets of the earth.*

She closed her eyes, listened to his voice, found her heartbeat, knew she was alive and whole. Knew she could make it through another minute. Another hour. Even another night. Destiny knew the truth then, accepted the truth. If she were to survive, then so must Nicolae. The nightmares haunting her were far too strong to conquer on her own. She might fight and win every other battle, but not the one for her sanity. Not the one for her soul. That was Nicolae's battle.

She took a deep breath and looked up at the sky, at the stars glittering like gems over her head. The tension was slowly draining out of her body, but the need was there, crawling through her with insistence. A craving she couldn't ever escape.

Your craving is natural, Destiny, like breathing. We are of the earth. We do not eat the flesh of living things. Is it so terrible what we sustain ourselves on? We harm no one. We see to the protection of humans. We live among them, do business with them. Just as you have learned to care for the people who live along these blocks, so will you care for our people.

Her first reaction was denial. More of them? Vampires? She shook her head, forcing herself to consider his words. Carpathians. A race of beings she now belonged to. Beings with special powers. Beings who could enter churches and stand under strings of garlic.

She suddenly laughed, the sound flowing down the street like music. She had a reflection. She knew what she looked like.

The tension began to drain out of her. Destiny inhaled deeply, thankful to be alone. A movement down the street caught her eye and she swung her gaze in that direction.

"Come here, girl!" Velda was imperiously waving at her, beckoning her up the street.

Destiny had forgotten to make herself invisible to the human eye. Velda shrieked again, waving so enthusiastically she nearly fell from her chair at Inez's side. Knowing she did not have it in her to deny the old lady, Destiny jogged along the sidewalk until she was a few feet from the two sisters. They were smiling at her with open, welcoming smiles, without guile, hiding nothing.

"At last! I've spotted you several times," Velda said with satisfaction, "haven't I, Sister? Haven't I told you such a pretty young woman shouldn't be out by herself so late at night? You need a young man. Don't worry, Inez and I have been giving it some thought, figuring just what man you should be with."

Destiny's eyebrow shot up and she blinked rapidly trying to assimilate what Velda was saying. Were the two women looking to hook her up with someone? "You don't even know me. I could be a horrible person. You wouldn't want to stick some poor unsuspecting man with me, now would you?"

Velda and Inez looked at each other, then beamed at her. "Now, dearie, you're a nice little thing. You need a man and a place to stay. We've been thinking about the little apartment across the street there. We think it would suit you just fine. I'm Velda, and this is my sister

Inez. Ask anyone—we have a reputation as match-makers."

Destiny had never thought of herself as being a "little thing," and a reluctant smile found its way briefly to her eyes.

"There, dear, so much better when you smile." Velda's pink-tipped hair swung breezily as her head bobbed. "I have the second sight, you know. I see a young man for you. Quite handsome, with nice manners."

"Rich, dear," Inez added. "Velda told me he's rich and handsome." She beamed, her purple hair glowing in the dark. "That should make you happy. Settle down, dear, have two or three children. You'll be happy. I wanted ten, but Velda stole my beau right out from under my nose."

Destiny gaped at the two elderly women as they patted an empty lawn chair insistently. They clearly expected her to join them. Not knowing how to decline graciously, she slid gingerly into the chair. She was aware of Nicolae's amusement at her uncomfortable predicament. Aware of the warmth of his laughter brushing her mind. Turning her attention to the two sisters, she determinedly ignored him, wondering fleetingly how they could be so closely connected. How could he touch her mind when he had not taken her blood?

Velda snorted, patting Destiny's arm. She didn't seem to notice Destiny wincing or drawing away. "Inez was such a beauty. All the men wanted her. She wouldn't choose, you know. She liked having them chase her. She's making up a story about my stealing her beau. I'm a true spinster. I never wanted a man in my life, and she certainly didn't want ten babies! Did you, Inez? You wanted to sing in a bar."

"I did sing in a bar," Inez returned haughtily. She patted Destiny's knee, unaware that Destiny was squirming to get out of reach. "I was a raving beauty, dear, not unlike you. But I had a real figure. I was no stick like you girls now. And I had a voice like an angel. Didn't I, Sister?"

"An angel," Velda agreed solemnly. She leaned close to Destiny. "Don't look at me, dearie. Pretend you're interested in the apartment over the dress shop there." She waved airly, so Destiny followed the direction of her pointing finger. Immediately Velda lowered her voice to a conspirator's whisper. "We're thinking of hiring a private eye. We've been discussing it. I think we need someone hard-boiled like Mike Hammer, but Inez thinks an intellect like Perry Mason would be better. What do you think?"

Destiny gaped at her. She had no idea what or whom the sisters were referring to. "Why do you think you need a private detective?" It was the only thing she could think of to say. She had no idea how she had ended up sitting between these two eccentric women. The thought of two seventy-year-old women needing a "hard-boiled" detective was laughable. Destiny had watched the women for the last few months. They were open and honest and so much a part of the neighborhood, she couldn't imagine the streets without them.

Velda looked around. Inez did the same. Simultaneously they hitched closer to Destiny. "There've been strange goings-on around here."

Inez nodded solemnly. "That's right, Sister, you tell her. Listen to her, dear—it's mojo. Bad, bad mojo."

Laughter bubbled up in Destiny's throat, but she blinked rapidly, battling to stay solemn. The two women deserved respect. They were gossips, but they were sharp. Destiny settled back into her chair. "I'm Destiny, by the way." She felt she owed them her name because they had spotted her on the streets often enough to recognize her. If they could see her as she moved rapidly along the streets at night, they had sharp eyes to go with their sharp minds. And more than that, they had restored a semblance of balance in her world. "Please do tell me."

"No one believes us, Sister," Inez cautioned. "They think we have bats in the belfry." She patted her bright hair, and Destiny noticed that her nails matched the amazing shade of purple. So did her tennis shoes. The laces were coiled and metallic purple.

"I doubt that," Destiny answered decisively. "You're very well respected by everyone. If you say something is going on, it probably is. I'd have to hear some details, though, before determining what sort of detective you'd need."

The sisters exchanged a long, satisfied look. It was Velda who took up the challenge. "It started a month or so ago. We began to notice small things, but at first we didn't connect them."

Inez nodded wisely. "Small things, you know?" she echoed solemnly while her head glowed purple and red from the odd lighting of the streetlamp.

Velda shushed her. "Sister, let me tell her."

"I was just verifying. An account must be verified or no one takes it seriously. Isn't that right, dear, don't you want verification? Two eyewitnesses are better than one, don't you think?"

Destiny didn't know if she reached out or if Nicolae was already a shadow in her mind. Or maybe she was a shadow in his. All she knew for certain was that she wanted to share with someone the extraordinary relationship these two wonderful women had. They were everything she had always wanted in a grandmother. They made her smile inside and lightened the burden she always carried.

She was pleased with Nicolae's reaction. Warmth flooded her, amusement, but not mocking laughter. He saw the sisters the way she saw them. It was the first time she could remember sharing something fun, lighthearted, a connection of warmth rather than pain and degradation. She knew that the moment would be etched in her memory forever.

Destiny took in every detail of the two women—their open, honest faces, their eccentric hair and attire. Even the green-and-white striped lawn chairs. The way the wind was riffling the leaves in the bushes and blowing small bits of dust and debris along the streets. This was as close to happiness as she had ever come.

"Destiny?" Inez prompted. "Velda's right about this. She has the second sight, you know."

"Do you, Velda?" Destiny asked curiously. She had never run across another person who had special gifts.

Velda nodded sagely. "I know things about people," she whispered. "That's how I can match people up. And that's why I know something's wrong." The whisper was dramatic, the voice theatrical. Destiny automatically scanned the minds of the two sisters, even though she knew it was an invasion of privacy. Velda was worried and so was her sister. They believed something had crept into their neighborhood, but no one would listen to them. They fully expected Destiny to laugh at them.

"I know things about people, too," she admitted, seeking to reassure the sisters. "It can be frightening to have information and not know how to convey it so that others listen. Please tell me what you've observed, Velda."

Velda patted her arm. Inez patted her knee. Neither seemed to notice that she squirmed uncomfortably, but Destiny knew them now. They were both good at reading people; they knew she didn't like to be touched, and they were determined to push past the protective barrier she erected around herself.

"You're a good girl, dearie," Velda said approvingly. "You were right, Sister—she's the one who will listen to us."

Destiny considered screaming in frustration. Couldn't they get on with it? This close proximity to others was unnerving. Her head was beginning to throb, and she was afraid there was danger of it exploding.

Male laughter echoed softly in her mind. Gentle. Teasing. So typical of Nicolae, amused by her self-inflicted predicament, but never malicious about it. Why was she softening toward him? Why was she noticing little things to love about his character? Vampires were deceivers, sweet-talking, cunning deceivers.

I do not like your thinking I am the undead. My heart is very much alive and in your hands. Do your best not to destroy it.

You are very lucky it isn't in my hands. She responded to him immediately. To his words that turned her heart over and left her helpless and vulnerable. *The only thing I know to do with hearts is incinerate them!*

Ouch! His laughter swept through her mind, moved through her body with the heat of her blood. Turned her to jelly right there in the silly lawn chair. His laughter should be outlawed. She'd thought that more than once over the years.

"It all started with Helena," Velda confided, dropping her voice and regaining Destiny's attention immediately. "Have you seen little Helena? Nice young girl, with a real figure, not like the half-starved bodies we see so much now."

Inez nodded. "She has a woman's figure, meat on her bones for a man to snuggle up against. And she knows she's a prize."

"True, Sister, Helena knows it. She has the confidence of a woman who can wait for the right man." Velda confirmed.

"The *right* man," Inez echoed, bobbing her purple head. Destiny knew the "young woman" they were speaking of. She was in her late thirties or early forties and was a bright spot on the street when she hurried along the walkways calling greetings to everyone. She had mahogany skin and straight hair as black as a raven's wing. Her eyes were a dark chocolate, and she was nearly always laughing. She did have confidence in her walk and a way of enticing men.

"I know who she is," Destiny admitted.

"She has a lover, a sweet man, John Paul. A great big bear of a man."

"A teddy bear," Inez explained.

Destiny had seen them together—Helena, a short woman with a ripe, curvy figure, and John Paul, a huge, burly man who looked at her as if she were the sun and the moon and everything in between. They held hands everywhere they went, and John Paul was always touching Helena, a small, stroking caress on her hair, on her shoulder, on her arm. John Paul seemed a gentle giant, well pleased that he had managed to capture Helena's attention.

"They've been together for years," Velda said. "Always in harmony, a perfect match. Helena is a flirt," she added.

"A terrible flirt," Inez affirmed.

"But she never goes home with other men. She talks and laughs, but it's always John Paul. She adores John Paul, really adores him. And he's wild about her."

Destiny knew they were speaking the truth. She had been watching the residents of the neighborhood for months, was a silent observer of their lives. John Paul lived for Helena. His every waking thought was for her.

"Helena was crying a few weeks ago, wandering around at night. She came over to us, and her face was swollen and bruised. John Paul had struck her several times. She said it wasn't like him at all. He came home from work and was 'different.'"

The nape of Destiny's neck prickled in alarm. A shadow crept out of the darkness, slid along the street toward them. Overhead, a sudden gust of wind carried swirling black clouds to obliterate the stars.

"John Paul is incapable of hurting Helena." She made it a statement. She knew his thoughts, knew his gentle nature. She knew how much he loved Helena. He would never risk his relationship with her. Helena was not a woman who would put up with a man striking her. "Are you certain?"

Velda nodded. "Helena believes him to be ill. She was planning to ask him to go to see a doctor. She thought he might have a brain tumor or something. It's just so out of character. The next day, when she confronted him, he didn't seem to remember what he'd done."

"Not at all," Inez affirmed. "He was horrified by Helena's injuries. He didn't remember yelling at her or hitting her or . . ." She trailed off, glancing at her sister.

Rape. The ugly word was unspoken but it shimmered in all of their minds. Destiny's stomach churned in protest. Helena loved John Paul. And John Paul was incapable of such acts. *What would cause such bizarre behavior?* She held her breath, waiting for the answer, waiting for Nicolae to confirm her worst suspicions.

Do not jump to conclusions. Our minds are always on the undead, but not all crimes are committed by vampires. Humans are capable of great atrocities.

She didn't want to be reminded of that. She wanted to think a vampire was responsible. How could a human be responsible for changing John Paul's entire personality? That didn't make sense to her.

"How is Helena?"

"She doesn't come out of her house much, and when she does, she is quiet and subdued. Not at all like her. And John Paul is upset and afraid of losing her. He told me he honestly doesn't remember anything about that day. It's sad," Velda said. "And, of course, there are other things."

The door to the bar opened, spilling light and loud music and laughter into the street. The three women turned to watch MaryAnn emerge with a man beside her. He was holding her elbow. Neither glanced toward the women, but rather turned toward the small alleyway leading behind The Tavern.

Destiny's heart nearly stopped beating for a moment, then began to pound fearfully.

Chapter Five

"Velda, Inez, I know this is important, and I do believe you. I want to hear everything you have to say about what's happening, but unfortunately, I have to go right now." Her breath was rushing into her lungs. *Don't you touch her!* There was no pleading, just a very real threat in her sharp command. She leapt to her feet, began jogging toward the alley, blurring her figure so that she could put on a burst of speed and the sisters wouldn't be able to see. The wind picked up, rushed down the street in a gale, pushing loose paper, sticks and leaves ahead of it, swirling dust eddies into towers of turbulence.

Her body moved with grace, with power, a lethal machine rushing to stop the inevitable. She tried to use the blood bond between them, reaching for him, attempting to immobilize him. She should have known he would never have given her his blood if it would give her complete domination of him. He was a true ancient with more power and strength, more battle savvy than she could hope to muster in her short years as a hunter. It was too late to stop him; she knew exactly the moment his teeth sank deep into MaryAnn's vulnerable neck.

Destiny hissed softly, a promise of retaliation, the taste of betrayal bitter in her mouth. Why had she allowed his voice to deceive her into believing he was something different? She burst around the corner, skidding to a halt as she saw them. MaryAnn was turned toward her, a small frown on her face. Nicolae's arms were around the woman, holding her in front of him like a shield. He lifted his head slowly, almost lazily, his gaze drifting over Destiny in a kind of challenge.

Destiny halted a few feet from them. MaryAnn was in terrible danger. Nicolae might easily kill her. Destiny was very aware that one wrong move on her part could be the deciding factor. "What do you want?" She would give him almost anything for MaryAnn. She prayed she wouldn't have to kill MaryAnn to keep her from falling into his hands. "Tell me what you want." She was moving in a slow circle as she stalked him. The air between them vibrated with tension. Overhead the darker clouds began to boil. Small veins of lightning arced from cloud to cloud. The wind began an eerie moan, rising every now and then to a shriek of anger.

Nicolae smiled, revealing his immaculate white teeth. He looked the predator he was. "I am no fledgling to be tricked, Destiny. Back away and listen to reason."

"She is under my protection."

"And mine," he said gently, his gaze steady on hers.

Destiny's soft mouth firmed, formed a straight line. She inched closer, angling toward the left of the couple. She was on the balls of her feet, ready for his single mistake, a single opening.

Without warning, a shadow dropped from the sky.

Silent. Deadly. A wicked beak and razor-sharp talons flew straight at MaryAnn's face. Destiny leapt to put herself between them, but the owl was already climbing, and MaryAnn looked terrified at the near miss. The beak had driven straight for her eyes.

"Don't move," Destiny cautioned MaryAnn. "Call him off, Nicolae. Call him off now."

"He is only protecting me," Nicolae explained gently. "He knows your intent and knows I will not hurt you. It is his warning to you. Should you harm me, he will kill her. I cannot stop him, and you know that, Destiny. He is my brother and seeks only to protect me. Think before you act." Nicolae kept MaryAnn firmly between them.

MaryAnn frowned. "Destiny, are you angry with Nicolae? I asked him to do this. I wanted him to take my blood."

Destiny winced visibly. "You have no idea what that means. You didn't want it. It isn't reasonable to think that you would. His voice is a weapon. It can deceive you into doing anything. His voice holds compulsion. Do you know what that is? It means you'll do anything he asks, anything he commands, anything he wishes. You think he gave you a choice, but he didn't. There was never a choice. You would have said yes to putting a gun to your head and pulling the trigger."

Lightning slashed the skies, nearly striking the owl as it circled above them, but the raptor dissolved in midair, leaving behind a trail of vapor. A shower of sparks scattered like gems, seeking a target, but just as quickly a fine mist blanketed the night, snuffing out the hot points of light.

"Do not do that again, Destiny." The warning was a

low growl. For the first time there was a distinct threat emanating from Nicolae.

"Wait, stop this right now!" MaryAnn shook her head decisively. "This was my idea, I reasoned it out every step of the way. Nicolae wanted to remove my memories, as a protection for you, for his people, and even for me. He said that my knowledge made me more vulnerable to a vampire."

That revelation penetrated Destiny's red haze of anger. The terrible pain of betrayal. There was truth in what MaryAnn said. A vampire could easily scan MaryAnn's thoughts and learn she had knowledge she shouldn't possess. Destiny took a breath, let it out slowly, trying to be calm while the wind whipped at her and lightning split open the sky. The crash of thunder reverberated loudly, shaking the ground, shaking the buildings.

The owl had settled on the rooftop above their heads, its dark eyes fixed intently on Destiny's face. It was silent, watching with a predator's rapt attention.

The wounds in her heart felt fresh and jagged. She had allowed Nicolae to get too close to her. She had let him inside.

I did not betray you, Destiny. I did what had to be done, what I knew you could not do. She is unharmed and now protected. It was her choice alone. I give you my word of honor.

His voice was always the same. So perfect. She lowered her lashes, indecisive again. She had come to the alley to kill him, but hope was swirling in her stomach and crushing her heart at the same time. She loved his voice and she hated it.

"Destiny—" MaryAnn could see tiny beads of sweat on the young woman's forehead. Only it wasn't sweat, it was beads of blood. "Look at me. Please look at me. If you can do what you say you can, look into my mind and see what happened between us. I wanted this. I don't want to forget you. I'm your friend. That matters to me."

Destiny's fingers curled into tight fists. "I don't have friends."

"Yes, you do. It might be frightening to have friends, but they're there for you. You know how I feel; you know it's real. I care what happens to you."

"I don't want you to care." Destiny snapped the words, her vivid eyes glittering, picking up the veins of lightning so that she looked dangerous. "I don't want any of this." She swept her hand to encompass all of them. The neighborhood. MaryAnn. The silent sentinel on the roof. Nicolae. Especially Nicolae. She wanted nothing to do with him. She hated him, hated the way his hands curved over MaryAnn's shoulders.

Nicolae allowed his arms to drop to his sides. If Destiny made a threatening move toward him, he was certain he was fast enough to escape danger, but he couldn't control Vikirnoff's response to an attack on him. *Do not hurt her.* He couldn't stop himself from warning his brother.

I am fully aware that if I attack, you will be forced to protect her from me. Vikirnoff was unshakable. *She will not be allowed to harm you. Should she attempt to do so, I will divert her by attacking the human woman.*

Nicolae sighed softly. "Destiny, come with me." He held out his hand to her. "This situation is dangerous and belongs between us and no one else. Come with me now before something happens that neither of us can control."

Destiny went pale. Her teeth bit at her lower lip. She glanced up at the owl, looked at MaryAnn. Took a reluctant step toward Nicolae. Another. Nicolae felt as if he could breathe again. He had known what she would think when he had made the decision to take Mary-Ann's blood, how Destiny would react, but he hadn't counted on how painful his apparent betrayal would be to her. Seeing her suffer shook him more than he had ever imagined anything could.

Destiny looked at his outstretched hand, wiped her palm on her thigh, as if she were afraid to be alone with him. "MaryAnn, will you be all right walking home alone?" She sounded as if she were pleading with Mary-Ann to save her.

"Perfectly all right," MaryAnn said firmly. "You go with Nicolae and talk things out. I'm certain the very interesting bird will see me home safely." She grinned at Nicolae, waved daringly at the owl.

Nicolae couldn't help giving an answering grin. He liked MaryAnn. Who could not? There was something special about her. Her courage and loyalty set her apart. He could see why Destiny had settled in the neighborhood, drawn by this woman who worked so diligently for others; she was a woman of great compassion.

Nicolae took Destiny's hand. He couldn't say she held it out to him, or even met him halfway. He had to reach out, shackle her wrist and bring her hand to him. Lace his fingers through hers. But she didn't pull away from him. A small victory, but one that he treasured. Her fingers were ice-cold. And she was trembling.

He didn't make the mistake of tugging her to his side. He went to hers, standing close so that his larger frame sheltered her body from the wind. So that she could feel his body heat. So that electricity seemed to arc between them, crackling and snapping with a life of its own.

The owl flapped its wings, took flight overhead. The movement seemed to calm the wild winds. Even the white-hot whips of lightning faded from the dark clouds as Destiny began to relax.

MaryAnn reached out and, to Destiny's horror, hugged her briefly before walking determinedly away. Destiny simply stood frozen in place, as still as a statue, unaware her hand was gripping Nicolae's so hard that he was afraid she would pulverize his bones. She watched MaryAnn walk out of the alley with the owl flying just above her as if guarding her. Or stalking her. "He won't hurt her," Nicolae said. It was in her mind to try another attack on the owl. Knock it from the sky so she could be sure MaryAnn was safe.

"He only threatened her to stop you from attacking me."

Nicolae stepped closer to her. "You have not fed." It was an invitation.

"I don't trust myself yet." She looked up at him then. Studied his face with its dark sensuality, its sharp angles and planes. The eyes had seen too many centuries. Faced too many battles. He was a man who had been alone for far too long. "I can't be what you want me to be." She had touched his mind often. She knew his thoughts. *Lifemate.* She understood all the word implied. Everything. *Lifemate.* Something she could never be.

His hand framed her face. Exquisitely gentle, his fingers trailed over her cheekbones, lingering with tenderness. "You are everything I want you to be. There is no need to worry about such things. You do not know me. How can you decide?"

His touch wreaked havoc with every cell in her body, caused a small rebellion of her senses. A mutiny of blood and bone and nerve endings. He confused her. Every time he came near her, she felt different from normal. Restless. Needy. His voice found its way into her body, wrapped itself tightly around her heart and lungs, so that each time he spoke, he robbed her of breath. Of life. Of the ability to hate. Him. Herself. What she was.

"It was easier without you."

"You have never been without me," he pointed out. He curled his fingers around hers, brought her knuckles to his mouth.

Her heart jumped at the touch of his lips against her skin. A whisper of velvet. A stroke of heat. He was so beautiful there in the night. Tall and strong and alive. Too real. Too masculine. Too strong. There was a lump in her throat that made it almost impossible to speak. "You are, you know. Too strong for me." Her voice came out husky, strangled, so unlike her.

His thumb feathered along her cheek, traced the path of an imaginary tear. His palm cupped her forehead, removed every trace of the tiny beads of blood. "You were honed in the fires of hell, Destiny. No one will ever be as strong as you are. I know you fear you will lose yourself by being with me, but that would be impossible. I am not asking you to join with me. I am not asking anything of you other than for you to grow accustomed to my presence. I have shared your mind for many years, shared your fears and every unspeakable evil that was done to you. I shared your battles and I know your every secret. It is my physical presence that is unsettling to you."

He leaned closer, so close that his lips skimmed over the corner of her mouth. Her blood heated and her stomach clenched. "I need you. To live. To save my soul. I am willing to wait as long as it takes."

Her eyes met his. She flinched away from the dark sensuality she saw there. From the tremendous intensity. "I know that you're willing to wait. But you can't really wait, can you? I've read your mind. I know that this thing you call lifemate is essential to keep you from turning vampire."

He didn't even blink at the accusation. He nodded, his gaze drifting possessively over her face. "I *can* wait, Destiny. If it is difficult, that is not your failing but mine. Let me worry about how I will manage it."

"I can't be intimate with you." Her chin rose slightly; her soft mouth trembled. "I could never be intimate with you, and that's a big part of what you want from me."

"We are already intimate, Destiny. Sex is not necessarily intimacy. We have shared far more than other couples, shared *intimate* details of our lives." He tilted her chin, studied her vivid eyes. "Come with me. Let me show you what you are, not what you imagine yourself to be."

"Why does everything you say sound like a temptation?" A faint smile gleamed for a brief moment in the depths of her eyes. "Can't you just be dull and uninteresting?"

He laughed softly, brought her hand once more to his astonishing mouth. His teeth teased the pads of her fingers. "At least that is a start. I would much rather be a temptation than dull and uninteresting."

"Where are we going?" She moved backward, a subtle retreat. "I haven't spent so much time with people in my entire life. It's"—she searched for the right word— "uncomfortable."

At least she was willing to come with him. He couldn't ask for more than that. When he was near her, his pulse pounded and his head throbbed. His body was hard and full, aching for her. The ritual words beat in his mind, and deep within, the crouching beast lifted its head and roared for release. Nicolae didn't flinch from the knowledge in her eyes. He had deliberately given her an advantage. She needed to be able to touch his mind at will. To feel she could know his true intent. He had no intention of hiding his difficulties from her. It was the Carpathian way of life, the male struggling to keep darkness at bay. It was a fact, and finding his life-mate created its own complications.

Nicolae dissolved without another word, streaking through the dark clouds, a heavy mist mixing with the fog and moving determinedly over the city. He didn't hesitate, once again giving Destiny a choice. She had to want to take the steps, want to give them a chance.

That's not what I'm doing, she replied, responding to his last thought. There was no chance of their being a couple. Together. Lifemates. Destiny leapt into the air, bursting into the sky like a rocket. Her body dissolved into a prism of colored molecules, tiny drops that slipped lightly through the veils of fog.

She knew what his response would be and she braced herself. His laughter slipped into her mind. Nothing could rob her of breath the way the sound of his laughter did. There was something incredibly sexy about his laugh. Destiny followed the streaking comet through the sky, away from the city, toward the mountains and the forest some distance away.

She allowed the joy of flying to absorb her completely,

to block out her every worry. There were certain unde-
niable pleasures the dark gift had given her.

More than a few, Nicolae pointed out. *Each species
has its drawbacks and incredible wonders. I do not
think you have fully appreciated what you are.*

Destiny tried not to flinch away from his words. She
knew what she was, what she had worked to become.
She hunted the undead and she was becoming very
good at killing them. *How is it you can read my mind
when my blood does not call you? I'm not in pain;
I didn't connect with you.*

*We've created a path over the years. That is my best
answer. We are two halves of the same whole. I think
we would be able to find each other however far apart
we are, no matter what the circumstances.*

The answer both pleased and frightened her. Even
without the ritual words that were always in Nicolae's
mind, they were already sealed to one another. She
could not imagine her existence without him. There
would be no sanity. There would be no reality. Her
mind would fragment and crumble until there was no
substance, no thought. The idea terrified her. It terrified
her even more that she relied on him for her sanity.

Nicolae's heart contracted as he read her thoughts. He
stayed a quiet shadow in her mind, just as she was a
shadow in his. She clung to him without being aware of
it. He was very much aware that he clung to her.

He found what he wanted, a small secluded spot in
the heart of the forest. The richness of the trees and
foliage beckoned. He settled to earth, taking his true
form, a tall, wide-shouldered man with a wealth of rich
black hair, a dangerous mouth and compelling eyes. He
leaned lazily against a broad tree trunk, watching in-

tently as the colored molecules began to mesh together to form Destiny's curvaceous figure.

She remained some distance from him, a lost, wary look on her face. Her vulnerable mouth was very much at odds with the warning in her vivid eyes. She paced back and forth with quick, restless steps. "Why am I here?"

Nicolae regarded her with his cool, serene gaze. He could feel the need for solitude beating at her. "Have you scanned this place?"

She looked at him, impatience swirling in the turbulent blue-green of her eyes. "Of course I scanned. Did you think I would allow you to lead me into a trap?"

He could see that she was ready, expectant, her body in a good defensive position. He had taught her well. "What do you find here?"

Destiny glared at him. As the fog swirled in long white streamers, darker clouds drifted across the moon to obscure its radiance. Heat and fire glowed and reflected red and orange in her eyes. Tiny flames seemed to burn there. She blinked and the illusion was gone. Keeping her wary gaze on him, Destiny inhaled slowly. Deeply. Taking the crisp, clean air into her lungs. Wind rushed through the trees, rustled the leaves and whispered to her.

"What do you hear?"

"So much. You know that. I hear animals and the stories of their lives. There are no humans close, not even in camps."

"This part of the forest is little traveled," he agreed. "Carpathians are a species of people in harmony with the earth. The soil here is rich, and when it embraces you, its healing properties rejuvenate you. The healing soil of our homeland is beyond anything you can imag-

ine. Like this, but a thousand times richer. I miss it."
His white teeth flashed briefly in the night. "Especially
after a particularly long battle."

"What are you trying to tell me?" She ran her hand
over the bark of a small branch. She could hear the sap
running in the tree. Insects swarmed over her head in
the canopy above. An occasional owl flitted to branches
near them out of idle curiosity. A few miles away, a
cougar hunted with hunger rumbling in its belly.

"I want you to know our world. It is not the depraved
world of the vampire. We are not all evil any more than
every human is evil. We have wonderful gifts and many
problems to overcome. We have longevity, yes. We appear immortal, yet we can be killed. Not easily; a
wound that should be fatal can be healed with our saliva
and good rich soil. The blood of an ancient has healing
properties. We use the herbs and plants that abound in
our world. We can command the weather should we
have need. But we must rest in the hours of the sun. We
have limitations."

Destiny regarded him carefully. "Tell me more."

"I have told you these things often, Destiny. Are you
finally ready to listen?"

"I thought they were fairy tales. I needed something
to live for, and you gave it to me. You turned me into a
hunter of the undead."

For the first time he looked sad. Nicolae raked a hand
through the dark silk of his hair so that it spilled around
him like a halo. "I know I did, Destiny. I could not think
of another way to stop the things the vampire was doing
to you. I could not find you. You would not speak to me.
I had to use you to kill him."

She lifted her chin, her eyes stormy. "Don't you dare

feel sorry for that. It's the one thing I don't feel sorry for, and I don't ever want to. He did things—things I still can't face. With your help, I found the strength to defeat him. Don't you take that away from me. I deceived him and I managed to rid the world of something evil. I was only fourteen when I did it." She averted her face, but he caught a glimpse of hell in her mind.

"I did not want death ever to touch you. I never wanted that for you."

"It touched me the day I first heard his voice." She turned back to him, her gaze moving moodily over his face. Studying him. Looking to see beyond the mask he wore. "A voice like yours. Beautiful beyond belief, but so dangerous. Compelling and intense and filled with promises. You have that same danger in you. The power to crush another with your voice. To lure someone to you and compel him to do your bidding."

He nodded slowly. "That is so; it is a two-edged gift that can be used for good or evil. You have that same gift now. You have employed it, Destiny." His gut clenched. "On the young man you used for sustenance. You called him to you, kept him calm with promises of paradise."

Destiny couldn't deny his charge. She knew her voice held enthrallment. It was easy to lure men to her, to hold them compliant while she fed. It was easy to leave them with pleasant memories, and somehow that lessened the guilt she felt.

Nicolae stirred, a rippling of muscle, of menace, instantly drawing her full attention back to him. He struggled to keep the demon leashed and under control. Jealousy was an ugly emotion. It had no place in his life, in his relationship with Destiny. She feared intimacy and the sharing of her body, and he knew why. He knew her darkest secrets. Jealousy was beneath him, and he refused to allow it to grow into a cancer when they already had so many obstacles to overcome.

"Thank you," she said simply, watching him with her careful eyes.

His grin was sheepish. "It is a male thing."

Her eyebrow shot up. "I thought jealousy was universal. I didn't like seeing your arms around MaryAnn, but I thought it was because I was afraid for her." She shrugged her shoulders, the movement strangely elegant.

Nicolae found everything about her intriguing and tempting. She touched him on so many levels, not the least of which was his instinct to protect. Destiny did not want a protector, didn't believe she needed one. But he saw the vulnerability around her soft mouth, saw so clearly the torment in her eyes. He could see the terrible struggle for sanity that she endured at each rising. Every cell in his body roared at him to take her into the shelter of his arms, to shield her with his body from every hurt. She stood there so bravely, admitting to him that it had bothered her when she saw him with MaryAnn in his arms. And she had confessed in order to make him feel better.

His grin widened foolishly before he could resume his customary mask. Warmth spread through his body and tugged at his heartstrings.

"MaryAnn is quite a woman. She has a gift or two of her own." He was careful in choosing his words.

Destiny nodded. "I think that's what drew me to her. MaryAnn isn't even aware of her psychic ability. I felt the small surge of power each time she connected with a woman to counsel her. I spent a lot of time standing on the balcony of her office listening to her. Even her group sessions touched me." She was admitting something to him she hoped he would comprehend. She recognized she couldn't live a normal life and had tried to find a way to heal herself.

"You are not a monster, Destiny. Our people face many problems. Our men lose their ability to see in color, to feel emotion after two hundred years. Everything fades. In the old days, when our people were plentiful and our lifemates were close, it wasn't so. Now we feel the scarcity of lifemates acutely. With no women to give us children, there was no hope for our dying race. Many of our males have chosen the momentary rush of power, the high of a kill over honor and a barren existence. That forces us to hunt them despite the fact that they are often family and friends. Each kill we make spreads the darkness until it consumes us. It is not an easy life, tormented by fading memories of color and laughter and what it was like to have genuine emotion."

Destiny rubbed her temples. She didn't like to think about his life, or touch on his memories. A barren life of gray and white, an endless desert stretching out in front of him. Until she had connected with him. She saw clearly his worry for Vikirnoff. She saw clearly his need of her.

"Some human women with psychic abilities are capable of being converted to our species. You are obviously one of those women. We need children. Our women, our children, are precious to us, true treasures. We protect them with everything in us. Our women and children are our only hope."

"And that's what the vampire did to me, right? He converted me. How?"

"It takes three blood exchanges, but with a lifemate, it's not painful or terrible in the way you experienced. When we make love, it's natural to share each other's essence. To want our blood to flow in each other's veins. It's almost a compulsion. When we are with our lifemates, kissing them, skin against skin, exchanging blood is a beautiful need."

His voice seemed to whisper over her, a soft temptation she couldn't think about. "I see what you're trying to say to me. I look into your mind and heart and I can see that you mean what you're saying. I only wish this were all true, Nicolae, but it can never be for me. I believe that what you say about Carpathians is fact. I sense goodness in you, along with the crouching beast. But you and I both know I wasn't converted by you. Or by a Carpathian male. I can smell tainted blood miles away. The stench is disgusting. Do you believe I can't smell it on myself? In the cave, they called me to join them. You heard them calling me. Even the undead recognize what I am. Perhaps if one of your kind had converted me, I'd be all that you say, but it was a vampire, and his blood runs in my veins."

"You can be healed."

"Can you heal my memories? Can you remove the things that were done to me? You think you made me into a killer, Nicolae, but it wasn't you. It was never you."

"I taught you to kill, Destiny. No matter how necessary I deemed it, killing was foreign to your nature. It is not to mine." He was not going to allow her to feel as if she were born a monster. "I touched your mind with mine. I still do. The shadows there are of a vampire's making, not yours. Already my blood has lessened the burning in your veins. With time we can overcome what he has wrought."

Destiny shook her head. "I've lived with this forever. If there had been a way to fix it, I would have done so already. I may be partially in your world, but I'm also in the world of the undead. I'm unclean. I know it before I open my eyes, before I take my first breath on rising. I've killed so many times, I can never remove the blood from my hands." She looked at him, unaware of the terrible sorrow on her face.

Nicolae saw it and it turned him inside out.

"I examined your memories, Nicolae. I've had so many years of studying your mind, the battles and techniques used to kill. You don't feel anything when you attack. You don't know hatred. And you don't know rage. You don't know satisfaction and joy in killing. I do. Is that what you want in the mother of your children?" She turned away from him, hating him for making her confess her failings aloud. Making her see herself so clearly. "You never felt; I felt too much. I *wanted* to kill. You had no choice."

He glided closer, his heart breaking for her. "You didn't have a choice either, Destiny," he reminded. "He didn't give you choices."

"There's always a choice. You said yourself that the males can give up their lives rather than become vampire. I see in your mind the steadfast resolve to do so if it becomes necessary . . . and yet I didn't make that choice."

His hand swept down the line of her hair, caught the nape of neck and held her still. "You were not made vampire, Destiny. You are Carpathian."

"Then why do I feel hatred and the desire to kill?

Why am I like him and not like you, Nicolae? Do you think it makes it easier to have you near me, knowing what I am, what I've become?" She placed her palm on the wall of his chest, fingers splayed wide, and tried to push him away from her.

He was as solid as a rock, unmoving despite her insistence. "You are not like the monster who stole a child from the safe haven of her home. You are not like the creature who destroyed a young girl's right to a world of innocence. You are nothing like the depraved one who reveled in torturing and killing others. I see into *your* mind just as clearly as you see into mine. I know who you are, Destiny. I will always know."

"Intimacy." She murmured the word and there were tears in her eyes. "You look into my mind and call it intimate. I call it hell."

He drew her into his arms. "Your hunger is beating at me. I feel it deep inside me, an endless, empty ache." His fingers bunched in her hair and he turned her face into the hollow of his throat so that his pulse beat strongly beneath her lips. "I feel how his blood burns like acid in your veins. Let me replace it with my blood. Let me give you that small gift. That is true intimacy, Destiny, knowing what you need and providing it."

"And what of your needs?" Almost helplessly she rested her head there against his throat. Her mouth was already moving over his skin, the temptation far too great to resist. She could remember the exact taste of him. The feel of his arms, his skin. The power flowing into her body. "What if I can never provide you with what you need? The thought of a man touching me is . . ." She trailed off, inhaling his scent, taking it deep into her lungs. It could never be. It was too late for the things in his mind.

She didn't want a man touching her, yet every nerve ending was on fire for him. An unfamiliar heaviness had settled in her body. Her breasts felt swollen and ached for his touch. Not a man's touch. His touch. Only his touch. Tears burned, threatened to consume her. If she cried, she might never stop. She might drown the world with her tears. "I don't need pity. I never asked for pity." She said it with her lips tasting his skin, his heat. Absorbing him into her. She actually felt his body hardening, his muscles taut against her softness, his heavy erection pressed tightly against her.

"I am not giving you pity, Destiny. This is love." He said it tenderly. Coaxing her. "Yours for the taking. This is unconditional love. Nothing more, nothing less."

His arms were strong and warm; her body fit perfectly into his. "Your body wants my body," she whispered, the terrible sorrow welling up in her like a fountain. Her voice was husky and ragged. She was damaged for all time, a broken thing, forever contaminated by evil.

His hand clenched in her hair, pushed it aside to expose the vulnerable nape of her neck. He ached for her. For himself. "Of course my body wants you. That is only right and natural, Destiny. You are my true lifemate. There is no other for me, nor will there ever be. Look beyond my body to see into my heart and my soul. See yourself the way I see you. Courageous and beautiful. You are everything. Look into my mind and see that I want only to be what you need."

She couldn't look into his mind. Or his heart. Or his soul. She was afraid she would find just what he said.

Happiness and hope. A glimpse of what might have been. She knew exactly what she was. She lived with her body and her mind and her scarred soul every rising. Dreams had no place in her world. Destiny closed her eyes and allowed her incisors to lengthen. She needed to feed. That was all. That was all there could ever be between them. He was prey like every other man. Nothing more. Never more than that. She meant to drive her teeth deep, hoping to hurt him, hoping to drive him away from her.

It was impossible to hurt him. She couldn't do it. Her tongue swirled over his pulse, her breath warm and soothing. Her body moved on its own, restless and with a sense of urgency, pushing close to his, her hands moving over his chest, his back, shaping the defined muscles while his skin grew hotter and his breath grew ragged.

Nicolae whispered her name softly, hoarsely, a plea for mercy, his body going up in flames. Destiny wrenched herself out of his arms. She was shaking, her expression a mixture of fear and anger. "Go away from me," she said. "Stay away from me. I'm afraid of what I'll do to you if you stay." She backed away from him. "Please, if you really care, just go to some other land where I know you'll be safe."

He watched her leave and made no move to follow her. The chaos of her mind was too turbulent. A boiling mass of violence and rage, hurt and fear. Nicolae remained where he was for a long time, his head down, breathing deeply to get through his sorrow. To get through her pain. When he touched his face he was shocked at the blood-red tears he wept.

Chapter Six

The moment Destiny placed her foot on the steps in front of the church, she felt the vibrations of violence. She had tried to leave Seattle, go back to being a no-mad, roaming the world, but after several risings, she had reluctantly returned. She had deliberately stayed away from the neighborhood, determined to move on. Determined not to care about any of them. Not purple-or pink-haired ladies or MaryAnn or Nicolae. None of them mattered to her. Not a single one.

But she was a woman of honor. She had unfinished business with Velda and Inez; she'd given her word, so she had no choice but to return. She told herself honor was her only reason, but it was a lie and weighed heavily on her heart.

Destiny stared at the church doors. She had come back to this place, her one anchor, her last refuge, her sanctuary. Even in this holy place, something evil had followed her. She moved up the stairs cautiously, her footfalls silent, almost gliding above ground. She moved with all the stealth of a hunter. Destiny's hand was steady as she pushed open the doors to the church. At once she scented blood. The smell was nearly overpowering, a dark richness that beckoned and warned. She felt her heart accelerate and her pulse jump. The palms of her hands were sweaty as she widened the opening. Her stomach knotted, and hunger heightened into a terrible craving.

She scanned the church, found no one hiding, but the reverberations of violence were strong. She lifted her foot and hesitated, trepidation filling her soul. "Father Mulligan?" She called out his name softly and resolutely stepped across the threshold.

Nothing happened. Not a single lightning bolt slammed down from the sky to incinerate her for such a sacrilege. Her heart settled down to a steady rhythm as she gained confidence. She could see easily in the darkened interior. Several candles lit in a small alcove to her left were dim pinpoints of flickering lights. She spotted the priest lying on the floor near the altar. In his brown robes he looked like a dark heap of rags cast aside on the marble stair leading to the altar. Destiny knelt at his side. "Father— not you," she whispered. "Who would hurt you?"

The priest remained motionless for several heartbeats. Destiny leaned close to him. She could hear his ragged breathing. He was alive, but she was afraid to touch him. He looked so fragile, she was afraid she might hurt him. And a part of her was afraid that if she touched such a holy man, she might be struck dead on the spot. The priest groaned, lifted his fingers to touch his bloody scalp. His lashes fluttered, and then he was looking at her.

"Father? Who did this?" She inched back, automatically seeking the shadows.

"Child, I'm afraid you're going to have to help me sit up. I'm quite dizzy." His Irish brogue was still thick despite many years in the States.

"Touch you, Father?" She sounded horrified. "What if I hurt you?"

He managed a smile. "I don't think you're going to do any more damage to my hard head than has already been done. Give me a hand."

Taking a deep breath, Destiny put her arm gingerly around his shoulders. When nothing happened, she took a firmer grip. Very carefully she helped him into a sitting position. He felt much thinner than he appeared in his robes, his bones protruding and fragile. His body was trembling, and he swayed as if he might not be able to sit alone, so she kept her arm around him. She realized he was older than she had first thought.

"When I realized he was going to hit me, I thought of you and all your late visits. I knew God would send you to me." He tried a wink and winced instead. "Just to stack the odds a bit in my favor, I sent up a little prayer to ask God to get a message to you."

"Well, he sent for me a little late." She was nobody's heroine. It angered her that anyone would hurt such a generous, compassionate man. "God must have been sleeping when you sent Him the message. He just now delivered it." She had no idea why she had come to the church but somehow she had felt an urgent need to visit.

"You're here—that's all that matters."

"Can you stand up?" His extreme pallor worried her. "Maybe I'd better call an ambulance."

"No, no, don't do that. Just let me sit here for a moment and rest." The priest patted her hand gently as if reassuring her. "If you call an ambulance, we'll have to explain all this, and it would be better to get to the bottom of it ourselves."

Destiny frowned at him. "You're not making any sense, Father. You have to call the police. Whoever did this should be punished."

He slumped closer to her, leaning more of his weight against her. "No, that's why I needed you." His voice sounded weaker. "You can't go to the police. It was one of my parishioners. He isn't like this. I don't know what got into him. He didn't need the money—there was nothing much to take—but there was no reasoning with him." He closed his eyes and sagged completely against her. "I'm counting on you."

"You're really hurt, Father," Destiny pointed out. "You need medical attention."

"What is your name?"

"Destiny," she said angrily, feeling murderous toward the priest's attacker. *Nicolae. I need you to come to the church.* She hated calling him. She knew he would be grinning like an ape when he received her call. Destiny glared at the priest. "You have no idea what you're forcing me to do."

"Yes, I'm afraid I do, child. I know you do not wish to be in contact with others, but I have a feeling only you can solve this for me. I don't want the police involved. Promise me you'll handle this yourself."

"I don't believe this." Destiny threw her hands up in exasperation, then quickly caught the priest to her to keep him from striking his head on the marble step. "First the sisters and now you."

You sound impatient for me. Male satisfaction purred in his voice.

Destiny pressed her lips together to keep from shrieking in frustration. The world had suddenly gone insane. *Well, don't puff up yet. Do you have any skills in healing humans?*

There was a small silence. Destiny couldn't help the small smile that flitted briefly across her face and found its way into her mind. And into his. *You want me to heal a human for you?*

Did you think I wanted your company?

His laughter came as always. Wrapping her up in warmth and tugging at her heart. *That is my woman, always so warm and welcoming. Is your human a male?* She caught that small hint of menace flaring in him.

Yes, as a matter of fact, he is, and important to me, so quit talking and get moving.

You amaze me. You know I will help you, yet you still keep yourself from me.

She rolled her eyes and took a firmer grip on the priest. *I'm saving your life, buddy. I really want to do something violent to you. You're in my territory.* A sudden suspicion hit. *You're some distance away, aren't you? You were hunting the vampire.* Fury accompanied comprehension. *That's my vampire! He's in my neighborhood. I don't need some second-rate hunter in here mucking things up.*

"Destiny?" The priest drew her attention with his thin voice. "Perhaps you could loosen your grip. You're crushing my bones."

At once she complied, a blush stealing up her neck. "I'm so sorry, Father. I told you I might hurt you if I touched you. I'm not good at this sort of thing, but I think you should be lying down." *If you laugh, Nicolae, I will murder you right here in this church.*

His laughter came anyway, a low whisper of a caress;

obviously, he was not in the least intimidated by her threat. It was a stolen moment of camaraderie and both recognized it as such.

"If you don't mind, I'd rather not move," Father Mulligan said. "My head is throbbing and I'm afraid I might be sick."

Nicolae! I think he has a concussion! There was fear in her voice.

At once Nicolae was soothing, all laughter gone. Destiny could face a vampire without flinching, but this situation was beyond her experience. *I am on my way and I will teach you what needs to be done. Keep him quiet.* Nicolae couldn't help the small dart of pleasure shooting through him that she had reached for him in her need. Counted on him. Accepted that he would be there for her.

"You need to stay quiet," Destiny said, hoping she sounded knowledgeable and confident. She stroked the priest's thinning hair and tried to ignore the way the scent of blood heightened her terrible hunger.

"Do you know Martin Wright? A nice young man. Marty. I've known him since he was a child. He was always a sensitive child and so loving and kind to others."

Destiny knew the man. He was Tim Salvadore's lover. Wright was always the quieter of the two. Destiny had observed him many times helping the older women in the neighborhood with heavy bags; he was the one who often slipped money to the young couple living in the small house next to Velda and Inez. "Yes, I know Martin," she admitted.

"It was Marty." There was deep sorrow in the priest's voice. "I told him if he needed the money, I would give it to him, a personal loan, but nothing I said got through to him. It made no sense at all. The only thing that mattered to him was getting the box where I keep the money for the poor. There was hardly anything in it."

"That's completely out of character," Destiny mused aloud. "And it doesn't make sense. Tim and Martin have plenty of money. They live carefully and they aren't spenders or gamblers. They don't use drugs, and Martin doesn't even drink. It's difficult to believe he would do such a thing."

She knew that Martin Wright and Father Mulligan were fast friends. They played chess every Saturday, and Martin often worked with the priest in his garden. Whenever Father Mulligan sent out a call for volunteers, it was always Martin who headed the project. "It's completely out of character," she repeated, frowning. This situation was too close to the story Velda had told her of Helena and John Paul.

"He has been coming late at night, working on plans for a gated community for the elderly. He's thought of everything seniors need—medical aid, access to a handyman, grocery shopping on limited means. But when he came tonight . . . well, it was Martin, but not Martin," Father Mulligan offered. "You see why I can't go to the police." He patted her hand with shaky fingers. "You find out what happened to him. I know you're the one to do it."

"I'll look into it," she said before she could stop the words. Another promise. Another thread tying her to this place. To these people.

"Thank you, Destiny. I knew this work was meant for you. After working so many years as a priest, I sense things about people." He patted her arm again. "I know you're very troubled."

She drew back, her mouth suddenly dry. "Isn't everyone?"

He smiled, his eyes closed, his head resting on her shoulder. "Tell me."

She took a deep breath, let it out and plunged in. "I looked into someone's heart and thought him a monster because he killed without emotion. I could feel darkness in him, yet he felt nothing when he killed. He did so out of duty to protect others from a monstrous being. He says I am not the monster I think myself, that I kill to protect others as well, but there is hatred in me. I hate, and *want* to kill. I don't think he does. He kills because he considers it his duty." Destiny waited until the priest opened his eyes and focused on her. "I kill because I *have* to kill."

Father Mulligan searched her face for a long time in silence. "Whom do you kill, Destiny?" He asked it softly, without fear.

Her gaze shifted away from his for a long moment. He caught the shine of tears in her eyes. "There are things in this world you can't possibly know about, Father. Monstrous beings. Not human. One took me away from my family when I was a child." She tasted death in her mouth, the bitter, vile essence of evil. There was no hope of explaining to the priest, no way of making him understand. There were moments she herself thought she was insane, living in a world of illusion.

Father Mulligan tightened his grip on her hand. Knowledge crept into the depths of his eyes. Wonder spread across his face. "You're one of them. I've heard rumors about you, but I doubted you existed. You're a hunter, aren't you, from the Carpathian Mountains?"

At once she felt the stillness in Nicolae, his wariness, his watchfulness. He was a dark shadow of menace the priest didn't know existed. Destiny immediately tried to sever her link with the ancient hunter. Unexpectedly, it proved to be impossible. She could feel Nicolae merging with her, waiting for her answer.

"Where did you hear of such a thing?" she asked carefully, all too conscious they might have to remove the priest's memories. *It isn't right, Nicolae. He's a holy man. We must not touch him.*

"I should never have said anything, but I was so surprised. Some years ago it was my privilege to be assigned to a certain cardinal. He was a great man, much loved by the church, his peers and his people. He was quite ill and subsequently died. In packing up his books and precious papers, his journals and letters, I found an old letter written by a priest in Romania. That priest also is dead, but in the letter he had written of a friend of his, a man by the name of Mikhail who lived in the Carpathian Mountains. That man was extraordinary, of a different species altogether. There seemed to have been a bit of a theological discussion back and forth between the cardinal and the priest on the placing of this species in the grand scheme of things. The cardinal was sworn to secrecy and methodically burned the letters from the priest. I know that because it was well known that he frequently burned correspondence from Romania. It was a matter of speculation why he would burn the letters from that particular priest. I came along some time after the letter burning and never witnessed it, but I did find the one remaining letter."

"Does it still exist?" Destiny looked directly into his eyes. *Don't you dare hurt him.*

Your trust is heartwarming. There was that same

mild amusement, no exasperation or frustration, just a patient waiting. Destiny tried not to let his voice invade her mind, wrap itself around her heart.

Father Mulligan attempted to shake his head, then groaned. "I burned the letter, although I wanted to keep it, just as the cardinal had. The contents were interesting and historically important, but I realized the priest had been reluctant to reveal his knowledge even as he was attempting to solve a theological question."

"Don't talk any more, Father, you're really hurt. We'll sort this out later." *He's slurring his words!* Destiny was already lifting him up, cradling him in her arms as if the priest's weight were no more than a child's. *Meet me at the rectory, and hurry up!* she demanded as she ran, using preternatural speed, to the priest's home.

I am right behind you. Nicolae's voice was strong and reassuring, completely confident, and she felt some of the tension leave her.

Destiny carefully placed Father Mulligan on his bed, ignoring the presence of the other priests out in the hallway. She had blurred her entry so that none of them had seen her. Nor had they seen Nicolae as he carefully closed the door and mentally directed the occupants of the small house away from Father Mulligan's room. Nicolae pretended not to notice that she let her breath out in a sigh of relief.

"Father Mulligan, you have taken quite a crack on the head." Nicolae's voice was gentle, but Destiny recognized the hidden compulsion in it. "Open your eyes for a moment and look at me." It was a command, and in spite of his grave injury, the priest struggled to obey.

Nicolae smiled in reassurance, but Destiny hovered

protectively just to show him she was watching his every move. Nicolae's infuriating smile became a smirk. Destiny couldn't look at his confident face. She melted inside. It was that simple, and that disgusting. A holy man was lying bloody and bruised from an unprovoked attack, and she was staring helplessly at Nicolae's beloved face.

Her stomach clenched. She pressed a hand to her abdomen tightly, alarmed at her thoughts. *Beloved?* Handsome. Sensual. Male. *Not* beloved. Where had that come from? "You're so annoying," she hissed indignantly.

Nicolae reached out, framed her face and looked at her for just a moment. It was only a brief second in time, but it was enough to rob her of reason. "You will hear the ancient healing chant in your head. Listen to the words, Destiny, and repeat them with me. Allow yourself to fall away from your body. It is difficult at first; we are always so aware of ourselves, but you can do it. Become light and energy and travel with me. Hold the mind merge firmly and use my images as a guide." The pads of his fingers trailed over her cheekbones, left a trail of fire behind. Left her shaken and confused.

Father Mulligan fumbled weakly until she reluctantly, gingerly found his hand. "I think you know the answers you are seeking, child. Have courage."

She watched him with admiration. Here was a man who gave himself willingly to be healed by a hunter of the undead. Gave his trust to a total stranger of a different species. A man who could think to comfort her when he was so injured. Destiny was humbled by his selfless, giving nature.

"Relax, Father," Nicolae said softly, his voice musical,

compelling. "You should not feel pain, only warmth. I think you have a concussion, sir, but I believe I can help you if you will allow me to do so."

The priest retained his hold on Destiny's hand, but he closed his eyes once again with a small nod.

Destiny felt the shifting in Nicolae's mind first. A freeing of his spirit from his body. She knew the way; he had taught her how to do just such a thing to heal her own body when she had suffered injuries in battle. She had never healed another. Destiny went with Nicolae, following his lead as she had for so many years. Merging with him, becoming part of him.

It seemed she had always been a part of him. Her life had really begun when she had crawled into her mind and found Nicolae with his soft, beguiling voice and his unfailing patience. Destiny had closed the door on her life as a human to help preserve her sanity; only Nicolae had been allowed into her world. He knew everything about her—the good, the bad, every dream, every nightmare. Her own private hell. He knew her, yet he stayed.

Looking back, she wondered that she'd ever thought him vampire. There was darkness in him. He hunted and killed. Yet he was unfailing in giving of himself and his knowledge to her. What vampire would do that? All along she had been afraid of what he would see when he found her. Broken. Damaged. *No salvation.* She breathed the words between them.

Stay with me, Destiny. His voice was steady. *Do not be distracted. You must concentrate on the priest, not on yourself.*

Destiny hesitated for one more minute, wavering with indecision. He was drawing her deeper into his world. Into his life. Into his soul. Destiny let go of the last remnant of her being and went willingly, allowing her body to slip away, feeling the freedom of becoming energy and light. This was a healing balm that was twice as strong as anything she had ever experienced.

The fracture was there in the skull of the priest, a jagged crack, a dark violation of his being. Destiny heard the soft chanting in Nicolae's melodic voice and added her voice to his so that they blended in perfect harmony. Words of healing. Ancient words she didn't understand but that were beautiful and right. She felt the peace and rightness of it, the energy flowing between them to the priest. Destiny observed carefully as Nicolae meticulously welded the edges together so that the skull was once again seamless. He paid attention to the smallest detail, removing blood clots and reducing the swelling as if the injury had never been.

Nicolae did not stop there, even though she sensed his weariness. He streamed through his patient, examining his heart and lungs, every vital organ, until he was completely satisfied that the priest would awaken healed and strong.

They emerged at the same time, returning to their own bodies, smiling at one another like old friends. "Thank you, Nicolae. You saved his life."

It was worth every ounce of his strength to see that look on her face. Soft. Accepting. Happy. She was looking at him with stars in her eyes. He had not thought she would ever look at him that way. Nicolae was careful not to allow any show of emotion to betray him. His hold on her was fragile. He didn't make the mistake of gathering her into his arms and drawing her close, even though that was all he wanted to do. She was pale, her hunger beating at him, yet he couldn't provide for her.

"He is a good man, Destiny. Did you have time to examine his memories to see what actually happened?"

Destiny nodded. "It was as he told me. Martin Wright came in and confronted him. Father Mulligan offered money, asked him to sit and talk, tried to reason with him, but Martin attacked him."

Nicolae sat on the floor beside the priest's bed. "That makes no sense."

"No, it doesn't. Velda and Inez told me a similar story about John Paul coming home and attacking Helena."

"I am not familiar with them. I have seen Wright in the bar, but not this other couple."

"John Paul adores Helena. He would never beat her." Destiny tapped her fingernail against the bed frame. "Something is definitely wrong." Nicolae looked pale and drained, appearing gray in the darkness as he rubbed his shadowed jaw thoughtfully.

"Do not look so worried, Destiny. We will figure it out. Are you certain Father Mulligan destroyed that letter? Mikhail Dubrinsky is the Prince of our people. We cannot afford to let anything or anyone endanger him in these tense times. Our very existence as a people is threatened."

She leaned toward him, needing to examine his features up close. Her fingertips moved over the angles and planes of his face, brushing at the lines near the corners of his mouth. "You need to feed." She hadn't meant it as an invitation, but it came out that way. Soft. Seductive. Unexpected. And it startled both of them.

Nicolae's body responded to the temptation of her voice, of her invitation; a relentless, savage ache hit him hard. Heat swept through him. Lightning streaked through his veins with white-hot intensity. His eyes met hers. He was lost immediately, drowning in the depths of her aquamarine eyes. She turned her head slightly, exposing her soft, vulnerable neck, an expanse of smooth, scented skin.

Nicolae reached for her, drew her close. She fit into his arms, her soft body lush and pliant. She was hot silk and satin, elevating his fever. Slowly he bent his head to her perfect skin.

No! It was no less than a command. His brother's voice was sharp with warning. Nicolae inhaled her scent, felt her pulse jump beneath his lips. The call of her blood was potent in his mind, in his heart. *She is tainted. You are not yet bound! Stop Nicolae, you endanger both yourself and her.*

Nicolae closed his eyes, wanting to shut out reason and thought. *You endanger both yourself and her.* It was true. Reluctantly he drew back, away from temptation. His incisors receded. He could not risk Destiny. Would not risk her.

Destiny sat very still with the warning echoing in her mind. *She is tainted. She is tainted.* It played like a terrible refrain in her head. Beat at her with the intensity of a horrific truth. She shoved Nicolae away from her as she leapt to her feet.

"Destiny." Her name was wrenched from his heart. "Stay with me."

The aching loneliness in his voice was haunting, soul destroying. For the first time she could see how much he needed her. It wasn't just wanting; he *needed*. Everything feminine, everything *human* in her struggled to be what he needed. *She is tainted.* The ugly refrain reverberated loudly in her mind.

She shook her head as she backed away from him.

"What do you think will happen if I stay with you, Nicolae? Do you believe in miracles? I prayed for miracles night after night when I heard him coming for me, when I huddled in a little ball in the corner of a dirty cave." She curled her fingers tightly into a fist so that her nails dug into her palms. "You belong here with Father Mulligan. With these people." She gestured toward the priest with her clenched fist. "I don't, and I never will. Please thank Vikirnoff for his warning. I wouldn't have wanted to infect you."

"Destiny." The ache in his voice was raw, real, expressing a pain far beyond her own.

"No." Someone had to have sense. "Answer me. I would have infected you if you had taken my blood, isn't that right?"

Her eyes were glittering like rare gems, sparkling with tears. She dashed the moisture away with an impatient sweep of her arm. Nicolae thought her the most extraordinary woman he had ever seen. The most courageous. He refused to be anything less. His gaze met hers squarely, and he nodded. "Yes, Destiny. And as I have no anchor to hold me to the light, it would be very dangerous."

She lifted her chin proudly. "That's me. Your anchor. What happens to you if I can't be what you need?"

"Destiny, this is not necessary. You are everything I need. Everything I want."

"Answer me, Nicolae. What happens to you?" Her voice was very soft but very steady. Her gaze never wavered.

A flicker of pain crossed his face before his expression settled once more into a stoic mask. "I am a Carpathian male, an ancient hunter very close to my time. If I am not bound to my lifemate, I must either seek the dawn or turn vampire. My choice is clear."

She pressed her fingertips to her eyes briefly in reaction. "Is there no other lifemate for you? There must be another."

Nicolae shook his head. "There is only one. You are the other half of my soul."

Destiny swung away from him, dissolving into a fine mist, streaming under the door and down the hallway into the night air. She rose fast, climbing high until she was well over the city, screaming in her mind so the shock waves wouldn't distress the people below her. *Did you know all along that I was your lifemate?* It was an accusation, nothing less.

No! If I had known, I would have told you. Come back to me, Destiny. You must feed soon. You need me.

He was right. Her strength was waning quickly. She hadn't fed in several risings, and lending her strength to Nicolae as he healed the priest had drained her of what little she had left. She landed, regaining her natural form. She knew exactly where to go to find what she needed. And it wasn't Nicolae.

Destiny was furious. Her entire life had been disrupted again. The world seemed to be spinning out of control. As she stalked down the narrow street, her fingers curled into fists and her lips pressed together tightly. She was looking for a fight. Any fight. A good old-fashioned fight would do. Where were all the criminals in the city? Had they all gone to bed early? Where was a vampire when you needed one?

Destiny sought out every back alley she could think of, stalking the streets trying desperately to look like a victim. A poor, lonesome girl caught out all alone in the dark. Her eyes glittered dangerously as she glared into the night, looking for anyone to attack her.

She huffed out her breath in a rush of indignation. She was strolling down a dirty street where it was known a person could be stabbed for a pair of shoes, yet not a single person tried anything. The buildings loomed up on either side of her, great ugly examples of crumbling neglect. Graffiti was thick on the walls, along with other things she preferred not to identify. Stairwells and alcoves abounded, perfect hiding places for someone with larceny on his mind. Destiny was certain she was the perfect target. A woman alone, defenseless. There were no streetlights to illuminate any crime. It was the perfect opportunity for mayhem, and no one was taking her up on the invitation. She was totally disgusted with the criminals in the city.

It seemed an eternity before she spotted three men leaning against a wall, watching her progress and murmuring softly to one another. She could hear them clearly discussing ideas on how to pass the rest of the night with her. Their conversation brightened her spirits considerably. At last, a chance to take out her frustration and aggression. Deliberately she slowed her pace, giving them plenty of time to make up their minds. She had stayed away from the neighborhood for three risings and she had not fed. Hunger was a living, breathing entity crawling through her body with a relentless demand. The pull of the neighborhood was incredibly strong. MaryAnn's gentle voice, the church, Velda and Inez. She shied away from thinking the word *home*. She had no home. She was a nomad. A loner. *Why wouldn't Nicolae get out of her head?*

She had no reason to worry about him or feel guilty.

Nicolae probably was making the entire thing up. Except she'd never caught him in a lie. She'd spent a lifetime looking for his lies to prove to herself he was a vampire. She glanced briefly at the men, then down at the ground, continuing her steady pace. She needed physical action.

One of the three men straightened, took two steps toward her as if to intercept her. Destiny let her breath out in a hiss of anticipation, eagerness coursing through her body like adrenaline as she turned toward him, waiting. Waiting. Even the wind seemed to hold its breath with her. Two rats scurrying near trash cans sat up on their hind legs, motionless, waiting expectantly.

She felt him then. Nicolae. Real, not imagined. Close. There was no beautiful voice, no soft words to turn her from her intended path. But when she swung her head, her gaze meeting her would-be attacker, he stopped dead in his tracks.

Destiny knew immediately that the hungry flame burning deep in her belly betrayed her, glowing red hot in the depths of her eyes. "What kind of idiot are you?" she taunted him, then glared at the others, daring them to attack her.

She heard Nicolae's soft laughter then. *You should have lured them with sex.* Something in his voice made her shiver, an underlying menace that told her it wouldn't have been a good idea. *Call me to you.*

Her breath escaped between her teeth, a hiss of anger. Before anything else, she should have asked MaryAnn if all men were such pains in the butt. She was *not* going to call him to her. She would not be enticed. Lured. Tempted. She would have left Seattle for good to escape him, but she had unfinished business. She had promised

Inez and Velda she would check into the problems in the neighborhood. "Cowards," she sniffed with contempt and turned her back on the three men, who were staring in outright alarm at her.

Had there been a small surge of power in the air? Had Nicolae interfered in some way, enhancing the fire burning in her, allowing the three men to see the danger they were in? Destiny whirled around, her vivid gaze seeking out every nook and cranny. The rats. They had hunkered down closer to the trash cans, staying small in an attempt to keep from being noticed. She glared at them until they hid in the midst of the trash. *Are you following me? Don't you dare try to follow me!* Nicolae wouldn't dare. Destiny paused at the entrance to the narrow street, tapping her fingernail against the wall. Of course he would dare. He was a hunter.

Her anger was fading. All she could think about was the aching need in his voice, the stark hunger in his eyes. Despair was a sharp knife piercing her heart each time she remembered the flicker of pain crossing Nicolae's face. She leaned her weight against the wall and looked up at the stars. The wind was blowing stronger now, shifting a blanket of gray fog so that it spread across the night, blotting out stars and muffling sound. A fine drizzle began to rain down on her.

She glanced at the rats scurrying for cover. Something in the way one of them moved caught her attention—the way it kept her in sight, the round, beady eyes shining with far too much intelligence. At once a chill went down her spine. She went still inside, her senses flaring out to discover the others. And there were others. This time she had been truly drawn into an ambush.

Chapter Seven

Destiny moved slowly, carefully positioning herself as she examined every inch of her surroundings. The wind was kicking up paper and small leaves and whirling the debris down the street. Her wary gaze slipped over the buildings, took in every detail, every shadow. She had come looking for a fight; she was in for an all-out war.

She needed room to maneuver. Smiling sweetly at the little rat, Destiny glided swiftly into the open, out from between the towering buildings into the middle of the street. "I see you are in your true form, Pater. Ever the nasty little rat. And you have all your little friends with you this time, running in packs the way ratty little creatures tend to do. What is it? A reunion? Old home week? A vampire's seminar and no invitation for me? I feel left out." She used her most compelling voice, so that those listening would reveal themselves, if only for a moment.

At once she saw them in their true form. Tall, gaunt figures with jagged, stained teeth and gray skin stretched tight over their skulls. The illusion of physical beauty was projected by their minds, while their bodies had decayed to match their rotted spirits. There were two beside the trash cans. One on the roof of the nearest building. One in the shadows of the alley itself. And the last one clinging to the side of the building looming just above her, hidden as a dark splotch, a spider waiting at the center of the web, to attack when the net was drawn tight.

Destiny's heart thudded wildly, then settled into her normal rhythm. She moved easily, casually, saluting the macabre figure crawling up the side of the building. He bared his teeth at her, his fetid breath fouling the cool air, so that she was grateful for the fine rain dispersing the odor of corruption.

Pater folded his arms, calmly regaining his illusion of beauty. "Indeed, my dear, we have an invitation for you. We have come to ask you to join us. What is the sense of fighting amongst ourselves?" His voice was soft and persuasive so that deep in her heart she cringed, remembering another voice calling to her, summoning her. And she had followed him. Her gravest sin. Why hadn't she confessed to the priest? Told him the truth while she had the chance?

Destiny shook her head to rid herself of guilt. She needed absolute concentration now if she were to have a chance of defeating the undead. "Why would I want to serve you when I can choose my own path?"

The vampire on the roof began a low chant, his feet pattering a rhythmic dance. The vampire beside the trash can to the right of Pater took up the singsong refrain, and the flash of his feet moving in the silver threads of rain was mesmerizing. Destiny gritted her teeth and resolutely pulled her fascinated gaze away, blocking out the sounds of the chant as she did so. It was an old trick, but one that often worked on the unwary.

"Do you think me such a fledgling to be caught so easily?" Her eyes flashed at Pater, a glinting promise of retribution.

He bowed low, in no way perturbed. A simple hand motion stopped the refrain and the dancing pattern. Once again the vampires were still and watchful. Waiting their chance. Watching for an opening, a mistake on her part. Just one moment of inattention. "You are a curiosity. You know much for one so young. You are a woman, yet you combat us successfully. You share our blood, yet you are a hunter. How have you not heard the news spreading throughout the world? We are emissaries of the strong one. I am one of his most trusted commanders. We are at war with the hunters, and yet you do not know this. We have entered a new era in which we band together and fight our enemy."

There was movement within the fog. She sensed it more than saw it. Nicolae. Of course he would come. And his brother would be guarding his back. She felt herself relax a little. "Fight for whom? For what? You make no sense, old one. Why would I fight to bring power to an evil one? My death is nothing to him. Your deaths are nothing to him. We are cannon fodder while he hides and gloats and waits for us to bring the hunters to their knees. I see no sense in dying for someone else."

"But we will defeat the hunters, attack in packs. He is wise, our leader. He will make the world ours." The voice held compulsion. She could feel it working on her mind, undermining her confidence, dragging her closer to the net of outlaws. There was something different in the compulsion, something elusive she could not quite assess. The cadence should have been recognizable, yet it wasn't; it was almost as if his voice were tuning itself to her personally, finding what tone would be the most pleasing.

Destiny lifted her hands, palms out, wiping away the intriguing sound of Pater's voice. Tilting her head to one side, she smiled again, a slow, sexy come-on, her small white teeth perfect and gleaming. "Why would anyone as powerful as you follow another?" Her tone was flirtatious, flattering, admiring. Her hands fluttered gracefully as she talked. Destiny noted Pater's chest swell visibly. Like all vampires, he was susceptible to flattery. "You look like a leader to me. You survived three hunters the other day. How many others could accomplish such a feat? Could your leader? He's hiding behind you, cowering, afraid, while you face the hunters."

"He has vision," Pater told her.

"Have you even seen him? Has he dared to show himself to you?" She sounded curious, feminine. Filled with admiration. Her hands were flowing as she spoke, a graceful swaying that matched the beautiful allure of her voice. She smiled, a conspirator's smile, lowering her pitch. Her voice was husky. Sexy. Tempting. "*You* join with *me*. We don't need an alliance with others. This is my territory. All of it. Share it with me. We can defeat the others."

At once the snarls and rumbling began; the vampires shifted tensely, fangs exposed, talons curling in anger. It didn't take much to drive a wedge between unholy allies. They were deceivers, betrayers, preying on each other as well as on human victims.

Pater again waved the others to silence, a sign of his leadership among the worst of abominations. He held out his hand to Destiny. "Come to me now, join us. You are weak with hunger. You cannot possibly defeat us all. Let me give you my blood to sustain your life. Join our family."

His words cracked open a door in her mind, spilled out a memory. A small, dark-haired girl crawling in the dirt, dragging herself along a damp cave floor, weeping useless tears and trying to drown out the sounds of begging, pleading. The horrible screams, the river of blood. The monster dropping his latest victim and turning to look at her in slow motion. He always turned in slow motion, his teeth still black from his victim's blood. A dark shadow looming over her. Maniacal laughter. *Take my blood to sustain your life*. Hands roughly squeezing and probing her small body. The slaps, the fetid smell, the teeth tearing at her tender skin. A brutish savage pounding into her, ripping her body in two, while burning, coppery-flavored acid poured down her throat.

Destiny couldn't think. Couldn't breathe. Her throat closed, her lungs seized. She began to choke. The violation of that child was more than she could endure. Sweat broke out on her body, a terrible trembling took over, one she couldn't control. She was no longer standing in the streets of Seattle, a full-grown adult, a powerful hunter; she was trapped back in that cave, mindlessly dragging her little torn body along the damp, blood-covered floor.

I am here with you. The voice came out of nowhere, was simply there in her mind. Calm. Steady. A rock that always anchored her. When there was nothing left, when there was no sanity and no reason, there was always that voice. *I will always be with you. You are hunted, Destiny. They are closing in from above and below. Come back to this time and place. Come with me now.*

She followed him out of the labyrinth of her nightmares. Out of memories that would never go away. *Nicolae.* Her sanity. Her life. When had it happened? Why hadn't she known? The wind hit her face. The clean rain was soaking her clothes and hair. She became instantly aware of her surroundings, of the vampires facing her, moving swiftly toward her.

Knowing how vulnerable she was at that moment, Destiny dissolved into mist, abandoning her attempts to weave a holding spell on Pater. She was certain he was the strongest of the band. He would orchestrate the battle. He was the one she must defeat if she were to succeed in ridding her neighborhood of the undead. At once she became part of the weather, mixing with the gray fog.

Pater snarled as he grasped empty air, his talons scraping at the mist all around him. At once he began chanting a spell to lure human victims to him. His voice was powerful, a call for blood. His followers took up the words, sending their call into the buildings and along the narrow streets. A retaliation for losing the female they had been so certain they would acquire.

Do not panic, Destiny. Nicolae's council was gentle and calm. *He is using this to draw you out. It shows he has studied you. He knows you will protect the populace here.*

I am not going to trade their lives for mine.

Vikirnoff will go in first. The two in the shadows are mine. You must remove the vampire from the side of the

*building. Do not worry about Pater. He is smoke. We
are not going to get him unless we are incredibly lucky.
If possible, keep Vikirnoff from having to kill any of the
beasts. He has reached his limit and will only kill to
save our lives.*

To Destiny's horror, doors began to open as human
prey answered the collective call of the vampire. She
could see the red flames blazing in the sunken eyes of
the undead, the grimaces of joy at the prospect of a
blood feast. The humans' adrenaline-rich blood would
give the vampires a rush of power and a tremendous
high. The creatures were leaping at victims, determined
to kill as many as possible and gather strength for the
coming battle.

Overhead the storm clouds were roiling, spinning a
witch's cauldron of black threads. Veins of lightning lit
the edges of the brew, momentarily lighting up the grim
scene on the ground.

Below her, Vikirnoff cut off one of the undead, a
large, bulky monster who was growling continually.
Vikirnoff glided in with such grace and elegance, the
vampire appeared clumsy and stiff in comparison. The
two seemed to explode into action, one moment per-
forming a ritual ballet of shadowing steps, the next
moment erupting into violence, lethal and ugly.

Nicolae waved his hand to calm the screams of the
victims as they became aware of the imminent danger,
immediately removing the chance of a false high for the
vampires. The vampires might be able to get the blood
they sought, but not the high of adrenaline. Two vampires rushed a couple of people standing in the doorway
of an apartment. Nicolae was there before the vampires,
thrusting the couple inside, out of harm's way, and turn-

ing to face the snarling undead. The two monsters
closed in on him, eager to finish off the hunter and
claim their prize. Nicolae exploded into action, a blur
moving so fast that Destiny couldn't follow him, fluid
and powerful and extraordinarily dangerous.

Destiny caught a glimpse of Pater as he slipped into
the shadows, retreating to allow his minions to fight the
hunters while he waited for an opportunity to attack
without risk. It was the tactic of a smarter, more experienced vampire. She would have followed him, but there
was movement on the second story. A young woman
wandered out onto the fire escape just above where a
vampire clung to the side of the building. In answer to
the creature's summons, her face was lit with rapture,
her arms outstretched as if embracing death.

Destiny saw the eagerness on the vampire's face, the
triumph as it slithered up the building rapidly, a dark
spider bloated with power and the need to inflict pain.
Destiny was already attacking, shooting out of the fog
like an arrow, dropping down from above as the vampire reached the fire escape, certain of his victim. The
creature turned at the last moment to face Destiny, his
face hideous, his teeth bared, his eyes red-rimmed and
blazing with hatred. He leapt at her, talons digging deep
into her skin as he attached his reptilian body to her,
raking with claws and sinking his teeth into her throat.

They tumbled through space, raking and clawing, the
vampire sinking his teeth deeper and deeper and tearing at her body with his claws. He was much stronger
than he looked, ripping through her skin to weaken her.
Destiny proceeded without faltering, driving her fist
deep through muscle and bone, her hand clenching the
blackened organ that provided life for the creature. His

scream was horrible, even muffled by her own throat as he gnawed off a great chunk of her flesh. They fell together, bounced off a projection of the building and hit the pavement. Destiny held on grimly to her prize.

Nicolae! She tossed the heart out onto the street so the jagged bolt of lightning Nicolae was conducting could incinerate it into black, foul-smelling ash. The creature gripping her went limp, talons still dug deeply into her side and arm. Teeth still sunk into her throat. Destiny threw him off her and with her remaining strength staggered out of the alley toward the open street. Her legs went out from under her and she sat abruptly on the pavement.

Destiny tilted her head to look up at the sky, at the white lightning and the clouds spinning madly above her. It really was beautiful. But cold. Surprisingly, she was very cold. For some reason, she couldn't regulate her body temperature, and she was shaking. She attempted to focus on Nicolae, to see if he needed help, but it was too much trouble to turn her head. She was shocked when she found herself lying flat on her back, her body heavy and feeling strange. She should have been afraid, but she was only mildly curious. Mostly she worried about Nicolae.

Far off, or maybe in her own head, she heard his voice. *Do not let go, Destiny. Do not let go!* She was unclear what he meant. She wasn't holding on to anything, but there was desperation in his voice, a tone she'd never heard him use, so she tried to stay focused on him.

Pater loomed over her, his gray features grim, a hint of his terrible anger showing in his red-rimmed eyes. "You should have joined with us. You are going to die a hideous death." He hissed the words at her, spittle ruining his civilized facade.

"That's no surprise. I lived a hideous life." She tried to say the words to him, but her throat was torn and raw, and no real words emerged. When she blinked to clear the haze from her eyes, Pater was gone, perhaps never really there.

Nicolae and Vikirnoff materialized on either side of her. Nicolae had a red streak down the left side of his face and an angry-looking wound on his chest. He lifted her into his arms as Vikirnoff guarded his back. She wished she could wipe away the anxiety on Nicolae's face, but no sound would come out of her throat and she couldn't find the strength to lift her hand to smooth away the lines of worry. She sighed softly, recognizing that something was terribly wrong, but it didn't matter to her. Destiny simply closed her eyes and let Nicolae take her away as he had always done, soaring high above the city into a dream world where there were no more monsters.

Nicolae kept his mind numb, blank, streaking through the sky toward their lair. If the undead gave chase, Vikirnoff would protect Destiny and him, guarding their back-trail as they hurried to safety. He should have known she would do such a thing. He should have known she would not be able to deal with the idea of being responsible for his life . . . or his death.

She had no such thought in her head. Vikirnoff was the voice of reason.

Anger flooded Nicolae's body, took over his heart and head. *How would you know? Why do you think you know her better than I do?*

Because I do not think of her day and night, my every

waking minute. I saw her defend the human. She was hunting as she believed she should. Nothing more. Nothing less. Vikirnoff was not in the least disturbed by Nicolae's outburst. Nothing seemed to provoke him these days. *Do not take that away from her.*

Nicolae was immediately ashamed that he had taken out his fear on his brother. *I am sorry I was harsh.*

Were you? I had not noticed.

Nicolae glanced at his brother's impassive face as they settled to ground deep within the earth. There was no humor, nor hint of reprimand; Vikirnoff really hadn't noticed his momentary anger. And that worried Nicolae. He packed Destiny's wounds with his own saliva and the healing earth, chanting softly as he worked. "She's lost far too much blood." He examined the wounds, nasty rips and bite marks, great gaping holes. The vampire had sought to destroy her as painfully as possible.

"That is good for our purposes, Nicolae," Vikirnoff said. "Instead of killing her outright, they tried to prolong her death, to torment her." He was collecting herbs from a small cache they had stored in the underground chamber. It took only seconds to light the flames of aromatic candles.

"Her enemies do not know her." Nicolae's voice was soft, filled with emotion held tightly in check. "She has lived with pain every moment of her existence. This is nothing to her." He blinked back unexpected tears as he carefully wiped her face clean. The wounds on her throat and shoulder were horrible to see. "This is nothing to her," he repeated. His hands were gentle on the gaping wounds in her throat. He leaned close to her, put his lips to her ear. "Stay with me, Destiny. I will follow where you lead this time. Let it be here, in this time and place. Stay in this world."

Nicolae allowed his body to drop away from him, transforming himself into an immaterial instrument of light and energy. It was much more difficult to shed the emotional storm that whirled within him. He needed to be calm and steady to save her. To heal her wounds. This was the most important task of his life. Her torn, mangled flesh was a mess, and, as always, the vampire had left behind a poison that would quickly destroy the cells around the area of the bites. The decay was spreading quickly.

Nicolae was meticulous in his work, fast and efficient but steady as he repaired the damage to her arteries and muscles and tissue. He paid attention to the smallest detail, ferreting out every drop of the vampire's poison. It wasn't an easy task. Her tainted blood made his job especially difficult because of the damage it had already done to the inside of her body, damage that tormented her continually.

Twice Nicolae thought something moved in her bloodstream, something microscopic, a shadow darting away from his healing energy, but when he went back to inspect, he could find no more of the bacteria.

He came to himself swaying slightly, his face pale from concentration and from expending so much energy. Pale with the knowledge of what she endured on a nightly basis. His eyes met Vikirnoff's. "I do not know how she has survived," he said softly.

Vikirnoff held out his wrist to his brother. "We are Carpathian. We endure. She is Carpathian and has honor and instincts as old as time. It matters little that a vampire converted her. He could not have done so successfully if she were not of the light. You think with your heart, Nicolae."

"And it is breaking." Nicolae bent his head to his brother's offering, drinking deeply to replenish his strength, to be able to pass the gift on to his lifemate.

Vikirnoff shook his head. "One of you must be whole. She searches for a way to you. Do not make the mistake of failing her because your compassion is too great."

Nicolae allowed the rush of ancient blood to fill his being. What could one say to Vikirnoff? His words were a double-edged sword. Painful but logical. Full of wisdom. As long as Nicolae could remember, Vikirnoff had spoken so. When he had carefully closed the wound on his brother's wrist, using his healing saliva, he gathered Destiny to him.

Cradling her on his lap, he opened his shirt and pressed her mouth to his skin. *You will take what is freely offered, that we both may live*, he commanded her, using the strength of an ancient, of a lifemate. And she obeyed. Her lips nuzzled him. Gently. Almost sensuously. He closed his eyes as a white-hot pain sent lightning whipping through his bloodstream, tightened every muscle in his body. Instinctively he held her closer, his arms protective.

Nicolae glanced up at his brother. "How do we remove the taint of the vampire? In all your years, have you ever encountered this problem?"

Vikirnoff shook his head slowly. "Destiny is not vampire, so there must be a way. I can only think to dilute the blood as you are doing. She has lost more than she can afford. We will both give her ancient blood and call to the healers. Perhaps the soil of our homeland would be of help."

Nicolae rested his brow gently against Destiny's. "She is a fighter, Vikirnoff. If anyone can beat this, she is the one."

"You do not object to my giving her blood?" The question was put mildly.

Nicolae shrugged his powerful shoulders as he looked down at the face of the woman he loved. "I will give her all I can; you will have to replace my blood as you have done so many times. It is one and the same. She has a need, and we can do no other than to meet it." His fingers flexed in Destiny's hair, crushed the silken strands in his fist. He wanted to take her away from this place, back to his homeland, where the healers and the soil would have a chance to work their magic on her.

You have always been my magic. I have no need of others. Her voice came out of nowhere, brushed at the walls of his mind like gentle butterfly wings. His gut clenched in reaction. His heart rolled over in his chest.

It is about time you admitted it.

Well, don't get a big head or anything. I still think you're annoying.

That sounded so much more like his Destiny that he breathed a sigh of relief. He felt the sweep of her tongue, closing the pinpricks on his chest. *You have not taken nearly enough to replace the blood you lost, Destiny.*

I feel you growing weaker. Go hunt. I can wait. A ripple of pain went through her body, a certain sign that she was waking. Her eyelashes fluttered, two thick crescents that lay like feathery fans against her pale skin.

Nicolae bent over her, brushed his lips across her

eyes. He trailed a series of kisses along her cheekbone, down the line of her small nose, then lingered by the corner of her soft, curving mouth.

You're taking advantage. I'm too weak to resist.

No, you are not. You do not wish to resist.

Maybe you're right. But if you are, it's because you mesmerized me while I was unconscious. It has nothing to do with the way you smell. Or the sound of your voice. Or the way your mouth is so perfect.

Nicolae teased her lips with his, rubbing gently, persistently until her lips moved under his. Softened. Accepted. He took her breath. Gave her his.

Destiny gasped, muffled a groan of pain, buried her face against his chest and held herself very still. "I'm sorry, it slipped out. It isn't that bad." The weakness was almost worse than the pain.

His hand stroked gentle caresses through her hair. "I know it hurts, Destiny. You need to go to ground and allow the earth to heal you. Vikirnoff and I will take care of your people."

"You're not at full strength. You gave me too much of your blood." Her voice was barely audible, even with his acute hearing. She opened her eyes to study his pale face. "Go feed."

There was too much pain in the depths of her eyes. "I thought I would just hold you for a while. I am not certain I will ever get the chance again. For once in your life you are being cooperative."

A small smile lifted her mouth. "Is that what I'm doing?" She winced as she shifted to get a better look at him. "I bet I look great."

His eyebrow shot up. "You look beautiful."

"I knew you'd say that. You're such a liar. Please go feed, I don't want to have to fight any more vampires tonight, and you're not in any shape to kick butt."

"You could not fight your way out of a paper bag," he pointed out.

"Hey! I destroyed my vampire," she said softly, her hand going to her raw throat as if it hurt her to speak. "What did you manage to do?"

"I bagged two of them. Vikirnoff took out his, although he should not have done so." Nicolae spared a quick glare for his brother.

"Do you have to do thát? Is it a man thing or something? I'll admit I don't know much about men, but it's so annoying."

Nicolae leaned closer, took her hand away from her throat because he couldn't bear to see her fingers fluttering helplessly there. She looked so vulnerable with her pale face and her torn body. "Have to do what?"

"One-upmanship. I kill one, you have to kill two. The big bad hunter flexing his muscles. It's annoying."

"You are not going to whine simply because I have superior hunting skills, are you?" He rubbed her knuckles along his jaw, wanting the contact. Needing to show her what he felt too deeply to say. "It did not occur to me you would whine."

"It's hardly whining to point out how annoying you are. And you aren't superior, just luckier." Her voice was husky, sounding far away, but she was grateful she could talk.

"I hesitate to mention I am not the one in need of healing."

"You don't seem all that hesitant to me. You pointed it out just fine. I'm sure your brother heard you." Her impossibly long lashes drifted down to cover her uniquely colored eyes. She turned her face toward him so that her lips brushed the back of his hand where he was holding hers. "Did you know that there are laws against stalkers?"

He felt the jolt of her soft mouth through his entire body. It was an accidental brushing, nothing more, not even a real caress, but his heart did a somersault anyway. "I know you are not about to accuse me of stalking you. You came after me. I merely followed wherever you led." He sounded reasonable. His fingertip traced her sculpted mouth, her full lower lip, sending a shiver through her body. Through his.

You have the most fascinating mouth I have ever seen.
What's so fascinating? It's a mouth just like any other.
I think it is your pouty lower lip.
Now I know you're crazy. I never pout and neither does my lip.

"I beg to differ." The sheer pleasure blossoming inside him spilled over into his voice. She was alive, his courageous Destiny!

She opened her eyes again to look directly at him. "So what do we do now, Nicolae? I did my best to protect you, but you just don't mind very well."

He brought her knuckles to his mouth, his teeth scraping back and forth, gently, insistently, over her skin. "Is that where I went wrong? I should have been obeying?"

"At least listening." Her fingers touched the shadow along his jaw, a weak, trembling movement that conveyed more to him than her words ever could. "I want you safe, Nicolae. It's important to me."

"I am safe, Destiny," he assured her. The lump in his throat was threatening to choke him. "As long as I have you, as long as we are together, I will be safe."

Vikirnoff cleared his throat, drawing her attention to him. He was looking at his brother. "You are not bound together, Nicolae. You will never be safe if you do not bind her to you in the way of our people."

Swift impatience crossed Nicolae's dark, sensual features. Before he could react, Destiny laid her hand across his mouth and looked up at his brother. "Those words always beating around in his head—the 'you are my lifemate' words." Secretly she thought the ritual words as beautiful as they were terrifying. "How would simple words bind us together or make Nicolae safe?"

His strong teeth nipped at her palm so that she yelped and glared at him. "You are not to think about that, Destiny. We have plenty of time."

"I don't believe I was speaking to you," she responded huffily. "There's no talking to you when you're in your ridiculous alpha male he-man mode. Sheesh! All you think about is protecting the little woman. I'm talking to your brother right now." She attempted to lift her chin but it hurt too much, so she suppressed a squeak of pain and had to be content to challenge him with her eyes.

Nicolae's heart melted beyond repair. She was so brave, so filled with courage. She lay in his arms, beaten, torn apart, her flesh shredded. Pain coursed through her veins and the taint of the vampire stood between them, yet she met Vikirnoff's gaze without flinching. It mattered to her that Nicolae was safe. He read the determination in her mind, her complete resolve, even as he read her fear of what Vikirnoff might say.

"He must bind you to him so that you will act as his anchor. Once the words are said and the ritual is complete, he cannot turn vampire. Unless you die. You will provide the light to his darkness."

Destiny stared at Vikirnoff for several heartbeats. A single sound escaped her. Muffled. Strangled. Somewhere between humorless laughter, hysteria and tears. "Are you crazy? *I'm* supposed to be the light to *his* darkness? Do you have any idea what you're saying? Nicolae is *my* light. My only light."

"Destiny." Vikirnoff's voice never changed. It was soft. Calm. Reasonable. "You have dedicated your entire existence to the protection of others. You think first of Nicolae even as you lie broken. Those are not the acts of someone who lives in darkness."

"Nicolae lives for the protection of others."

"He was bred to do so. It is his right and his honor. It is his way of life. It was not so with you."

"You can't see what's inside me." She turned her face away from him, only to find Nicolae. Always Nicolae. He was there in her mind. There in her heart. He held her safely in his arms.

"Nicolae sees what is inside you. Nicolae is no easy man to be twisted around a woman's finger. He is an ancient hunter of the undead. A dangerous predator who is capable of destroying more than you could ever comprehend. You could never fool him. Never, Destiny. You are exactly as he sees you. His light."

"Have you forgotten that you had to warn us I was tainted?"

"Your blood is not who or what you are. It merely runs in your veins. If a human has cancer growing in his body, does that make him a tainted being? Do not allow this vampire to run your life any longer. He does not own you. He is long gone from this world. Let him stay dead."

Destiny let her breath out slowly. Her gaze met Nicolae's, and she felt instantly lost. He had to stop looking at her like that. He just had to. Before she could stop herself, her fingertips were rubbing away his frown. She could bear pain better than she could bear his frown.

"You know he is right," Nicolae said gently.

She rolled her eyes. "You just had to point it out, didn't you? Couldn't stay quiet. Totally annoying." If she didn't joke she would cry, and that would be too humiliating to be borne. This man had already seen her at her worst. She didn't need to have tears running down her face and her nose all red.

For the first time, something made sense. Vikirnoff actually had given her something to hold on to. Her blood didn't dictate who she was. Or what she was.

She looked across the cave at Nicolae's brother. "Thank you for what you did, Vikirnoff, battling the vampires with us. I know it is hard for you to kill. Had you not been with us, they would have destroyed many people. You look a bit on the pale side, too. Did you give me blood?"

Vikirnoff nodded toward his brother. "In a way. I gave to my brother." It was easy to see that Destiny was holding on by a thread.

"Pater seems to be losing all his little children. They're dropping like flies. I doubt if he can father enough to come looking for us. Both of you go hunt and regain your full strength. I'll be fine while you're gone." Destiny attempted to shift herself out of Nicolae's arms. The movement wrenched a groan from between her teeth. "Ignore that. It slipped out without permission." She hadn't managed to move more than an inch; she felt like a wet dishrag held up only by strong arms.

Above her head, Nicolae glanced at his brother. Some

communication clearly passed between them, but Destiny was far too tired to read Nicolae. The pain was almost more than she could take. Her injuries were severe this time, and the wounds burned, as always when inflicted by a vampire.

Vikirnoff bowed from the waist toward her in the elegant way of the ancients. "I will leave you so that I may hunt." He vanished into a stream of mist, already on the move, streaking upward toward the narrow chimney leading out of the cave.

Destiny looked up at Nicolae's set features and managed a hesitant smile. "You're just spoiling for a fight, aren't you? I don't have the energy. I'm not going to complain if you want to stay. Well, not too much. I won't mention how pale you look. Or that I can feel your hunger. Or that you're being silly."

He stopped her easily, stealing the air from her lungs. Robbing her of speech. Of thought. Of reason. Leaning forward, he locked his gaze with hers. She read the desire there. The absolute need. He took his time, slowly lowering his head to hers. Watching her. Drinking her in. His long hair, wild from the battle, tumbled around his shoulders and skimmed her bare shoulder.

Her heart flipped; her insides turned to mush. Liquid heat rushed through her bloodstream, pooled low and throbbed for recognition. None of it mattered. There was only Nicolae in her world. In her mind. His arms tightened, nearly crushing her to him, yet all the while he was careful of her injuries.

And then his mouth fastened to hers and her world turned upside down for all time.

Chapter Eight

Time stopped. The world dropped away, simply disappeared. He tasted wild. She tasted exotic. The mix was a form of perfection, creating a powerful addiction. His mouth was firm and certain, her mouth was velvet soft and trembling with uncertainty. Nicolae was infinitely tender, murmuring to her as he gathered her even closer so that his body was imprinted on her softer one. Claiming her. And she melted right into him as if made for him.

Her heart was beating with the rhythm of his. Electricity seemed to arc between them. Whips of lightning danced in her bloodstream. Destiny was vaguely aware of the steady roar that thundered in her ears as his mouth took possession of hers. His gentleness was her undoing, the exquisite care he took with her. It was his tenderness that enabled her to merge with him completely.

Nicolae allowed the need to wash over him, through him. How did one survive when the body went up in flames and burned so cleanly? So completely? When the mind roared with need and every muscle was swollen and hard with a craving beyond bearing? Colors danced behind his eyes; fireworks burst through him, shooting sizzling sparks into his bloodstream. He deepened the kiss, feeding on her exotic taste. Possession and obsession were intertwining.

It was her small wince of pain that brought him to his senses. Reluctantly he lifted his head, needing her, craving her, but mindful of her terrible wounds. He rested his brow gently against hers, struggling to regain control of his breathing.

Destiny's long lashes fluttered and lifted. She regarded him with a dreamy, unfocused gaze. Her breath was coming in ragged little gasps. Nicolae deliberately slowed his breathing, coaxed her into following his rhythm. His white teeth flashed in a small, smug display of male arrogance. Of satisfaction.

Her palm skimmed his jaw, framed his face. "You learned a few things in all those years hanging around on earth, didn't you?"

His smile widened, his eyes glinting with humor. "I do not believe I ever experienced anything quite like this. Believe me, I would have remembered. It was rather like stepping off a cliff and free-falling through the heavens."

Destiny was pleased in spite of herself, but too exhausted to keep her hand up. It slipped away from him and she snuggled against him, shifting her hips to a more comfortable position in his lap. At once she came into contact with his fully aroused body. Her blue-green eyes went wide with shock.

"Do not panic, little one," he soothed gently. "I am

not asking for anything." The pad of his thumb slid over her lower lip to trace the perfection of her mouth.

Destiny's gaze drifted over his face for a long moment, lingered in the dark depths of his. "You don't ask for anything, yet you're asking for everything."

"In your time, Destiny," he answered gently. "It will happen; we have all the time in the world."

A faint smile curved her mouth. "Do we? You'd like me to believe that, wouldn't you? This isn't the first time the lifemate ritual has come up. You know, if what you say is true, it won't matter one way or the other if you say the words and bind us. You're already fixated." There was faint humor in her voice.

His eyebrows shot up. Nicolae found he wanted to kiss her again. He was fascinated with the way her mouth curved and tempted him when she smiled. "I wouldn't say fixated."

"Sticking to me like glue, then," Destiny insisted. A soft laugh escaped and immediately was choked off as pain slid over her fragile features. "Just do it. Get it over. Otherwise that idiot brother of yours will sit around glowering at me."

"Vikirnoff does not glower."

"Oh, yes, he does. He has those eyes and he gives me the 'get it together' look. It's annoying."

"What is annoying is that you are noticing his eyes. I do not think there is any need for you to be noticing his eyes." He scowled at her.

She stared up at his face, a slow grin spreading. "You are jealous. Oh, my gosh, you are totally jealous because I noticed your silly brother glowering."

"I am *not* jealous. And it is not that you noticed his

glowering, it is that you noticed his eyes, which is an altogether different thing."

"You are so jealous. That's too funny. As if I'd look at the silent caveman. It's bad enough that I have to put up with you. Just say the stupid words so I can go to sleep."

"Destiny." Nicolae sighed in exasperation. "You are missing the point. This is supposed to be romantic. There seems to be something lost in the moment."

"Romance? We are definitely, absolutely not having a romance." She looked panic-stricken.

This time he couldn't resist. He leaned down and kissed her very gently. His lips lingered over hers, teased, feather-light for just a moment or two. Not long enough to get him slapped, just long enough for her eyes to go dreamy again. "What are we having?" There was amusement in his voice.

She looked confused, staring up at him with a kind of hunted look that made him gather her closer. "Just say the dumb words, Nicolae. Let's see if it works."

"Well then, if you insist, I can do no other." He was very obliging. "But I must insist on a little romance."

Destiny narrowed her gaze. "I'm not always going to be lying here helpless," she warned.

"I should hope not. Once was enough to give me heart trouble." His hands stroked her face, caressed the jagged tears in her throat. His voice was so tender, it sent liquid heat coursing through her body and little butterflies winging in the pit of her stomach.

His arms gathered her even closer, cradling her in his lap. She closed her eyes as his face came closer, as his breath warmed the cold of her skin. Destiny felt her body turn to liquid heat. That warm breath felt like something she'd never thought she would find, not even if she lived for centuries. His lips were velvet soft, feathering down her cheek to the corner of her mouth. She felt tears burning behind her eyes. He was stealing her heart, and he wasn't stopping there. Her soul was craving him. Truly craving him. She hadn't thought she would ever have anything worthwhile for herself.

Destiny. Her name shimmered in her mind. The way he said it was musical. He always made her feel beautiful even though she knew she wasn't. But he made her believe, whenever he was with her, or when he was speaking to her, that she was beautiful and worthwhile. That she could dream and hope. That she could belong. That someone saw her as a woman and not a monster.

Her hands were shaking as she placed her palms against his chest to push him away. She couldn't handle this. She couldn't be with people after being alone for so long. She couldn't do it. But her hands just lay there helplessly. Her fingers curled into the silk of his shirt.

For a moment his breath caught in his throat. She was giving herself into his keeping without a thought for herself. Nicolae felt humbled by her generosity. "I am not people, little one, I am Nicolae, and I belong with you. You have been sharing your life with me for many years now." The kisses trailed to her ear. "I claim you as my lifemate." His teeth teased her earlobe, sent a shiver through her body, heated her bloodstream. Left her breathless. Without words to protest. "I belong to you."

Destiny's stomach somersaulted. Nicolae did belong to her. She knew he belonged to her. He was her sanity. Her savior. His mouth slid along her neck, gently, tenderly, to linger over the vicious wounds in her throat. "I offer my life for you. I give you my protection, my allegiance, my heart, my soul and my body. I take into my keeping the same that is yours."

She felt it, the difference inside her, the sudden wrenching deep within, turning, forming, completing something that had long been torn in two. Fear shook her, but she still didn't push at his chest or loosen her hold on his shirt. She clung to him instead, digging her fingers into his shirt, holding him close to her.

"Your life, happiness and welfare will be cherished and placed above my own for all time. You are my life-mate, bound to me for all eternity and always in my care."

His lips settled on hers, robbed her of air, gave her his own breath. Took her heart and gave her his. His mind settled into her mind. His teeth teased her bottom lip until she opened to him. Yearned for him. His tongue swept inside the sweet recesses of her mouth, teased hers into an erotic duel. He gave her no time to feel the ties strengthening between them, drawing them closer so that they became one soul. Two halves of the same whole. It would only panic her.

Nicolae took his time, making a thorough job of kissing her. His body was hard and painfully full. The demon roared for release, roared to continue the ritual, to claim her fully, make her irrevocably his. His fangs threatened to lengthen, wanting to taste her blood, wanting a true exchange as it was meant to be. His heart and soul sang with complete joy.

Nicolae. There was a faint ache in her voice, betraying her own deep needs and cravings. He felt her strength ebbing.

"You need to go to ground. Once more, Destiny, take my blood." He murmured the words against her lips.

You are weak. It was a faint protest, but her mouth left his and traveled along his neck to his throat. His entire body clenched as her teeth teased the spot over his pulse. *Will you have time to hunt before you go to ground?*

I will feed. The anticipation strained his muscles till they were rock hard, defined clearly beneath his thin shirt. His breath slammed out of his lungs as her fangs sank deep. White-hot erotic pleasure. He closed his eyes and let it happen. Fire spread through his blood straight to his heavy erection. The heat threatened to be his undoing. He shuddered with the effort to maintain control.

Destiny was careful to take only enough to sustain her through recovery. Her tongue swirled over the tiny pinpricks, lingered for a moment before she lifted her head. She was all too aware of his discomfort, the terrible need gripping him. She gave him the only thing she had to give. *Put me in the earth and set the safeguards, please, Nicolae. I am very tired.*

Nicolae went very still. He had been certain he would have to force her compliance, but she surprised him. He didn't make the mistake of allowing her to think too long about her request. He seized control immediately and sent her to sleep.

Nicolae held her for a long time, staring down at her face. She looked young and vulnerable, an angel with features that were far too seductive for his peace of mind. Or for the peace of his body. He felt humbled by her trust. He had never supposed she would trust him enough to sleep in the same chamber with him, no matter how severely injured she was. He sighed softly and lowered her into the rich bed of soil. Destiny. His world.

She lay so still, her breath stilled in her lungs. His hands lingered on her as he surveyed her injuries.

The air in the chamber stirred gently and he whirled around swiftly, a dark, dangerous predator, menace in every line of his body. His eyes flashed a hot reprimand at his brother. "You did not warn me."

"It is good for you. You have spent so much time sharing her head, I think it best to test your skills now and then."

Nicolae relaxed slightly. "Very funny. Your sense of humor has warped over the centuries."

"I did not know I had a sense of humor." Vikirnoff studied the lines of strain in his brother's face. "You are arrogant and you do not even realize it. You do not even seek to hide her resting place from me."

"I trust you."

"You do not trust me with her life, Nicolae. I am in your head just as you are in mine. You know how strong you are; you believe I am not a threat to you because you know you can protect her."

Nicolae raked a hand through the black silk of his hair, leaving it more disheveled than ever. "I believe in you, Vikirnoff."

Vikirnoff shook his head. "You believe in yourself. She has no idea how dangerous you are. How strong you are. After you connected with her you shouldered part of her physical pain, lessened her emotional pain, all the while going from continent to continent hunting for her. You battled the undead where you found them and avoided all contact with our people as Vladimer requested. You went on her hunts with her, helping orchestrate them, feeding her your own strength and power from great distances and shielding her from that knowledge. I know of no other Carpathian who has accomplished such a feat. Why do you hide your strength from her? And why do you allow this?" His hands gestured toward the bed of soil where Destiny lay, bruised and torn. "Why do you not forbid this behavior and simply put an end to your suffering? You are a Carpathian male. This is hell for you."

There was no reprimand in Vikirnoff's voice; there never was. He was mildly curious about behavior he couldn't fathom. Vikirnoff clearly found it incomprehensible that a Carpathian male would allow his lifemate to live in constant danger.

Nicolae shrugged his broad shoulders. The simple movement sent a ripple through his powerful muscles, a subtle warning to those who might see only his unfailing elegance. "She is my lifemate. I will do what is necessary for her, no matter what the cost. Destiny needs to be in control of her life more than she needs my protection."

"That makes no sense. We have few women. She is needed, alive and capable of giving birth to a female child. Why would you allow such unnecessary danger to her? Take her to our homeland where she belongs."

"A vampire robbed her of her life, forced his domination on her. Should I do the same?" Nicolae shook his head. "You know she would never stand for such a thing."

"You can take control of her. Once she is healed—"

"Vikirnoff, she will never be completely healed, you know that. What was done to her is there in her mind for all time. She must come to me of her own free will."

"The cost to you—"

"Does not matter. Will never matter. The physical

danger to her is nothing in comparison to the danger of losing her to her own demons. They are more real and more lethal than any vampire she chooses to fight. I know you cannot understand, but you and I have stood together for centuries. You know me. You know my strength. There is no danger of my failing her by turning vampire. If she chooses another world, another time and place, I will follow her."

"Do you remember all those years ago when our Prince called us to him? We were already aware our lifemates were not in the world with us. Most of us had already fought battles and had seen brothers and friends turn to a corrupt existence. We accepted that we would not have our lifemates, that something had happened to prevent their birth or that they had died before they had a chance to grow." Vikirnoff casually tugged at his wrist with his teeth.

Nicolae would never leave Destiny unprotected while she lay helpless in the healing sleep he had commanded. Not even with Vikirnoff to guard her.

Nicolae accepted the offering just as casually, nodding before bending his head to his brother's wrist.

"I have given this situation much thought," Vikirnoff said. "We accepted our lives as guardians of the world. We asked for nothing in return, and we did our duty and upheld the honor of our people." Vikirnoff glanced at the woman lying so still, her body battered and bruised, the tears in her skin still ragged. "This is not right. She should never have suffered like this. It is the very thing we gave our lives and our hopes to prevent. Of all people, it should not have happened to your lifemate. The undead should never have touched her."

"And yet he did," Nicolae said with resignation, closing

the laceration in his brother's wrist. "Thank you for your help in this difficult situation."

"It is easier to continue when I see your lifemate and I know there is hope for our race. That there is hope my brother will live on and continue our line."

"Perhaps Prince Vladimer knew that some of us would find our lifemates in this century rather than in our own. He did have precognition. If there is hope for me, surely there is reason for you to continue your existence, Vikirnoff."

"Perhaps that is why he chose certain ones to stay and others to go. Our Prince was a great man and saw far into the future. I thought at first he was wrong not to tell his son of our existence, but Vlad was right. Mikhail drew our people together as no other could have. They were few, and they fought hard for the preservation of our race."

Nicolae nodded his agreement. "Our people would have become divided had we not remained hidden. Vlad foresaw much, and that is why it is so important that all of our males continue to hold on."

"How is it that one who is so strong, so skilled a hunter and so intuitive, did not know the child he communicated with was his lifemate?" The question was casual, but Nicolae's gaze immediately sharpened, focused on his brother. There was a hidden significance to this question, but when Nicolae touched his brother's mind lightly, it was closed to him. He thought over his answer carefully, choosing his words.

"I believe I could not know she was my lifemate," Nicolae replied candidly. "Had I had that knowledge, I would have lost my sanity knowing she was being tortured and raped and forced to witness his murders. I tried, once or twice, to use her sight, to kill the vampire, but there was no blood bond between us and it was not possible. I was too far away to help her. The knowledge that I could not protect my lifemate would have sent me over the edge. Because I did not know for certain, I could still function, protecting her as best I could. It has occurred to me that on some level she knew the truth. Oh, not as we know, but still, she protected me in the only way she could, by not speaking. I might have found her sooner, but maybe not. She was so frightened that she kept moving all the time."

"She is a strong woman and very courageous. But she is in constant danger fighting the undead. She does not value her life."

"But she values my life. She has always valued my life, and she knows our lives are intertwined. She will not willingly give up her life in a fight, and she is not careless. I will not, I *cannot* force my will on her. She will find her way to me in her own time."

"I am in your mind, Nicolae. The only emotion I can feel is yours. The battle for her weighs heavily on you. Take her to our homeland. You are far stronger than she is, far stronger than most ancients, most hunters. She would have no choice but to obey," Vikirnoff urged. "She might be upset for a while, but at least she will be safe."

Nicolae shook his head. "She would not be safe. She would not tolerate such behavior on my part. In her eyes I would be no better than the vampire, forcing my will on her. My comfort is not important to me, only her life and her sanity."

"You have bound her to you. You live or die together."

"We lived or died together before I said the words.

She agreed to the ritual to protect me, anchoring me to the world of light."

Vikirnoff leaned his hip against a rock and studied his brother's face. "You insist, then, on remaining here in this place overrun with the undead?"

"I know what is in your mind, although you are attempting to close it to me. You cannot sacrifice yourself by hunting the vampire here. We both know you are too close to turning to continue killing. Go to our homeland and we will follow as soon as we are able."

Vikirnoff shrugged, the gesture very close to his brother's mannerism, a casual display of sheer strength. "One of us must continue our line."

"I believe you have a lifemate somewhere, Vikirnoff. I think Vlad sent us into this century with the foreknowledge that we had a chance of finding our lifemates. Why it has taken so long, I do not know, but this is no time to choose the end. We had no hope, no belief that it was possible, yet we hung on. Now that there is hope, you cannot give up."

Vikirnoff regarded Nicolae for a long moment in silence. He shook his head slightly. "She will eventually find out that she only thinks she can read what is inside of you. That you hide what she cannot handle. What then, Nicolae? If she chooses the dawn for the two of you and I have waited too long, then I have nothing to anchor myself to the world of light. You sentence both of us if she is not able to overcome these terrible scars on her soul."

Nicolae reached out, laid a hand on his brother's shoulder. "She will survive."

Vikirnoff was silent again while water dripped continually from the walls of the cave. Finally he nodded once, then swept his hand over the earth to open it a short distance from where Destiny lay surrounded by rich soil. "The undead has gone to ground. I suspect he will flee the area or at least pull back to regroup. Her friends are safe for a time." He floated across the chamber to lie in the earth.

Nicolae watched the dirt pour over his brother, watched as the surface smoothed and settled as if undisturbed for eons. He set safeguards at the entrances to the cave and up along the steep, narrow chimney. Nicolae would take no chances with Destiny in his care. He set an intricate safeguard over his brother's resting place, one that for the first time would alert him should Vikirnoff rise first.

Nicolae lay in the dark, rich soil beside Destiny's body. Still uneasy over the shadows in Destiny's blood, he decided another thorough inspection was warranted. Once more he shed his own body to become light and energy, entering hers to check the repairs he had made, to meticulously go over the cells where the vampire had injected his poison. He inspected her blood, wanting to see if his ancient blood was slowly fighting off the vampire's tainted sludge. Her blood was different. He felt it, sensed it, but no matter how carefully he searched, he could not find the poisonous bacteria. At times he had the sense that something was there with him, aware of him, but he found nothing to substantiate the feeling. He was gratified to see the blood flowing much more freely in her veins. Some of the long-term internal damage had been healed. It gave him hope that there would be a way to cure her completely. Finally he gathered her close to him and allowed the soil to pour over them, his lips brushing her cheek as the earth enfolded them into its care.

Destiny woke fighting. She knew she wasn't alone the moment awareness came to her, still deep beneath the earth as the soil opened above her. Her heart began to beat, and air found space in her lungs. She felt the body next to hers—hard, muscular, male. Strong. Too strong to fight, but she tried anyway. She was on her side, and the instant she became aware she turned, the edge of her hand slamming down with the force of a hammer toward the throat she knew was close to hers. But it was no longer there.

As her hand passed through empty air, Nicolae shackled her wrist, brought her hand gently to his throat to rest over his pulse. "You are safe, Destiny. Always safe with me. Each rising from this night until the end of our days, you will never wake alone or at risk. I will be here."

Destiny wrenched her arm free and launched her body out of the earth, her heart pounding so loudly it sounded like a drum in the confines of the cave. She landed some distance from him, fully clothed, her hair neatly braided and her gaze moving continually, restlessly in all directions.

"Where's Vikirnoff? He has not risen?"

Nicolae took his time rising, deliberately pausing before he clothed himself so she could get a good look at his sinewy body. He swept his hair back, using human means, securing the thick mass at the nape of his neck with a leather thong. "Are you nervous, Destiny? Surely not. You cannot be nervous with your lifemate."

Destiny tried not to stare at the perfection of his masculine body but she couldn't stop. He had incredibly broad shoulders, a narrow waist and hips, long, lean legs and well-defined muscles. He was fully aroused and quite casual about it as he dressed.

She began pacing, quick agitated movements that betrayed her inner conflict. "I can't be with someone all the time. I need space."

"There is a world waiting outside this chamber, Destiny." Nicolae gestured toward the entrance. "The night is waiting."

Her hand went to her throat. The ragged tears were healed. Her skin was without a single blemish. Her heart was beginning to settle down again, finding the exact rhythm of his. She forced a small smile, a brief curving of her mouth, yet her blue-green gaze continued to jump around the cave. "I think this might feel like my first one-night stand."

"One-night stand? I am offended. You planned to use me and throw me away after one night, did you? I am not that kind of man, Destiny. I am in for the long term. Eternity. You slept with me. It would be wrong of you to toss me out."

A reluctant smile touched her mouth, gleamed for an instant in her eyes. "I've watched a lot of movies—I don't think we slept together."

He grinned, a slow, teasing grin that swept away the lines etched into his darkly sensual features and managed to give him a boyish look. "We definitely slept together, Destiny. And as you can see, it was sleeping, not making love." He brushed his palm over the thick fullness stretching his trousers.

She blushed. She felt the color rising steadily, and no matter how hard she tried to stop it, it swept up her neck and into her face. She had been looking. Speculating. Maybe even admiring. "I was naked. You were lying beside me and we were both naked."

"That is common practice, I believe, when one goes to ground, especially to heal wounds." He looked totally unrepentant.

"I told you there would be none of that." She gestured with her chin toward his erection.

He laughed softly, pure male amusement. "I do not think we have much chance of controlling certain portions of my anatomy. You will just have to be understanding and pretend not to notice."

Her eyes widened. "How am I supposed to not notice *that*?"

"Well, fine, then." He sighed heavily. "I guess you can notice, but there will be no touching." His voice lowered an octave. "Or stroking."

For some insane reason her breasts ached and her body throbbed. It was his voice. The thought of his hands moving over her body, cupping her breasts . . . She could picture his thumbs teasing her nipples into hard peaks, could *feel* it. Her mouth was unexpectedly dry, and her incisors threatened to lengthen. Destiny backed a few steps farther from him. She *wanted* to feel the weight of his erection in her palm, the thick hardness of his desire for her. She wanted to kiss him, to see the desire flare in his eyes. She wanted to stroke him.

"Stop it." His voice was husky. "I mean it, Destiny. I am your lifemate, not a saint. You cannot have erotic images in your head and expect me not to react to them."

She did have images in her head—her hands moving over his body, her mouth trailing kisses. She closed her eyes, wanting to shut out the pictures, but they were still there and her body was still in need. Hot and heavy and burning for him.

"What did you do to me?" She glared at him accusingly.

"I healed your wounds; I did not take advantage. You know that."

"I've never felt this way before in my life!"

"That is a relief. I doubt I would be happy if you had wanted many men, Destiny." There was the merest trace of laughter in his voice.

"I'm glad you're finding this amusing."

"Come here." He held out his hand to her. "Let me feed you. You have been to ground for two risings and have not fed."

Her chin went up. "Neither have you, and you gave me blood before we went to ground. I can find my own prey." She felt strange. Divided. Wanting to be close to him. Wanting to run from him. He made her feel out of control. And vulnerable. She hated feeling vulnerable.

"Why would you prefer to feed from humans when you can have the blood of an ancient to sustain you? Can you not feel the effects of my blood? Your suffering is far less on this rising."

"Don't tell me my suffering is far less." Her eyes flashed at him, glinted a red fire in the darkness of the chamber. "I can handle that kind of pain. I know what to do, how to cope with it." *I don't know how to cope with you.*

She didn't wait to hear what he had to say. She bolted from the cave, fleeing as if pursued by demons. She knew exactly where she was going. To the church. Where she always went before feeding. Where she could find some semblance of balance. Of peace. She had entered the church and it hadn't fallen down. A bolt of lightning hadn't come out of the sky to incinerate her. She had touched the priest. And she wanted to look into a mirror again.

You look fine. I do not think you need to become vain. You have enough bad habits. Nicolae was laughing at her again, but she didn't care. There was something new and unexpected in her life. She found she was looking at the world differently. The stars were glittering like gems over her head and she couldn't help noticing and appreciating them. The wind blew gently over her body like the whisper of a lover's voice. It cooled her body, ruffled the silk of her hair. Lightened her heart.

For the first time in years, her blood wasn't burning her from the inside out. For the first time in years, she hadn't awakened with the thought of killing. She was wide awake, and her mind was filled with Nicolae. As hard as she tried, she could not extinguish the tiny ray of hope growing deep within her.

The church doors were unlocked, and she knew before she pulled them open that Father Mulligan was inside, hearing confession. With her acute hearing she could distinguish soft words and the strangled sob of a woman as she spoke with her priest. In the pew close to the confessional was a big bear of a man. John Paul. His head was bowed, and Destiny could see his big shoulders shaking. Tears slid down his face.

Destiny entered the church suppressing a small shiver of trepidation as she crossed the threshold and slipped into the poorly lit interior. Candles flickered in the alcove and cast strange, shifting shadows on the stained-glass window above it. She studied the depiction of the

Madonna and Child, the sweet face and the way one hand held the infant to her while the other was outstretched toward Destiny.

John Paul didn't look up, didn't seem to notice her, so Destiny slipped closer, wanting to get a feel for the man. Had he been touched by a vampire? Was that the explanation for his bizarre behavior toward Helena? Destiny scanned his mind, looking for the blank spots that would reveal the presence of the undead.

John Paul was filled with sorrow and confusion. He feared losing Helena and he believed he might be losing his mind. His thoughts were jumbled and mixed with wild plans of carrying his beloved off to a secluded place until he could convince her he loved her and would never harm her.

Father Mulligan and Helena emerged from the confessional, and the priest put his arm around her shoulders. Even in the dim light, Destiny could see Helena's swollen eye and cut lip. The damage was fresh. She was still crying softly. The priest helped her to a pew and beckoned solemnly to John Paul. The huge man hunched his shoulders as if struck, but like an obedient child, he rose. His tremendous bulk made the slight priest look small and thin and very frail.

Destiny waited until the two men disappeared into the privacy of the confessional before gliding silently to the aisle near Helena, scanning the woman's memories as she did so. Helena certainly had memories of John Paul attacking her. He was terrifying, a tremendously strong man with hamlike hands and a body like a solid oak tree. Helena believed John Paul was insane. She planned to leave him, fearing for her life, yet she loved him fiercely, protectively.

Her heart unexpectedly twisting in sympathy, Destiny laid a tentative hand on Helena's shoulder. "Velda and Inez asked me to help you, Helena. I hope you don't mind." She wished she were MaryAnn with her gift for saying what Helena needed to hear.

Helena shook her head without looking up. "No one can help me. I've lost John Paul. I can't stay with a man who would do this to me."

Destiny gently took her chin and lifted her face on the pretense of examining it. She waited calmly until Helena was caught and held in the depths of her eyes. She saw the relationship clearly; Helena and John Paul were nearly inseparable. Two people wholly devoted to one another. *I didn't know anyone could feel as strongly as they do about one another.*

You just did not want to know, Destiny.

Destiny scowled, wishing Nicolae were standing in front of her. She sent him a visual just in case he didn't get the fact that he was *annoying*. Destiny sighed. She couldn't let Helena and John Paul lose something so rare and precious. Continuing to look deep into Helena's eyes, she planted the idea of working things out with John Paul. Helena needed to allow MaryAnn to put her in a safe place until Destiny could figure out what was going on. Destiny would make certain John Paul understood and agreed with her plan.

I don't detect a vampire, she told Nicolae.

Are you certain? John Paul is a simple man. Perhaps he is so shaken, you are not receiving a reliable brain pattern.

Destiny frowned. *Does that happen?*

It is possible. If the vampire had a soft enough touch

and made the suggestion from a distance, you might not encounter the blankness they leave behind.

Destiny tapped her finger lightly on the back of the pew. *Is there a possibility that there is no vampire? Is there an illness that would cause John Paul to become violent? I don't know much about illnesses. I was only a child when I was converted, and I haven't spent much time around humans.*

She could feel Nicolae weighing his answer carefully, thinking it over. *Do you detect a tumor or a brain bleed, something physical that would affect his behavior?*

No. His brain patterns seem normal enough. He is very focused on Helena. I don't think he is capable of hurting her this way.

Why? Nicolae prompted. *Everyone is capable of violence.*

Destiny sank into the pew. Nicolae was right. John Paul was a huge bear of a man, quite willing to indulge in a brawl if the opportunity presented itself. *But not violence toward her. Never to Helena. He loves her.*

A wave of warmth flooded her mind. Her heart. Her very bloodstream. *I understand how he feels. I believe you, Destiny. We will figure it out.*

Chapter Nine

Nicolae couldn't miss the purple-haired woman waving at him, as much as he would have liked to. She was flapping her arms and jumping up and down on the sidewalk while the small, pink-haired lady beside her shouted out a welcome to him. He found himself returning to the small neighborhood near the bar, seeking out MaryAnn. The counselor for battered and abused women meant much to Destiny. MaryAnn also had some psychic ability; he wanted to know more of her.

Destiny might have run from him physically, but he could feel her, a quiet shadow in his mind, sharing her fears, talking over the puzzling problems of "her" humans, laughing with him. She didn't give him any sympathy as he deliberately shared the embarrassing vision of two elderly ladies in neon colors jumping up and down on the sidewalk and making frantic noises and wild gestures.

Their antics were drawing undue attention to him, something no Carpathian desired. Resigned, he turned away from MaryAnn's office to saunter down the street toward the two older women who obviously wanted his attention. He heard Destiny's muffled laughter brush at his mind. It lightened his heart. They would always be connected.

There are times when being invisible comes in handy. You could have warned me.

I think a good dose of Velda and Inez is exactly what you need.

He gave an exaggerated groan just to hear the sound of her laughter. After so many years of pain, it was a miracle to hear the amusement in her voice, to feel the lightness in her heart. She was slowly coming to terms with what she had become, slowly accepting that she might not be the evil creature she had been led to believe.

I am uncertain what I did this rising to deserve such punishment. Flashing his most charming smile at the two women, Nicolae bowed low over Velda's hand, skimmed Inez's knuckles with brief, old world courtesy. Both women fluttered their eyelashes and giggled like schoolgirls. "What can I do for you?"

Stop with the voice! Do you want to give them heart attacks? Destiny was really laughing now. She sounded so carefree, he felt a strong burst of emotion.

The women introduced themselves and patted the chair waiting between them, gushing over his name, his foreign accent and wonderful manners.

"What brings you to our neighborhood, Nicolae?" Velda asked curiously.

"We saw you with our dear MaryAnn," Inez added.

"I have come courting," he announced, devilishly sharing the conversation with Destiny. "The beautiful woman you were speaking with the other evening.

Destiny. I am doing my best to make her my wife, but she is attempting to resist my charm. I do not suppose either of you would have any suggestions to further my cause?" he added hopefully.

The women made cooing noises and Destiny hissed at him. Nicolae settled back to enjoy himself. Turning the tables on Destiny was no easy task, and he was determined to make the most of the opportunity. *Go attend to your business, little one, and leave me to mine. I think these women might have invaluable insight into the female psyche.*

"I think that's so romantic," Inez burst out, clasping her hands. "Don't you think so, Sister? Romance is just about gone from today's society. But romance is what you need to court her."

Velda clucked, shaking her head in disapproval. "We have to be practical in this day and age." She leaned close to Nicolae, pinned him with a sharp gaze. "You can't get by on good looks and manners, young man; you need substance. What kind of a job do you have?"

Destiny's laughter heated his blood and robbed his lungs of air. It was not only musical, but also held a latent sensuality that whispered promises of hot, silken nights.

Sheesh! Do you have a vivid imagination! Keep your mind on the business at hand, Nicolae. Tell them you hunt vampires and see if they think you're a safe bet as husband material.

Nicolae smirked. A predatory, smug, superior smirk guaranteed to set Destiny's teeth on edge. "I am in law enforcement, a special branch, but I am also independently wealthy, so she would never want for anything." His long fingers stroked his jaw, drawing attention to the singular masculine beauty of his face. "I have searched the world for her. I know we are meant to be together."

The two sisters exchanged a long look as if well pleased with his answer. It was Velda who took charge while Inez sighed over the sheer romance of true love finding a way. "Why is the girl dragging her heels? You're an attractive man."

"Oh, my, yes," Inez agreed, earning a fierce scowl from her sister. "Well, he is," she defended indignantly. She patted Nicolae's thigh. "You are, dear, just the type of beau I had in my heyday." She leaned close. "I was a wild thing, you know," she whispered in confidence.

He removed her hand by simply raising it to his lips. "Thank you, Inez. That is a true compliment coming from a woman such as yourself. I would be grateful for direction with my wayward bride."

What BS you're shoveling, Nicolae. You should be ashamed of yourself.

There was her laughter again, winding his body tighter and tighter until he was afraid Inez was going to have something to grab hold of if he wasn't careful. He shifted his position in the chair. The sound of Destiny's happy voice was a powerful aphrodisiac.

"Flowers," Velda said firmly. "You must find out her favorite flower and give her as many as you can afford."

"Don't forget chocolates. No woman can refuse a man with chocolates," Inez added. "And you can do so much with chocolate, all warm and melting—"

"Pay Inez no mind," Velda said. "But it is important you court Destiny properly, let her know you have strictly honorable intentions. Sweep her off her feet. Take her to a dance. There's nothing like a man holding a woman close to him and dancing with her." She raised an eyebrow, pinning him like an insect with her steely stare. "You do know how to dance? Not that rot the young kids do today, but dancing like a real man. There's nothing sexier than a good waltz or tango."

"It is a large part of my education," Nicolae assured her. "You have made some wonderful suggestions. I will follow them to the letter."

"And report back immediately," Inez reminded him. "Isn't that right, Sister? We need a report to know how it is going."

"Absolutely," Velda agreed. "Oh, look, there's Martin. Have you noticed he's been looking a bit down lately, so unlike him. Poor dear must be working too hard." She stood up, waving so violently, Nicolae was afraid she might fall over. "Martin! Martin! There's a good boy, do come over and talk with us."

"It's that project of his. He and Tim work night and day on it even though they have regular jobs," Inez said. "Those boys work much too hard."

Nicolae watched the man approach, noting the pale skin and dark circles under his eyes. This was the man who had so viciously attacked the priest. Nicolae scanned Martin's memories and found no remembrance of the assault. Only the recollection of sitting on his bed holding the wooden box from the church and turning it over and over in his hands in complete bewilderment. Nicolae could find no malice within the young man, only a heavy sorrow and utter confusion.

Exactly what John Paul was feeling, Destiny pointed out. *Can you find the blankness of the mark of the vampire?*

Nicolae was an ancient, far stronger than Destiny, one

well versed in the arts of the undead. He was certain he would detect the presence of a vampire had the creature touched Martin in some way, but there was no evidence of such a violation. Nicolae stood up, drawing instant attention, holding out his hand as Velda introduced him to the young man.

Martin did his best to be polite in spite of his distraction. Nicolae could see he was naturally a friendly and outgoing person. His affection for Velda and Inez was obvious, as was their affection for the young man they had seen grow to adulthood.

"I have heard such good things about you, Martin. You are an advocate for the elderly and have a new project you are working on with Tim Salvadore. Father Mulligan tells me it is a wonderful opportunity to provide independent living in a safe environment for people on limited means. He believes you to be quite brilliant. The two of you must be great friends." Deliberately Nicolae used the priest's name, kept his voice soft and friendly and engaging. He knew the power of such a weapon. Few could resist the invitation to talk.

Martin's shoulders sagged. "Father Mulligan's a great man. I've known him all my life." He lifted his head and looked directly at Nicolae, anguish plain in his eyes. "Did he also tell you someone assaulted him? Struck him over the head repeatedly and stole the box of money for the poor right out of his hands?"

Velda gasped. Inez shrieked. Both women crossed themselves, lifted a silver crucifix each wore and in perfect synchronization kissed the cross. "That can't be, Martin," Velda protested. "No one would hurt Father Mulligan."

"There's never any money in the poor box, is there,

Sister?" Inez added, wringing her hands. "What is this world coming to that someone would attack a priest in God's own house?"

"Maybe Inez and I will have to move to your community after all, Martin," Velda said. "If things have gotten so bad in this neighborhood that a thief would harm Father Mulligan, no one is safe."

"Is the poor man going to be all right?" Inez asked. "Sister dear, we must make some of our famous chicken soup and take it to him immediately." She tapped Nicolae's arm. "No one can make such perfect chicken soup as dear Velda. Of course I have to remind her what she's doing or she wanders off on one of her research projects. Velda hunts for proof that vampires and werewolves exist."

That snapped Nicolae to attention. He had been watching Martin closely for any reaction, barely registering the conversation flowing around him. His dark gaze found Velda, settled there thoughtfully.

Velda patted her hair and smiled at him. "An old hobby of mine. I dabble a bit in magic spells, but I'm not very good at casting. Inez is much more accurate than I am. Martin, dear, do sit down. You look like you could use some feeding up. I'll make a double batch of my soup and give some to you. We'll have you fixed up in no time."

Martin, still partially under the thrall of Nicolae's voice, slumped heavily into the chair Nicolae had occupied, frowning up at him. "He thinks I did it. Father Mulligan thinks I bashed him over the head and took the poor box." The confession came out in a rush, ended on a choked sob.

Velda and Inez instantly turned their attention to him,

patting and stroking his hair soothingly and making clucking noises. "Father Mulligan must have suffered a concussion. He knows you would never do such a thing, Marty. I'll go talk to him at once," Velda said supportively.

"Oh, yes, Sister, we must go at once," Inez echoed. "Father must be hurt badly to accuse poor Marty of such a thing."

Martin Wright stared at his hands. "What if I did do it? Father Mulligan would never lie to me, and Tim said I came home covered in blood that night. He said I had the church box in my hands and I wouldn't talk to him. That I just sat there, staring at the box." He looked up at Velda, tears shimmering in his eyes. "I don't remember. Could I have attacked Father? I've never hurt anyone in my life."

"Martin." Nicolae hunkered down so he was eye-to-eye with the man. Distress was emanating from Wright in thick waves. "What do you remember about that day *before* the assault on Father Mulligan? Where did you go? Who were you with? What did you do? Do you remember anything at all?"

"I did all the usual things. I went to work, I met Tim for lunch. We discussed the project like we normally do. He had his astronomy class, so I went down to the project site to talk to the contractor. I was there a long time. I remember thinking I wanted to show Father Mulligan the plans again because I was worried about a series of steps and a ramp leading to the gardens from the west side. I was afraid some of the residents might have a difficult time maneuvering them. The contractor insisted that the slope wasn't that steep, but Father Mulligan knows a great deal about the hardships of people using walkers or canes because he talks with the elderly on a daily basis. I wanted a second opinion."

"Oh, Sister!" Inez caught at Velda. "He did go to see Father Mulligan that night. You are right. There is something going on in the neighborhood."

Velda nodded grimly. "Something evil is afoot. We should activate the neighborhood watch immediately."

Nicolae winced inwardly. He had visions of little old ladies with shocking hair marching up and down the streets with magic potions and garlic wreaths. "Martin, before you went to the church to see Father Mulligan, do you recall going anywhere else? Did you stop to speak to anyone, even casually, or eat dinner? Did you drop by the neighborhood bar?"

Martin frowned, rubbed his temples. "I must have. I left the work site just after six o'clock. Father Mulligan was assaulted much later than that. He always goes to the church around eight thirty or nine, I wouldn't have tried to catch him before that."

When did you discover Father Mulligan? Nicolae asked Destiny.

It was close to ten, between nine thirty and ten.

Nicolae turned once more to Martin. The sisters were fussing over him, leaving Martin somewhere between amusement and tears at their staunch support of him.

"Sister, you must make him a talisman," Inez insisted. "Something to ward off evil. Martin, Velda can give you a powerful totem to wear around your neck."

"Do you think vampires are involved?" Nicolae asked Velda with a straight face.

Velda glared at him. "Mock me, I don't mind. I've lived with the knowledge of the supernatural world for years and the unbelievers who insist on making light of it. I know my duty."

"Velda," Martin interrupted. "It had to have been me. Tim wouldn't lie, and neither would Father Mulligan. Tim says it isn't the first time I've acted oddly and not remembered. I promised him I'd go for a checkup at the clinic."

"Velda." Nicolae's voice was impossibly gentle, completely compelling. "I am so sorry you misunderstood me. I have no idea if vampires exist or not and I would never make fun or mock you. I was asking your opinion."

Velda blushed a bright shade of scarlet. "I thought . . ." She trailed off, her hands fluttering helplessly. "I'm so used to someone making fun of my beliefs, I jumped to conclusions."

"I think Martin should go to the clinic and I think we should do a little investigation into this matter. I do not mind looking into it for you. After all, I am in law enforcement. Father Mulligan prefers to keep this as quiet as possible. He believes something happened to you that night, Martin. He doesn't want the police brought in. He is a personal friend and I am here to help out. And, of course, Destiny asked me to help."

"That sweet girl," Inez said. "Sister dear, isn't she a sweet girl?"

Velda's attention was on Nicolae. "Yes, I believe you've been sent here to help us." She continued to stare at him, her eyes glazing, her expression becoming dreamy and faraway. Her gnarled fingers, clearly damaged by arthritis, moved in a complicated pattern before his eyes.

Nicolae felt his breath slam out of his lungs. Destiny's

heart skipped a beat, then began to pound far too hard. Nicolae lifted his hand toward Velda, palm out.

No! Don't stop her. You can't stop her. Let her "see" you.

It was the sheer desperation in Destiny's voice that stopped Nicolae from preventing the reading Velda was so obviously capable of. Her talent was deep and well hidden and thinning with age, but it was there nevertheless.

Velda gasped aloud, staggered backward and shook her head as if clearing her vision. At once her trembling hand went to the silver crucifix around her neck. "I'm not well, Sister. Take me inside." Her voice shook and she avoided looking at Nicolae.

"Look at me, Velda." It was a command and the woman turned to face him, looking her age for the first time. She seemed to have diminished in size and was frail and sunken in. "You know you will never have anything to fear from me. I have come to this place to help you and your friends. You believe that."

Velda nodded solemnly. "Yes, I know," she murmured.

She knew too much. Nicolae suddenly realized that nothing was what it appeared to be in this quiet neighborhood. The ground shifted and rolled beneath his feet. *Destiny! Come to me now.* The command was made by an ancient in full power; it was a compulsion impossible to resist. He didn't even think about the repercussions of bending her to his will. He couldn't think about it. There was a strand of evil woven into the very fabric of the neighborhood, and he needed to find its root. The preservation of his race could very well be at stake.

Nicolae released Velda from his enthrallment and

watched as Inez helped her sister into their home, leaving him alone with Martin.

"She looked ill," Martin said with genuine concern. "Do you think we should call Dr. Arnold? He supervises the clinic, and I know he'd make a house call for Velda or Inez. They're sort of an institution here."

"I think she just needed to rest." Nicolae's glittering gaze moved broodingly over the man sprawled out in his chair. "Where did you have dinner that night, Martin? You never said."

Martin frowned and rubbed his head as if it pained him. "I always go to the bar. I must have gone there. I knew Tim wasn't going to be home, and I always go to the bar for company when he has classes. I don't remember. How could I lose an entire night?"

"We will figure it out, Martin," Nicolae assured him, using a soothing voice. At once, some of the anxiety eased from the man's face. "It will be easy enough to ask at the bar if you were seen that night. Everyone knows you."

"Tim is upset. He doesn't know what to think or believe, and I can't reassure him," Martin said wistfully.

"Velda and Inez seem to know what they're talking about when they give advice, Martin, and so does Mary-Ann. Maybe you should talk it over with someone you trust and see what they have to say."

He could feel the surge of power as Destiny flew swiftly through the night sky toward him. *Destiny.*

Martin pushed himself up out of the chair and thrust out his hand toward Nicolae. "I was feeling pretty hopeless until I talked with you. Thanks, man. I think you're right. I saw MaryAnn going in the direction of her office. Maybe I'll go hash this out with her."

You summoned me? The words were bit out. Destiny wasn't happy with the way he had drawn her to him. Or the fact that he could draw her. *His* blood ran in her body, yet he was the one who commanded her.

"Excellent idea, Martin." Nicolae lifted a hand in farewell and sauntered around the corner out of sight. He knew exactly where she waited for him, seething and determined to pick a fight.

Destiny glared at him when Nicolae appeared next to her, shimmering into solid form on the highest rooftop above the neighborhood. "Would you like to explain your arrogant behavior to me?"

Her eyes were smoky green, with turbulence swirling in their depths. She looked wild and unpredictable. Her body was poised and ready to fight, coiled like a spring, yet as still and as watchful as a tigress. The wind was ruffling her hair like the touch of fingers and her mouth was . . . tempting. His gaze dropped to her full lower lip. Its slight pout didn't mean she was sulking. It meant trouble for someone.

His entire being reacted to the sight of that pouty lower lip. His arousal was swift and hard, accompanied by a punishing ache that wouldn't quite leave him even when he was away from her.

Destiny was furious. Not just furious. She was frustrated and restless and strung tighter than a bow. Anger roiled in the pit of her stomach, mixed with an age-old excitement she couldn't contain. It was a reaction to the way he was looking at her, his hooded gaze hot with desire and an intensity of need and hunger he didn't bother to try to hide.

"Was my behavior arrogant?" His gaze never lifted from her mouth.

The power of his voice sizzled in her stomach, throbbed lower. She recognized need for what it was, and it frightened her that she could be so caught up in the force of his power. His voice stroked her skin like a velvet glove, making her intensely aware of every inch of her skin.

"Are we going to talk about this?" Her own voice sounded husky, strangled, as if she couldn't catch her breath. "You used your power against me. That's entirely unacceptable." She had to look away from him. Up close he was stealing her very reason, putting erotic ideas in her mind that should never have been there. Destiny closed her eyes and inhaled, hoping the cool, crisp air would clear her head.

"Is that what you think I did? Used my power *against* you? When has anything I have ever done been against you? I have lived for you for more years than I care to consider, Destiny. You have to meet me somewhere, if not halfway then at least make a few concessions, take a few steps toward me."

She inhaled his scent. The beckoning call of male to female. Her breath exploded out of her. "Nicolae." His name came out an aching whisper. "I have tried. I swear to you, I have tried."

He reached for her, unable to prevent himself when there was raw pain etched into her face and such urgent need in her eyes. "Come here to me. Nothing can be done until we resolve what is between us." His hands settled around her, gathered her into the shelter of his body, and he took to the air.

She knew she should protest. Wherever he was taking her was a place in which they would be alone. She couldn't afford to be alone with him and the temptation he represented. Her hand was already splayed over his chest, feeling the heat of his skin through his thin silk shirt. She reached around his neck to loosen the mass of his long, thick hair so that strands blew around her face and over her arms.

Nicolae felt the shiver that ran through Destiny as he took them far away from the city to one of the larger underground chambers he had found in his explorations of the area. His lips skimmed her throat, lingered for a moment over her frantically beating pulse, feathered up her neck to press against her ear. "We need a private place to speak on this matter. I do not altogether trust what is happening within the neighborhood. Anything could be listening to us."

He placed her on her feet, waving his hand so that flames leapt to life in the carved urn he had left behind days earlier. Golden light flickered and danced on the walls of the cave, illuminating gems buried in the rock so that the chamber seemed to sparkle. A ring of boulders captured a pool of shimmering water that bubbled up from the ground and fizzed like a Jacuzzi.

Destiny moved away from the sheer potency of his larger, masculine frame. "What happened back there with Velda? Is she like me?"

Her eyes were begging him to give her the right answer. Nicolae touched her mind very gently as she shared with him that first dangerous memory. The little girl with a mass of ringlets falling around her shoulders and eyes too big for her face smiling up at a handsome man. The stranger bent down to her level, speaking softly, and her smile widened. She nodded her head several times, took his hand and walked him back to a small house. A woman stood on the porch, frowning a little as she watched her daughter speaking animatedly to a tall, rather beautiful man who slowly took on the form of a monster. His perfect skin became gray. His thick dark hair grew white and hung in strings. The slash of his mouth revealed jagged teeth stained black with blood, and long, sharp talons bit into the child's arm.

Immediately, Nicolae realized he was looking at the vampire through the eyes of the child Destiny had once been. "How could a child of six recognize a vampire? How could she know that one even existed? A child is innocent of such things."

"I drew him to my family. You can't say different. Velda is in her seventies. In all this time, why hasn't she drawn a vampire to her or her family? And what of MaryAnn? She is also psychic. We've destroyed several vampires in this area, yet none of them were drawn to these women."

Nicolae could feel the tears burning behind her eyes, although she held her chin up and her blue-green gaze was as steady as ever. "A better question might be why are all the vampires congregating here? That disturbs me immensely. Three women with varying psychic talents are here together. Is that really a coincidence? And Father Mulligan knows about our people, and he just happens to be here too. In this city of so many, we just happen to meet him and become involved in his life. Does that not disturb you? And we have two men, John Paul and Martin, behaving in a manner totally out of character for either one of them. I examined Martin. He has no darkness in him at all. He is incapable of harming another human being, yet he must have assaulted the priest. Or someone pretending to be him did so. How could one person play the part of John Paul, a large, muscular man, as well as Martin Wright, a slender, much shorter man?"

"A vampire could. He could assume any shape, any role," Destiny pointed out.

"And play the part well enough to fool Father Mulligan?" Nicolae's eyebrow shot up. "A man of the church? A man of such wisdom?"

"Of course, a vampire could fool Father Mulligan. I could do it. I could take your shape and make anyone believe I was you." She shrugged her shoulders with casual disdain. "Well, almost anyone. Maybe not Vikirnoff."

There was a small silence while Nicolae watched her closely with his unblinking stare. He saw the moment she understood what he was getting at. A vampire could fool any human. There was no way that she, an innocent child of six, could have recognized the monster who'd destroyed her family.

"I see what you're saying, Nicolae, and I know you're right. In my head I know you're right. I tell myself to stop placing the blame for my parents' deaths on my shoulders, but my heart doesn't listen."

"At least you are hearing me," he said quietly. "It was not a vampire that entered the church. No vampire would do so, nor would one of their ghouls. They are unclean and would not dare to enter a sanctified place."

"I know that." He had trapped her very neatly into admitting to herself that she was not unclean, for she had entered the church. She wanted that truth to sink into her heart and soul and live there, freeing her from the weight of guilt and self-hatred. She lived. It mattered little that her life had been a form of hell. She was alive, and the vampire who had murdered her family and countless others was dead at her hand.

Nicolae's face was hidden by the shadows recess of the cave, but she could see his eyes. Hungry. Intense. Needful. Burning with desire. He robbed her of every protest. Robbed her even of self-preservation. She tasted his desire in her mouth. It spread through her blood-stream and pooled into molten liquid, pulsing and throbbing for release. Her body felt strange, not her own. Heavy and aching.

Nicolae's gaze locked on hers. He could smell her beckoning scent. He could read the confusion in her eyes. It didn't matter how much his body was scream-ing at him. His heart was melting, even as his body craved hers with an obsession he couldn't overcome. "You have not fed, Destiny. Why is that?" His voice was a whisper of sound in the confines of their under-ground chamber. A husky invitation that nearly brought her to her knees.

Destiny went weak at the sound of his voice. She watched his fingers slip the buttons of his shirt loose. Watched in complete fascination as he tossed the silk aside to reveal his powerful chest. His muscles were subtle, but well defined. She couldn't tear her gaze from the wide expanse of skin. The breadth of his shoulders. The thickness of his chest. His narrow waist. The strength in his arms.

"I can't breathe." She lifted her gaze to his face. "I can't breathe, Nicolae."

Destiny looked so fragile, so vulnerable, so lost. Nicolae stepped toward her and caught her face in his hands. He bent his head to hers, taking possession of her mouth, breathing for her, sharing his air. Sharing his strength.

At once the fire raged. Deep. Hot. Elemental. It flashed between them, in them, burning from the inside out. She simply surrendered to his dominance, her tongue dueling with his, a wild tango of mating. Of its own accord, her body went soft and pliant, molding itself to his, her breasts pressed tight to his chest. Her hands moved over him almost helplessly, as though moved by a compulsion to feel his skin beneath her fingers. The kiss went on and on. Neither could get enough; each wanted to crawl into the other's soul, into the other's skin, into the other's body.

It was sheer possession. A wild branding. Lust and love rising up swift and fast, intertwining, spinning out of control to create a firestorm, turbulent and white-hot. A soft sound escaped her throat, a keening mixture of fear and need. When he heard, Nicolae reluctantly began to exert his control, pulling back slightly to allow her to escape.

Her arms circled his neck and brought him back to her hungry mouth. He had been alone so many centuries, searching, waiting, needing her. She had been cut off from the world. Yearning for him. Clinging to him. Pushing him away at the same time to protect him. To save him. Her mouth was wild, fanning the heat up another notch. There was no saving either of them. She was helpless under the onslaught of his mouth, needing to be closer, demanding to be closer.

I am not going to be able to stop. There was a plea for mercy in his voice. His hunger for her consumed him. He fed on the honey of her mouth, taking rather than asking, a dominant male in the full grip of passion, yet there was a tenderness in the way he held her that only added to his appeal.

Don't stop, then. "Never stop." She whispered the words into his mouth. "I don't want you to stop." And she didn't. She was beyond being afraid. She was terrified. But that was nothing to her in the firestorm of her need. It consumed her, this obsession for him. Her body burned and throbbed and pulsed for his. Pleaded for his. And when he was kissing her, there was nothing else in her mind. No monsters. No deaths. No guilt or memories of wailing victims. There was only pure feeling. There was only Nicolae.

His hands slipped from her face to follow the smooth line of her neck. "Are you afraid of me, Destiny?" His teeth tugged at her lower lip, the one he found so intriguing, so impossible to resist. "I feel your heart slamming so hard." His hand lay over her heart, fingers splayed wide so that her breast ached and her heart pounded into the very center of his palm, as if he were holding it. "I do not want you to fear me, or to fear our joining. Coming together in love is a beautiful thing, not an act of despicable violence, but something unbelievably wondrous. Do you trust me enough to join your body with mine?"

Before she could answer, his mouth took hers again, his hunger ravenous. His hands slid lower, cupped the weight of her breasts, his thumbs caressing her nipples into hard peaks right through the material of her shirt. Destiny gasped as the sensations plunged her body into a volcano of need. Her legs threatened to give out. Her clothes were too tight, too heavy on her body. "Nicolae." Raw sensual hunger was in her voice. She opened her eyes to look at him, to search his dark gaze.

Passion stamped an erotic sensuality into the perfection of his masculine features. He was no boy, but a dangerous, powerful being, yet she saw his vulnerability.

"Say yes to me, Destiny. Let me make you mine."

She was drowning in need. In hunger. In what had to be love. If it wasn't love, why were tears shimmering in her eyes and clogging her throat? Why was she fighting to save him? "You know what will happen. You know, Nicolae. You'll want to take my blood, and I would let you. I would never be able to find the strength to stop you." She whispered the words while his hands slid over her ribcage to find her waist. His hands tugged at the hem of her shirt, his knuckles skimming bare flesh. She burned and pulsed and waited for his rejection. It was the only answer for them. His enduring strength.

Chapter Ten

The sound of water dripping mingled with the accelerated rhythm of their hearts. The flickering flames in the stone urn danced over their bodies and bathed them in mystical light. There was a heartbeat, two, while his eyes locked with hers. His fingers bunched the hem of her shirt into his fists and he drew the light material over her head in one swift motion.

Destiny heard the hitch in his breath as his gaze dropped to her body. His hands went to her waist, a burning brand that seemed to melt through her skin. She reveled in the intensity of his gaze, the way it moved over her body, hot, possessive, claiming her very soul. She knew his mind was firmly entrenched within hers, allowing her to experience the extent of his hunger for her. He hid nothing from her—not the way she made his body feel and not the way he wanted to touch her. Not the way he needed her so desperately. So urgently.

Destiny felt an answering wildness rising in her. Clothes seemed a foreign intrusion, a heavy weight she could no longer bear against her sensitive skin. The thin lace of her bra chafed her skin, prevented his heated gaze from caressing her. Even as his hands caught her waist and he bent his dark head, dragging her body to him, she reached behind her to undo the tiny clasp.

His mouth closed over her breast, wildly hot and moist, suckling right through the thin lace, his teeth scraping gently, expertly so that she cried out and cradled his head to her. Destiny's knees nearly buckled, the sensation was so strong, so overwhelming. Her fists clenched in the thick silk of his hair, holding him to her while his tongue danced and stroked and his mouth pulled strongly, creating a burning, throbbing pool of need in her deepest core. The friction of the lace and the heat of his mouth drove her crazy. She arced into him, giving herself up to sheer pleasure.

When he lifted his head to attend to her other breast, the scrap of lace floated freely to the ground. His lips found bare flesh, ravishing her with his mouth alone. His tongue lavished attention on her, teeth teasing until she cried out, her fists tugging at his hair. She really was going to fall. There was no way to stand up; all strength had drained from her legs. Only his arms held her up.

He bent her back slightly, teasing, lapping, suckling, loving, lusting after her. Going up in flames. His hands shifted, tracing the contours of her body. She had full breasts, a narrow waist and flaring hips designed to be cradled by his body.

"How can it be like this?" she gasped. "I never knew it would be like this." A wildfire out of control. A fierce firestorm neither could ever put out. They had started it, and it burned bright and hot and perfect. She was melting, her body soft and pliant with need. She wanted his touch—more, needed it. There was never going to be enough time for them to be together. She was in another world, another time and place, far from the realities of what her life had become.

She heard her own gasp as his tongue lapped the underside of her breast. Her stomach clenched. There was only feeling, wonderful, pure feeling.

"My clothes," he said against her flat belly. "My clothes are killing me, Destiny. Take them off for me."

It was his voice again. That perfect sensuality. That urgent need. Destiny found it impossible to resist him. Her gaze dropped to the front of his pants. The material was stretched far too tight. Her heart leapt. In fear or anticipation? Destiny wasn't certain which emotion was predominant, but that thick bulge drew her attention immediately. She couldn't resist brushing her hand across the hard evidence of his need. When he jumped, she closed her hand over the bulge, pressing into him. He was hot, throbbing. He grew larger, swelling into her palm.

Keeping her hand in place, she removed his clothing in the manner she had grown accustomed to, using her mind, rather than her hands. Her palm found hot flesh, hard, iron in velvet. Nicolae sucked in his breath, murmured something against her soft skin. His teeth scraped erotically, tugged and teased, his tongue swirling to ease every ache.

"Your clothes." His voice had dropped an octave, was huskier, a little rougher than before. The touch of his mouth on her stomach left behind a trail of fire everywhere he touched. "Get rid of them." His hips were pushing forward, thrusting deeper, filling her palm. "I need them off of you." His hands were pushing at her clothing, trying to be gentle when he wanted to tear the offending material from her lush body.

Her fingers squeezed, danced, played lightly over the hard length of him, taking pleasure in what she was doing to him, feeling the bursting fire in his veins through their mind merge. Colors seemed to sparkle around them; there were tiny sparks behind her eyelids. She allowed herself to drift further into the world of sensuality, into Nicolae's world of heat and passion.

Destiny felt the heat of the flames, watched the shadows they cast on the wall. A man bending over a woman's body. Her breasts thrust upward in invitation, his head down as he explored her offering. It was an erotic image, a shocking one when she considered she was part of it. Watching the shadowy figures, she allowed her cotton jeans and scrap of lace underwear to slide away from her body, watched them simply disappear, leaving her skin to skin with Nicolae.

His hands moved possessively over her hips, her buttocks, smoothing, kneading, exploring. His fingers nestled in tight curls, causing her to gasp, her body tightening in anticipation. The need was building to a terrible urgency.

Destiny had no choice but to circle his neck with her arms. Her knees buckled as his finger dipped lower with a long, caressing stroke. *Nicolae!*

He waved his hand toward the earth and flowers sprang up, thousands of soft petals to cushion her body as he floated them easily to the waiting bed. She could feel the petals on her skin, velvet soft, rubbing against her body. Nicolae's weight settled over her, his mouth once more fastening to hers.

At once they were melting together, fusing with heat and fire. Somewhere between love and lust. His hands were everywhere, claiming her body for his own. She felt helpless under the onslaught, nearly sobbing with the urgency of her body's need. It was an unfamiliar, alien feeling, as if someone else were in her skin, in her mind, and she was going along on this journey of erotic sensuality.

His mouth hardened, taking command, driving out all thoughts until she was back to feeling. His hands skimmed her body, rested between her legs so that she throbbed and pulsed and shifted restlessly, forever seeking more. She needed more.

Destiny was in a world of feeling and love. It surrounded her, embraced her, a perfect paradise. But the snake began an insidious attack, slithering into her perfect world and bringing images she couldn't stop: the feeling of being held down, locked beneath another, much heavier body; her soft cries of pleasure were drowned out by the agonized scream of a child. She forced her mind away from the nightmare images, determined to recapture the perfect sense of sharing with Nicolae.

Nicolae was in her mind, heightening her pleasure when her heart began to pound too hard and fear thrust its way back into her world. When the nightmare images strayed too close, he kissed her again and again, pushing the memories back. He kissed her, his hands gently exploring until she was hot and moist with wanting him, her body accepting of his. Still he was careful, taking his time when the beast inside roared for more, roared for possession. Very gently he pushed his finger into her, slowly, careful of her tightness, not wanting her to experience discomfort. Her small muscles clenched around him and her body shuddered with the intensity of pleasure. Her hips pushed against him instinctively.

Nicolae bent his head and kissed her stomach as he slowly, inch by inch, slid two fingers deep inside her. She gasped, caught at his silken hair as it slid over her sensitized skin. Her hips began a slow rhythm, following the lead of his hand.

Sizzling heat swept through her. She wanted to grind her body against him. And when he withdrew, she cried out, needing him to fill her. His hands pushed her thighs apart; his hips took their place between hers. At once her heart jumped. She felt vulnerable and open. His weight as he stretched out above her pinned her in place. Instinctively she shifted out from him, but his leg stopped her sudden movement. He was strong. Far stronger than she'd first thought. His leg pinned her thigh, holding her down.

The strange roaring in her mind became louder. The mouth on her was tender, loving, but it couldn't prevent the memories of teeth puncturing her flesh, biting unnaturally, the all-powerful man ramming something far too large into her tiny body over and over, slamming her to the ground, throwing her over a boulder, taking her from behind, uncaring of her screams, reveling in her pain and humiliation. She recalled the blood she'd slipped in, lain in, all around her, the dead body with the open eyes staring into hers as he took her over and over again.

She gasped, cried out, stiffening in shock. Her breath was coming far too fast.

"Wait—please, I'm sorry, just wait a minute." Destiny tunneled her fingers in his hair. "Wait, Nicolae. We're going too fast. Slow down." She didn't want to slow down. She was burning up. Even as she pleaded with him, her hips moved against him, a blatant invitation she couldn't prevent. She needed him buried deep inside her; that was the only solution for the terrible building pressure she felt. But the images in her mind were tenacious. She wanted Nicolae's hands and mouth to remove the images for her, not invoke them. She wanted the ecstasy of his body to take away every nightmare memory.

Nicolae felt the disturbing images of death and madness moving through her mind, moving through his. He felt her partial withdrawal, felt her tremendous physical need so at odds with her mental hesitation. At once he lifted his head, moved his leg to allow her freedom. "We can slow down. I could spend hours just touching you. Or holding you. Or kissing you." He found her mouth with his, blazing his brand of possession straight on her heart.

Destiny was stiff beneath him, but his mouth held familiar heat and his hands were gentle as they wandered over her body. He was patient, starting over, kissing her until she was breathless and kissing him back. Until her body slowly began to relax. Until she was hungry for him again. Until the brush of his fingers on her skin sent tiny flames dancing and singing through her body.

Nicolae shifted once more, his knee sliding between hers, nudging her legs apart so that he was pressed tightly against her. She could feel him there, at her entrance, where she was ready with a moist invitation, beckoning and tempting him to her. A small sound escaped. She couldn't find enough air to breathe.

"What is it, little one?" His voice came out of the

darkness, velvet soft, his hands skimming her body with exquisite tenderness. "Where are you going?" She was tensing up beneath his hands and he couldn't bear it, couldn't bear to let her go. He fed her his heightened awareness, his own desire, slowing his own heartbeat to aid her in accepting him. He moved his body away from hers to give her time to accept what was between them.

Fighting his instinctual need to exchange blood, he feathered a trail of kisses from her throat to her abdomen. His mouth was on her flat stomach, his tongue swirled around her belly button, that intriguing sexy dimple he had so greatly admired. Her hands stroked his back, her body softening slightly, once more preparing to surrender to him.

Destiny was determined to give herself wholly to him, to take him for herself. She had been alone too long, needed him too much. He was everything she had ever dreamed about. She would do this!

Laughter hissed in her ear, evil and taunting. The monstrous creature was dragging her by her hair as she fought him, pounding into her, heedless of his size and strength. Uncaring of her broken bones. Uncaring of tearing her body in half. The pain was beyond anything she had ever experienced, and it was endless, trapping her there. She felt the taste of blood in her mouth as he forced her to drink from that dark, corrupt well. It was an acid burning her throat, her stomach, a blowtorch burning her from the inside out. *You will be like me.* The stench was overwhelming, part of the madness of her existence. Evil permeated her pores, seeped into her from him.

Abruptly she pulled her mind away, tears leaking out of her closed eyes. She wanted this. She ached for Nicolae with every fiber of her being. He was as necessary to her as breathing. She wanted him, but darkness was descending and her lungs refused to work. A heavy stone was crushing her chest; hands seemed to be gripping her throat, strangling her. She could have stopped Nicolae long ago, but she had insisted. She was unclean. She would always be unclean. Nicolae's love couldn't make her whole again. Pure again. She would only disappoint him, hurt him, risk his becoming as she was.

"I'm sorry. I'm sorry," she whispered, turning her face away, jamming her fist into her mouth to keep from screaming. She was humiliated beyond imagining. To tease Nicolae, bring him to this point and not be woman enough to give him what he needed, was intolerable. She tried to pretend, to recapture the intensity of her desire, but the walls of the chamber were shrinking, threatening to suffocate her. She knew she could not be what Nicolae so desperately needed.

"I can't do this." Destiny shoved hard at the wall of his chest, panic-stricken, fighting just to breathe. "I tried to tell you I wouldn't be able to be intimate, but you wouldn't listen." She shoved again, desperate for space, desperate to breathe.

Nicolae shuddered with the effort to control his body, to contain his passion. Her blue-green gaze shimmered with tears, darkening with turbulence, a foreshadowing of her rising instincts to fight her way out of a situation she couldn't handle. He felt her resistance in his mind, in his body. She was rigid, straining away from him, trembling. And there was fear, waves of fear swamping her, clouding the air between them. The childhood memories of atrocities were sharp and terrible, poised like a knife over her heart. Over his. He forced air through his lungs, through hers. Nothing else mattered to him but that she be comforted and reassured. Her eyes, enormous and shadowed with memories, held so much sorrow it nearly broke his heart.

"Destiny, slow down, take a breath. I am not going to do anything you do not want. We are intimate each time we look at one another. Each time we draw breath. That will never change between us. You think yourself tainted, but there is no greater light for me than you. If we can only have what we have right now, it is enough." Sensing that the feel of his body pinning hers down was a large part of the problem, he rolled off her onto his side. She felt helpless against his enormous strength, and he knew that emotion was triggering her fight responses.

Nicolae's arm circled her waist firmly, possessively, his body curving protectively around hers. He made no move to hide his erection, thick and hard, hot and rigid, pressed against her buttocks. "I do not expect the memories of things done to you in violence to disappear. But that was not making love. It was an abomination of what is meant to be. Here, between us, we are only expressing with our bodies what we feel in our hearts. Lovemaking may be rough or tender, may be fast or slow, it may be many things, but it should always be an expression of love."

She lay curled beside him, taking comfort from the heat of his body when hers was so cold. Listening to the sound of his voice, Destiny closed her eyes. She loved his voice, the one anchor she could cling to in every storm. "Do you think I don't know that, Nicolae, that I don't feel the same things you do? I know making love with you is the most natural thing in the world. My body . . ." She trailed off. Was on fire. A liquid cauldron of heat and fire spinning almost out of control. She wanted him more than she had ever thought possible. Her fist clenched. Tears burned her eyes and clogged her throat. She felt completely out of control, when she so desperately needed to be in control.

He lifted the heavy mass of hair from the nape of her neck and pressed his lips to her skin. "Why did you withdraw from me? I could have aided you when you were panicking."

"Don't use the word panic. It's so humiliating." She was very aware of his hand at her waist, his fingers splayed wide over her skin. His palm was a brand, burning into her stomach, right through to the hot, wet core of her desire. She shifted so that his fingers came in contact with the underside of her breast. The slight brush of sensation shook her, left her trembling for more. She *wanted* him. Wanted him with every fiber of her being. Her very cells were crying out for him. Yet there was that terrible knot in her gut, that block in her mind.

"I want to disappear." She murmured the words softly. "Just disappear so I never have to face you again."

"Destiny. Do not say that. Do not ever feel that way." His teeth grazed her neck, a small punishment, a seduction of already drugged senses. "I do not need the physical expression of love as much as you seem to think I do. I can wait. Come on. You are not going to lie here crying and shatter my heart into a million pieces. That I cannot take." It was the first time he had ever deliberately told her a lie. He hoped he would never again need to do so. He needed the physical expression of love more than he needed to breathe. His body was hot and

uncomfortable, so hot he was afraid he might spontane-
ously combust. His features remained impassive, his
mind serene, while his belly knotted with frustration.

Nicolae was on his feet, easily lifting her so that she
had no choice but to wrap her arms around his neck.
Her vivid gaze met his. "What are you doing?" They
were locked skin to skin. Her awareness of him heightened immediately.

There was a small silence while their hearts beat out
a rhythm of hunger. His gaze roamed her face possessively, dropped to view the lush enticement of her full
breasts. "A woman's body is a miracle."

"You're embarrassing me." Her breasts were embarrassing her, jutting up at him, aching for attention. Her
nipples were hard peaks, so sensitive his breath alone
sent desire spiraling through her body.

"It is a miracle. You can carry life in your body." He
bent his head to her, giving her no choice but to meet
him halfway.

She lifted her face to his, drawn by shared desire,
drawn by need beyond her knowledge, as elemental as
time. His mouth fastened on hers. He said there was life
in her body; if it were so, he gave it to her. She wanted
to be everything he needed. She had been inside his
mind so many times in the past. She'd lived there,
sought refuge there, and she knew him inside and out.

Nicolae. She sent his name fluttering like a butterfly
through his mind. A whisper of sound, of aching love.
Of commitment. Just the touch of his mouth, his hands,
weakened her, sent her soaring. Dreaming.

"Why do you feel such sorrow, Destiny?" He kissed
her chin, his teeth scraping gently over her skin. "I feel
tears in your heart."

Because she carried death in her body. Disease. A corruption not meant for the earth. How could she say that to him when he was looking at her with such love? Instead, she swallowed the words and buried her face against his throat to prevent him from reading her expression. "I want to be what you need, Nicolae. I want to be your lifemate."

His lips were on her hair. "You are my lifemate, Destiny. We are bound together, two halves of the same whole. You feel it. I know you feel it."

She lifted her head to look into his eyes. "I know it, yes—how could I not? But what kind of lifemate would do what I've done to you?" She wanted him to see her. Really see her, not what he wanted to see.

He waded out into the pool, cradling her in his arms. "What have you done to me, little one? Everything I have asked of you and more. You share my mind. Do you see me thinking I have been cheated? I share your mind and what you think is nonsense."

She tightened her hold on his neck and reached up to feather a line of kisses along his jaw, grateful for his unrelenting loyalty. His absolute faith gave her hope, melted her heart, made her feel beautiful. "I don't think you'd ever ask anything for yourself if you thought it would make me uncomfortable or unhappy, Nicolae."

He laughed softly. "I am not the wonder you are making me out to be, Destiny. I want you with everything I am. I can afford to be patient. We have eternity. I may feel the urgency of wanting to unite physically with you, but if we wait, I know it will happen eventually."

"Total confidence in yourself?" Her eyebrows shot up. She attempted to tease him, wanting to find a way to salvage something of their time together.

"Total confidence in *you*," he corrected, slowly lowering her feet into the pool.

The water felt amazing. Warm and wet, with tiny bubbles bursting and fizzing over her skin. She sank down into the depths immediately, delighted with the sensation. "This is fed from underground, isn't it?"

Nicolae was very aware of her eyes on him, drinking him in shyly, warily. In the clear bubbles of the pool he could see her body, enhanced by the shimmering water. She looked more seductive than ever, a water nymph bent on bewitching him. His body hardened to the point of pain. He had thought that being in the pool would relax him, but it seemed to have the opposite effect. The bubbles felt like tiny fingers caressing his erection, bursting and fizzing over him until he couldn't think straight.

"Tongues." Destiny swam closer to him, her body stretched out so that her shapely buttocks flashed through the water. She ached for him all over again. Just looking at him made her restless and edgy with need. And more than that, she wanted to please him, to do something to express the way she felt about him. Something to show him how much he meant to her.

Nicolae remained unmoving, still as a statue, watching the water caress her skin. The flickering light of the flames cast shadows across the pool, heightening their awareness of one another. "Tongues?" he echoed. The word came out a husky blend of need and urgency.

She nodded, swimming very close to him. "It feels like tongues on your body, not fingers. On my body too." She stood up. Water ran off her body, ran down the valley between her breasts to the tight curls just below the water line.

His hungry gaze followed the beads of water like a man parched and thirsty, greedy for moisture. Nicolae realized that she was right. If it were possible, his body swelled even more at the thought. He became conscious that she was reading his mind again, that she caught every erotic image, every sensual thought. "You know what I want to do, Destiny. What is it you want? Just tell me. Say it out loud. There is no one here but the two of us. Tell me what you desire most at this time." He wanted that much from her. He wanted the words even if he couldn't have the action.

She blushed, the color delicately staining her cheeks. "I want to touch you, to feel my hands on your skin. The need is as strong as any compulsion I've ever been under, but it isn't coming from you."

His fingertips traced the line of color in her face. "Need between lifemates is strong, Destiny, as it should be. We live long in this world. If what was between us were a weak thing, it would never last. I have given my body into your keeping. What you choose to do with it is always right. It is good. If you feel the desire to touch me, to learn to know me physically, it is not an intrusion or a violation. I would welcome it."

She turned her face away from him. "It can't be, Nicolae."

His hands framed her face, gently turned it back to him. "You are in control of this, Destiny. What we do is with *both* our consent. It is not for me, not to satisfy me alone. You have to have the courage to take what you want. Stay merged with me as you are touching me. You will always know what I am feeling, whether you are heightening my senses or making me uncomfortable."

There was a small silence while the water lapped at their bodies, the tiny bubbles bursting against their skin. Now that she had put the image in his mind, the feeling definitely reminded Nicolae of tongues stroking and caressing every inch of him, and he nearly groaned under the strain of erotic sensation. He wasn't altogether certain he was going to live through this experience with her.

Destiny might have nightmare images and memories struggling to break free, but she didn't lack courage. She wanted her time with Nicolae. She refused to allow a monster to rule her life, to rule Nicolae's life. She wanted to be able to enjoy fully what was her right. She wanted to have the complete freedom of exploring her lifemate's body. And she wanted his hands and mouth on her body. She wanted all of it, the complete fantasy.

She allowed her gaze to drift slowly over his body, to dwell on his defined muscles, his powerful chest, his narrow waist and hips, to drop lower and study the thick, heavy erection he had never once attempted to hide from her.

A sound escaped his throat. A small groaning plea for mercy that produced a leaping fire in her body. Destiny smiled. "So if I tell you to keep your hands on the rocks and off of me while I see if I can do this, you won't touch me?"

She was going to kill him for certain. Nicolae thought his body couldn't get any harder. Or any hotter. Yet it did just that at the sight of her teasing smile. At the images in her mind. He stepped back so he could rest his hands obligingly on the large boulders slightly behind him, leaving most of his body exposed and out of the water.

There was a heartbeat of time when she didn't move. While she summoned her courage. The only sounds were the lapping of the water at their bodies and the pounding of their hearts. She lifted her eyes to his face. Found him waiting. Saw his terrible hunger. He didn't move, didn't attempt to persuade her, allowing her complete freedom of choice. Destiny chose Nicolae.

She stepped close to him. So close her nipples brushed his chest as she lifted her arms to circle his neck. Her fingers plunged into his hair. "I love your hair." It was thick and long and it slipped between her palms, caressing her skin like fine silk. Her body slid up against the cradle of his hips. She was slick from the pool, water beading on her skin, as she rubbed against him like a purring cat. Her lips trailed over his eyelids. Followed the line of his cheekbones. Found his mouth.

It was far easier to express her love, her hope, when she was standing free, making all the moves and decisions. When he was keeping his promise not to touch her. Her body ached for his, and what she was doing only deepened her desire. There was joy in locking away demons. In not allowing them control. She reveled in giving Nicolae pleasure and in doing so, allowing herself that same pleasure.

Her tongue slid along the seam of his lips, teasing, testing, licking delicately. Each stroke of her tongue sent an answering fiery throb straight through the head of his shaft. Nicolae groaned, his fingers digging into the rocks as he opened his mouth to her. They melded together, fused, devouring one another, each ravenous for more.

While her tongue dueled with his, her hands slipped from his hair to find his shoulders and then moved down, her fingers stroking every inch as if committing his body to memory. Her mouth left his so she could nibble at his stubborn jaw. Her tongue swirled over his throat, found his pulse. The breath slammed out of his lungs, his gut clenched and his erection throbbed and swelled until he was afraid he would burst.

"Not yet," she whispered, as if to caution herself. Her tongue lapped at his pulse a second time, her breath warm with promise. "You taste so good, Nicolae."

His entire body shuddered. "Are you with me, Destiny?" His voice was husky, evidence of his terrible need. "Do you feel what you are doing to me? Stay merged with me. Stay with me." If she merged with him, felt what he felt, felt his hunger and his overwhelming love and admiration for her courage, she would not be able to stop, she would give herself completely to him.

Destiny hesitated only a moment before she did as he asked. Her mind merged completely with his. The intensity of his pleasure robbed her of breath, of the ability to do anything but shudder with need. The depth of his love and respect for her lodged in her soul, allowed her to see herself through his eyes. It was a view she had never expected, entirely different from her own. Courageous. Honest. Compassionate. Beautiful. Seductive. She held his heart in her hands. He was incredibly vulnerable to her. To her pain, to her fears, to her rejection.

Her mouth left his pulse, her breath swirling over his skin as her palms slid along his chest, her fingertips smoothing the lines of his muscles. She tasted his skin, lapped at the ridge of his collarbone, found his flat nipple, flicked it experimentally.

The air left his lungs in a rush. His body went rigid. Destiny, merged deep within his mind, could feel the fire coursing through his bloodstream, the whips of lightning burning from the inside out. That same fire was burning deep inside her, a conflagration she wanted to lose herself in completely.

Her hands wandered lower while her mouth feathered kisses over his chest and along his ribcage. She found his back, each defined muscle. The dip at the small of his back was intriguing. His buttocks were firm and hard as she kneaded and explored.

Nicolae shuddered with pleasure. Her fingers were driving him insane, as was the occasional brush of her body, skin to skin. He was all too aware of her mouth as it wandered over him, a slow torment he never wanted to end. He was grateful he'd had centuries to learn control; otherwise he would yank her to him to do his own exploring, to bury himself deep inside her. He also wanted to fist his hands in her hair and drag her head to him, thrust deep into her mouth to end his torment. Instead, he held himself very still, allowing her total control. Allowing her exploration.

Her tongue lapped at the crease of his hip, her hands sliding around him to cup his sacs, squeezing gently. Her breath was on the head of his shaft, a merciless torture. Nicolae dug his fingers into the boulder. "This is dangerous, Destiny." He managed to get the words past his clogged throat.

She was in his mind. She could feel the bursting pleasure. "I don't think it is, Nicolae. You're enjoying this." Her tongue lapped at the salty moisture experimentally. He jumped, every muscle straining and locked. "I know *I* am." There was pure seduction in her voice; the fear had been pushed aside by intense pleasure. Every nerve ending in her body was alive and pulsing. She could feel the welcoming moist heat dampening her body in anticipation.

Her mouth was a silken cavern of heat and moisture as it closed tightly over him. Nicolae's head fell back, and he gasped out her name. Wave after wave of pleasure swamped him. Swamped her. He tried not to move, tried to stay still under the onslaught of her clever mouth, but it was asking the impossible. He was losing control, his hips thrusting helplessly as her mouth tightened and withdrew, then tightened again, drawing him deeper and deeper under her spell.

"Destiny!" Her name burst from him, a plea for mercy.

She lifted her head, smiled as she licked her lips to remove every drop of his essence. Her mouth found his belly, her wet braid sliding against his far too sensitive shaft so that he cried out, catching her arms to give her a small shake.

"I am not going to live through this."

"Oh, I think you are." Her hands circled his neck, and she slid her wet body over his, rubbing like a cat. "Because I want you deep inside me where you belong." There was absolute resolve in her voice.

Nicolae didn't wait. He lifted her to the rock he had been hanging on to for his life, his body wedged between her legs. His hands positioned her on the edge of the small shelf just at the water line, so that water continued to bubble over their most sensitive parts. "You are ready for me, Destiny?" He needed her to be. He was so ready for her, he didn't know how gentle he could be. Already he was pushing into her, the head of his erection meeting the tight resistance of her body as he inched his way into her channel. She was so fiery hot, velvet soft, tightly gripping him, that he wasn't prepared. He shared his penetration with her, the pleasure-pain of it, the white-hot ecstasy bursting through him.

Destiny shifted, drawing up her knees, allowing him better access, watching his face as he slowly buried himself deep inside her. The magic was almost too great, too intense. She had never experienced anything remotely like it. There was resistance from her body. He felt too large, and she was too tight, but there was also such beauty and wonder and fire that she wanted more. She wanted much, much more. He stopped several times to allow her body to adjust, to accommodate his length and thickness. Each time he pushed deeper into her, she felt silk and steel sliding against each other, the friction lashing them with whips of dancing lightning. She heard herself laugh, a small, happy laugh of acceptance. She wanted him; she had taken what she wanted and he was deep within her.

Nicolae bent his body over hers, his hands gathering her bottom to him. "Are you all right, Destiny? Are you comfortable?" There was still a plea in his voice. Need. Hunger. Lines of strain were etched there. But it was her choice. Even with him buried deep inside her. Even with his every cell and nerve ending screaming for possession of her, even with the demons roaring in his head, it was her choice.

"Absolutely. I want this. I want you." She gave him acceptance, tears shimmering in her eyes. Tears of gratitude that Nicolae was her lifemate, and not some other who would never understand her needs. Or her inadequacies.

And then he began to move. Robbing her of breath. Of the ability to speak. Or think. There was only Nicolae, his body surging in and out of hers. Pulsing with fire and life and absolute pleasure. She felt his love so strongly, warming her from the inside out, filling her mind and heart as his body filled her emptiness.

Destiny looked up at his face, the lines etched there, and she knew she had put them there. He would have little signs of aging but for her. And she loved him for that. For always being there, a breath away, a heartbeat, when she needed him.

He was driving up. And up further, climbing fast and high, taking her with him until her body was wound tight, the pressure building with the force of a volcano. She gasped and clung to him, afraid of coming apart, afraid she would never be the same. Still he went on, driving deeper into her until she felt him touch her soul.

His chest was looming over her, close and tempting. Instinctively she reached for him, lifting her head the scant inches that separated them. Her tongue tasted his skin. Flicked his pulse. His fingers sank deeper into her hips, holding her still for his body to drive into hers. She felt his need, his silent pleading, as she put off the inevitable, heightening his awareness, his pleasure. Her own pleasure. She knew how he would taste. She sank her teeth deep.

At once lightning flashed, arcing through their bodies, through the chamber, sizzling and dancing and snapping. Colors burst like fizzing bubbles all around them. He took her up further, higher, to someplace where she teetered on the edge of a cliff overlooking paradise. His blood was ancient and contained the very essence of him. Tasting him, she made them one. Sharing the same body, the same heart and soul and mind.

Let go, Destiny. Come with me. Stay with me. An enticement. A temptation. His voice luring her as it had always done. And she trusted him. Her small tongue closed the pinpricks on his chest. She caught his arms firmly and gave herself up to him, her body wound so tight it was a coil, gripping his. And then they were both exploding together, Destiny safe in his arms, soaring together, shattering, free-falling through time and space.

She lay staring up at his face, his perfect face. Her lungs were searching for air, her mind at peace. Perfect peace. How had he done that? Her fingers trailed over his mouth in wonder. "You are the miracle, Nicolae," she whispered.

Still locked to her, he bent his dark head toward her throat. Her body clenched around his. Small after-shocks shook them both. What little air remained in her lungs rushed out of her at the first touch of his mouth on her skin. His tongue swirled over her pulse. Felt her heartbeat there. So frantic, matching the rhythm of his. His eyelashes drifted down as his teeth teased the small, throbbing pulse.

His hand found her breast, claimed possession, his thumb feathering over her nipple. Each stroke sent shock waves through her body and into his where they were so intimately connected. Destiny reached for him to draw him closer. White-hot pain lanced her throat; ecstasy showered her body with dancing flames.

Suddenly she hit him with every ounce of her strength, palms flat on his shoulders, knocking him back into the bubbling water. "No!" she cried. "What are you doing? What are we thinking? Nicolae!" Blood trickled down her throat and across the slope of her breast, mingling with the beads of sweat and water. Her insides ached and throbbed for the loss of him. She felt empty, bereft, without him.

Nicolae sank beneath the surface of the water, the bubbles closing over his head. He pulled his mind firmly from hers. Not wanting to think. Not wanting to feel. Bereft.

Destiny reached for him anyway. She found terrible loss, the pain of heartache. It swamped him. Swamped her. Threatened to bury them both. *Nicolae. I'm so sorry. I had to get you away from me. Don't you see? You can't take my blood.* She was pleading with him for understanding. *I wasn't rejecting you. My blood is dangerous to you. Please don't be angry with me.*

She was choking on a sob and it was breaking his heart. He surfaced, shook his head to clear it, flinging water across the pool as his hair flew back. She sat on the rock, naked, her knees drawn up, her hands clasped around them, tears glittering in her eyes. She was watching his every move, judging his mood, feeling totally inadequate.

With a small oath, Nicolae waded through the pool to crouch low in the water so that his head was the same height as hers. "How could I be angry with you when you were protecting me, Destiny?" He tugged at her hands until he freed them, drawing her into the depths of the pool with him. Drawing her out into deeper water, where he could stand but she had to cling to him to stay above the surface. "I withdrew my mind because it was necessary. The intensity of my emotions was overwhelming, and you did not need to experience them. I did not mean to hurt you."

Nicolae bent his head and followed the trickle of blood from her breast to her throat, lingering over the pinpricks to close them. "Wrap your legs around my waist."

He murmured the words against her ear as he gathered her closer, fitting her bottom into his palms.

Destiny found that when she did so, she was positioned over his waiting erection. She could feel him nudging her entrance, eager to join with her. Circling his head with her arms, she laid her cheek on his shoulder. She closed her eyes as he lowered her over him, fitting into her like a sword into a sheath.

He was gentle, loving, taking her again with more care than ever. He kissed her breathless, his mouth wandering over her face and throat. His teeth nipped occasionally, but he held a tight rein on that particular need. "I love you, Destiny. The way you are. With or without your blood. You will always be mine. You will always be everything I need and want. Do you understand me? You are everything to me." It was his apology for wanting more. Maybe needing more. But it was also the truth. He wanted her to see that, deep inside his soul where it counted, it was the truth.

Destiny threw back her head, riding his body with a long, slow rhythm of delight. She heard his declaration, read it in his heart and soul. He meant it. What they had was enough. But it wasn't everything. It wasn't the way they were meant to be. He could give it all to her, but she would never be able to provide for him. He accepted that shortcoming. She could not. And deep inside she wept for him. For both of them.

Chapter Eleven

The moment Destiny entered MaryAnn's office, she felt the shuddering vibrations of evil in the air. Horrified, she paused with one hand to her throat, her mind racing. Standing just inside the door, Destiny scanned each of the three small rooms that made up MaryAnn's office.

MaryAnn sat calmly behind the desk, her usual serene smile of greeting in place as Destiny entered. "I was hoping you would come by this evening," Mary-Ann said. Her dark eyes were soft and welcoming as she rose. "Come in, Destiny." She waved toward a large, comfortable chair. "Have a seat and talk with me."

Destiny's heart was pounding as she glanced carefully around the office, looking for hidden traps. At the same time she scanned MaryAnn's mind, hoping to find evidence that all was well. Instead she found blank spots in the woman's memory. Destiny's alarm grew. MaryAnn looked the same—sweet, gentle, compassionate.

The undead have found MaryAnn, Nicolae. One has been here, in her office. Why did you not sense it through your blood bond? There was accusation mingled with fear in her voice. More than that, she realized, wincing; there was a plea for help.

"I came by because I'm becoming one of those witless women who think they can't tie their shoes without a great big he-man to help them," Destiny announced with disgust, realizing that she was counting on Nicolae's help, when before she would never have thought to rely on anyone but herself.

The green fire flashing in Destiny's eyes fascinated MaryAnn. A slow smile spread across her face. "And here I thought I was in for a boring evening. Do sit down. I have never once thought you would find yourself unable to tie your shoes without a hunk to help. Who is he? Nicolae? Has he managed to interest you, after all?"

"Don't sound happy about it." Destiny glided closer and perched on the edge of the desk, looking into Mary-Ann's dark, expressive eyes. There were no shadows there, and no pinpricks or lacerations marred the smooth skin on her neck.

I feel his presence, although he has tried to hide it. He examined her and he has given her a command. Destiny sensed that Nicolae was close by.

"You don't want me to be happy when you've relieved me of a tedious evening catching up on paperwork? You don't do paperwork, do you?"

Destiny permitted a small grin to escape. "Well, no. Luckily, hunting vampires doesn't require that yet."

"Not even a permit? In this day and age one would think you'd need a permit and a hunting license."

Destiny's laughter bubbled over, humor keeping fear at bay. Nicolae was on his way, and he had much more experience than she did. He would know what to do to protect MaryAnn. "Actually, if word got out, it's more likely that vampires would be put on the endangered species list and we'd be forbidden to hunt them," Destiny pointed out.

The door opened without even the pretense of a knock and Nicolae sauntered in, looking so handsome it annoyed her all over again. "Speaking of devils."

Nicolae leaned over and kissed the nape of Destiny's neck. "She is absolutely crazy about me," he assured MaryAnn.

Destiny rolled her eyes heavenward. "She is definitely *not* crazy about him," she denied. "She doesn't even like him."

Nicolae pressed his body suggestively against Destiny. It was the briefest of contacts, but it sent a shiver feathering along her spine.

"MaryAnn, I couldn't stay away," he said, turning to the other woman. As she rose to greet him, he took her hand, bent gallantly over her fingers.

"See?" Destiny's eyebrows arced. "Is he full of crap or what?"

MaryAnn laughed softly. "I don't know, Destiny, I rather like his manners." She withdrew her hand and looked up at Nicolae. "What brings you here to see me besides wanting to make Destiny crazier than usual?" She went very still, put a hand defensively to her throat. "Is something wrong?"

"Don't encourage him, MaryAnn. He's already puffed up beyond belief." Destiny made a face, determined to keep the worry from her friend's face.

"I was wondering if you've had any visitors lately, MaryAnn," Nicolae said easily. "Destiny and I are looking into this business with John Paul and Martin."

"Oh, that's good, Nicolae. I've been worried about them." MaryAnn looked confused, rubbed her temples as if they were suddenly throbbing. "Somebody was here earlier, right before you came in, Destiny. A very nice gentleman. He asked me a lot of questions and seemed very interested in our sanctuary."

Destiny exchanged a long look of alarm with Nicolae. *She carries no visual memory of this man. She remembers the conversation, but not his appearance. He did not seem to ask questions about you or me.* Nicolae gave a barely perceptible shake of his head, warning her to remain silent as he turned the full power of his voice and gaze on MaryAnn. "Had you ever met this man before?"

Aslight frown tugged at MaryAnn's mouth, put little lines around her eyes. "I don't think so, Nicolae. I can't remember—isn't that strange? But I keep notes. He must be in the notes. He wanted something . . ." She trailed off again, looking more bewildered than ever.

She has the classic signs of memory tampering. Every time she tries to picture him, she feels pain. Nicolae waved MaryAnn back to her chair, soothed her with his touch alone, trailing his fingers along the top of the desk so that she followed the hypnotic gesture.

"What did he want?" Nicolae sounded casually interested, but there was a hidden compulsion in the velvet tones of his voice.

Destiny scowled at him. *She can't remember him. It hurts her to think about him. Don't push her like that.* She thumped the desktop, her fingernails tapping out a rhythm of warning.

Nicolae reached out and gently laid his hand over Destiny's, stilling her nervous fingers. *You know this is necessary. I will protect her from pain, little one. I can just imagine you with our children. I would never dare to correct their behavior.*

Destiny's heart thudded. Her eyes widened in shock. *No one said anything about children.* She hissed the words at him. *You never said a single word about children.* There was panic in her voice, in her eyes.

MaryAnn leaned back in her chair, but neither Carpathian looked at her. Their gazes were locked on each other.

That would be a natural progression, I would think. Nicolae pried Destiny's fingers from the desk and placed her palm over his heart. *I am beginning to realize that you have more fear of what is natural than you have of the undead.*

Destiny didn't dare answer him. She didn't know how to answer him. He was in her mind, reading her every thought. He knew the idea of home and hearth and family was terrifying to her. Her eyes flashed at him, daring him to be amused.

MaryAnn saved him. "He was looking for someone. A woman with a special talent. He wanted me to call him if she happened to show up here. She was traced here, to Seattle, but she's disappeared." MaryAnn opened a drawer and removed a business card to hand it to Nicolae.

He leaned close to Destiny so she could read it with him. So she could inhale his masculine scent and feel the brush of his skin against hers. Her tongue traced her suddenly dry lower lip, and the action immediately caught his attention. Destiny lowered her gaze from his sculpted lips to the card.

"The Morrison Center for Psychic Research." She read the words out loud. "Have you ever heard of them, Nicolae? MaryAnn?" She turned the card over. "They have several addresses in several cities, none here in Seattle. Why would they be following a woman into a sanctuary for battered women? Did she run away from them?"

"MaryAnn," Nicolae said. "The gentleman asked you to call this number if the woman showed up here asking for help?"

MaryAnn smiled with the innocence of a child, nodding her head. "It was strange. Afterward I wondered why I hadn't thought of Destiny. She doesn't fit the description, but she is talented. I thought it strange that she didn't come to my mind."

The protections held, Nicolae observed with some relief. There was a certain underlying arrogance in his tone. Destiny glanced warily at him, aware on some level that there were many things Nicolae was capable of that she was not. His hand slid down her arm, a gesture of camaraderie. *I am an ancient, my love, and your protector. There are many things I have learned over the centuries.*

I'll just bet there are.

"MaryAnn, tell us something about the woman this man is seeking," Nicolae prompted.

MaryAnn frowned again. "He gave me a photograph of her, a reprint from a computer. That's how I knew it wasn't Destiny." She rummaged through two drawers, confused that she couldn't remember where she had placed the picture. She found it in her notebook, pressed between two pages of writing. "This is the woman. Do you know her?" In spite of Nicolae's persuasive commands, MaryAnn handed the picture over almost reluctantly.

The woman could have been anywhere from twenty to her mid thirties. She had a lush, full figure and a mass of dark hair falling in a cascade of loose ringlets. She was looking back at the camera, and there was a hunted, anxious look in the depths of her eyes. Destiny felt an instant kinship with her. She knew what it was like to be alone and hunted. Whatever the woman was running from, a violent boyfriend or husband, she now had much bigger problems with a vampire tracking her.

"What is her talent?" Destiny asked.

"She can hold an object and know who has touched it and the past history associated with it. A wonderful gift, and very rare."

He asked her if she knew of any other people with such a gift. Why is the vampire more interested in the talent than the woman with the talent?

Destiny could feel his confusion. The vampires were not acting in expected ways at all.

MaryAnn swept her hair from her face and smiled at them. "Velda can see people's auras. Did you know that? We don't talk about it, of course, because no one would believe us, but she knows about me and I know about her."

"What about you, MaryAnn?" Destiny asked curiously. "What talent have you been gifted with?"

She smiled innocently, without any guile whatsoever, still completely under Nicolae's compulsion. There was no way to hide the radiance of her inner heart. "I have a small gift, one barely discernible to most people but useful when clients need help. I know when a woman is telling the truth. Like poor Helena. I know John Paul did attack her. And I know she loves him more than anything on earth. When women come here seeking refuge, I screen them. More than once, a woman has come for the wrong reasons. And worse, there have been a few who took money to act as a spy to find another woman already in a safe house."

"This gentleman who came to see you, MaryAnn— what were his specific instructions?" Nicolae asked quietly.

Again she frowned slightly and rubbed her brow. "I am to call him at once if she comes here. A reasonable request. He wants to help her. The research center has money and counselors, and they are very willing to hide her from anyone wishing to harm her. He says her talent is valuable, and the center will do anything it can to help her. He believes she is trying to find an underground avenue to South America."

She cannot tell us anything more. I cannot see even a hint of what this vampire looks like.

Pater? Could it be Pater? Destiny stared down at the face in the picture, the haunted eyes. *What are we to do for her?*

She must be found and protected. There is no other choice. She will be found.

A terrible black stone weighed heavily on Destiny's chest. Jealousy. It rose, sharp and appalling and unexpected. She fought down the unfamiliar emotion, exerted control on herself, made certain she didn't meet Nicolae's sharp gaze.

I cannot leave you, Destiny. I would not leave you.

Vikirnoff must find and protect this woman. She must be escorted to our homeland and placed under the protection of our Prince. Nicolae framed Destiny's face with his hands and bent his head to hers, kissing her thoroughly.

And then he was gone, leaving her to face MaryAnn, who sat behind her desk, one eyebrow raised and a faint smirk on her face. She fanned herself. "Well, well, well." Free of Nicolae's compulsion to speak of the stranger, she was once more completely at ease. "What in the world were we talking about? The two of you were so darned hot, you fried my brain."

"Not the two of us, MaryAnn," Destiny said with disgust. "He's like that. Impossible." She began to pace back and forth like a caged tiger, prowling through MaryAnn's office, carefully skirting the comfortable chairs for clients. She moved with elegant grace, fluid, like an animal on the hunt rather than a human. Gliding. Her feet made no noise, her movements were a whisper in the still air of the office.

Leaning her chin into her hands, elbows on the desk, MaryAnn watched her solemnly, mesmerized by the beauty of Destiny's movements. "Are you just going to wear a hole in my carpet or are you going to tell me what's wrong?"

Destiny glared at her. "It's *him*. *He's* what's wrong." She shoved a high-backed chair out of her way and made another circuit around the room.

MaryAnn nodded her head. "I see. I presume by him you mean Nicolae."

Destiny whirled to face her, hands curled into tight fists. "Don't you dare laugh, MaryAnn, and don't use that tone. I know what you're thinking. I don't need you laughing at this; it isn't funny at all."

MaryAnn kept her features carefully blank. "What exactly is it about Nicolae that is upsetting you, Destiny?"

"Everything!" Destiny threw herself into one of the offending chairs and stretched out her legs, still glaring at MaryAnn. "You saw him. You saw the way he acts with me. Everything about him drives me crazy."

There was a small silence. MaryAnn picked up a pen and began to trace patterns in her notebook. "Could you be a little more specific? Perhaps narrow it down for me?"

"Okay." There was challenge in Destiny's voice. "He looks at me." She lifted her chin belligerently, silently daring MaryAnn to laugh.

If MaryAnn's eyebrow could have risen any higher it would have reached her hairline. Her mouth twitched, and she hastily bit the end of her pen. "Oh, my. The bastard."

Destiny steepled her fingers and looked pointedly at MaryAnn. "Could you try to be serious? You're supposed to be a professional. It's the *way* he looks at me."

MaryAnn gestured with her hands. Beautiful hands, Destiny noted. Graceful. Perfect nails. The fingers weren't very long, but they were shapely, like MaryAnn. Destiny always found herself fascinated by MaryAnn's movements. By her innate goodness. "Please continue, Destiny. I'm certainly intrigued."

"He looks all goofy at me," she elaborated reluctantly. "Like I'm beautiful. Like he thinks I'm incredibly beautiful and smart and everything he ever wanted."

MaryAnn smiled at her. She leaned closer. "Is it possible that to Nicolae you *are* beautiful, and smart and everything he wants? Why is that so threatening to you?"

Swift impatience crossed her face. "I didn't say I was threatened. Did I say that? He's nuts to want me. I'm not normal."

MaryAnn sat back in her chair, her gaze on Destiny's face. "Normal? What is normal, Destiny? Why should he settle for normal when he could have you? What is normal to you?"

"You know, normal. Not me. Not what I am." Impatiently Destiny jumped to her feet and resumed pacing, quick, restless movements that revealed more than her short, snappy sentences.

"What do you think you are?" MaryAnn persisted.

"There you go again. You're using your counselor voice on me. You know very well what I am. I turn into vapor and fly on wings and run on four feet. Does that sound normal to you?"

MaryAnn smiled, a quick gleam of humor. "Actually, Destiny, it sounds very normal when we're talking about you. Or Nicolae. Isn't he the same as you?"

"Don't take his side. He's acting ridiculous. I'm trying to save the situation here, and the two of you and Velda and Inez have some idiotic idea of romance. Can you really picture me in the middle of a romance?" Destiny waved her hands around in a kind of fury. "It's absolutely silly. I don't do that sort of thing."

"I suppose it's true if you say so. You've never done that sort of thing, but that doesn't mean you can't. There's no reason not to try new experiences." MaryAnn leaned her chin into her palm and tapped her pen on the desk. "I think of you as very adventurous, Destiny. Maybe you should view Nicolae as a new page in your life."

Destiny stopped pacing, kept her back to MaryAnn. "Well, he isn't a new page in my life. He's been in my life nearly as long as I can remember." She pushed a hand through her thick mass of hair, lifted the weight of it from her neck.

MaryAnn noticed the slight trembling and sat up straight. "How did you meet Nicolae?" Because that was what this was about. Something in the past was causing perfectly controlled Destiny to pace like a caged animal. Causing her hands to tremble and her soul to reject a wonderful partner.

Destiny's shoulders hunched slightly. A small signal, but MaryAnn noted it. She watched the younger woman examine a painting on the wall. The silence stretched between them until MaryAnn was certain Destiny wouldn't respond.

"He came to me when I was a child." The voice, usually so beautiful, was strangled, a choked whisper of sound. "I might have been six. It's hard to remember. Time isn't the same for me anymore. It's endless and stretches out forever."

"Is it difficult to remember because it was a painful time?"

Destiny touched the painting, traced the outline of the child. "I prefer not to remember it. I closed the door on that part of my life."

MaryAnn nodded. She laced her fingers and regarded Destiny over her hands. "That's a self-preservation technique that abused and traumatized children often have to employ to survive. They have compartments in their minds to safely put things away in so they can move on." Her voice was without judgment. "Do you associate Nicolae with that time in your life?"

"Nicolae is . . ." Destiny hesitated, searching for the right word. "Magic. Not real. A dream that can't possibly be true. He's like a white knight. The hero in an action film, larger than life and only a figment of the imagination."

"Destiny." MaryAnn waited until the other woman turned to look at her. "What would happen if Nicolae was real and not a dream at all?"

Destiny lifted her hand to eye level, held it out for MaryAnn to see. They both watched it tremble uncontrollably. "He could take everything away from me. Everything I am, everything I've worked so hard to achieve, to become. He could rip me apart, and I would turn to ashes in the sun."

"You're saying you're very vulnerable to him, and that frightens you. He is capable of hurting you if you let him in."

"I'm saying he could *destroy* me. I've been destroyed once and I rebuilt my life into something." Destiny ducked her head. Nicolae had given her back her life, had made her into what she was. And now he was asking her to change all over again.

"I think it is natural for anyone entering into a relationship, a partnership, to be frightened of being hurt, don't you, Destiny? When we allow ourselves to love, we're always vulnerable. Everyone is, Destiny. It wasn't that long ago that you were leery of having a simple friendship," MaryAnn pointed out.

"Because it would bring you into a dangerous world. It *did* bring you into that world." Destiny sighed and took another turn around the office. "I could destroy him."

There it was. Out in the open. The words had slipped

out before she could stop them. Maybe she'd wanted to tell MaryAnn all along. Maybe that was why she had been drawn to this place of peace. To tell the truth to someone who mattered to her.

MaryAnn pushed back her chair and moved around the desk to lean her hip against the edge. "That's what you want to talk about, isn't it? You're worried about Nicolae."

"You said you have a talent. That you can read women. What do you see in me?" Destiny lifted her chin almost belligerently, her gaze steady on MaryAnn's.

MaryAnn allowed her breath to escape her lungs in a rush. "Seeing things is not always comfortable. You're certain you want me to tell you?"

Destiny shrugged with studied casualness. "I could just as easily read your mind, MaryAnn. But I respect you and, unless it is for your own protection or the protection of others, I would never violate the trust between us by reading your mind without permission."

"I know you are tied in some way that I can't understand to Nicolae. It is beyond the boundaries of the earth. And I know you were hideously abused and you fear that staying with him will somehow cause his destruction. Nicolae is a strong man. I've never encountered anyone with his sheer power." MaryAnn tilted her head to one side, regarding Destiny carefully. "Why are you so certain you're not just what Nicolae needs? I think you are. I think you're *exactly* what he needs. I know you're what he wants. Every time he looks at you that longing is in his eyes."

Destiny waved MaryAnn's remark aside. They had come full circle. She had already ranted about the way Nicolae looked at her, she didn't need MaryAnn to point it out to her. She knew he wanted her, that he needed her. She also knew the price might be more than either of them could afford. She swept her hair away from her eyes. "There aren't just a few small problems, Mary-Ann."

MaryAnn watched as Destiny threw herself carelessly into a chair, her legs stretched out in front of her. "I'm going to speak very plainly with you, Destiny."

"Please do." Destiny intended to speak plainly with MaryAnn.

"Women who have been raped or sexually abused as children have problems with intimacy. Those problems don't just go away. And even when you think you've beaten the past, it will suddenly be there, between you. That's a normal reaction, Destiny, and one to be expected."

"I do expect it. Well, the chemistry between Nicolae and me is much more explosive than I had counted on. I had no idea it could be so strong. I also realize I don't want to surrender control in any way. I'm honest enough with myself and with Nicolae to admit that."

MaryAnn looked pleased. "As long as you understand that, you should be fine. Nicolae seems man enough to give you the space you need when you need it. You should be able to work out that aspect of your relationship."

"You would think so." Destiny sighed heavily. "But our attraction to one another is far more than just physical. We *need* to be together. We need to come together, physically as well as mentally. It's part of what we are. I can't explain it other than to say it's intense and sometimes uncomfortable."

"You find it uncomfortable?"

Destiny nodded, her small white teeth tugging at her lower lip. "He takes everything in stride. I'm the mess. It's just so intense. There's no other word. When I'm with him, I feel so out of control. It's so frightening to be like that, to want someone so much you don't care about anything but being with him."

MaryAnn laughed softly. "Destiny, you don't know yourself at all. You obviously care a great deal about this man or you wouldn't be so worried that you're in some way going to harm him. Do you think loving him or wanting him so intensely is going to hurt him?"

"My blood is tainted." Destiny blurted it out, leaping to her feet to pace around the room again. Movement enabled her to avoid MaryAnn's eyes.

There was a small silence. "Would you mind elaborating?"

Destiny gestured rather helplessly with her hands. "The vampire converted me. His blood was tainted and he tainted my blood. Sort of like a disease."

MaryAnn frowned. "Sit down, Destiny. You're making me nervous with your pacing. This is important and out of my realm of knowledge. Is the tainted blood dangerous to you?"

"To Nicolae." There was only acceptance and the need to understand in MaryAnn's voice; the terrible knot in Destiny's stomach relaxed. She returned to the chair. "I don't know all that much about Carpathians, but there is a darkness in the males, from what Nicolae tells me. That darkness is what allows them to turn vampire. They fight it, of course. Nicolae has been fighting for a long time."

MaryAnn hitched her chair closer. "And your blood somehow makes it more difficult for him? What are you saying?"

"I don't know what will happen if he takes my blood. When we make love, it's difficult, nearly impossible not to"—she hesitated, searching for the right word—"*indulge* that side of our craving too. It becomes erotic. Nicolae's need is very strong. I don't think there's a cure for me. If we're together, we aren't going to be able to resist the lure of that side of our hunger." She passed a hand over her face. "I couldn't bear to be his destruction, MaryAnn. I wanted to walk away from him, but it's too late for that."

MaryAnn immediately rose to wrap a comforting arm around Destiny's shoulders. "Have you discussed your fears with Nicolae?"

Destiny touched MaryAnn's mind, afraid of what she must be thinking of her revelations, but MaryAnn was as centered as always. She accepted the things Destiny told her with her usual equilibrium and was struggling to understand.

"We talked about it. He doesn't worry about himself; he only thinks about me." It set her teeth on edge, his total commitment to her. Destiny wasn't comfortable with devotion. Or love.

"People search their entire lives looking for what you have, Destiny. Don't be afraid of it."

Destiny glared at MaryAnn in disgust. "You sound just like Father Mulligan. I ask him a question and he gives me some sort of philosophical Zen answer. What kind of advice is 'have courage'? What does that mean? Have courage to do what? Isn't a priest supposed to give spiritual advice? You know, MaryAnn, I'm beginning to think you make it up as you go along, you and Father Mulligan."

MaryAnn's eyebrow shot up. "Are we supposed to have the answers? You don't have the answers—how would we? You can only keep moving ahead, Destiny. You keep your eyes open and with luck you see the pitfalls before you step into them, but you embrace life and live it as best you can."

"Tell me something, MaryAnn. Do you think your life has been changed, knowing there are such evil creatures in the world as vampires?"

"Of course my life has changed. But am I going to live it in fear? I hope not. I hope I face each day with courage and dignity. You do that. I wouldn't mind being like you."

The shock of those words was tremendous, shaking Destiny to the very core of her existence. She found herself gaping at MaryAnn, nearly choking on her protest. MaryAnn was everything Destiny had ever wanted to be. "Are you crazy? I'm a mess."

MaryAnn patted her arm. "That's normal, Destiny. We're all a mess in our minds. Welcome to the world of human reality."

A faint smile lit Destiny's eyes. "Well, I guess we didn't solve the world's problems, but I sat in a chair and talked for the first time in years without feeling like I couldn't breathe." The moment she said the words, her smile faded. *It was you, Nicolae. You are helping me to be able to be inside this structure, conversing with her, aren't you? I've never been able to do this.*

There was an impression of warmth surrounding her like strong arms. Destiny leapt out of the chair as if it were a viper threatening to bite her. Her eyes darkened to a brilliant green. "That man is a total jerk! Why did I ever think I might want a relationship with him?" Her hand flew defensively to her throat. She could feel his lips brushing just there over her pulse. At once her skin throbbed and her body burned. *You aren't helping your silly courtship. I am not a baby to be aided without my consent or knowledge. I don't want your help, and I don't need it!*

You are just angry because you did not sense my touch. There was smug male amusement in his tone. *I am merely keeping you on your toes. We have something taking place here we do not understand, and we both should be vigilant.*

Destiny snarled. "Nicolae is the most annoying man on the face of the earth. Why would I want a smug, arrogant, pain-in-the-butt male creature like him in my life? Answer me that, MaryAnn!" *I am always vigilant!*

"Sex." MaryAnn answered succinctly. "It's sex, Destiny. He reeks of sex. I take it he's telepathic."

"He's annoying, that's what he is." *There is nothing sexy about you. I know you're all puffed up and smirking but I don't think you're the least bit sexy.*

I had no idea you were such a little liar, Destiny. You think I'm sexy.

"I do think he's sexy," she admitted, wrenching open the door to MaryAnn's office, "but I don't like him very much."

"Destiny," MaryAnn said quietly, halting her flight. "Everyone needs help now and then."

Destiny turned her back on MaryAnn, on Nicolae and all relationships. She didn't want help, she decided as she fled the office. She would work things out her own way. And there was that little nagging question that kept popping up. She kept pushing it down, not wanting to face it, but there were all those little things that she couldn't ignore forever. Why could he find her at will when he had never taken her blood? And how was he able to be in her mind, actively aiding her, yet she felt no surge of power? No push? Why was she unable or unwilling to fight the compulsion to obey him, even when she knew it was a compulsion?

How powerful are you? There was accusation in her voice rather than admiration. She slammed her mind closed to him and took to the skies. It was the only place she felt absolutely free. She soared through the clouds, reveling in her ability to do so. She didn't want to know how powerful he was. She didn't want to think too much about what she had done with him.

Nicolae hadn't pressured her. She couldn't even blame him. She had insisted on the words. He would never have made love to her except that she had insisted on that too. The wind rushed at her, cooled her skin and soothed the chaos in her mind. Nicolae. He belonged to her, and she had no idea what to do with him.

It was so easy for the priest to tell her to have courage. He didn't have nightmare images walking through his mind every waking minute. He didn't have scars on his body and etched into his soul. He didn't have poison in his blood that could corrupt and twist something good into evil.

"I am so lost." She murmured the words aloud, listened to the wind carry them away from her, wishing it could take her pain so easily.

I can take away your pain.

There he was again. Just as if she had summoned him. He was always with her when her world was in turmoil. The wind tore tears from her eyes as she streaked across the sky. *And what must I do in return for you?* There was despair in her heart when she wanted to show him joy. She wanted to be different. She wished she could go to him clean, without distress, without scars. Without the terrible weight and sin of what she was. What she couldn't change. She hated feeling sorry for herself; she didn't want his pity.

You exist. You love me. You are beginning to surrender yourself into my keeping. It is enough. He was calm even when he was tearing out her heart.

It wasn't enough, and they both knew it. Her cry of sorrow echoed across the skies.

Chapter Twelve

Surrender herself into his keeping. Such simple words. He said them with calm, with conviction. Destiny raced across the skies with no idea of where she was heading, only the need to fly high and fast and far.

I never wanted this.

She detested whining. She detested feeling sorry for herself. She really detested being afraid. She hadn't feared her battles with the undead. If she had died then, it would have ended the suffering, the agonizing problems her tainted blood caused. If she were the victor, the world would be rid of another monster. Now she feared destroying the only person who mattered. The only one who had managed to find his way into her soul. Nicolae.

I want you with all my heart. With every breath in my body.

He was relentless in his pursuit of her. She understood suddenly. He had always hunted her, not for the reasons she had thought, but to satisfy a terrible need and hunger, the same craving she now felt. An addiction that would never stop. She couldn't find the strength she needed to free them both of this dangerous liaison.

"Where are you, God?" She cried the words out among the clouds as she had done so many times before.

The wind carried back the answer. It caressed her skin with a loving touch and affectionately ruffled her hair. The wind surrounded her, enfolded her in the beauty of the night sky. The clouds shifted to allow her to pass through them, trailing a fine mist in her wake, dusted her skin with cool vapor so that if there were traces of tears, it was impossible to see them.

Come back to me, Destiny. His voice offered comfort. Offered paradise. Offered everything.

Why do you want me? Because I'm the light that burns so brightly you will not turn? Is that all there is between us? That and chemistry? I don't know you at all, do I?

The wind murmured to her, a soft, consoling lullaby. She could feel the wildness subsiding deep within her, settling back to allow her heart and lungs to work without effort. A small sound, faint and far off, caught her attention, so that without conscious thought, she changed direction, veering back toward the city.

You have only to touch my mind, Destiny, to find the things you wish to know. To really love, you have to choose intimacy. You have to choose to know your life-mate. You have not made that choice.

I was intimate with you! She was angry that he could accuse her of holding back. It had been difficult to commit herself physically to him. How dare he even think such a thing!

Intimacy is far more than physical, little one.

The lights of the city twinkled like thousands of stars, drawing her back toward humanity. Back toward Nicolae. She knew he waited. That he watched. Just how powerful was he? Had he somehow directed her feelings for him? Amplified them in some way she couldn't detect? Was she already in his power? She knew the answer. She was totally captivated by him. Completely. Utterly and completely.

Destiny shimmered into her human form, landing easily, lightly. She was already moving, scanning, hurrying out of the secluded alleyway onto the street. Somewhere close by was the soft, discordant note that had disturbed her flight. A child's muted crying tugging at her heartstrings. She hurried, her footsteps silent, her posture completely confident.

There were only a few people on the street so late at night. She scanned as she walked, checking the various apartments for the location of the child. Most of the buildings were dark and quiet. She could hear televisions blaring in a few apartments and music playing in others. The child was broadcasting sharp waves of grief. Unerringly Destiny turned down another side street where the apartment buildings gave way to small houses set close together. Rickety fences set a few of the properties apart, but duplexes and smaller single dwellings were built tightly against one another. Paint was chipped and peeling from the thin siding. Doors sagged, and gates were cracked and falling off their hinges.

Destiny vaulted a low fence easily and made her way around to the back of one house. Cardboard boxes and bundled newspapers were piled high, mountains of them, taking up most of the space in the tiny backyard. She should walk away, leave the city and get as far away from Nicolae as she could. But her mind was already tuning itself to his. Needing to be immersed in his.

Was it really the ritual words that had bound them together, or had her need of him started long ago? She had reached for him at every rising. His calm, his presence in the world had been her sanity. For years she had used him, forced him to share her pain, her damaged soul. She had sentenced him to a life in the shadows, forever seeking her. She had punished him with her silence, all the while sharing with him every aspect of the vampire's torture and abuse.

I was already of the shadows, Destiny. You pulled me into the light.

His voice. His beautiful voice could take her into dreamland. Could weave fairy tales and bring hope. Could absolve her of all guilt. Her lashes drifted down as she paused beside the rotting back stairs. There was always so much guilt. Would it never go away and leave her in peace?

The sound of the hopeless weeping dragged her out of her own despair. A child should never experience such heartbreaking emotion. Destiny could feel the vibrations of violence, the aftermath that lingered in the air. And she smelled blood. She hunkered down to peer beneath the wobbly stairs. The boy couldn't be more than nine or ten years old. He was so thin, his clothes were far too wide, although his bony wrists and ankles were showing. He wore no socks and had holes in his shoes. Tears made muddy tracks in the dirt on his face. He rubbed his face continually with his knuckles, but he couldn't stop the sobs that shook his young body. There were smears of fresh blood on his clothing, but she could see no open wounds.

"Hi there," she said, using her gentlest voice, afraid of startling him. She had learned those soft, silvery tones from Nicolae. It always came back to Nicolae. "Is there room under there for me?" There was compulsion in her voice, a small "push" to make it easier for the boy to accept her presence.

He looked frightened, his eyes widening with shock, but he obligingly moved over to allow her enough space to squeeze beneath the stairs. Destiny sat tailor fashion, her body heat helping to warm the child.

"Bad night?"

The boy nodded mutely. Destiny could see the scars on the backs of his hands and arms. Defensive scars. She recognized them for what they were. "My name is Destiny. What's yours?" She held out her arms, palms down so that he could see the slash marks on her arms. The same defensive wounds. "We match."

He bent close in the darkness to examine her scars. "You have more."

"But they've faded," she pointed out judiciously. "And they don't hurt anymore. At least not on the outside. What about yours?"

"Mine don't hurt either." His gaze locked with hers. "Well, maybe a little on the outside. I'm Sam."

"A lot on the inside, right, Sam?" She brushed the pad of her thumb over the worst of the scars, leaving behind a soothing balm. "Tell me. This didn't happen tonight. Tell me what's wrong."

He shook his head, the code of the streets keeping him silent for a moment, but it was impossible to resist the lure of her voice. His lower lip trembled, but he squared his thin shoulders. "I didn't wash the dishes. I knew he'd be mad at her if I didn't wash the dishes, but

Tommy wanted me to play basketball. All the kids were playing, and I thought I'd only play for a couple of minutes." His lashes were wet and spiky from his tears, and the weight in his chest was like a stone in hers.

Destiny already knew. The horror was seeping through the rickety floorboards and pervading the air beneath the stairs. *Nicolae.* She reached out to him as she always did. As she had done for years. And he was there. In her mind. As he had always been. Surrounding her with warmth. Giving her courage. Holding her in strong arms and giving her a refuge, a shelter when the pain of the world was too much to bear alone.

I'll bring him to Father Mulligan, but the police will have to be brought to this place of death. She knew Nicolae would hear the sorrow in her voice. He would feel it in her heart. And he would share it with her and shoulder part of her burden.

"It was my fault." The thin shoulders shook, and the boy covered his face with his hands. "She came home from work and she was tired. I heard her call to me to hurry, and I ran, but I was down the block and it was too late. I saw him go in. I knew what he was going to do to her. He was always so angry. He wanted money for his drugs and he took it out of her purse. She was crying because we needed it for food. That's when he saw the dishes."

"Sam, you don't need to be in this place. I'm going to take you to a friend of mine," Destiny said gently.

Sam shook his head. "I can't leave her. He was so mad about the dishes. He kept hitting her and throwing plates on the floor. I tried to stop him, but he pushed me and she threw the coffeepot at him and told him not to touch me or she would call the police and have him arrested. That's when he picked up the knife."

She drew him to her, rocking him gently, letting him talk.

"If I had washed the dishes, the knife wouldn't have been on the sink. It would have been in the drawer. He wouldn't have picked it up. I should have just done the dishes instead of playing basketball."

"It wasn't your fault, Sam. He was ill, and he is responsible for hurting your mother, not you. Never you. We all put off chores. Everyone does. Procrastination does not cause one human being to murder another. *He* did it, not you. Your mother would never want you to think that. Come with me. Let me take you to Father Mulligan. He'll make certain you're all right. The police will come and they'll take care of your mother."

"They'll lock me up. He said the police would lock me up 'cause I don't have anyone else."

"Father Mulligan won't let anything bad happen to you. And police don't lock up children who have lost their parents, Sam. They help them. They find them a home with people who care about them. Come with me now." She wanted to get him away from the house, away from the man who might return at any time. Sam didn't need to see more violence. He didn't need to feel responsible for things adults did to one another.

She drew the boy out from under the sagging stairway and urged him quickly away from the house. She felt the first stirrings of apprehension as they hurried along the narrow pathway by the side of the house. The boy stopped abruptly as they gained the front yard. She felt the tremor that ran through his thin body, and she turned her head to see the man half sitting against a column on the front porch.

Her fingers tightened on the boy's shoulder, and she raised a hand to her lips to indicate the need for silence. It wasn't difficult to take control of the child's mind, shielding him from further fear. The man was obviously in a stupor, his head lolling back, his mouth wide open, his arms and clothes splattered with blood.

A low hiss of anger escaped her as she silently watched the man twitch and jerk, his fingers clenching into tight fists, then opening again. She was so focused on the murderer, she failed to notice the mist streaming into the yard, or feel the surge of power as Nicolae shimmered into solid form.

"Take the child and leave this place, Destiny," Nicolae said grimly. His palm caressed the back of her head with the briefest of touches, but it provided a comfort she didn't expect.

Destiny pulled the child closer to her. "This should never have happened. A child should never have to live this way, Nicolae. He thinks he's to blame."

Her enormous eyes were begging him to do something. Held confidence that he would. His heart turned over. Nicolae wanted to drag her into his arms, to point out that when she was a child, she thought herself to blame for things she had no control over, but he knew she had to come to that knowledge on her own. The realization had to be more than intellectual, it had to be in her heart, her soul, right where the scars were.

"Take him away from here. Father Mulligan is expecting you, and the police are on their way. They will not find me in this place." His voice was very gentle.

Destiny met his gaze. Some of the tension eased out

of her. "Thank you, Nicolae. I'm grateful that you're here." She reached out and touched his arm. A mere brush to answer his, but her heart was swelling with joy as she turned away. She couldn't help the way she felt every time she looked at him. There was pride and confidence and chemistry and a curious melting deep inside her. A part of her might always fight to avoid admitting how deeply he had entwined himself around her heart, but she could admit to herself he was a large part of what was good in her life.

Destiny lifted the boy into her arms. The child circled her neck trustingly, leaned into her for shelter. The childish gesture of trust disarmed her. She tightened her arms protectively and took to the skies. She wanted to give this boy something to counteract the terrible memory of his mother's death. Placing him in a dream-like state, she flew through the sky, drifting through clouds and allowing the joy of flying to fill the boy's mind and heart. He would always carry the dream with him, always have a sense of soaring free through the night sky.

Destiny had little else to give him, and it bothered her. She wanted to be able to free him of the weight of guilt. To somehow make him understand that he was a victim, a survivor, that his life could be rebuilt. As she took him around the small church's steeple, she wondered how her life had gotten to this point. It wasn't long ago that she had lived a solitary existence, yet now her life was intertwined with so many people.

Father Mulligan was waiting for her in his garden. He smiled a gentle greeting as Destiny released the boy from the shield. There was a soothing quality to the priest that even the distraught boy couldn't fail to notice.

"This is Sam. Sam, my friend Father Mulligan." She hunkered down to the boy's level. His fingers were digging into her arm, clutching at her for protection.

The boy made a strangled sound as the priest turned his attention on him. He stepped closer to Destiny and her heart turned over. "Nicolae explained?" she asked Father Mulligan.

The priest nodded. "Sam, you'll be safe here. A friend of Destiny's has spoken with the social service worker, and she has agreed to allow you to stay in the rectory with the other priests and me for the time being. There is a priest here that you will find very easy to talk with. He's waiting for you now. There are also two police officers who need to speak with you about what happened. Just tell them the truth. I will be with you if you like while you explain what happened."

Sam squared his thin shoulders and nodded, but his gaze was pleading as he looked at Destiny. She smiled encouragingly at him. "Father Mulligan is a priest, Sam. He doesn't lie and he's greatly respected. He'll make certain you are well cared for."

"What if Jerome finds me?" Sam asked anxiously.

"Is Jerome your father?" Father Mulligan inquired.

Sam shook his head adamantly. "He moved in with us a couple of years ago. I don't have a father. It's just me and my mom."

Destiny felt shaken. She had had a mother and a father. She remembered her mother's face. Her smile. Her scent. She remembered her father tossing her high into the air so that she squealed and laughed and begged him for more. The memory was vivid and tore at the carefully built locks on the doors in her mind.

Why is this happening? I put all this away. She turned to Nicolae, the one person she believed in.

How could you not identify with this child? He had a decent life with his mother until a monster found them. It matters little that the monster was human. The monster found them, and the child could do nothing to change the outcome. He blames himself for something he had no control over. You look at him and you see yourself.

It was only the complete calm in his voice that steadied her. There was far too much truth in Nicolae's observations. "You'll be okay, Sam. Father Mulligan will look after you, and I'll come often to see how you're doing. Please do talk with the priest Father Mulligan has waiting for you, and tell the police officers exactly what happened." She couldn't help giving him another little boost to help him accept the priest's aid.

Sam lifted his chin bravely. Destiny ruffled his hair. "I will come back, Sam, I promise. Tonight, there are some things I must do. I want you to get some sleep after you talk with the police." She wanted to turn back time and save Sam the years of fighting for his life and sanity in a world that a monster had turned upside down. "I'll come back," she whispered again.

"I'll take good care of him," Father Mulligan assured her. "There's no need to worry, my dear."

Destiny nodded, biting her lip as she turned away. She could feel Sam watching her as she walked away, so she smiled at him over her shoulder and lifted her hand. She felt her mind tuning itself to Nicolae as it seemed to do every few minutes. Her need to know that he was alive and well was a further annoyance to her.

She valued her independence highly, and it didn't sit well that she had to continually reach for him.

She chose to walk down the street, needing the normalcy of human life. The time it took to walk would help her gather her thoughts. She had promised Velda and Inez and Helena she would help John Paul. She needed to investigate further. It was difficult to force her thoughts away from Sam. She hadn't really thought that there were human monsters in the world. She had focused so completely on vampires, she hadn't given a thought to other kinds of threats.

Deep in thought, she barely registered the change in the wind as it shifted direction, blowing away from her, stirring dirt in the street. A streetlight blinked, faltered and abruptly went out in a shower of sparks. She lifted her head alertly, looking around her warily. John Paul was just entering The Tavern, his head down and his feet shuffling along the walkway, his body posture betraying his despondency. Farther down the street, a second streetlight shattered as if hit by a rock, raining glass on the ground.

John Paul hesitated as he went to pull open the bar door, looking up at the streetlight with a small frown. He glanced down the street at the other shattered light on the corner near Destiny. John Paul allowed the door to close as he shuffled along the street toward Destiny. He was looking not at her but at the shattered glass. He seemed drawn to the pieces of the large lamp.

Destiny observed him, the way he seemed drawn to the glittering pieces. His expression was blank, his eyes slightly glazed. He stood over the glass, his great shoulders shaking, his chest heaving with every breath as if he'd run a race. His hamlike hands were opening and closing into tight fists.

She searched the skies. The skies were darkening as gray threads spun wildly to spawn larger, more ominous clouds. Small dust devils spun in the street, dissipating as cars roared by. A fog bank began to seep onto the street, hovering a foot above the ground. First streamers, just tails of vapor that thickened quickly into a murky soup.

John Paul continued to stare down at the glass, his gaze narrowing as he studied the sharp pieces scattered on the sidewalk as if they held some deep fascination for him. Destiny glided closer, scanning while she kept a wary eye on the hulk of a man. Something wasn't right, but she couldn't detect a surge of power. The storm had come in a little too fast to be a legitimate weather front. There was no movement in the whirling, darkening clouds. The blanket of stars disappeared beneath the storm. Black clouds moved across the moon to completely obliterate it, a lacy black shawl wrapping the orb in a thin dark fringe.

"John Paul," Destiny said softly. She didn't want him exposed out on the street. He made far too big a target.

John Paul whirled around, silent and deadly, impossibly fast for a man of his size. Her shocked astonishment held her motionless for the few seconds it took him to attack her. It felt like the hit of a charging rhino, his body slamming into hers with terrific force, driving her to the ground. As she hit the sidewalk, the air rushed out of her lungs. A part of her wanted to laugh as his body landed on top of her, slamming her body into the sidewalk.

Destiny fought vampires, creatures of immense power and strength. It was ludicrous to think a human had managed to knock her off her feet. The fog was swirling heavily around the two of them, as if it had suddenly been given life. The vapor streamed over and around them like jungle vines.

John Paul sat on her stomach, his giant hands around her throat, his face a grim mask as he began to squeeze. His fingers dug into her windpipe, cutting off her air, crushing her throat.

Destiny hit him hard, her palms flat, carefully positioned high on his shoulders to keep from injuring him even as her enormous strength sent him flying backward. "Get off, you oaf! Sheesh! You weigh a ton." She leapt to her feet, landing lightly, hands up, her eyes glittering with warning. "Back off, John Paul. Do you even know what you're doing?"

John Paul had landed on his backside. He sat on the sidewalk, stunned, shaking his head to clear it. Destiny watched him carefully, aware he was not in his right mind. She could only read the need for violence in him, violence aimed at her. She wasn't certain she had been the original target, but he seemed a puppet doing someone else's bidding. There were no blank spots in his mind to indicate a vampire, but she didn't believe John Paul was aware of what he was doing.

A wisp of fog swirled around her neck, tugged at her ankles, bit deep like tiny teeth. She felt a fiery pain lancing unexpectedly through her leg. She looked down and saw tiny drops of ruby-red blood. The air left her lungs in a rush of shock as she attempted to dissolve into mist, but the vapor held her fast. She was locked in the mysterious circles as surely as if they were shackles.

Her heart broke into a thudding rhythm, but she blocked out the pain and fear, concentrating on her imprisoned ankle where the white tails of vapor were solidifying into tiny wires with serrated edges, digging deeper and deeper into her flesh. Her ankle and foot contorted, thinned so that the coils slipped off.

She looked up just as John Paul attacked again, slamming her to the ground with the force of a human freight train. Destiny didn't give him much thought other than as a nuisance. She could handle John Paul, but her unseen enemy was another matter. The fog was alive with tendrils, little wormlike creatures rushing toward her, alive with teeth and seething with hatred. Again she tried dissolving, but the holding spell she was caught in could not be broken.

The worms ignored John Paul, rushing at her with ravenous appetites for her blood. *As if her blood drew them to her.* The answer hit her hard. Her tainted blood was once again betraying her. Worse, they reminded her of the microscopic creatures she occasionally caught glimpses of in her own blood. They sickened her. She hissed her defiance at her enemies, hastily throwing up a barrier between her body and the wriggling worms. Some had already gotten through, biting at her arms and legs viciously.

John Paul swung his hammerlike fist at her face. Before he could connect, he was jerked backward, his huge body tossed through the air as if he weighed no more than a child. Nicolae's grim features stared down at her.

"You look as if you could use some help." He pulled her to her feet, ignoring the worms slithering around her.

"Don't flatter yourself, hotshot," she snapped, yanking

one of the creatures and hurling it off of her. She kicked another as it tried to crawl up her leg. "I am perfectly capable of handling these things."

"Hmm, I can see that," he said, one eyebrow arcing as he lifted his hand toward the sky. At once the dark clouds swirling overhead lit up with veins of white-hot lightning. "A little out of sorts this evening?"

"You'd be cranky too with these *things* sinking their teeth into you." The truth was, the ugly creatures turned her stomach. Shuddering, she pulled viciously at two more, hurling them away. The fog was flowing around the barrier she had erected, the worms erupting into a frenzy as they tried to get to her. "They're disgusting." The white worms boiled up out of the fog, writhing ferociously, smashing into the invisible wall, their teeth tearing at it.

"Women." Casually Nicolae lifted his arm to direct the whips of lightning to the fog. Black ashes burst from the spinning vapor, and a foul odor permeated the air. Destiny plugged her nose against the stench.

Nicolae could barely look at her. She was seething with anger—justifiably so, after such an attack. She hadn't called him to her. His heart was still trying to recover. The sight of her, covered in tiny pinpoints of blood, sickened him. He could feel the demon in him roaring for release, fighting for supremacy, needing to protect her, needing to destroy anything that dared to jeopardize her safety. He kept his face carefully turned from hers, knowing his eyes would betray his inner struggle.

She was his lifemate, and more than any other thing, her health, happiness and protection mattered to him.

Yet securing her happiness and protecting her seemed to be dramatically opposed to each other.

Destiny scanned the area, searching for her enemy. "Coward," she spat, into the wind. "A woman defeats you and you hide. There is no greatness in you. Slink away. Be gone. You are not worth the time to hunt you down." She waved her hand, a gesture of disgust, of disparagement, pure scorn in her voice and manner. She sent the wind out over the city, into every hole and every cemetery, into any place the undead might choose to call his lair.

Nicolae reacted immediately, stilling the wind, calming the fog, his glittering gaze capturing hers, allowing her to see the fierce flames burning there. The depth of his displeasure. "Enough! You will not challenge this vampire. You will not, Destiny."

Her chin lifted belligerently. "I'm a hunter. That's what I do. I find them any way I can, and I destroy them. You taught me that, Nicolae."

She was bleeding from countless bite wounds, tiny gashes and gouges from razor-sharp teeth. There were lines of strain around her mouth. Her eyes were more wary than angry. She tilted her head to one side so that her long, thick braid fell over one shoulder as she studied his set jaw.

He looked intimidating. Ruthless. And she was right in thinking him far more powerful than he had ever shown her before. A trembling started somewhere deep inside her. Even her mouth went dry. She feared him more than the vampire she hunted. Nicolae could hurt her so easily. Destroy her with the wrong word.

"Do not!" He spoke harshly, his voice, always so unfailingly gentle, was completely different now. "I will not hear your meager excuses. You were heedless of the danger. If you hunt the undead, you must not do so with half your attention. I did not teach you to be careless or scattered. And I did not teach you to be foolish. You have skills and you have a brain. I counted on you to use both."

Her fingers curled into fists at the reprimand. Color stained her cheeks. "I would have handled it. I didn't ask for your help, and I didn't need it."

"You sound like a defiant child. You're a grown woman, a hunter of skill." He turned away from her, striding over to John Paul, his quick, fluid movements betraying the anger still seething deep within him. He glanced at her, his features set and harsh. "You should have called me to you immediately. You know you should have. You were being childish, angry because the lifemate you thought your equal in strength turned out to be more than you bargained for. That is no reason to place our lives in danger."

Nicolae reached down and caught John Paul by the back of his shirt, jerking him to his feet and waving a hand almost carelessly to still any protest.

Destiny stood in the street, watching warily. "I didn't think it necessary, Nicolae. I'm telling you that in my judgment, it wasn't necessary."

The full force of his glittering gaze hit her as he turned back to face her. "Are you so foolish as to think those creatures were the actual attack on you? Why would a vampire waste his energy?"

The disgust in his voice brought tears burning behind her eyes. "Of course I didn't believe that. I knew he was trying to weaken me. He used a holding spell to keep me there. He would have shown himself if you hadn't arrived." He had always respected her, respected her abilities. His words had hurt more than the teeth biting into her flesh.

"He poisoned you, Destiny." He spat the words out. The wind rushed down the street in a gust of rage. "You let him poison you."

Her heart stuttered. "My blood's already tainted, Nicolae. It doesn't matter what he does to my blood." There was a strange mumbling in her ears. Words she couldn't catch, but the voice was tearing at her insides like sharp talons.

Nicolae yanked John Paul around, looked deep into his mind, into his memories, shook him in sheer frustration. "He has no memory of what led up to this. We have no time for this. Go home, man, and sleep this off. I will attend to you later." Much later. His mind was consumed with the immediate problem.

John Paul looked at neither of them but obediently shuffled away, toward his home, looking neither right nor left, uninterested in the world around him.

Nicolae scanned the area carefully. The clouds overhead spun in thick threads of black, but there was no wind. He moved, gliding with incredible speed, his fingers settling around Destiny's arm. "We need to go now."

"I don't want the vampire to hurt someone here, not even John Paul, because he's angry he missed me." Destiny tried not to sound as if she were pleading. The buzzing in her head was getting worse, a million bees stinging her from the inside out. It took a great effort to keep from covering her ears or tearing at her head to remove the voice.

The long fingers tightened around her arm like a vise. "Destiny, the vampire has *not* missed you yet. His poison is in your bloodstream, destroying your cells while we waste time talking. We must seek shelter, a place we can defend."

The urgency in his voice told her, even more than the raucous sound in her head, that they had to hurry. Taking the image of an owl from his mind, she immediately began to shift her shape. Only it didn't work. Her form shimmered, but nothing happened. "Get out of here, Nicolae." She shoved him hard with the flat of her hand. "He's using me as bait to trap you. Get away from me."

Nicolae swore in the ancient language. "What happens to you happens to me. We stay together."

She shoved him again, this time hard enough to rock him. "That's what he wants. I'm weighing you down, a stone around your neck. Get out of here. If you care about me at all, leave me here." The worm stings were getting worse, not only in her head now but spreading through her body until she thought she might go mad. She couldn't tone it down, or control the pain at all.

More than the madness, more than the pain, her one thought was his protection. She knew she was right. The vampire had realized that Nicolae was his most powerful enemy. Though she had failed to detect Nicolae's power, the undead had sensed it. The vampire recognized an ancient and knew that if he were to succeed in his plans, it was important to destroy Nicolae.

Nicolae ignored her protests, simply blocked out the sound of the tears in her voice. He couldn't afford to feel emotion. He swept her up in his arms and took to the skies. She went still, knowing better than to fight him, sensing his utter resolve. He would force compliance from her, and both of them knew that if he did such a thing, she would be unable to view it as anything other than a complete violation.

She slipped her arms around his neck and concentrated on their back trail, trying to focus despite the strident voice shrieking in her head and the fiery stings in her body. She would not leave the entire fight to Nicolae, no matter how difficult it was to concentrate.

Her pain was excruciating. Nicolae could feel it coming from her in waves. He shared her mind and heard the hideous voice of the vampire. Her heart was beating far too fast, galloping with the effort to overcome the strain of the poison and the stinging army attacking her from the inside. She was fighting to stay focused, to weave holding spells and throw up flimsy battlements to delay the vampire following them. To give Nicolae more time.

Nicolae buried his face for one moment in her throat, inhaling her scent, whispering softly to her.

Without warning, the world darkened around Destiny, so that only small pinpoints of light burst behind her eyelids. Then all light faded, all sensation. The voice in her head ended abruptly, and the world dropped away.

Chapter Thirteen

How much time do you have? It was Vikirnoff, calm as always. He was far off, but moving rapidly toward his brother. *Her blood calls to the undead like a bright beacon. You will not be able to hide her from them.*

I have no intention of hiding. Nicolae sounded grim. Supremely confident. Merciless. He sounded exactly like the brother Vikirnoff had known for centuries. His power filled the skies, bursting into bolts of lightning, zigzagging whips attacking in every direction. Nicolae was taking the offensive. The skies opened up and torrents of rain pounded the earth. *Let them come for us.*

In the distance, Nicolae heard the echo of a cry of hatred, of rage. A second and a third cry followed as his weapons found targets. The skies lit up with fire, and thunder shook the earth. The ground heaved, buckled and rolled. Below, in a small lake, a huge wave crested high, racing across the surface in foaming madness. Stars seemed to explode around him, an answering war call from the vampire.

Nicolae swept one hand across the sky, stirring the wind to a furious assault on the white-hot bursts of light, blowing them away from the woman in his arms. He raced straight for the mountains, away from humans, where others might be caught in the coming battle. Deliberately he took her far from their chamber of pools, not wanting the vampire to find their resting place. Deep underground he flew, where a series of caves opened into the earth. Steam rose through vents, and the smell of sulfur was strong, but the minerals in the soil were exactly what he was looking for.

He built safeguards in haste, mere stalling tactics to give him the time he needed to drive the poison from Destiny's body. The tiny bite marks were already festering, dark, evil stains, the mark of the beast. Nicolae took Destiny deep beneath the earth to one of the smallest caves, a chamber where the walls were close and there was barely room for their bodies. It was not a place for battle, but far more defensible than one of the larger caves. He waved his hand to open the rich earth, settling Destiny's body into the cool soil. She was hot to the touch, and blisters were forming on her skin.

She has little time. It is a fast-acting poison and one I have not yet seen. They are almost upon us. Nicolae was not disturbed by the gathering vampires. He felt the weight of their anger and determination. They thought him trapped in the mountains, unable to move with a woman to watch over, but they did not yet know his Destiny. Nor did they realize Vikirnoff was streaking across the skies, determined to join the battle.

Using saliva and the rich soil, Nicolae hastily packed each laceration. The tiny, razor-sharp teeth had bitten deep to find Destiny's veins and inject poison into their victim. He worked swiftly but methodically, not taking a chance on missing anything. The vampire who had orchestrated the attack had been clever and quick, using the cover of the fog and waiting for the moment when Destiny's inattention made her vulnerable. At no time had the vampire exposed himself to danger or injury. It was a smart move, and Nicolae acknowledged the enemy was a dangerous adversary.

It was the poison moving through Destiny's body that alarmed him the most. "Wake, my love. Wake with the knowledge of our coming battle."

Destiny obeyed his command with a gasp of pain. Her gaze, darkened with suffering, met his. "They seek you, Nicolae. They come for you."

He waved the information away casually. "Let them come. They have underestimated you. They will come to their own doom. I must drive the poison from your body as quickly as possible, and I will need all of your strength and aid."

She nodded, trust shimmering in the depths of her eyes. "Tell me what to do and I'll follow your lead."

Nicolae forced his mind away from the absolute trust in her gaze, in her words, and how much it meant to him. How much *she* meant to him. He slowed his heartbeat to a strong, steady beat designed to hinder the swiftness of the poison. He had sent her to sleep for the same reason. He took her hand and placed it over his heart. "Like this, Destiny. Keep your heart rate exactly the same." His thumb caressed the back of her hand while his heart beat directly into her palm.

She became aware of the rapid pounding of her heart. It filled the chamber with the sound of thunder, a powerful drum that beat a rhythm of death. At once she slowed the beat, taking control of her body, following the slower, much steadier beat of his. She felt sluggish and drained, tired beyond belief as her heart slowed down.

"You will be shocked when we are inside. Do not panic, and do not fear for me. I have dealt with poison many times. Concentrate on what must be done. Fear is our biggest enemy."

Destiny nodded her understanding. "I won't let you down." She was very aware of the danger they were in. She was in Nicolae's mind, even felt the presence of Vikirnoff. He didn't bother to shield his presence from her any longer. She knew he was racing to their aid.

Nicolae allowed his body to drop away, become light and energy so that he could enter Destiny's body to survey the damage. He spent precious minutes studying the chemical compound used to poison his lifemate. It was replicating itself quickly, and mutating as it spread through her body. The mutant form seemed to sense him, an army of hostile intent, ready to attack his light.

Pull out! Destiny didn't wait to see if he listened to the order; she struck with every bit of strength she had, driving him from her body, using their blood bond to draw him with her.

The move was so strong, so unexpected, it caught Nicolae unawares. He found himself back in his own body blinking at her.

If I had a sense of humor, I would be laughing right now. Vikirnoff sounded the same as always. Calm, undisturbed by the fact that they were being stalked by an unknown number of vampires, and a bloody battle would soon take place.

Nicolae sighed. "You should not have done that, Destiny," he reprimanded. "The poison must be driven from your body; we have no other choice. We have no time for arguing."

"No, we don't," she agreed. Beads of sweat dotted her skin. Some were pink, the first traces of blood. "You will have to delay them, defend us while I do this myself. The poison was designed to attack the healer. Both of us cannot be infected." She laid her hand on his arm. "You know I'm right, Nicolae."

She does actually make sense once in a while.

"I heard that," Destiny said. "Nicolae, we don't have time to argue about this. Even your brother agrees I'm right, and you know he's totally living in the Dark Ages when it comes to women."

Nicolae swore eloquently in the ancient native tongue. He included Vikirnoff in his litany just for good measure. The poison was a virulent strain. He bent his head to rest his brow against hers. "Being your lifemate is not the easiest on a man's ego."

Her hand cupped his cheek, her thumb feathering a caress over his lips. "The hounds are at the front door."

His mouth skimmed hers. "You be careful, Destiny. Do this right. You do not have much time. I will need you on your feet and ready to go. They must be kept from this chamber if possible. I will meet them above."

"Go." She squeezed his fingers, let her hand fall away. Nicolae was already dissolving, streaming away from her and up the chimney to burst into the night sky. He would go out to meet their enemies. His lifemate's blood was a bright beacon summoning the undead straight to their location. It was his job to keep them away from her until she was able to move and hunt on her own.

Destiny wasted no time, and he could detect no fear

in her as once more she allowed her body to slip away. She became light and energy, marshaling her waning strength to fight the army of invading microbes in her bloodstream. Nicolae remained a shadow in her mind, ready to give her strength should there be need, ready to aid her in any way.

He climbed high, taking stock of his surroundings. He hoped the vampires would be careless in their attack, certain he was too busy with Destiny to go on the offense. This had been a carefully prepared battle, and Nicolae was certain Pater was behind it. Pater was determined to bring the vampires together, uniting them against the hunters.

It might work if they can keep from killing one another, Nicolae observed.

Vikirnoff thought it over. *I did not believe there was a vampire powerful enough, not even an ancient, to accomplish such a thing as uniting vampires to a common purpose, but our enemy seems to have managed such a thing here.*

It has been done before, but not with ancients. Always there has been one who has power, the rest only sacrificial pawns. This bodes ill for our people. Nicolae hid his being in the tiniest of molecules, spread out across the sky in the roiling clouds. Vikirnoff was in his mind, and deeply merged with Destiny also, waiting to lend his strength when there was need.

Destiny was unaware of either of them. She concentrated entirely on her own war, trusting Nicolae to fend off the undead until she could join him. She recognized she had lost too much blood through the many bites on her skin. The compound in her body was wreaking mass destruction, mutating her cells at a rapid rate. She noted the wiggling parasites that were always present in her bloodstream, familiar to her, but somehow abhorrent. Even they tried to hide from the attacking poison. She searched quickly through her bloodstream, found natural antibodies and began replicating them, hastily throwing her own army at the microbes to slow down their reproduction and give herself more time to come up with something to destroy them permanently. She glimpsed a bubble, nearly hidden behind the swarming cells. It was reddish-black, a large clot rolling in the wake of the microbes. She could fight the mutant cells, programmed to attack the surge of energy she radiated, but she had the feeling the real demon was that unknown mass.

She ignored the lesions forming on her organs everywhere the poison touched. She ignored her tainted blood, burning and scalding so that the walls of her veins seemed thin and weak, ready to burst. In places they bulged alarmingly, just as some of her organs did.

What weapons did she have to fight such a thing? Energy. Light. She stopped wasting her time creating antibodies that merely slowed the army of mutants. She waited, watched the surging swarm of cells bent on enveloping the essence of her life.

Destiny held her position, aware of time slowing down. She felt no one near her, heard nothing, not even the beating of her own heart. Her entire focus was on that mass of malignant cells. She waited, gathering her energy until it was white-hot, a pinpoint laser, zeroing in on the deadly microbes. She allowed her power free rein, and it became a concentrated lethal pulse of energy, so great she knew it wasn't all her own.

She couldn't let the knowledge distract her. She was

watching the cells shrivel and die, watching as the thing behind them appeared clearly for the first time. It was only about the size of a walnut, lodged in her stomach. Her heart stuttered. She couldn't use fire or heat with this. It was some kind of explosive chemical waiting for a detonator. The chemicals had been attached to the first compound injected into her body through the teeth as they bit into her flesh. When the cells mutated to the second generation, the chemicals had rushed through her body from every direction to bond together as they were meant to do. She had been made into a living bomb, aimed and directed straight at Nicolae should he attempt to heal her.

Destiny inhaled sharply, knowing Nicolae was with her now, seeing what she was seeing. Fearing as she was fearing. *Do what you have to do, Nicolae. I will find the answer to this.*

Nicolae felt his heart stutter. *You must hurry, Destiny. The malignant cells are damaging your body. You need a healer.* He sent calm reassurance and total belief in her, even though deep in his heart he raged against having to fight the enemy when he wanted to rush to her side.

The skies lit up with fireballs, missiles of spinning orange flames that sought him out in the darkness. As they whistled through the air, hot threads spun off and lashed at the space around him, seeking a target.

Calmly Nicolae swept the fierce wind in front of him, hurtling the lances back toward his enemy, announcing his presence. *Come to me, all of you seeking the justice of our people. I will help you depart for the next world as you should have done long ago. Come to me now. I grow weary of your tantrums.*

Cries of hatred and rage echoed across the sky in answer. Nicolae was already on the move, knowing the vampires would attempt to pinpoint his location by the direction of the terrible wind. He heard a highpitched chatter, and then the air to his left, where he had just been, erupted with an army of bats. Large creatures much like vampire bats, these were minions of the undead with long fangs, seeking his blood. They flew at him, so many the skies were filled with their furry bodies. All the while, the squeaks and chatter continued as they transmitted his presence to their master.

Nicolae blasted the area with lightning, supercharging the air so that whips danced and zigzagged, shedding radiant sparks as they sought their targets. As the creatures were incinerated, they gave off a foul-smelling odor that stung Nicolae's eyes and burned his throat and nose. The night sky, black with ominous roiling clouds, was lit up by the phenomenal lightning display. Thunder followed, a clap that shook the earth below but also carried a hidden attack, bouncing sound waves as strong as any earthquake through the sky to shake loose the undead.

Harsh screeches hurt his ears as one of the vampires tumbled from above, shimmering a grayish opaque as the hideous form materialized from the mist, caught itself in midair and quickly streaked behind the clouds, fearful of attack. As the vampire threw spears of pure sizzling electricity toward Nicolae, Vikirnoff emerged into the open.

Nicolae slammed into his brother hard, driving him out of range of a white-hot lance. It skimmed his own shoulder, burning through muscle and tissue as it whistled by him.

You are getting too old for this. The reflexes are going, Nicolae taunted his brother even as he circled around to get behind the vampire.

Just checking to make sure you were in this battle and not with your woman.

Nicolae grunted as he blasted through the thin cloud straight at the vampire. Immediately the sky erupted from three sides with monstrous lizard creatures, much like the ones in the cave where he had first faced Pater. Clearly the ancient vampire had orchestrated this battle as well. The hideous creatures attacked even as the vampire shifted to the same shape, reaching for him with enormous, wicked claws, its huge head swinging toward him.

Fetid breath smelling of rotted flesh was hot in his face, but Nicolae drove forward, slipping away from the claws by a hair's breadth. He put on a burst of speed, and his fist shot out toward the beast's scaly chest. At the last moment, the vampire spun, whipping with its spiked tail, the barbs tipped with a paralyzing poison.

The other three beasts lunged at Nicolae, snapping with crushing jaws, their great wings flapping hard, creating a windstorm, stirring up dust in the sky. Clouds swirled and churned; blackened bits of debris torn up from the earth below towered high in a tornado funnel. The force of that wind created its own weather; a storm of ice like splinters and spears of crystal hurtled out from the center, looking for a target.

In the instant when Nicolae would have dissolved to allow the whipping tail and crushing jaws to pass harmlessly by him, one of the creatures opened its hideous mouth wider to reveal the prize in its mouth. His legs held prisoner by the rows of teeth, a man screamed helplessly, flailing his arms wildly, his horrified gaze locked with Nicolae's as the giant beast began to exert pressure.

Vikirnoff dropped from above, emerging out of the dark clouds to land on the lizard's back. In his hand was a spear glowing red-hot. He thrust the weapon straight through the back of the neck of the reptile. As it screamed in pain and hatred, the great jaws opened, releasing the human inside. The man plummeted toward earth, his cry a thin wail of terror.

Nicolae plunged straight down, chasing after the falling man as he dropped toward the rising funnel cloud. The splinters and spears of ice targeted both Nicolae and the victim of the undead. Nicolae hastily constructed a net woven of silken strands below the falling man while at the same time moving his hands in a complicated pattern, drawing fire from the sky to melt the ice weapons.

The vampire's victim hit the net, bounced and caught desperately at the thin strands, hanging on grimly. He was fully aware of the bizarre happenings and yet he was fighting to stay alive. Needing him conscious, Nicolae chose not to shield him as he swept him into the comparative safety of his arms.

"Hang on!" Nicolae ordered. He recognized Martin Wright. The man clasped his hands around Nicolae's neck, sliding around to his back, then closing his eyes against this terrifying reality. Blood dripped steadily from his legs where the teeth had bit into him.

Don't let anything happen to him. Destiny's plea was strong in Nicolae's mind.

Nicolae glanced down toward the mountain even as the reptilian creatures lunged after him, streaking away from their fallen companion. The giant lizard Vikirnoff had lanced was falling through the sky, somersaulting with Vikirnoff stubbornly clinging to its back. The vampire was roaring in rage and terror, but the others did not go to his aid. Instead they were hurtling toward Nicolae and Martin at an alarming rate of speed.

Evading them with blurring speed, Nicolae almost missed the shadow near the entrance to the mountain. A dark shape slithered over the ground silently, moving from shadow to shadow. Nicolae barely caught the sliding tail disappearing into the ground far below him. His heart slammed hard in his chest. The undead knew that if he managed to kill Destiny, he would destroy at least one of the hunters for certain. Her lifemate would never continue without her, and it was possible both hunters would follow her or turn.

Destiny!

I feel the evil one approaching. I have smelled his stench before. There was a confidence in her voice Nicolae did not feel. Pater was a powerful and dangerous adversary. Destiny was seriously injured, ill and fighting the poison in her body.

Nicolae, let the human go. You will need your full strength to fight off the undead. Vikirnoff was always the same, his voice without inflection, even when he was sentencing a man to certain death.

You will not! Destiny was furious with Vikirnoff. *Do not listen to him, Nicolae. I do not need your help with one slimy vampire.*

The boiling chemicals that had mixed together in her stomach to form the explosive device were beginning to burn through her insides, as if releasing some terrible gas. Destiny studied the compound, felt Nicolae, and Vikirnoff through Nicolae, studying the chemicals with her.

The first is nitric acid or something similar, Nicolae identified.

And they have found a way to introduce glycerin, uniting the two chemicals, Vikirnoff pointed out.

Destiny winced. Nitroglycerin. Unstable. Dangerous. Sitting inside her and waiting for some signal to explode. Even a change in her body temperature could set it off. The virus itself could be the detonator if it raised her body temperature. Destiny controlled her panic, thinking, determined to use her brain. Their kind existed on blood. Blood would have no effect on that raging mass. A laser blast of pure energy would ignite it. The vampire would expect her to think like a hunter, not a human. He would never expect her to ingest anything other than blood.

Pater was drawing closer, making his way stealthily down through the caves to the chamber where she rested. Destiny could feel his evil presence spreading through the mountain, a soft rumble of protest from the soil, from the insects and cave dwellers. The shadow lengthened, grew, a feeling of impending doom that began to invade her mind with insidious strength, shaking her confidence.

The poison was doing its work, overcoming the antibody defense she had set up and breaking down her body's ability to fight. Tiny droplets of blood began to seep from her pores.

Destiny closed her mind to everything but the problem within her. Nicolae must be protected at all costs. This thing, this trap that had been set for him, had to be destroyed. She could think of only one way to do so. Carefully weaving her spell, she called on the earth's minerals, looking for what she needed. Sodium carbonate. Lots of it. She could neutralize the acid in the system and break the glycerin down naturally; neither was toxic alone. She prepared a drink using the mineral water, making certain it was the exact temperature of her body.

She had to fight to ingest it, to keep it in her body when everything in her rebelled. Once again, she entered a bodiless state in order to direct the sodium carbonate mixture where she needed it. She watched it closely as her only hope raced to do as she bade. If it didn't work, she intended to wait until the vampire was upon her, raise her body temperature as high as she could as fast as she could, and detonate the bomb, taking him with her. She would not allow him to get his hands on her. The chemicals touched, mixed. She knew the precise moment when she'd won.

Nicolae sighed with relief. Vikirnoff's presence disappeared.

The vampire was still coming and she was still weak. But she was a hunter. Destiny held the compound in her body as long as she could stand it, then expelled it as quickly as she could, crawling to a corner to be violently sick.

She turned her head when a soft slithering betrayed the intruder. "Pater. How nice to see you've taken your true form. The scales suit you. I'm very impressed with the reptilian head. It screams success. Bet you drive the ladies wild in that form."

There was little room to maneuver, and Destiny doubted she had the strength to shape-shift. She sat back, looking at the huge beast as it smirked at her, the cold, dead eyes triumphant. "You think you've won some sort of victory, but you don't know me. And you don't know Nicolae. You will never live through this."

The vampire retained the body of the beast, but the crocodilian head contorted, wavered, solidified into the head of a man. It was an ugly amalgamation, Pater's head attached to the neck and body of a dragon-lizard. He flashed his jagged teeth at her, not bothering to sustain an illusion of beauty. "Neither will you live, my dear. I gave you a chance to join us. More than one chance. They will never accept one such as you. Never. If the hunter takes your blood, lifemate or no, it will strengthen his dark side. What is the use of suffering, only to be cast aside? What do you think the Prince will do when he sees you? And what of Gregori? Do you believe they will accept you into their keeping? Allow you to associate with their women?"

Her heart fluttered. The truth of his words was like an arrow piercing her heart. Sharp. Lethal. Terrible. She would always be an outcast. Always. Even Nicolae's brother recognized her as such. She glanced away from the beady, accusing eyes, ashamed.

Keep looking at him, Nicolae said. *It matters little to me what the Prince or Gregori or any other thinks. And it should matter little to you. This evil one is a vampire and he lies. He is using the oldest trick in the book on you, undermining your will to fight him.*

It was a stern reprimand, and she took it to heart. The scrape of a claw on rock warned her, and she locked her gaze with the vampire's. At once she felt power and strength moving through her. Enormous strength. The power was astonishing.

Pater screamed, contorting, attempting to spin around

in the small confines of the burrow, his spiked tail lashing, but his very bulk defeated him. Flames danced over the scales, sizzled and bubbled the reptile's skin, searing down to the bone. Fire raced the length of his body, blackening the scales, fouling the air with a terrible stench. The carcass split open, spilling the vampire onto the cave floor. He was hissing in rage, crawling toward her, his eyes glowing a fiery red, fixed on her with malice.

Destiny tried to gather herself to meet the attack, but her body failed her, useless without nourishment, her strength spent on the battle to drive out the poisonous virus.

Just look at him. Nicolae was completely confident. His certainty struck a chord deep inside her. He was engaged in his own life-and-death struggle, with a human in his care, evading vampires while he aided her, yet he was supremely confident of his ability to protect her. And she believed him.

Destiny didn't take her gaze from Pater. A small, grim smile touched her mouth. She looked exhausted and weak, but she was also relaxed and certain.

Pater read her expression, saw her eyes, the power swirling in the blue-green depths, power not her own, and he knew he had failed. His minions had not kept the ancient occupied. He was staring at death. In desperation he threw up a barrier, burrowing into the ground as he did so. Inches from Destiny, vines erupted from the ground. Giant tentacles reached for her, flowers opening to reveal tiny piranhalike teeth snapping close to her legs.

She drew away from the plants with her last remaining strength. Even as she did, she felt the power moving through her, saw the vines wither and die, dropping in the dirt to disintegrate into lifeless black strings. Destiny slumped against the wall of the cave, breathing a sigh of relief. Pater had escaped a second time, but he hadn't managed to use her to destroy Nicolae.

The battle in the air was fading, the vampires retreating at their master's call. Vikirnoff had managed to destroy one of the undead, calling on lightning to incinerate his black heart.

Nicolae had managed to evade the other three, even while keeping Martin safe and fighting off Pater's attack on Destiny. He was worried, though. He could sense Destiny's weakness.

Take Martin back to the city for me while I see to Destiny, Nicolae said to his brother. *He must be healed and his memories removed.*

He is your human. I do not deal well with such people. They make no sense to me. I must feed if I am to supply you with what you need. You should take what you need from that one before you go to your lifemate. But you will not because she will be angry if you do. It makes no sense. Prey is prey.

Nicolae glared at his brother, but the gesture was lost on Vikirnoff. *Destiny. I must see that Martin's wounds are healed and that he gets home safely.*

Of course you must. There was something new in her voice. A soft note of warmth, of love that hadn't been there before. Nicolae was certain she was unaware of it, but it spread fire in his belly and sent his heart leaping with joy. *I'm a little tired, but I'm all right. Do what you have to do, then come back and get me. I'll even let you play the big hero. You can pick me up and carry me home.*

Nicolae found himself smiling as he whisked Martin across the sky, back to the comparative safety of the city. *You like it when I carry you around. Especially if you do not have any clothes on.*

Her laughter bubbled up, soft and melodic, warming him even more, filling him completely with happiness. He also heard the note of utter weariness in her voice when she spoke to him. *You like it when I have no clothes on. That mind of yours is a minefield of erotic images. It is true what they say about men thinking of sex every few seconds.*

I have been in your mind too, Destiny.

I have an excuse, though. You have all those images in your head and I'm thinking them over. Memorizing them.

Her teasing voice caressed his skin, fanned the flames of urgent need, even when he knew rest and the healing soil were the only thing he would allow his lifemate this night. *I am proud of you.* He had to tell her of his pride, could not keep it to himself. The intensity of his emotions swept through him until he thought he might burst. She had done the impossible, the unthinkable.

You did rather well yourself this night, although your speed could use improvement. Do not think I haven't noticed the wound on your shoulder when you were just a bit slow shoving your idiot of a brother out of harm's way.

You are critiquing me? He injected shock and horror into his voice to make her laugh. He loved her laugh. *I thought frying the lizard was a nice touch.*

I was taught by a master. Really, you could use a few tips. The amusement was already fading from her voice, leaving her sounding drowsy. *I'm tired, Nicolae. I must rest until you return.*

He shared her mind as she set safeguards; they would be easy enough to unravel now that he knew the complicated patterns. *I will return swiftly.*

No need. I will rest in the soil.

Just like that she was gone from him. He knew she was safe, that she had gone to ground, allowing the earth to welcome her, but he needed to hold her, to see for himself that she was safe from all harm. He wanted to carry her to the cave of pools, to perform the healing ritual on her and give her blood before placing her in the rich soil of their lair.

Nicolae controlled his descent so as not to alarm Martin further. He chose a small park a short distance from the man's home.

Martin trembled uncontrollably. "What were those things? You saved my life."

Nicolae helped him to sit on the park bench. "It is not necessary to explain. You will not remember them. You will not remember any of this."

At those words, Martin jerked away from Nicolae. "Like I don't remember the attack on Father Mulligan? Did you have something to do with that? Did those . . . those *things*?"

"I do not know why you cannot remember what happened, Martin," Nicolae answered honestly. "I cannot find evidence that one of the undead touched you in any way. Either a vampire has grown more powerful than anything I can conceive of, or it was not the influence or work of one. I do not know what happened to you, but I am trying to find out." He examined the wounds on Martin's legs. "Fortunately, you were not injected with poison. You were very lucky this time."

"Lucky?" Martin looked as if he might cry. Then he began to laugh, almost hysterically. "I guess you're right. If you hadn't come along, that thing would have eaten me alive. What was it?"

"Martin? Nicolae?" Father Mulligan came up behind them, startled to see them in the park. He had walked right past that bench only minutes earlier and no one had been in sight.

Nicolae heaved a sigh, sitting back on his haunches. The world was conspiring against him. "How are you tonight, Father?"

"What happened to Martin's legs?" The priest peered anxiously at the gaping, bloody lacerations. "Should I call an ambulance?"

"I can take care of it for him," Nicolae said. "What are you doing out so late?"

"The storm over the mountains made me uneasy." The priest's gaze was shrewd and assessing as he studied Nicolae and then Martin. The blackened wound on Nicolae's shoulder and Martin's shredded legs told him more than either would admit in words. "That was no natural storm. Who won?"

Nicolae pushed a hand through his hair. "I would have to say it was a draw. I cannot stay long. Destiny is ill and I must return to her." He glanced sharply at the priest. "You did not feel a compulsion to come here now, did you?"

"You mean as if I couldn't stop myself?"

Nicolae nodded. "I do not like the fact that you were attacked. That Martin was used to attack you and that he was out tonight. And now I find you here."

Father Mulligan shook his head firmly. "I woke when

the thunder was so loud. Believe me, I was in complete control of all my faculties. I knew something was wrong, and I was worried about my parishioners."

"It is much safer to stay inside, Father," Nicolae pointed out. He turned his attention to Martin's leg. "How did they manage to get their hands on you?"

Martin frowned. "I had a fight with Tim. We never argue, but this thing with my losing my memory and nearly killing Father Mulligan is ruining our relationship. I think Tim's a little afraid of me. I keep telling him I'd never hurt him, but then I would never hurt you, Father, and I did. So that doesn't mean much."

"Do you know John Paul, Martin?"

"Sure. Everyone knows him. He looks like a brute, but he's really a gentle giant. He'd give you the shirt off his back if you needed it."

"He beat up Helena. Not once but twice," Nicolae said, watching Martin's face carefully.

Martin paled visibly, looked genuinely shocked. "I don't believe it. He *adores* Helena. He would kill anyone who touched her. I don't believe you." He looked at the priest for confirmation. "It had to be someone else."

"He doesn't remember it either, Martin," Father Mulligan said gently.

Martin dropped his face into his hands. "I don't understand any of this. Why is this happening? Does it have something to do with those creatures?" He dragged his hands over his face twice as if wiping the memory away. "Am I going insane? Tell me if I am. I swear I'd rather let that creature bite me in half than hurt someone I care about."

"I don't think you're insane," Father Mulligan said,

dropping a comforting hand on the man's shoulder. "Neither is John Paul."

"I was out walking tonight. I didn't want Tim to see me cry. I didn't see the thing coming at me. One moment I was alone, and then it had me." He shuddered with the memory of the hot jaws crushing him. "Some animal, Father—a cross between a Komodo dragon and a crocodile, but with wings. I sound crazy even to myself." He slumped against the back of the wooden bench. "I don't know whether to go to the nearest hospital and check myself in or put a gun to my head."

Nicolae leaned close, staring directly into Martin's eyes. "You will do neither. You will not remember the creatures you saw tonight, or my presence or flying through the air. There was no battle in the skies. You sat here in the park and spoke with Father Mulligan. He calmed you down and told you to have faith and wait it out. There is an answer, and you will be exonerated."

Martin nodded, his eyes glazing slightly as he slipped deeper under Nicolae's compulsion. Nicolae healed his legs, making certain there was not even a tiny scar to draw attention to the incident. He looked up at the priest. "You will have to take over from here, Father. See that he gets home. Maybe talk with Tim and ask him to ease up on Martin. He is not dangerous."

"Neither is John Paul, yet he hurt Helena," the priest said. "I was told that tonight he went berserk in his home and tore it to pieces, destroying furniture in a terrible rage. A neighbor wanted to call the police but called Velda instead. She advised against it. Helena is safe, and he can't get to her for the time being. If he goes into the system, he'll have a record for life."

"I saw him earlier; he was not himself, more like a zombie, programmed for violence, but I could not detect the undead," Nicolae said.

"You are talking about vampires. Individuals who drink the blood of the living and have given up their souls to continue their immortal existence. Those are the creatures you hunt. And Martin saw them." Father Mulligan's voice was filled with awe. "It is difficult to believe such creatures could exist. Are they wholly evil? Beyond redemption? This is certain?"

Nicolae surged to his feet, looming over the priest, his eyes glittering dangerously. "Do not dare try to save them, Father. They would delight in getting their hands on you. You are in the business of saving souls. They do not have souls to save. Vampires are capable of making you commit depraved acts you cannot even conceive of. Must I give you a command, Father?"

Father Mulligan glanced at Martin, who was slumped on the bench with a slack expression. He drew away from Nicolae. "It isn't necessary. I'll keep my distance from them."

"Make certain that you do." Nicolae "pushed" with his voice, making sure the priest would stay away from the vampires. He waved his hand to wake Martin even as he dissolved, streaming away from the city in a trail of vapor.

Chapter Fourteen

Destiny lay as still as a corpse in a grave so shallow, it was a testament to her weakness. He had known she was exhausted, but she had hidden the full extent of it from him. No hunter, knowing vampires were in the area and the resting place compromised, would have gone to ground in such a way.

Nicolae waved aside the thin layer of soil and closed his eyes at what he saw lying there. Anger swirled through him. Mixed with heartache. She looked terribly young and vulnerable lying there with her skin translucent, almost gray. Droplets of blood had seeped from her pores, and in her exhaustion she had been unable to summon the strength to heal her body any further. The poison had been dealt with, but it had come from the infected vampire and her tainted blood had embraced the dark gift. She looked as if she were slipping away from him.

Nicolae didn't awaken her there. He wanted her out of the damp, tiny space, a crawl space of near death where the odor of blood held the stench of the vampire. The blackened carcass of the lizard remained along with the black strings of tentacles, a reminder of the double attack. Destiny didn't belong in this place of death. He gathered her into his arms. She seemed light and insubstantial. The confrontation with evil had weakened her beyond her limits. He held her to him, against the breadth of his chest, wanting to shelter her from every struggle. He looked down at her face and felt the sting of unexpected tears.

Destiny had been through so much in her life. As her lifemate, he wanted to protect her from all harm, shield her from all adversity. He was an ancient warrior. His protection was considerable, yet he could never bring himself to force Destiny to give up hunting the undead. She needed to know she was strong enough. She needed to know she had control. She needed to be able to rid the world of as many of the vile creatures as she could. He knew Vikirnoff didn't understand. Most likely no Carpathian, male or female, would understand. But he knew Destiny. He knew her heart and soul. He knew every scar in her mind. The wounds were deep, and he couldn't get rid of them for her. In truth, he didn't want to get rid of them anymore. He realized that those memories, that horrendous life she had endured and survived, had made her the courageous woman she was. She had been shaped and honed in the fires of hell and she had come through it, a compassionate woman who sought to protect, with every breath in her body, those she allowed into her life.

He took her from the underground burrow out into the open air so that the gentle wind slipped over her body, ruffled her hair and clothes, breathed a clean scent over her. Nicolae, aching with love, took her out over the mountains, made his way through the series of chambers until they were home in their cave of shimmering pools and glittering gems. He waved his hand so that the carved urn leapt to life, flickering and dancing, casting shadows on the walls and across the surface of the water. Healing aromas filled the space, mingling together to provide a soothing peace.

Nicolae removed his clothing, removed hers and carried her down into the deepest and hottest of the pools. With his lips against her skin, he whispered to her softly to awaken. "I love you, my lady," he murmured. Needing to say the words to her. She could reach inside him and find the emotion, deep and real inside his heart and soul, but he wanted to declare it.

She stirred. Her heart beat into his hand. Air rushed through her lungs. Her lashes fluttered. Lifted. Unbelievably, she smiled at him. "I was dreaming of you."

He kissed her. He couldn't help himself. His mouth lingered over hers, robbing her of breath, of air. "That would be impossible, little one. The sleep of our people is a mortal death. There is no brain activity."

"Nevertheless." She said it complacently. Her gaze drifted over his face with a touch of possession. "I was worried about you." Her fingers found the blackened slash in his shoulder. "I felt this hit you. Does it hurt?"

He shook his head. "I am going to sit down in the water. It is hot, but it will do you good. I need to replace your blood."

"You did not feed." It was a chastisement.

"Vikirnoff wanted me to use Martin, but I thought you might give me a lecture. Having never experienced such a thing, I thought it better not to start off our life together that way. Do not worry, my brother will provide. He is feeding now."

He sank into the water, taking her with him, holding her close as the heat pushed the ice cold from her veins. She gasped, stiffened, holding herself slightly away from him, trying not to struggle. The hot water on her chilled skin wasn't comfortable, but within a matter of minutes she relaxed, subsiding against him, her body snuggling close, fitting into the cradle of his hips.

The water lapped at her breasts, fizzing over the tips, bubbling and cleansing, removing all traces of blood, all remnants of the poison. She closed her eyes and allowed her head to fall back, enjoying the sheer luxury of the hot pool and Nicolae's strong arms. "Vikirnoff needs a swift kick where it will do him the most good," she murmured, not bothering to lift her lashes. "But I'll forgive his egotistical arrogance because he looks after you. You should have fed."

"He will feed me. He went out hunting."

"As soon as possible, I want to give him the picture of the woman MaryAnn told us about. We should also ask Father Mulligan and Velda and Inez if they have seen her. They seem to be the eyes and ears of the neighborhood."

She nuzzled his throat. Hunger was rising, sharp and demanding. Her insides were burning, a terrible scalding from the inside out. The bubbling water and Nicolae's nearness helped considerably. She inhaled his clean, masculine scent. Took his scent deep into her body. Held it there. She had been in a storm, a whirling, turbulent storm, but she had made it safely home. Nicolae was home. She settled in his mind. Her one refuge.

She could admit it to herself now and not feel ashamed and humiliated.

"I did my best to push you away. I should have been stronger, but right now I'm glad that I wasn't." Her lips skimmed his throat. Her tongue swirled over his pulse. Her bare buttocks were nestled in his lap and she could feel there the strong reaction of his body to that small, erotic movement of her tongue. He hardened. Thickened. Pulsed with need. She savored the feeling, wanted to remember it forever.

His hand skimmed over her hair, tugged her long braid. "I would not allow you to push me away. I am tenacious when something matters to me."

She smiled against his skin. She kissed the small, steady pulse in his neck. "Is that the word? I thought stubborn suited you better."

"You are not in the best condition to try to do battle," he reminded her.

She won the battle without a single word.

His head fell back as she took what he offered. The air rushed from his lungs, a soft sound of ecstasy escaping as the white-hot pleasure-pain rushed through his body. The intensity of his love for her shook him. His arms tightened possessively. She swamped him with warmth, with her need of him, the way she wanted him.

Beneath it all, he felt her sorrow, the weight of Pater's words implanted in her mind and heart. She would never believe the Carpathian race would accept her with her tainted blood. If Nicolae called the healer, Destiny would never allow him near her. She would run. There was no way to erase what the vampire had wrought. Nicolae could remove all traces of the virus. He could restore her strength. He could give her unconditional love, but he could never remove those words.

Because his words are true. Her hands found his hair, tunneled her fingers deep into the mass of silken strands. She wanted to lose herself in sensation. She couldn't make the words false, but she could put them somewhere in a little corner of her mind, replace them with something that consumed her: the bubbles popping against her bare skin; the silken strands of dark hair sliding through her fingers. *I love your hair.*

You are supposed to love me. And it is not true. Vampires twist the truth until you can no longer see what is. You know that, Destiny. More than most, you know what they do.

In this instance even a grain of truth is far too much. She swept her tongue across the pinpricks, closing the tiny wounds with her healing saliva, lifted her head and met the dark intensity of his gaze without flinching. "You can love me with your heart and your mind and your soul. You can be my salvation when the memories come to haunt me, Nicolae. You can be my everything, but you cannot change what I am. A vampire put something hideous deep inside me. It is evil and dark and dangerous. I've lived with it most of my life, and I know. You can love me, even with that terrible flaw inside me, but you can't change it. I can't change it. It isn't going to go away because we want it to. I recognize darkness in others. Others will recognize it in me. Like calls to like."

Her voice was a thread of sound. Exhaustion lined her face. Nicolae couldn't bear the way she was looking at him with such a mixture of love and regret. His hands moved over her body with exquisite tenderness, washing the remnants of blood and poison from her skin. "Destiny, I've found you to be stubborn and independent but never dense. Are you deliberately not understanding that we are two halves of the same whole? We are alike. Like did call to like, and I am it. I am what you got."

She was warm and safe huddled in the shelter of his arms, cradled by his body. The water lapped pleasantly against her skin, bubbling and fizzing against every sore spot. The flames flickered and danced and released a fragrance conducive to healing and comfort. Destiny lifted her gaze to Nicolae's face, studied the hard angles and planes. A slow smile found its way to her mouth. "Lucky me."

Her words twisted his heart. "How do you do that, little one? It bodes ill for our future. One moment I am determined to chastise you severely as you so obviously deserve, and the next all I want to do is kiss you senseless."

Destiny framed his face with her palms. "It's a gift. I much prefer the kissing." The pad of her thumb moved over his jaw, traced his chin. "You have such shadows in your mind. You think I was wrong not to call you to me, but I wasn't. Why would you think yourself less important to me, less to me in some way than I am to you? Do you think you're the only one with rights? I do not want your protection at the expense of your life. *You're* the target here, not me. I'm merely the bait used to draw you out. Fortunately, one of us is able to think in tight situations."

His breath escaped in a hiss of impatience and frustration. When her soft mouth began to curve in amusement, he gave her a little shake. "Now is not the time for you to laugh, Destiny. I am still shaking from your near miss on the street and in the cave."

"Did you know that when you are exceptionally upset with me, your eyes darken to the most beautiful black? It reminds of the midnight hour. So perfect when the air is still and the stars are out and you can see the night sky. Your eyes are like that."

Deliberately he sighed. His hands continued to wash her body, lingering on her curves. "My eyes should be making you tremble. I am giving you a most disapproving look. It is meant to intimidate, not make you think of the sky at midnight."

A laugh slipped out. That small carefree sound that was so rare for her. "I can't help how you look. It's tempting to upset you just to see that particular color."

"I am not amused." He tried to sound as grim as he felt. She might turn him inside out, even melt his heart, but he was staring down at her ravaged face, looking at her body where dark bruises marred the pale coloration of her skin. He knew how close he'd come to losing her and . . . *it could have been prevented*.

She wanted to apologize. She touched lightly on the memory in his mind, the moment he realized she was in danger but would not call him. She felt the terror welling up in him, shaking him. Turning his stomach and seizing his lungs, robbing him of breath. Then there was a dark, brooding rage, ugly and menacing, a dangerous demon lifting and stretching, unsheathing claws as it opened its mouth to roar a protest.

Deliberately Destiny lay back in his arms to allow the water to close over her face, hiding the tears burning in her eyes. His anger ran deep. It simmered just below the surface. He held her tenderly, washed her, murmured beautiful things, but the rage was there all the same. She had succeeded in scaring him. And hurting him. His emotional pain was deep and sharp, and that was far more painful to bear than his anger.

"A little pain isn't going to hurt me, Destiny, and certainly is not worth your tears." He lifted her up higher, bringing her head out of the water. "Your tears tear me apart. Stop." He made it an order, leaning over her to kiss both eyelids.

Her arms tightened around his neck. "You just aren't as tough as you like to think." She forced a brief smile, wanting to please him. Wanting to show him that he mattered to her.

He carried her out of the pool, waving his hand to open the earth, a quick, impatient gesture. Nicolae knelt to lay her gently in the dark, rich earth. The soil was cool and welcoming on her hot skin. At once she felt a semblance of peace washing over her. Her lashes drifted down. "Tell me how it is you can speak to me when you have never taken my blood."

"It is necessary to heal you." His voice was gentle, a soft, melodic persuasion.

"I know. But how is it we are so strongly connected?"

"You are a much more powerful talent than you realize. Telepathy runs strong in you. As a child you reached for me and connected. I am an ancient with talents of my own. My need to help you was the strongest compulsion I had ever experienced. Once we had connected, you were an obsession. I could do no other than find you." His fingertips stroked back her hair.

She reached up, caught his hand. "You're not giving me an answer."

"You know the answer."

There was silence in the cave. The bubbles in the pool sent waves against the boulders, lapping gently at the rock, providing a strange music.

"How can someone be so powerful? How can you reach through time and space without a blood bond?"

"I have always had certain gifts. Once you connected with me, you were imprinted on my mind." *And in my heart and soul.* He bent his head to kiss the corner of her mouth. "Each time you connected with me, the imprint became stronger. I believe I have some sort of telepathic ability beyond the blood bond of our people."

A small shiver went down Destiny's spine. "How do I know you aren't enhancing my feelings for you? I have to know this is real."

The ache in her voice tugged at his heart, but his face remained expressionless. "That is something I cannot help you with, Destiny. You have to find out some things for yourself. Do you think I am so powerful I can make you feel desire for me?"

Her blue-green gaze drifted over his face. He found his muscles were tight, clenched, waiting. She looked ethereal, her skin translucent and her body somehow smaller. He wanted to gather her into his arms and shelter her from every further hurt. It made him crazy to see her this way, hurt and spent, all energy drained from her body. His brother was right, he should have taken charge, thrown her over his shoulder like a caveman of old and taken her to his homeland without her consent.

A small smile curved her mouth, drew his instant attention. At once the pad of his thumb brushed the velvet-soft lower lip.

"I'm reading your thoughts, Nicolae. There is a blood bond between us. The first thing, above all else, is *never* listen to that idiot brother of yours. The man never climbed out of the cave. You do all right on your own." She wanted to kiss him. He thought he was so stoic, yet she could see the hungry intensity in his eyes. A terrible anxiety that could only be real. He might be tremendously powerful and capable of all sorts of things, including controlling her, but she could see the genuine need in him, the genuine love.

"I think your pouty lower lip is extremely sexy." He bent his head to hers, brushed her mouth gently, almost reverently.

He could send butterfly wings through her stomach without trying. "You have rocks in your head," she told him lovingly, tangling her fingers in his hair. "There's nothing sexy about me." Laughter danced in her eyes. "I'm lying here in the dirt, covered in it, and you're looking at me like you might eat me. I think you need a few counseling sessions with MaryAnn. You're a bit on the kinky side." But he took her breath away and started a warm glow that wouldn't go away. He had a way of making her feel beautiful in the midst of her nightmares, even when she knew it wasn't so. He had a way of taking her out of death and violence and bringing her to a paradise she hadn't known existed. Most of all, she was never alone.

"You are obviously hallucinating and quite ill." He kissed her again, lingering over the pleasure. He showed every restraint. He didn't kiss her possessively. He didn't devour her, or pick her up and shake her. His insides were roiling like the clouds had been, a turbulent storm that wouldn't die down. He could control it, keep it from spilling out and shaking the earth around him, but he couldn't make it go away.

Her fingers involuntarily slipped away from his hair, her arm dropping to her side. "I'll agree with the quite ill part. I'm not doing a very good job of controlling my body temperature. First I was freezing, then hot, and now I'm cold all over again."

"I am going to do my best to heal you, Destiny, so lie still and do *not* give me any trouble. A man can only take so much."

His voice was far too loving for her to worry. She smiled as her lashes drifted down. "I wish I were human so I could dream about you all the time."

"I thought you did dream about me." That drowsy note in her voice caught at him. He bent his head once more to brush a kiss over her mouth. "Go ahead and sleep now, Destiny. I will put you in the shelter of the earth when I am certain all traces of the vampire's poison are gone."

She didn't answer him. The choking lump blocking her throat came out of nowhere. No matter what he did, there would be no way to erase the taint of the vampire. She had accepted it as a fact, but she wasn't certain Nicolae ever would. Or even if he could. Destiny had no idea how to resolve the problem and she was far too tired to think about it any more. She allowed herself to drift, lulled by the soothing rhythm of the water and the warmth spreading through her body as Nicolae began the slow, meticulous healing process of their kind.

Nicolae worked for a long time, repairing the damage done by the microbes, checking every organ, every vein, ensuring that there were no infected cells lurking in wait to attack again when she was at her most vulnerable. Despite his painstaking care, he felt uneasy, as if he had missed something.

He knew the moment his brother began to unravel the safeguards to enter the chamber. He heard the musical voice of his brother join with his as he chanted. As always he felt grateful for Vikirnoff with his strength and loyalty, guarding his back and ready to aid him in times of need.

Nicolae pulled out of Destiny's body, swaying with weakness. He flashed his brother a quick glance, mostly to check that no harm had come to him while they battled their enemy.

"How is she?" Vikirnoff asked courteously.

"Stubborn. Gutsy. Impossible." Nicolae's voice was clipped as he sent Destiny into a deep sleep. Only then did he allow his suppressed rage to swirl dangerously close to the surface. The earth beneath their feet rolled slightly and the water in the pool bubbled ferociously. "She should have called me to her side the instant there was a hint of trouble. If she had, none of this would have happened. Instead, her life was endangered and I nearly lost her."

Vikirnoff shrugged his shoulders with casual strength. "It makes no sense to get angry with her for not calling you to her. I see no reason for your anger."

"You were reprimanding me for allowing her to hunt in the first place, Vikirnoff. Now I am not supposed to be upset with her when she throws herself directly into the path of danger?"

"She had no one to raise her, to guide her. She was taken from her family at the age of six. Everything she has ever learned she learned from you. You taught her to hunt, to rely on herself and her own judgment. You would not have thought to call *her* to *you*. You did not think to call me to you. She does not fear death, only

capture by the undead, and you know she is determined
that will never happen again. She is like you. Independent. Courageous. Do not fault her for those traits. They
are admirable. You are the one capable of stopping her.
Force her back to our homeland."

Nicolae wanted to argue with his brother. He wanted
to point out he was far more experienced, far less vulnerable and much more powerful than Destiny, but none
of that changed the truth of Vikirnoff's words. She was
acting just as he had taught her. She hadn't called him
because she was accustomed to relying on herself. She
hadn't sensed the immediate danger because she had
been thinking about Nicolae. He knew a good part of
his reaction was fear for her, but another part was based
on the incorrect assumption that after he made love to
her, she would turn to him naturally.

Sighing, Nicolae raked a hand through his hair, leaving it more disheveled than ever. "I am not going to say
you are right because I could not take it if you smirked."

"I do not smirk," Vikirnoff claimed.

"Yes, you do. And I detest that after all these centuries, you are making sense. Frankly, it is scary."

"It is only that you are not making sense since you
acquired a lifemate. I hope that does not happen to all
men. It would be a shame."

"Your sense of humor is not improving," Nicolae
pointed out dryly.

"I do not have a sense of humor," Vikirnoff answered.

"I had not noticed," Nicolae teased. His smile faded
quickly. "She did well."

Vikirnoff nodded. "Yes, she is a worthy lifemate to
you. I did not think I would think so with her tainted

blood and her wild ways, but she is courageous. A call was put out not long ago. The lifemate of one of our people was with child and lay dying. Healers were sent for, and our people were called to join together to help perform the healing ritual, even from afar."

Nicolae's heart leapt with hope. "That is so. It was not far from here. The healers must still be with the woman. One of them was Gregori."

There was silence between them. Vikirnoff shared his brother's mind during their battles with the undead, making it easier to coordinate their battle plans. They both had heard the vampire whispering his cruel words to Destiny. He had told her the Prince would not accept her. That Gregori would hunt her. That no one would want her near the other women. They both had felt the answering shame in Destiny. The vampire had known exactly what to say to play on her fear and humiliation.

"She will not accept him. She will run."

Vikirnoff shook his head. "You have no choice but to call him here. He will soon leave for our homeland. You will never get her to go there after what was said. She believes there is no cure for her. Call him. He can do no other than answer. You will find a way to persuade her to accept his healing power."

Nicolae turned the idea over in his mind. Vikirnoff made sense.

"It is possible there is no cure," Nicolae pointed out.

Vikirnoff shrugged. "One can only try."

Before he could change his mind, Nicolae sent the call on the common Carpathian path. *Hear me, healer. We have great need. The blood of the vampire torments my lifemate on every rising. I do not want to lose her. It is a beacon for the undead and prevents our complete joining. I ask that you come when you have assured the life of the woman you are aiding.*

There was a space of time. Water bubbled and the flames flickered on the cave walls. Gems sparkled in the ceiling overhead one moment, then were gone the next. The answer came. There were no questions. No demand to know who Nicolae was or how his lifemate had gotten into such a condition. *I will come at once. We will start out next rising.* It was the Carpathian way of selfless service, and Nicolae's heart was so full he could not reply.

"Thank you, Vikirnoff. He will come." Nicolae reached inside his shirt, extracted a rumpled photograph. "A vampire visited MaryAnn in her office and planted a compulsion to call the number on his business card if this woman should come to her seeking sanctuary. I think we need to find her and do our best to protect her. I cannot leave at this time. Will you begin the search? We can make copies of the photograph— MaryAnn has such a machine—and distribute them among our people."

Vikirnoff took the photo, glanced at it without much interest, stiffened and swung his gaze back to the photo, studying it carefully. "Who is this woman?"

"He did not give a name. There was little memory of the conversation and no memory of the vampire himself. I could not 'see' him in MaryAnn's memories. Why? Do you recognize her?"

"Is this photograph in color, Nicolae?" He didn't look at his brother, but continued staring at the picture as if mesmerized.

Nicolae watched as the pad of Vikirnoff's thumb

caressed the face looking back at him from the glossy paper. "Yes, it is. Do you recognize her?" he asked again, never having seen Vikirnoff exhibit interest in any woman.

"I have seen her face. Her eyes. It was not real; it was in a dream. Long ago, Nicolae, in a dream. Her hair was as black as midnight and her eyes were as blue as the sea when it is clear and calm. It is the only color I remember, that deep blue of her eyes. I never let go of that memory. Are her eyes blue? In the photo, are her eyes blue? A striking, vivid blue?"

Nicolae's heart surged with hope. "Yes, Vikirnoff. Her eyes are blue and her hair is midnight black. You never told me of such a dream."

Vikirnoff shrugged, but his gaze was glued to the photograph. "There was no reason to tell you of such a thing. A dream only. What do you know of her?"

"We believe she is human and has psychic talent. The vampire indicated she had the gift of psychometry. That is all we know. He claimed he was from a research center for psychics and that they wanted to help her. She is running from someone, probably the vampire. I think it best our people find her first."

"It could take years, Nicolae. I cannot leave you now, while you are surrounded by vampires and hampered by a lifemate who could very well endanger you without realizing it. Her blood is tainted. We do not know if it can be fixed. I do not want to lose you, Nicolae. You know how close I am to the end. Should something go wrong here with you and your lifemate, it will also go wrong with me. Here, I can aid you. Searching for this mythical woman, I can do nothing for you."

Nicolae waved the protest aside. "I'm a hunter, a protector of our people, as are you. We can do no other than what is expected of us. Our honor demands it."

"I will begin the search in a rising or two. It is best to show her picture to some of the local people. If she was in the area, or is expected, perhaps someone knows of her. It will give me a starting point."

"It is possible the vampire managed to get to Mary-Ann before this woman made her way to Seattle," Nicolae mused aloud. "Velda would be the one to ask. Nothing gets by Velda and Inez."

Vikirnoff visibly shuddered. "Perhaps you should speak with them. It is best if I stay in the background."

Nicolae's eyebrows shot up. He remained silent, watching his brother with evident amusement.

"I see no reason for your new, strange humor, Nicolae. It is a matter of logic. The women know you and will tell you things they would not reveal to me."

Nicolae snorted. "You are a coward. You are afraid of a couple of sweet elderly ladies. I had no idea."

"Speaking with little old ladies is enough to shake the very foundations of a man," Vikirnoff pointed out reasonably. "They flap their arms and screech like chickens. In truth there is no fear involved, only the painful reality that they will draw undue attention to my existence."

Nicolae sat abruptly on the edge of a boulder. "There is some truth to what you say. I must confess I feel some small affection for Velda and Inez, although I do not know how it happened. They are frightening to me also. Velda has talent. She knows things I would like to better explore. Do you have any idea what is causing these humans to behave at odds with their true nature?"

Vikirnoff shrugged his shoulders. "I cannot detect

the touch of a vampire. It is unsettling. The poison used on your lifemate was much more sophisticated than I have ever seen. I do not like the fact that there is some semblance of order among the vampires and someone is orchestrating a great war plan we have never before seen."

"It is possible Gregori knows of this. He is second to the Prince and shares all his information. If they can use such a trap to attack me, it can also be used against our Prince, and he should be alerted to the possibility."

Vikirnoff studied Nicolae's pale face. "You are not taking proper care of yourself. It is necessary for you to be at full strength to fight the call of her blood. If you succumb, we do not know what will happen. I have never heard of such a case before, and we have no way of knowing what to expect." It was a reprimand, delivered in Vikirnoff's usual forthright manner.

Nicolae sighed. "You just have to act the older brother with me."

"If finding one's lifemate means throwing away all reason, I am uncertain whether it is such a good thing." Even as he uttered the words, his thumb slid once more in an unknowing caress over the face of the woman in the photograph.

Nicolae held out his hand. "I will take the picture to MaryAnn's office and make copies for you and show it to Velda and Inez."

Vikirnoff hesitated uncharacteristically. He shoved the photograph inside his shirt. "I will make the copies myself and give you one to show the human women." Vikirnoff stepped forward. "You must feed." He tore his wrist open with his teeth, extended his arm to his brother.

Nicolae bent his head to the life-giving fluid. *This is becoming a regular habit.*

"I have noticed. I am fast gaining the reputation of being a glutton, feeding for both of us," Vikirnoff said dryly.

The ancient blood, strong and healing, rushed through Nicolae's body, filling shriveled cells, bringing strength and power to muscle and tissue. He took what he needed, knowing he would be replenishing Destiny on the next rising. Carefully, respectfully, he closed the wound.

"Thank you for always being my brother," he said formally.

Vikirnoff nodded without replying, his form already shimmering. *I will find my own resting place, close enough to be called should there be need, but far enough to afford privacy.*

The flames from the urn sputtered and went out as if a small breeze had moved through the chamber. A wealth of healing aromas filled the cavern and drifted deep into Nicolae's lungs. He stretched, feeling the tension in his body slowly begin to fade. There were still remnants of anger and fear at the thought of what had been, what could have happened, but Vikirnoff had managed to calm the turbulent storm.

Nicolae began the complicated weaving of difficult safeguards at all entrances to the mountain and the network of caves. He didn't want to find himself sharing their resting place with a vampire this night. Deepening the resting place so that Destiny had even richer soil to welcome her, he floated down into the arms of the earth.

At the next rising he intended to find a way to lock Destiny closer to him, find a way to force her acceptance of a healing by the Prince's second-in-command. He could be as ruthless as the next hunter if the situation called for it, and he believed this one would. Destiny was not likely to welcome Gregori, nor would she thank Nicolae for summoning the healer.

Nicolae gathered Destiny into his arms and waved his hand to command the earth to close over them. The soil was warm, welcoming and soothing. He held her close, brushed the top of her head with his lips and allowed his heart to cease beating.

Chapter Fifteen

She woke to the scent of flowers. She was no longer in the earth but lying on a bed with silken sheets. She could feel the silk on her bare skin, already arousing her body as the silk rubbed against her with every movement. Her hair was unbound and fell in a mass around her on the pillows. Destiny inhaled deeply, drawing the fragrance of flowers and her lifemate's masculine scent into her lungs. A small smile curved her mouth.

"Nicolae. You're here with me." She opened her eyes, turned her head to look at him. Drank in the hard angles and planes of his face. The sensuality of his mouth. The beauty of his eyes.

"Where else would I be but with my lifemate?" He was sitting on the edge of the bed, his gaze drifting lovingly over her face like the touch of fingers. His voice was a caress, a velvet stroke that reached deep within her and sent every nerve ending into overdrive.

With an effort, Destiny tore her eyes from his, her

amazed stare moving around the chamber to take in what he had done for her. There was no chance for the stench of evil to enter their hidden world. Roses were everywhere. Climbing up the walls of the cavern. Forming an overhead canopy of flowers. Some floated on the surface of the coolest pool. Others sprang up among the rocks. Roses of all colors with soft, inviting petals and beautiful fragrance to please her.

Destiny's smile widened and she turned back to Nicolae. "You took Velda and Inez seriously, didn't you? Should I expect chocolate and the interesting things that can be done with it?"

His fingertip traced her soft skin from her throat, down the valley between her breasts, to her flat stomach. The small caress sent a curling heat spiraling through her body. "I was very afraid to ask Inez for the details of what exactly to do with the chocolate, so I skipped that part. I liked their idea of flowers, though."

There was a note in his voice that turned her heart over. "I like it too." She was very much aware of lying naked on the bed, her body soft and open to his inspection. A part of her wanted to cover up, feeling suddenly shy, but there was another, much stronger side that whispered of seduction. That reveled in the way his eyes were dark and hungry as his gaze moved possessively over her. She loved to see his body, so hard and aggressive, reacting to the sight of her. And she loved knowing that he liked what he saw.

Nicolae picked up her arm and turned it over as if inspecting the thin white scars marring her skin. The scars shouldn't have been there after her body had been repaired by Carpathian blood, but she had been converted by a vampire and those scars would remain for all time. Her heart accelerated in reaction. He bent his dark head and placed his lips gently against the scars, feathering kisses along her sensitive inner arm and wrist.

Destiny felt her stomach somersault in reaction. His lips traveled to her fingers, drawing first one, than another into the searing heat of his mouth. Her mouth went dry. His gaze suddenly locked with hers and she caught a glimpse of the flames burning in his belly, tightening his groin, hardening every muscle in his body. At once she caught fire, her own body restless and hot and needy. Without meaning to, she moved her hips against the silken sheets, her legs shifting in invitation.

It was shocking to her that she could catch fire so quickly, need him so much, want him in every way. A part of her would always hesitate, remain linked to her violent past, but looking into his eyes, Destiny was willing to be lost in him. In his fantasies. In his possession. She was willing to trust him with her body because she could feel the depth of his love.

He bent his head to hers. His hair caressed her skin with thousands of silky strands. Tiny flames seemed to leap over her skin. Electricity arced and sizzled between them. His mouth found hers. Hot. Hard. Totally possessive. While his hands were gentle and his movement slow and leisurely, his mouth was wildly possessive. Taking hers. Devouring hungrily. Feeding on her as if he would never get enough.

His kiss ignited a like storm of need and urgency in her. Her temperature rose several degrees. Her mouth took his just as hungrily, matching him kiss for kiss. She arched into him, her breasts thrusting upward invitingly. She felt tight and swollen and ached desperately for his touch.

His hand found her throat, slid lower to capture her breast. A soft sound of contentment escaped her; the sensations were so strong, so right. Her hips lifted in blatant invitation. He raised his head to look at her. "Have I told you that I love you?" he asked softly in his beautiful voice. The one that always melted her insides.

She went boneless. Helpless under his spell of enchantment. "If you haven't, you've certainly shown me." He had shown her what love was supposed to be. Unconditional. Loving without reservation, with total acceptance. "I feel very lucky at this moment," she confessed.

It was a great concession for her, an admission not made lightly. She wanted him with every bone in her body. Every nerve ending screamed for his possession.

He had other ideas. "I want to get to know you the way a lifemate should." His tongue swirled around her nipple, his breath warmed her. "I have a need to explore every inch of you."

His mouth closed over her breast, hot and moist and unbelievably possessive. She cried out, unable to contain the blossoming fire exploding in her belly. She could feel her body tighten relentlessly, mercilessly. She had never felt such a buildup of pressure so quickly, so fast. "Exploring should wait."

He smiled against her soft skin. "Leisurely exploring. Did I mention leisurely? I want to take my time."

She closed her eyes as wave after wave of sensation rocked her. "How much time?" She gasped out the words. "I don't know if I can take it."

There was silence as his mouth pulled strongly at her

breast. His tongue laved and lavished attention on her nipples until she cried out again, circling his head with her arms to cradle him to her. There was no room for anything other than joy. Need. Sheer physical pleasure. The sensations rushed through her, filled her with fire and left her breathless and craving more.

Nicolae's hands began a slow, intimate search of her body. The pads of his fingers smoothed over her skin like a blind man memorizing texture and shape. It was the most shattering experience she'd ever had. Her body fragmented beneath his caresses, came apart, the sensations so powerful she couldn't hold still beneath his seeking hands. If he had not managed to tie them completely together before, he was doing so now. She would never be able to be apart from him, never be free of the craving for his touch.

She felt as if she were bound to him for all eternity, body and soul. There was not a place on or in her body that did not crave him. Her mind sought his. Her body throbbed for his possession. He was everywhere, finding every shadow, every hollow. Taking his time almost reverently, committing her to memory.

His mouth followed his hands. Tiny little kisses designed to drive her out of her mind. He paid particular attention to every trigger spot that made her gasp and writhe on the silken sheets. Every soft hidden shadow that brought her hips up off the bed. His tongue dipped into her intriguing belly button, one of the many places that fascinated him, even while his hands found the tight thatch of curls, the tiny triangle guarding her treasure.

He felt the first ripple of unease from her. Nicolae was prepared this time, knowing she felt intensely vulnerable and open to him. He stroked her gently, his hand cupping her dampness. "This is for me, Destiny, your body welcoming mine to you. Can you imagine how this makes me feel? The sight and scent of your welcome when I have been alone for so long? The way you make me feel that you really want me, that you have to have my body in the same way I need yours?" He whispered the words, bending his head to the junction between her legs as if seeking nectar.

Destiny could feel his breath warm on her moist feminine channel. He blew softy, and her body rippled with pleasure instead of fear. Nicolae parted her thighs, his finger pushing slowly, gently, into the hot, wet core of her. At once her small muscle clamped around him, gripped with hot, slick velvet. She shuddered in reaction and pushed against his hand, needing him deeper inside her. His tongue tasted her. It was the smallest of caresses, but she nearly jumped out of her skin, her cry one of pleading more than of objection.

Then his tongue probed boldly, a strong, demanding stroke that sent her skyrocketing. She screamed, catching fistfuls of his hair to anchor herself as her body burst into a firestorm without end. There was no way to quench the fire. She could only hang on to him as he drove her ever higher, a little ruthlessly, without mercy. Claiming her, branding her, taking her for his own.

She let go, she had no choice, allowing him the intense satisfaction of driving her over the edge. Her orgasm was so strong she shuddered with it, writhing beneath him, keening his name in an inarticulate sound.

Destiny was barely aware of his knees pushing hers further apart, of his thighs settling between hers. She felt him, large and thick and hot, pulsing with life and need, pushing into her body. He was bigger than she remembered, filling her as he invaded, pressing tightly into her as he slowly began to settle his weight over her. The feel of him inside her was beyond pleasure, beyond her previous experience with him. He belonged. She knew it. She knew she was made for him alone. They fit. No matter that there was some slight stretching and adjusting, no matter that he had to tilt her hips to accommodate him. They fit together as if one single body.

Once deep inside her, he stopped moving, to look down at her, to assure himself that she was unafraid. He was pinning her down with the weight of his body, his hands curled around her hips. She felt his power and strength, knew in that precise heartbeat that he could dominate her will, take over her life. That she would fade to nothing without him.

Fear clouded her eyes. She blinked it away. She had the same power over him. She would not allow fear to keep her from what she wanted. This man. This one man. Her dark and wonderful hunter. It was Destiny who moved first, committing her body to his. Pushing into him, setting a rhythm, inviting him to take her as he wanted.

Nicolae sensed the wildness rising in him. His body was hot and far too tight, his belly and groin burning with urgent need. He moved, surging forward, burying himself deep inside her. A long, hard stroke that shook both of them. She lifted her hips to meet him, unafraid of the strength of his body as he picked up the rhythm, driving hard and fast, needing to empty himself. She was everything. Her body so lush and soft and inviting. He could feel the ebb and flow of her blood, calling him, enticing him.

Her breasts rocked with each hard stroke, drawing his

attention so that twice he had to dip his head to lap at her nipples. He was rewarded with her muscles clenching even tighter. Her sheath was fiery hot, so tight he could barely breathe with the intensity of his pleasure.

He'd known from the moment he awakened what he was going to do, and the excitement of it, the anticipation, had been unbearable. Now she was his. He was going to make her completely his. Destiny was made for him alone, and he wanted her, body and soul. Without reservation. He built the exquisite fire between them, taking them up to the edge over and over until she whimpered for mercy.

"I want my blood flowing in your veins." He whispered the temptation. "I will not give us release until you have all of me. I want to be here, buried deep in your body. I want my mind merged deeply with yours and I want my blood in your veins."

There was no way to resist. The craving was already on her, lengthening her incisors so that she lifted her head toward the broad expanse of chest he was offering her. His scent enveloped her. His body was swelling more. The friction was scalding, searing her to her soul. She stroked his skin with her tongue and without further preamble sank her teeth deep, connecting them in the way they were meant to be.

He cried out, his voice strained with the pleasure-pain, the white-hot ecstasy pouring into both of them like molten lava. The flames danced over skin and muscles. Her body tightened around his, her muscles clenching strongly, demandingly. His life force, his ancient gift, filled her as his body filled her.

His hips drove harder, plunged deeper. He knew the moment she reached the pinnacle. The moment her

body clutched his, taking him with her over the edge.
Her tongue swept the pinpricks to close the tiny holes,
to allow her to breathe, to cry out her pleasure to the
roses, to the gods. He went willingly, pouring into her,
allowing her to take the last drop of his essence.

Nicolae lay pinning her to the silken sheets with his
larger, stronger body, his arms tightly around her. Their
hearts were pounding together, her body rippling around
his, still tightly gripping him. He moved the thick mass
of her hair from her shoulder, baring her skin, her breast
to his gaze. Very slowly, as if afraid of frightening her,
he lowered his weight more fully, burying his face in
the soft column of her throat.

He cupped her breast in his palm possessively, his
breath hot on her skin. They were locked together, his
body unbelievably as hard as ever. As thick as ever.
As in need as ever. "Hold me, Destiny." The words were
whispered against her ear. He nuzzled her neck, his lips
feathering over her skin.

Her arms circled his neck immediately. Her body was
still alive with aftershocks. When he moved she could
feel her muscles clenching and unclenching, making her
gasp each time with renewed pleasure. She drifted in
the pleasure, the complete harmony between them, holding him close to her, loving the feel of his masculine
body against the softness of hers.

Without warning his arms became hard and immov-
able, his teeth sank deep into her pulsing neck. Lightning struck, arcing and sizzling through her body,
through his. Pain and pleasure mingled, gave way to
ecstasy, a dazzling fire that consumed them both. He
drank deeply, his body once more moving in hers. Hard.

Insistent. Thrusting deep as if he were attempting to reach her very soul.

Nicolae! No! She wailed the words, fought to stay focused on the danger. The pleasure was so intense, it was difficult to think straight. To remember that what was happening was wrong.

She didn't want the fever again, the desire that was fast becoming obsession. She didn't want the urgency that was already taking hold of her. One of them had to be sane in the world of erotic pleasure. Destiny needed to protect him more than she needed her own pleasure. She tried to pry his head away from where it was clamped to her neck.

Nicolae! Stop! You don't know what you're doing. You must stop. What you're doing is dangerous.

She tried to be the cool voice of reason in the midst of the leaping flames. It was impossible to penetrate the sweeping ecstasy overcoming his senses. Destiny fisted her hands in his hair and tugged hard, but his mouth pulled strongly at her neck. Her body reacted wildly to his, spiraling out of control before she could prevent it. Every nerve ending was alive. Her skin was on fire, her insides erupting with pleasure, shaking her as he took them over the edge so fast and hard she could barely catch her breath.

"Nicolae! Please. Please listen to me." He was too strong. She couldn't prevent the disaster, and her body betrayed her, caught in the fiery tango with his. Tears beaded on her lashes as she pleaded with him. "Do this for me. Stop and think."

It is already too late. Your blood flows in my veins. We are the same. His voice was completely calm. Completely accepting. His tongue swept across her throat, and he lifted his head so that his gaze glittered down into hers.

Black obsidian. The words were in her mind as she stared up at his eyes. The rush took them both, a tremendous, mind-shattering orgasm that shook them, yet they stared at each other without blinking. The release rocked them both; they allowed it to slide away. Neither moved. Neither spoke.

Very slowly the terrible hardness of his arms melted away and he reluctantly released her so that she could move her head. Her neck throbbed. "You knew what you were doing." She said the words aloud. Tested them. Even thinking the words made her feel guilty. She had been so caught up in making love, she was certain he must have been overcome by the temptation of the moment.

"Of course. You are my lifemate. We belong together as one. Where you are, so am I. You fear the Prince will not accept you. Now I share your fate. What happens to one happens to the other."

Her stomach rolled. She pushed hard at the wall of his chest. "Get off of me! Get off now!" When he rolled off of her, she scrambled up from the bed and glared down at him. "How could you do that? How could you deliberately take what we had and twist it into something so wrong?"

He sat up, watching her calmly with dark, thoughtful eyes. "What is it you think I have done, Destiny?"

"You took him inside you!" she yelled at him. "You *invited* his entry. If you really knew me, really knew how I felt, you could never have done such a thing. The loathing. The sickness. He lives in me. I can't make him go away. You let him win." She stumbled against the cave wall, mindless of the roses, and slid down to the floor. "Nicolae, you let him win." She began to weep quietly, her knees drawn up, her head in her hands.

Nicolae sighed softly. He could have taken anything but her tears. He had expected anger. He could easily deal with her anger, had been prepared to deal with it. But not her tears. And not just any tears. She wept as if her heart were breaking. As if there were no hope. How was a man supposed to handle such a thing without his heart shattering into pieces?

He glided across the distance between them to sit carefully beside her. Close. But not touching. She didn't look up at him. "Destiny, I had to find a way to make you understand how much you matter to me."

She made a small sound, shook her head and looked up. "This is your answer? This is what you thought you'd do to show me you care? Are you crazy or just stupid?"

"I thought about it a long time. There is no other way. You do not see anything but the difference in your blood."

She swept the cloud of hair from her face and glared at him. "It's no small thing, Nicolae. It isn't as if we're talking about my family tree here. We're talking about tainted blood. Don't you get it? It calls the undead to me. You cannot ever creep up on them and surprise them. Not ever again. They will always know when you are in the vicinity. You're a hunter, and you just lost your edge and put yourself in terrible danger." She rubbed her hands over her face again. "Oh, Nicolae, how could you do something so ridiculous?" There was despair in her voice.

"Destiny." His voice whispered over her skin. "Look at me, little one. I have only bound us together more tightly. Our blood bond will not harm me. I am strong, able to fight any darkness. I have you as an anchor to hold me."

"You were *my* anchor," she cried, looking up at him. It was a mistake. She was instantly caught and held in the dark depths of his eyes. He was looking at her with such love, she couldn't look away from him. She couldn't condemn him. "I *needed* to know I could keep you safe."

He smiled at her, reached down to lace his fingers through hers. He brought her hand to the warmth of his mouth, brushing kisses along her knuckles. "I am safe. The moment I heard you cry out all those years ago, I was safe."

"You don't understand. I wanted to know we could be together and I wouldn't be the one to harm you. I wanted the vampire far away from you." There was a terrible sadness in her voice.

Nicolae shifted closer to her, his bare thigh settling next to hers. "You must hear me in this. He was never far away from me. Never. I was there with you from the moment you first merged with me. I felt the pain and the humiliation of what he did to you. I *chose* to share all of it with you, so I would know firsthand what it was like to be so helpless and vulnerable to a powerful and evil being. All the while, I was ashamed I could not find you and protect you as I should have been able to do. That vampire walked in my thoughts and in my body and ate away at my soul. Every time he put his filthy hands on you, he tore out my heart. He was never far from me."

Destiny hung her head, shamed. "I couldn't let you

go. I knew I should, I knew I should never have connected in the first place, but your voice saved me. Even as a child I knew I should let you go. I needed you desperately."

"As I needed you. You do not seem to be able to comprehend that I needed you just as desperately. The beast was strong in me. I had come to the end of my days. You gave my life purpose and meaning. And you brought love into my world. I now see colors where there was only barren gray. I feel emotions, where my life was endless monotony. Your need was no greater than mine."

"I still feel ashamed that I brought him into your life." *She had led a monster to her parents. And now she had allowed him to find Nicolae.*

Nicolae tugged at her hand until she lifted her head. He brought their clasped hands to his heart. "I have seen this tragedy so often over the centuries. The things we think of as our sins as a child cannot be released even as adults. It is sad we cannot let go, because those things color our lives. Think of that poor little boy who will always believe he was responsible for his mother's death simply because he didn't do the dishes. He will never feel worthy of love."

Destiny leaned into the wall of flowers. She knew very well what he was saying to her. "Where are the thorns?"

"Thorns? What are you talking about?"

"On the roses. Where are the thorns?"

Nicolae looked puzzled as he nibbled on her fingers. "I would never leave thorns on the plants. You might be injured."

Destiny burst out laughing. She couldn't help it. "Nicolae, do you have any idea how absolutely silly that is? We hunt vampires. We have tainted blood flowing in our veins. I don't think getting scratched by a thorn is going to harm me."

He shrugged his shoulders. "I do not like your hunting vampires, and I hope to rid you of the tainted blood. It is unnecessary to risk your getting scratched by a thorn if I can prevent it." He sounded perfectly reasonable.

Destiny groaned, trying not to notice the way her heart was melting at his words. Trying not to notice the brush of butterfly wings fluttering in her stomach at the touch of his lips against her skin. "You're going to be one of those overprotective idiots who are always tripping over their own feet trying to rescue the fainting little woman, aren't you?"

He winced visibly. "I do not much care for the image you are conjuring up. I would put it in a much better way. I do feel it is my duty and right to protect you."

She rolled her eyes and heaved an exaggerated sigh. "You are one of those he-man kind of rescuers. Something in *your* childhood maybe. Perhaps we need to explore your psyche a bit."

His eyebrows shot up. "I do not think it is necessary. Protecting one's lifemate is as necessary as breathing."

"Really?" Destiny stood up, pulled him up beside her. "Next time you decide to make a decision like taking tainted blood, you might want to consult me first. I might hit you over the head if you pull something like that again."

He found himself grinning down at her exasperated expression. "You have problems with authority."

She tossed her head, her eyes sparkling with mischief.

Waves of dark hair spilled around her face and down her shoulders. "Fortunately, I don't acknowledge anyone as an authority, so there's no problem whatsoever." She clothed herself in the manner of the Carpathian people. She did so smoothly, naturally, without hesitation. She had been six years old when she'd been taken from her family. She knew more of the Carpathian way than the human way. "If the Prince doesn't like me all that much, well"—she shrugged—"it's perfectly fine with me."

He caught her chin, lifted her gaze to his. "You need to perfect the art of lying if you are going to be telling such tales."

She shrugged, unrepentant. "I'm going to have to figure out what to do with you, Nicolae. I hadn't planned to let you in my life, and you've turned everything upside down. What exactly are we supposed to do? It isn't as if we can have any kind of a normal life. We certainly can't have those children you seemed to want."

"Why not?"

Her eyes glittered with sudden fire. "Your blood, thanks to your being so stubborn and impetuous, is *tainted*. Or had you forgotten?" There was still a trace of accusation in her voice, and for a moment the flames leapt in her gaze.

He clothed himself in his usual elegant style, turning away from her to hide his amusement. She wouldn't be pleased that he thought her humorous when she was scolding. "I am stuck on the word impetuous. Surely that does not describe my carefully thought-out action."

She did glare at him then. "Don't remind me you weren't overcome with passion; it was the only excuse I had for you. What were you thinking, Nicolae? We don't know what that blood might do to you. It burns and corrupts, and you have darkness lurking in you. I've seen glimpses of it more than once. I'd hate to have to rip out your heart in the early morning hours when you least expected it, but if you give me any trouble and start exhibiting any vamp behavior, you're gone." She said the last with more glee than reluctance.

Nicolae couldn't help the laughter spilling out of him at her audacity. "I will be certain to watch myself."

"Seriously, Nicolae, if you thought about it ahead of time and planned it out so carefully, what good did you think would come of it?"

There was a sudden silence. He made no response, but all at once he seemed different, no longer the relaxed lifemate lounging in his lair. She could feel waves of power, of strength; she recognized the danger in him. And he was watching her with the unblinking stare of a predator. For a moment she stood blinking up at him, her heart jumping in her chest. She found herself taking a step backward, away from him.

Nicolae reached out to recapture her hand. "Do not look at me with fear in your eyes. You are my lifemate, bound to me for all time. I would never hurt you, Destiny. It would be impossible to do such a thing."

"We're joking about tainted blood, but what if it's not a joke? What if you turn? I couldn't really kill you. I know I couldn't make myself do it."

His smile softened the hard angles of his face. "I am pleased to hear such a reluctant admission. Never fear, Vikirnoff would take care of such a matter should there be need. I am not worried. If I must live with tainted blood, so be it. I believe the healer can rid us of it, however."

Her stomach somersaulted. There it was. Out in the open at last. "The healer," she echoed. "You keep speaking of a healer. You tried to heal me, but the tainted blood is still there." Nicolae was a miracle worker. She had seen firsthand what he could do. If he was unable to succeed in ridding her body of the vampire's contaminated blood, then no one could do such a thing.

"Our people have healers much greater than I will ever be. They are born into a line of ancients who carry this talent. They are the true miracle workers for our people. There is one close to us. The call went out for healers to save a pregnant woman with heart disease. I believe the woman and the baby are alive and doing well. I summoned one of the healers to us."

Her hand went to her throat defensively, as if she expected wolves to tear it out. "This is another one of your brilliant arbitrary decisions?"

"I thought it best. If he can heal us, we will have a normal life together." He ignored her disbelieving snort. "If he cannot, you will never feel alone in this world. If our people choose to condemn us, we will still be together."

She closed her eyes, turned away from him so he couldn't see the expression on her face. "You took the chance of living the rest of your immortal life as an outcast? Just so I wouldn't feel alone?" She wanted to shake him until his teeth rattled. She wanted to kiss him until they both fell back on the bed senseless. She wanted to weep for the strength of his love and commitment.

"You are my life, my very soul, Destiny. I could do no other."

His simple words shook her. Could someone really love another that much? So selflessly? She let her breath out slowly, trying to regain a semblance of composure. "Who is this paragon of virtue with such a talent?"

"He is called 'the dark one.' He is a descendant of a great line of hunters, and second-in-command to our Prince. He guards our Prince and is a renowned healer. He holds power in his mind and hands. I believe he is the one who will be able to help us. He is called Gregori."

Destiny couldn't prevent the involuntary shiver of fear at the dreaded name. She had heard of Gregori. Every vampire feared him, feared his judgment. She had grown up with the whispered curses of the undead if the name was spoken aloud. She squared her shoulders. "What if he can't help us and he tells his Prince we're vampire, Nicolae? He'll hunt us, and he's said to be very powerful."

Nicolae shrugged his shoulders casually. "I am an ancient, Destiny, older than Gregori. He cannot defeat me. I live by the code of the Carpathian people. He would not condemn me for tainted blood."

"You're always so sure of yourself, Nicolae. This was your decision, and because you took such a chance with your life, I have no choice but to agree. I would never have called this man into my life." Comprehension blossomed. "You took my blood so I would be forced to accept this healer. You knew I wouldn't otherwise."

Nicolae looked unrepentant. Destiny glared at him. "I have things to do tonight. I want to see Sam, and I'm hoping to talk to Velda and Inez about what's going on in the neighborhood. You might undo the safeguards for me." She didn't want to talk to him anymore. Or look at him. Delivering a swift kick might have eased some of her frustration, but she doubted it. He had outmaneuvered her and she knew it.

She had no choice but to accept Gregori's ministrations, although she feared him. She cared nothing about herself, but Nicolae was everything to her. She didn't want the tainted blood to begin its ugly work on him. He might have only a small amount, but eventually the blood would start its corruption, burning like acid. The pain would begin at every rising. He would grow to hate her. He would hold her in contempt. How could he not?

"Because it was my choice, Destiny," Nicolae assured her, easily reading her thoughts. He had not considered that she would think such a thing.

"It won't matter, Nicolae. As time goes on and your people do not accept you, as the pain spreads and the corruption grows so you have to fight it every single moment of your existence, you will forget the why and how of it and only remember you did it because of me."

"I fought the growing darkness, an evil far stronger than this tainted blood, every moment of my life from my two hundredth year. It crouched in me, waiting for one moment of weakness. Why would you think, now, when I have you, that I would succumb to such an abomination?"

She paced across the floor, caught between tears and anger. "I don't know, Nicolae. You shouldn't have done it; you shouldn't have taken such a chance with your life. With your soul. I *lived* with such a monster. I feel like he's reaching for us from his grave, reaching to rip us apart."

"Nothing, no one, will take you away from me," Nicolae stated in his perfectly calm voice. There was no bragging note or false bravado; it was simply a statement of fact.

Destiny looked up at the hard planes of his face. She saw his raw power and complete confidence, and some of her tension melted away. She allowed her breath to escape in a little rush. "I hope you're as good as you think you are, hotshot, because if this Gregori person is coming to pay us a visit, you might need to be." She held up her hand. "I have things to do, places to go, people to see."

"Are you *dismissing* me?"

"You have trouble with separation issues too, don't you? I think you should go visit MaryAnn. I'm going to see Inez and Velda. I suppose you could come if you really insist. They'll love the roses."

He groaned aloud, caught her firmly and kissed her until she was breathless and kissing him back.

Chapter Sixteen

Destiny found the sisters in their usual spot on the sidewalk with their lawn chairs set out and ready for company. They hugged her with far more enthusiasm than she would have liked, especially with the echo of Nicolae's laughter in her mind. Destiny was still uncomfortable with physical contact, but Inez and Velda hugged and kissed her, patting her encouragingly as if she were a child they adored.

You do not dislike physical contact with me. Nicolae deliberately teased her, knowing she would react, but she would laugh, too, and the exchange would leave her amused and relaxed.

I still want to kick you, Destiny said, shutting him out firmly. Inez was already attempting to teach her a dance step she'd just learned from a video.

"Come, dear." Inez took her hand, attempting to force Destiny's hips into swaying appropriately to the metallic music screeching from the boom box beside their chairs.

"Sister, she should learn the tango, not that step. It isn't romantic enough," Velda objected. "Your young man is quite fond of you, Destiny. He's learning the ways of true courtship, very rare in this day and age."

"I can't thank you enough for giving him pointers," Destiny said. "He admitted you were the ones who thought of the roses. They were lovely." She moved carefully away from Inez, smiling as she did so. "I'm not much of a dancer, Inez, but you move so beautifully."

The sisters twittered, pleased that Nicolae had taken their advice to heart. "Did you get your chocolates, dear?" Inez asked slyly.

"I'm looking forward to that pleasure," Destiny lied, blushing for no other reason than that the two women had such wicked thoughts in their heads.

Inez looked dreamy. "It will be a memory to treasure," she advised.

"What I really came by for was to get more information about these strange incidents. Nicolae is helping me look into them, and I thought you might have some more information for us," Destiny said hastily. "Do either of you remember similar events happening in the past?" Destiny asked. She seated herself in the chair between the two elderly ladies. "Something weird? Someone acting completely out of character?"

Inez made clucking sounds as she thought it over. "Why, yes, dear, now that you ask. Sister, you remember poor Blythe Madison. She's in the mental institution now. What a sweet girl she was."

"Oh, yes, Inez, I had forgotten that poor girl. We visited her a few times, but she was unresponsive and her husband told us our visits only seemed to upset her. We should have continued to make inquiries, though."

"Sister, how awful we are." Inez's hands fluttered to her throat. She looked distressed. "We haven't even asked about her lately. Poor Harry, he probably thinks everyone's forgotten about her. Poor, dear man, carrying such a burden alone."

"Blythe had no other family," Velda continued. "Just poor Harry. He was so bewildered when she cracked up."

"Blythe was a meek little thing," Inez added. "She would hardly speak without permission. That's why it was so difficult to believe it when she began doing bizarre things. Wasn't it awful, Sister? Why, she ran down this very street waving a butcher knife, threatening everyone."

Velda nodded. "It wasn't the first incident, but it was the one that finally convinced Harry she was dangerous to herself and others. I must go visit her."

Destiny patted her arm. "I'm certain Blythe would appreciate that, Velda, but could you give me a little more detail? What was the first odd thing she did?"

"It was right after they made such a success of The Tavern," Velda said. "Blythe had the idea of making it a deli-bar, hoping to bring in the neighborhood after work and in the evening as a visiting place. It was a wonderful idea. Everyone loved it, and we all gravitated toward The Tavern in the evenings. Her idea turned the entire business around."

"You liked her," Destiny guessed.

"Very much," Velda admitted, while Inez bobbed her head with enthusiasm. "A dear, sweet girl—she'd give you the shirt off her back. She was always rescuing animals and bringing soup to anyone who was sick."

"A lovely girl," Inez reiterated wistfully. "Perfectly sensible. Everyone liked her. We should have continued to visit her, Sister."

Destiny hung on to her patience. "Do you remember what started it all?"

"We were in The Tavern to celebrate Inez's birthday," Velda said. "I remember because we were wearing party hats."

"It was my sixty-fifth birthday, a true milestone," Inez put in.

Velda rolled her eyes. "It was your seventieth birthday, Inez. You're five years older than you tell people."

"Why, Sister! Surely not. I am certain of my age."

"You're two years younger than I am."

Inez looked shocked and began to fan herself. "I am certain you're wrong, Sister. I am at least five years younger."

Velda took a breath, patted her sister lovingly. "Now that you say so, I believe you're right. I was mixed up for a moment, dear, do forgive me."

"You were telling me about the party hats," Destiny said to redirect the conversation, but she was looking at Velda with far more respect. There was genuine love and compassion in the woman's eyes as she looked at her sister.

"Well," Velda went on. "I had tried one of those new perms and my hair was all curly and sticking out from under the party hat. I was looking at myself in the mirror and laughing. Blythe was laughing with me. We pointed to each other in the mirror. She'd had a perm, too, but her hair wasn't sticking out like mine. It looked pretty. Didn't you think so, Inez?" Deliberately she drew her sister into the conversation, taking her mind off the distressing subject of age. "Didn't you think Blythe's hair was really pretty all curled the way it was?"

"Oh, yes, Sister, she looked so young."

"But the mirror shattered. It just shattered. Nothing touched it. I was looking right at it." Velda frowned. "There were slivers of glass everywhere. The mirror must have really meant something to Blythe. Maybe it was an heirloom. She just went for the closest person. She picked up a chair and smashed it over his back. Who did she hit, Sister? Do you remember?"

"That tall friend of Harry's. He isn't around much anymore. I haven't seen him but once or twice since," Inez answered. "Davis something."

"Morgan Davis." Velda pounced on the name, proud of her memory. "Of course. I didn't like him, much too cold for me, but the young girls went for him." She glanced at Destiny. "I didn't like his aura. It was off color. He worked with Harry on and off for a few months and then left town."

"That's right. Davis is very tall, and Blythe smashed that chair right over him." Inez grinned at the memory. "Everyone wanted to laugh, a little thing like her breaking that chair. But then she picked up a piece of the leg and began to hit him all over. She didn't make a sound and she wouldn't stop. Harry restrained her, didn't he, Sister?"

"The next day she didn't remember anything at all," Velda said. "When we asked her about it, she denied it. She cried. I believe she began to think there was a conspiracy against her. None of us could convince her she had actually hit Davis with a chair. She just seemed to give up after a while. She withdrew from everyone, and eventually we rarely saw her. There were four incidents about a month or so apart. Finally Harry took her to the hospital. No one's really talked to her since." Velda's hand trembled as she reached for the talisman hanging on a chain around her neck. "I was her friend. I should have continued to visit her." She looked down at the ground. "I all but forgot her."

"Velda," Destiny said in a soothing tone. "Blythe knows you're a good friend. She's unable to cope at this time, but perhaps we'll find some information that will help her." She was turning Velda's words over and over in her mind.

A mirror shattered, Nicolae. The other night, just before John Paul's strange behavior, the streetlights shattered. There must be a connection. She reached for him easily, naturally. Nicolae. Her other half.

I knew you felt that way.

His voice was far too complacent for her liking. *You are my other half, I'll admit, but you're the worst half. The ridiculous, impetuous half that must be monitored continually.*

Ah, that word again. Impetuous. Spontaneous, reckless, a lover without measure.

Destiny laughed out loud. *Where did that come from? You're dreaming again.* "Thank you for telling me, Velda, I know it isn't easy to bring up difficult memories. You're always so generous." Destiny studied the two eccentric women. The pink and purple hair. The flashy tennis shoes. Inez with her overdone makeup and Velda with a cleanly scrubbed face.

"You're extraordinary women." Destiny knew it was true. They gave service to others, watching over and caring for the people they loved. Some thought them busybodies, others thought them silly, but those were the people who didn't take time to know them. To see who they really were. "I feel privileged to have met you."

"We're not extraordinary at all, dear," Velda denied. "We live life very simply, without fear of rejection. Others don't have to understand us." As if realizing they were getting close to the topic of her hidden talents, she completely changed the subject, patting Destiny's hand as if that would distract her. "I heard what you did for that little boy. Father Mulligan came by this morning and mentioned you brought him the child. Inez and I would gladly give him a home, but we're too old." She glanced at her sister. "I'm too old, and Inez must take care of me. She has her hands full with that, don't you, Sister?"

"You're never a bother, Velda. Of course we'll take the child if he has no one else. Velda fusses and spoils them, but I'd see to it that he ate properly and went to school. She'd be useless, taking him for outings all the time and giving him junk food."

"Father Mulligan has a family in mind," Velda said. "A couple who have always wanted children and could never have any. He's helping them fill out the necessary paperwork and talking with the social workers now. I believe he was meeting your young man and taking him along."

So that's what you're up to, smoothing the way. Hope blossomed in the pit of her stomach, a starburst she tried hard to squelch. She had lived most of her life without hope, without allowing others into her life. Velda and Inez lived their lives without fear of rejection. They dressed the way they wanted to dress, and they chose to have fun in their lives. Father Mulligan had told her to have courage. She was beginning to realize that meant the courage to actually enjoy her life.

She suddenly wanted to be with Nicolae, to feel his arms around her. He had had the courage to take tainted blood from her. So she would never feel like an outcast, never feel alone. She was afraid to allow the full scope of such a magnificent sacrifice into her mind, into her heart, because she feared she might love him too much.

Destiny was instantly ashamed of herself. Nicolae deserved better than what he was getting. Impulsively she leaned over to kiss Velda, and then Inez, on their cheeks. "Thank you both. You're the best! I'm going to go grill MaryAnn. Have you seen her?"

"Well, no, dear. This is Thursday. She always does her books on Thursday and isn't fit for company."

Destiny's eyebrow shot up. That sounded intriguing. She never paid attention to what day of the week it was, but Thursday with MaryAnn sounded interesting. Destiny found the woman in her office, scowling down at a book filled with numbers. "You don't look as though you're having fun, my friend," she greeted with a sunny smile.

MaryAnn glanced up at her, a frown on her face. "I detest accounting. I always find I need far more money to go out than I managed to take in. I've stared at this page until I'm cross-eyed and I can't make the numbers change."

Destiny studied MaryAnn's large, chocolate-colored eyes. "You do look a bit cross-eyed. We can't have that. How much do you need?"

MaryAnn laughed and tossed down her pencil with a

little gesture of defeat. "Let's just say robbing a bank is beginning to look like a way out."

Destiny leaned onto the desk with both elbows and propped up her chin in her palm. "I could do that for you," she offered, straight-faced. "It's rather a specialty of mine. Walk in, sight unseen, collect what I need and get out. No one's the wiser. And doors don't stop me; neither can a safe. Where do you think the money I've donated came from?" She widened her eyes to look as innocent and sweet as possible.

There was a moment of silence. The smile faded from MaryAnn's face and she looked horrified. "Destiny, surely you didn't steal that money? I used money from a bank robbery for my sanctuary?" There was a squeak of alarm in her voice.

Destiny blinked rapidly. MaryAnn wadded up paper lying on the desk and threw it at her. "You're awful! Why do I think I like you? You almost gave me a heart attack."

"Shame on you for even thinking such a thing. Although, now that you mention it, the possibilities are endless."

"Don't even joke about it. That would really be the end of my sanctuaries. Funding is so darned difficult and with all the government scrutiny I have to make doubly certain every 'i' is dotted and every 't' is crossed."

"Are you really worried about money, MaryAnn?" Destiny asked.

"Well, of course, isn't everyone? The sanctuaries are expensive to maintain, and I try to do job training and help each family get started. A woman on the run is difficult to hide, especially if children are involved. I have some help, but it isn't easy to keep the funding going. Grants can only cover so much and we do fund-raisers, but people tend to forget if we don't keep our cause in the spotlight. When you're hiding women from violent, determined husbands, the last thing you want is publicity. It's just complex, that's all." MaryAnn sighed softly. "Don't mind me, Destiny. Thursday's are my complaining days."

Destiny grinned at her mischievously. "Actually I knew that. Velda warned me to avoid you at all costs this evening."

MaryAnn groaned and rested her head on the table. "Don't tell me the entire world knows I'm a grouch."

"Only on Thursdays," Destiny pointed out helpfully. "Come on, don't be so down. Tell me how much money you need and I'll get it for you."

MaryAnn lifted her head to regard Destiny with deep suspicion. "You *cannot* rob a bank. I'll find a way to pay this month's bills without that."

"Actually I was thinking more about robbing the drug dealer a few miles from here. He's a nasty, slimy little man and has far too much cash for his own good. Just for the fun of it, from time to time I go and destroy all his drugs."

MaryAnn sat up very straight. "You don't really do that, do you? Those kinds of people are dangerous."

Destiny shrugged. "Not to me. They can't see me. I detest them—little worms destroying lives and thinking they know what power is. Why shouldn't a sanctuary have the money? It ought to be put to some good use. I just have to be careful to keep from starting a drug war, or allowing anyone else to take the blame."

MaryAnn stared with shock at Destiny's decidedly wicked smile. "How do you do it?"

Destiny's grin widened. "I plant memories in his nasty little mind. Every now and then he has way too much to drink or he suddenly gets an attack of acute remorse. That's my personal favorite. He thinks he gave the money away but can't remember to whom, and he thinks he destroyed the drugs."

"You really do this, don't you? Does Nicolae know?"

Destiny straightened abruptly. "Did you have to bring him into this? He has nothing to do with it. I sneak into the movie theater, too, and I don't have his permission for that either." There was a note of defiance in her voice that made her sound a shade childish. It annoyed her. She didn't need to answer to Nicolae, and she wasn't apologizing for her independence. She had no idea why she was feeling guilty.

The warmth flooding her body only increased her irritation. She knew he was secretly amused. Worse, he always managed to elicit a response from her, whether physical or emotional. *I used to be a perfectly reasonable person before you got hold of me.*

"Sneaking into the movie theater is hardly the same thing. One is dangerous, one is not," MaryAnn said severely.

Is something romantic playing at the theater? I will take you there. We could have an interesting time in the back row in a dark corner. His voice was soft and seductive, playing over her skin like the caressing touch of his fingers. *I would be happy to keep you away from trouble.*

In spite of her determination, she couldn't help her

melting response. She was happy. She had never really experienced happiness. *It sounds like definite trouble to me.* But she wanted to go with him. It would be fun sitting in the theater pretending they were a regular couple madly in love and wanting to sneak a few moments together in a dark corner. *But I'll go with you.*

I think Velda and Inez are on to something here. Maybe we ought to pick up the chocolate, after all.

She loved the teasing note in his voice. *I'll let you surprise me.* She loved sharing with him. Reaching for him and having him be there with her.

"Are you listening to me, Destiny? Dealers are dangerous criminals. They think nothing of killing people. You can't do things like that, even for a good cause."

Destiny turned her attention to her friend. *Friend.* She savored the word. When she had first encountered MaryAnn, it had never occurred to her that she would one day be in her office, perched on her desk, teasing her. "Let me take a look at what you need. Fund-raising is my particular forte." She reached casually across the desk and snagged the offending book, quickly scanning the open pages before MaryAnn could snatch it away.

"No, you don't. You're impossible. Do you really like to go to movies?"

"It's my favorite thing," Destiny admitted. "I've gone to every vampire movie made. The old ones were very cool. I found them in a small theater that seems to be geared mainly for cult movies. It got to be an addiction. I'd go through every single newspaper looking for what was playing. Sometimes I'd sit through the movie twice."

"Is that where you got your fear of garlic and churches?" MaryAnn teased, pleased to turn the tables.

"Since we're talking about it, why did you accept my

being different, a vampire . . . well, a Carpathian . . . so easily?" Destiny demanded. "It really bothers me that you have no sense of self-preservation, MaryAnn."

MaryAnn threw back her head and laughed. "Easily? You think I just accepted the existence of vampires so easily? You forget I couldn't leave the church. I sat there all night long. Praying. Screaming. Crying. Wanting to run for my life. In the end, I realized that you seemed different."

"I still don't understand why you accepted me, Mary-Ann," Destiny insisted. "You should have condemned me. You should have hidden yourself from me."

MaryAnn shrugged. "I already knew you. I'd looked into your eyes. If you were going to hurt me, you would have done it a long time ago. Your eyes were . . ." She broke off, searching for the right description. "Haunted. Your eyes were haunted, and I didn't want to turn my back on you no matter what you were."

"I'm glad you didn't. Thank you, MaryAnn." Destiny was humbled by the truth. She couldn't imagine Mary-Ann turning her back on anyone.

Even as they were smiling at one another, the dark shadow of violence slipped into her mind. She sighed, slid off the desk, turned toward the door, all too aware of the man hurrying toward the office. "Stay behind me, MaryAnn." Her tone had changed completely, was authoritative and firm.

Before MaryAnn had a chance to respond, the door smashed open, bouncing against the wall, splintering the door frame. John Paul stood in the doorway, his breath coming in hard gasps, his eyes wild, his huge, hamlike fists clenching and unclenching at his sides.

"John Paul," MaryAnn said quietly, "what can I do for

you this evening? It's after hours and I was just leaving with my friend."

John Paul didn't even glance at Destiny. His glassy stare was fixed on MaryAnn as he shuffled closer. "Where is Helena? I need her, MaryAnn. Give her back to me."

Destiny touched his mind. It was filled with his intense resolve to get to Helena. He had no real plan, no idea of what he would do when he found her, only a deep need to find her. She could sense the shadow of violence embedded deep in him, but there was no taint of the vampire. No surge of power, however slight, that might indicate he was a puppet of the undead.

"John Paul, you know Helena is somewhere safe. You wanted her to go, remember? You wanted her to be safe." MaryAnn was firm but still soothing.

John Paul shook his head adamantly. "Give her back to me." He shoved a large, deep-cushioned chair out of his way and stepped closer to MaryAnn. He didn't even glance at Destiny, didn't appear to notice that anyone else was in the room.

John Paul was so close to her, his jacket brushed Destiny's shoulder. She cleared her throat experimentally, to draw his attention, but it was wholly centered on MaryAnn.

"I didn't take Helena, John Paul. She *needed* some time away from you while she thought things over. Do you remember coming into this office with her? Both of you cried. You begged me to take care of her, and I promised you I would."

Without warning, John Paul swept his heavy arm across the desk, sending papers and the lamp scattering in all directions. The lamp flew across the room, hit the wall and shattered. Tiny slivers of glass fell like rain to the carpet. John Paul's attention was immediately caught and held by the glittering pieces of glass.

"MaryAnn, very slowly back into the next room," Destiny said softly. "He's under some kind of compulsion, and there's something about the shattered glass that's the trigger." She couldn't read anything in his mind other than the sudden need for extreme violence. It was an ugly roar, a need to grab and smash anything or anybody close to him. The roar was all she could distinguish at first, but Destiny dodged his swinging fists with blurring speed and concentrated on the sounds bellowing in his mind.

John Paul slammed his fist into the wall, punching a hole through the middle. Spiderweb cracks appeared from floor to ceiling, radiating out from the center.

MaryAnn groaned. "Repairs. Oh, no, repairs are so costly."

John Paul's head snapped around toward the sound of MaryAnn's voice, his brows drawing together, his fists swinging.

Destiny tapped his broad back to draw his attention away from MaryAnn. "Hey, big fella, I thought you wanted to dance with me. I'm the jealous type."

Stop playing around, Destiny. If that besotted idiot lays another hand on you, I will tear him into little pieces. I am not in the least amused, nor am I joking with you.

In spite of Nicolae's grim tone, Destiny wanted to laugh. *Pitiful male. I'm not slow dancing with him. There's no need for jealousy.* She ducked John Paul's fist and slipped just out of his reach, staying close enough that the large man kept his attention on her.

"What do you want me to do? Shall I call the police?" MaryAnn asked anxiously, wincing as John Paul struck at Destiny again.

"No, don't talk, I want his attention on me at all times." Destiny was working at deciphering the code in his head. He was fast for a big man, but she was much faster and not worried about getting hit. The noises in his head were nearly unbearable. Loud roars and growls, piercing whistles and shrieks. A buzzing like a swarm of bees. She separated the sounds, filtering them as she dodged around the small office always just inches out of John Paul's reach.

Something planted these sounds in his head, and it wasn't nature. She shared with Nicolae as she always did.

Someone. He has been programmed much like a bomb might be. If shattered glass is the trigger, what is the target? What is the point of this violence?

Now she could hear it, a voice, low, mumbling something over and over. It sounded as if it were on fast forward, demonic, speaking a command. Puzzled, she amplified it for Nicolae. John Paul was unaware of the command, unaware of the voice at all. It was only part of the terrible roaring in his head.

Destiny waved her hand and silenced the voice, silenced the roaring. John Paul stood in the center of the room, blinking at her with blurry eyes. He looked puzzled. His great shoulders were shaking and he broke out in a sweat. He lifted his head and looked past Destiny to MaryAnn.

Destiny blurred his vision to make certain that he would not catch a glimpse of the shattered slivers of glass on the floor. "John Paul." Her voice was melodic, silvery, the compulsion buried deep. "You must go back to your home and stay there. You want to sleep, not listen to music or tapes or talk on the phone. You just want to go to sleep."

I am going through his house now, Destiny. There must be something that sets him off before he is given the trigger. I will find it. Vikirnoff is on his way to MaryAnn's office to make copies of the photograph of the young lady the vampire is hunting.

John Paul muttered something and rubbed his eyes. He looked more confused than ever. When Destiny touched his mind, she felt sorry for him. He was totally bewildered, had no idea how he had gotten to the office or why he was there.

"MaryAnn?" He sounded like a small child seeking reassurance. "I think I'm losing my mind. I'm so sleepy, and I don't know what happened." He peered around her, squinting to get a better look. "Did I do this? Did I wreck your office?"

Destiny patted his arm in a gesture reminiscent of Velda. "Go home and sleep, John Paul. Everything will be fine."

MaryAnn watched him go, her eyes troubled. "Will it be fine, Destiny? Does this have something to do with a vampire? Do you have any idea what's going on? This violence can't keep happening. It's ruining everyone's lives."

"Velda told me of a woman, Blythe Madison, who had similar problems a while back. She was put in a hospital by her husband."

"Harry's wife. She's a wonderful woman. I go to visit her twice a month. She doesn't remember anything of what she did. She stays voluntarily in the hospital. I didn't even consider that her breakdown was anything like what happened to John Paul and Martin. How could the events possibly be connected?" MaryAnn knelt near her lamp and began to carefully pick up the pieces, tossing the slivers of glass into the wastebasket.

Destiny could see that MaryAnn's hands were trembling. Tears glistened in her eyes. Her reaction shook Destiny as nothing else could. MaryAnn cared deeply about these people, and it was painful to her when they were in trouble.

"We're much closer to finding out what is going on," Destiny assured her. "I don't know who's behind this, but John Paul was under some sort of command."

MaryAnn looked up at her, blinking back tears. "Like hypnosis?" There was sudden speculation in her voice.

"Is someone around here into hypnosis?"

"There's a doctor at the clinic. He comes in a couple of times a month. He believes in hypnotism for things like pain management and quitting smoking, that type of thing. I went to him once and couldn't quite get over his bedside manner. He's related to Harry, a cousin or something; that's why he even bothers to come to our lowly little neighborhood. He has offices uptown and also at the hospital."

Destiny frowned, trying to assimilate this new information. "I don't know what you mean by bedside manner."

Deep inside she heard Nicolae give an inelegant snort.

Well, I don't *know,* she insisted.

He probably came on to her. Made a pass while he was examining her.

He's a doctor!

Destiny, vampires are not the only monsters in the world. Many of them are human.

Destiny sat down abruptly beside MaryAnn. "Was the doctor inappropriate with you? Did he—"

"Touch me inappropriately? Yes. And he was a slimy little worm with a charming smile and a handsome face. Obviously, women have said yes to him and been thrilled by his advances. I was not, and made it abundantly clear. He thought hypnotism would work well on me and wanted me to let him try. What a jerk."

"But you didn't report him?"

MaryAnn ducked her head. "No one else was in the room. To make that kind of accusation against a professional with his reputation and money is risky. I didn't want to risk what I do here. I just never went back to him."

"I wonder if John Paul went to him for any reason. Or Martin. And before them, Blythe Madison."

"If Harry is the doctor's cousin, wouldn't it be natural for him to ask him to take a look at his sick wife?" MaryAnn wondered aloud.

Destiny was more inclined to think the culprit was a vampire. All along she had concentrated her energies in that direction. The legions of the undead had to be involved. To Destiny, whoever was behind these bizarre character changes was deliberately tormenting and hurting people for amusement. She couldn't conceive of a human committing such atrocities. Demons were vampire, not human.

At once Nicolae was there, sensing that her thoughts were beginning to shake the very foundations of her worldview. His arms were strong, his body sheltering, his mind firmly merged with hers. Her anchor. Nicolae was always with her. She could count on him endlessly. In spite of the crouching darkness that he had fought most of his life. In spite of the tainted blood now flowing in his veins, Nicolae was unfailingly good.

Nicolae. She breathed his name in a sudden overwhelming surge of love. He was slowly handing her back her life. A little piece at a time. And all the while he was there, comforting her, reassuring her as he had always done.

"Destiny?" MaryAnn's voice shook her out of her reflection. "If the doctor is somehow involved in this . . . if he actually has done something to harm Helena and John Paul and Martin and Tim and Father Mulligan . . . and poor Blythe living in a hospital thinking she lost her mind . . . I could have prevented it. I could have brought charges against him. What if I could have stopped him?" She looked lost, sitting there on the floor with her large eyes and horror in her mind.

"No! MaryAnn, what are you thinking?" Destiny gathered her close, hugged her hard in protest. "You know better than to think anything so ridiculous. How could you be responsible for something a madman chooses to do? We don't even know if this doctor has anything to do with what's happened. All the facts aren't in yet, but even if he is waving a magic wand and casting spells throughout the neighborhood, you cannot possibly be to blame."

"You sound like me. That's all well and good in theory, but if I had brought charges against him, maybe he wouldn't have been able to touch any of my friends."

"Or, more likely, he would have moved his deviant behavior somewhere else where no one would notice the difference in their friends. Don't you see, Mary-

Ann? This neighborhood and the people in it are so close, they don't readily accept that someone like John Paul who loves Helena so very much would suddenly turn on her and try to hurt her. They don't accept that Martin would attack Father Mulligan. All of them began to watch one another and try to figure out what was going wrong."

"Please find out who is doing this and stop it, Destiny," MaryAnn pleaded.

Destiny hugged her again. "I intend to do just that."

Chapter Seventeen

Nicolae was waiting outside the office, his long, sinewy frame leaning negligently against the banister. Destiny paused to look at him. The breeze was coolly ruffling the long silk of his hair. The moon cast a silver beam across the angles and planes of his face, illuminating the sheer sensuality there. His body was hard and powerful, a dangerous blend of predator and seductive male. He turned his head and smiled at her, robbing her of breath just that easily.

"You're very good-looking," she said judiciously, tilting her head to study his magnificent physique. "Are all Carpathians as good-looking as you?"

His black eyebrows arched. "I do not think that is a safe subject for you." He held out his hand to her. Destiny studied it carefully, as if examining it for a trap. How in the world had she become so obsessed with him that the sight of his outstretched hand could send her heart somersaulting? Her fingers laced almost reluctantly with his. Up close, he would be able to feel the way he made her pulse elevate, the way her heart beat a little unsteadily. Her entire body ached for him if she ventured too close to his sheer magnetism. A humiliating fact, and one impossible to hide when he was touching her.

"Silly woman," he said affectionately. "There is nothing at all to hide from a lifemate. There is never any need. I am in your mind as you are in mine."

"Well, if you're in my mind, then you should be perfectly aware that I'm having a difficult time accepting our weird relationship."

He brought their linked hands up to his mouth, his lips teasing the skin of her inner wrist. "You accept our weird relationship; you just are afraid to trust it. Or yourself. It makes you happy, and you do not trust that."

She glared at him. "Have you been hanging out with Father Mulligan again? He's always handing out that two-cent advice of his."

"He only charged you two cents? He made me fill his poor box," Nicolae said, straight-faced. "And he didn't offer a single word on marriage. He just said to have courage, whatever that meant."

Destiny burst out laughing. "The old fraud, he probably said that on purpose just to make me crazy. Where's Vikirnoff?"

Nicolae tugged on her hand until she began walking along the street with him. "He is out seeking information on the woman in the photograph. The healer is on his way, and my brother is determined to keep the cities free of vampires. We do not need Vikirnoff cluttering up the skies tonight. I have plans."

The three little words set butterfly wings fluttering in the pit of her stomach. She had already been too long away from him. Desire shot through her, shaking her very foundations. Her mouth grew dry, and her body hot, just hearing his words. Just the thought of his hard body made her tremble. She didn't dare look at his mouth; her knees would give out.

"What kind of plans?" She had no idea how she managed to get the words past her strangled throat.

He moved closer, his larger body brushing against hers so that electricity seemed to arc and crackle between them. Little dancing whips of lightning sizzled in her bloodstream. Just walking with him was a miracle to her.

Nicolae glanced down at the top of her bent head. She was the miracle to him. He still couldn't quite grasp the fact that he had found her at long last. The endless search for her was over and she was with him. A part of him. The intensity of his feelings shocked him at times. "You said you wanted to go to the movies. I found an all-night theater."

She glanced up at him from under her long lashes, rewarding him with a small smile. "I'd like that, thank you."

The thought of sitting with her in a darkened theater was a reward in and of itself. He couldn't stop the erotic fantasies filling his mind. Destiny blushed wildly, catching his thoughts. She had never considered what one might do in a dark corner of a theater.

Destiny cleared her throat, searching desperately for something to say. Searching desperately for a safe subject. "MaryAnn is worried about money again. She didn't want me looking at her books, and now John Paul has wrecked her office. She tried to act as if it were no big deal, but it obviously is."

"I do not want you robbing a bank or risking your life taking money from a drug dealer."

"You sound just like her." Destiny laughed at his severe tone.

"She had a point. I will get her the money she needs. Living in the world for centuries, we Carpathians have a certain expertise in acquiring money. There is no need for you to do anything illegal or dangerous to help MaryAnn."

"I'll hold you to that. I don't like her worrying so much."

"Good. I'm an expert fund-raiser. Count on me, Destiny."

Of course she could count on him. She had known, on some level, for most of her life that he would always be there for her. Now he was real. Solid. Beside her sharing her life and her thoughts. She did count on him.

He bent his head, feathered kisses down her cheek even as they walked along the darkened streets together holding hands. "I share your body too," he murmured wickedly.

His voice whispered over her body, made every muscle clench with urgent need. A rush of liquid heat surged, spread, pooled low in anticipation. She didn't know how he had managed to become so firmly entrenched in her heart so quickly. "I still think you've used some black-magic spell on me," she said gruffly.

"Is it working?"

"Don't sound so happy about it." A fine drizzle had begun. Destiny lifted her face to the skies, allowing the vapor to bathe her face. "I love the rain. I love everything about it. The air always smells so fresh after it rains, and the sound is so soothing. I sometimes lie under the covers and just listen to the way rain sounds likes music."

"Do you want to drop in at the rectory and see Sam?" Nicolae ventured. "Two hours from now I would not want you to suddenly worry about him."

"You were reading my mind again." She smiled up at him because she couldn't help herself. Nicolae. Sharing her life. Giving her hope. Binding his life to her life, so that she would never be alone again. It was almost more than she could take in and accept. Happiness. She had never dared to believe it could be hers. Belief seemed to trickle into her mind and take hold a little bit at a time.

Still hand in hand, they launched skyward, shifting shape as they did so, two owls flying toward the windows of the rectory. They shifted a second time, became vapor streaming through the night to find the opening in the window, no more than a crack, but it allowed them entry. Twin ribbons of colored mist poured into the house, moved quickly through the darkened hallway to find the crack beneath the door.

Father Mulligan appeared to be dozing in a chair by the bed. Sam was asleep, tears still marking his pale face. Destiny's heart went out to the little boy. She materialized beside him, her fingers stroking back the thatch of hair tumbling across his forehead. "Poor little boy," she murmured softly.

Father Mulligan sat up with a start, clutched dramatically at his heart as he glared at them. "Do you go through walls? You nearly killed me coming in like that."

Destiny looked instantly repentant. "I'm so sorry, Father. I thought you were really asleep. I should have been more careful."

"His heart rate did not even rise," Nicolae pointed out. "He should be an actor, not a priest."

Father Mulligan grinned mischievously, looking for all the world like a small boy. "I did rather well in the school plays when I was a young lad, much to my father's chagrin. He thought acting a perfect sin. I was expecting you two this evening."

"We would have come earlier but we have been looking into the strange, unnatural behavior of your parishioners. Are you certain the wine you are serving is not a bad one?" Nicolae inquired with a straight face. "All of them do attend this church."

"I hadn't thought of that," Destiny agreed, glaring accusingly at the priest.

"You two are treading quite close to blasphemy," Father Mulligan warned, attempting to look severe. His eyes were twinkling merrily, ruining his credibility as an actor.

"Well, I suppose we can rule you and your wine out, but I do have a question," Destiny said. "The night Martin took the poor box, do you recall if any glass was broken? Before he became violent."

Father Mulligan frowned. "How strange you should ask that. I spoke with Tim and he told me that he had given Martin medicine, and the glass of water dropped onto the floor as Martin handed it back. Tim said Martin just stared at the slivers of glass, shoved Tim out of his way and left their apartment. Evidently, Martin came straight here to the church."

"Has Martin ever used the little clinic, the one just down from MaryAnn's office?"

"Yes. There's a doctor who comes twice a month. He's noted for being brilliant in pain management.

Martin was in a terrible accident a couple of years ago, shattered all kinds of bones and twisted his back. He had been going to the doctor for help, and it seemed to be working. But Tim said they had some kind of falling-out and Martin decided not to go back. It was too bad, because his pain was under control."

"Do you have any idea what the falling-out was over?" Destiny asked. Seeing the priest hesitate, she continued. "I wouldn't ask, but I think the doctor may be involved in all of this in some way. The more information I have, the easier it will be to solve the entire mess."

"It had to do with their business. Tim and Martin are planning a community for older citizens. They are trying to make it unique and safe and yet affordable. A great deal of money is involved. The doctor wanted to be added to the staff for a high consultant salary. Martin overheard him treating an elderly patient and thought his manner impatient and insulting. I heard several complaints about his treatment of the elderly, and when Martin asked me my opinion, I told him what some of my parishioners had said."

"So at his next session with the doctor, Martin probably told him politely they would pass on his services," Destiny mused.

"I don't want to give you the wrong impression," Father Mulligan said. "The doctor may not be very good with the elderly, but he's helped others tremendously. I know he visits poor little Blythe Madison on a regular basis. I've seen him leaving when I go to see her."

"Is Blythe an attractive woman?" Nicolae asked.

"Strikingly so," Father Mulligan answered readily.

"Just as Helena is," Destiny pointed out. "Is Harry as crazy about his wife as everyone claims he is?"

"Absolutely," Father Mulligan said. "He's devastated. Not a single day goes by that he doesn't visit her at the hospital. He's begged her to come home to him, but he says she's become even more withdrawn."

"Perhaps we should pay him a quiet visit," Nicolae suggested. He held up his hand when Father Mulligan might have protested. "Do not worry, he will not even know we were there."

"Thank you for taking care of Sam, Father," Destiny said. "I'm sorry I had to turn him over to you."

"I don't mind. Nicolae helped the social workers see things my way, so I think we have Sam's future well taken care of, including a trust fund that Nicolae set up for him. The couple who want him are wonderful people, and we're cutting through the red tape nicely."

Nicolae. It always came back to him. His thoughtfulness. His attention to detail. For some reason, the thought made Destiny blush wildly and she had to duck her head to conceal her thoughts from the priest. There was no concealing them from Nicolae.

Details are important, he agreed in his black velvet voice, implying all sorts of things.

Lightning is going to strike you if you keep that up in front of a holy man.

Let us go where I am much safer, then. But first we must stop by The Tavern.

Destiny murmured a goodbye to the priest, brushed back Sam's hair once more and started for the door.

"Go out the same way you came in," Father Mulligan pleaded. "Just one more time, for me."

Destiny glanced at Nicolae, who raised an eyebrow at her. His lips twitched with suppressed laughter. Together they melted into vapor, then rushed out beneath the small crack in the door while the priest laughed delightedly.

Harry had already closed The Tavern and had climbed the stairs to his apartment above the bar when they arrived. He was slumped in a chair with a framed photo in his hands, his forehead resting on the glass. He sat there unmoving, clutching the picture of his wife. The sight of him sitting so alone and unhappy wrenched at Destiny's heart.

We will fix this, Destiny. Now that we know what Blythe looks like, we can find her. I feel as if we are very close to solving this mystery. The doctor is very much involved in these attacks.

They left Harry and flew out of the city. Destiny looked down at the sparkling lights. *It's so beautiful here, Nicolae. I love this city. I love the people.*

She could admit it to him now. He had given her that gift. She wasn't so afraid to allow herself to care about others. She was beginning to believe she wasn't responsible for the death of everyone she had ever loved.

Is that the hospital where Blythe is living? Destiny was already heading toward the grounds, certain of the direction, almost as if Blythe were calling to her.

"Maybe she is," Nicolae said with understanding. "She has suffered greatly. I think it best if you speak with her alone. I will be close, but unseen."

Destiny was grateful for his sensitivity. Nicolae could easily force Blythe's acceptance of him, but Destiny was reluctant to compel cooperation from someone who was most likely suffering, and Nicolae shared her view.

Destiny blew him a kiss as they walked through the halls of the hospital invisible to the human eye. She found Blythe huddled on a window seat, rocking back and forth, her tormented gaze riveted on the door. She didn't appear to notice Destiny at first; her entire concentration was focused on the door.

Destiny cleared her throat to bring the woman's attention to her. When Blythe turned her head, Destiny recognized the look in her eyes. She had seen it over and over on the faces of the abused and battered women who had fled their lives and gone to MaryAnn. There was despair and shame and hopelessness. Blythe was drugged, but there was awareness in her, a strong spark of life despite her situation.

"Who are you? How did you get in here?" Blythe asked nervously, but she was looking expectantly toward the door, not at Destiny.

"Is he coming? The doctor?" Destiny asked softly.

Blythe focused more fully on her. She nodded. "If he sees you here, you could be in danger." At the mention of the doctor, Blythe's heart rate increased dramatically.

"He hypnotized you, Blythe, didn't he?" Destiny asked softly.

"I suspect that he did." Blythe's voice was surprisingly strong for a woman everyone believed to be mentally ill. "There's no way to get away from him and know Harry is safe. He uses drugs and hypnosis." She shrugged. "Everyone thinks I'm crazy." She added the last as an afterthought.

Destiny noted that Blythe was becoming increasingly agitated. Her fists were clenching and unclenching. Destiny felt the same presence she'd discerned earlier that day. Evil. It was moving toward them, the footsteps

hard on the hallway floor. Blythe whimpered and hurried to her window seat, pressing one hand hard against
her mouth to keep from crying out.

Destiny slipped back into the shadows. "Get him to
talk, Blythe," she said softly. "Give me something to
work with." She could easily take the information from
the doctor's mind, but she wanted Blythe to participate
actively in freeing herself.

The lock clicked and the door burst open. Destiny
was half expecting a vampire, but the man glaring sus-
piciously around the room was wholly human and yet as
vile as any monster she had vanquished. Destiny could
see through the illusion a vampire projected with his
voice and his looks to the rotting malevolence beneath,
but this man shocked her. He was incredibly good-
looking, a tall, blond man with a shark's smile. Even
looking closely, Destiny could not *see* past his surface
good looks to the evil lying beneath.

"I heard you talking to someone." He closed the door
with deliberate finality. "Or are you so far gone that you
talk to yourself now?"

Blythe huddled closer to the window as if she might
throw herself out, except the way was blocked by bars.
Her gaze shifted to the corner of the room where Destiny had disappeared. She lifted her chin. "I won't let
you touch me again."

He laughed, the sound chilling. "Of course you will.
You'll do exactly as I tell you, just as you always have.
You wouldn't want to kill your husband, wonderful
Harry. Slice him up into little pieces while he slept in
bed, now would you? I could make you do that, Blythe,
and you would deserve it for cheating on me with that

nothing of a man. A *bartender*, for God's sake. I am a genius, a man of greatness, and you turned your back on me and slept with a common nothing. You let him touch you."

Blythe lifted her chin. "You can come here every night and rape me, drug me, force yourself on me, but I will never want you. I'll always belong to Harry, never you."

Destiny could feel her stomach churning with bile, with a fierce rage as cold as ice and as hot as an out-of-control fire. She heard the humiliation in Blythe's voice, the utter despair even as she defied her tormentor. Destiny looked at the doctor and saw only a monster. Without thinking, she waved Blythe to silence, sent her to sleep so that she slumped over on the window seat, her eyes closed.

The doctor swore. "You little bitch, do you think that's going to fool me?"

Destiny came out of the shadows, her eyes flaming a fiery red. She hissed softly, drawing his attention. "You do not deserve to live."

He spun around, stepped back and quickly put up his hand. "You have no proof of anything. I was attempting a form of therapy. How dare you come into this room?"

"You hurt John Paul because Helena turned down your sick advances. You harmed Martin because he refused to give you your way in his project. You use your profession to hurt people, don't you, Doctor?"

He shrugged carelessly once he assured himself they were alone in the room. "I'd like to see you prove such an accusation. I have an impeccable reputation." He pulled a syringe from his pocket, smiling at her as he did so. "You shouldn't have stuck your nose in where it didn't belong." He walked to her, completely confident that he could subdue her.

Destiny allowed him to take her arm in his viselike grip. She smiled coolly at him while inside she smoldered with outrage at his complete lack of remorse. "I don't have to prove it, Doctor. I'm not human." For one moment she allowed him to see the rage, the fury, the red flame of retribution.

The doctor went white, his mouth opening to emit a high shriek of terror. Destiny waved her hand to stop the sound, catching it in his throat, cutting off his airway. She blinked, suddenly realizing what she was about to do. *Nicolae. I will not be like the undead. I may have their blood, but I will not join their ranks and terrorize this disgusting excuse for a man. I will not do the very thing they do. He deserves to be brought to justice and I will do so, but . . .*

She released the doctor as Nicolae materialized, pulling the syringe out of the doctor's suddenly nerveless fingers. "I think I would like you to write out a full confession for us, Doctor. And include why and how. You must tell the world in general that you could not live with the guilt of your crimes." His voice was so soft and pleasant, Destiny backed away from him, away from the power of the compulsion. She was shaking with the need for justice, grateful that Nicolae had intervened with a cool head, remembering they would need proof for all the victims.

It was terrifying to think how much she had wanted the doctor to see death coming. Destiny wanted him to feel everything Blythe had felt. Everything she herself had felt.

She put her arms around Blythe, whispering to her, promising her that everything would be all right. *We cannot leave her like this, Nicolae.*

Do not worry, we will provide for her.

The doctor turned as if sleepwalking and left the room. Nicolae put his arm around Destiny and together, at a much more sedate pace, they followed the doctor down the hall and out of the ward. Both watched as the man sat at the desk in his office and carefully wrote out his confession. He left it on the desktop and once again was on the move, climbing the stairs to the roof, several stories up, where he simply stepped off the edge. They did not watch him hit the sidewalk below, but hurried away, stopping only to allow Nicolae to whisper to a security man and the nurse at the desk. They sought the peace of the quiet streets, easily gaining entrance into Harry's home. Destiny watched Nicolae, her heart swelling with pride as he bent to give Harry a soft command.

Harry dressed quickly and hurried down to the street, heading for the hospital, uncertain why it was so important to him, but needing desperately to spend the remainder of the night in the hospital room with his wife.

Destiny shivered, buried her face against Nicolae's neck. "I never once thought it was a man. A doctor. Someone who is supposed to be a healer. Why would anyone choose to be so evil?"

Nicolae brushed a kiss onto her hair, wanting to take away the pain of her memories of other monsters. "I cannot give you an answer, little one, but do not be sad. Blythe will learn to be happy with Harry again, and eventually all of these people will be able to live their lives in peace, thanks to your caring enough to listen to them and piece it all together."

"Thank you for thinking of sending him to her. I knew we couldn't remove her from the hospital, but I couldn't bear the thought of her being alone." She tangled her fingers in his hair and nuzzled his neck, aching to hold him to her and make love to him. He always contrived to make sense out of a world that was never quite sane. *How did I ever manage without you?*

He kissed her. Hard. Possessively. *Come with me. We have done what we could for our friends. I wish to do something for you. Let me take you to that movie.*

It was the last thing she expected, and it made her laugh. "You're crazy, you know that?"

She couldn't stop smiling. Joy seemed to start in her soul and spread through her body until her lips curved in complete happiness. She and Nicolae shifted shape once again, materializing in their true forms on the sidewalk together in front of the movie theater. Nicolae immediately drew her into his arms, pulling her tightly against the hard strength of his body. His long, lean fingers tunneled deep into the thick mass of her hair. "I have waited for hours to get you alone."

"Really?" Pleasure blossomed through her body. "I wanted to be alone with you too," she confided. No matter what he said about the darkness inside male Carpathians, Nicolae would always be her light.

A cool breeze slid over her body, bringing the inevitable mist with it. Laughing, happy, they slipped into the dark of the theater. Only a few couples were scattered around the large room. Nicolae found the darkest corner, up in the balcony where they were all alone. It wasn't a vampire movie but an action movie.

Destiny had seen it advertised, a popular video game made into a movie, and she particularly loved the actress. The balcony seats were wide and comfortable, and she settled into one with a little sigh.

"Did you really summon the healer? Gregori?"

"Do not sound so worried," he answered, sliding his arm along the back of her seat to rest on her shoulders. "He has a lifemate, and it would be impossible for him to be other than good."

Destiny shifted, leaning close to him. "What's he like?"

He waited to answer, framing her face between his hands, finding her mouth with his. Fire poured into her. Into him. His tongue danced and dueled with hers. He had already waited too long to have her. His body was hard and aching. His mouth said it all to her, taking command, a hard possession, a declaration of his intentions.

He lifted his head and stared down into her enormous eyes and smiled. His voice was very calm when he answered her. "Gregori comes from a revered lineage. His ancestors have always guarded the Prince of our people, and most of them had a tremendous ability to heal. All of us can do so when called upon, of course, but the talent runs strongest in his line. I do not know him, but I knew his father, a man of loyalty and integrity who always stood by our people."

She was beginning to know Nicolae well. "A warrior. A hunter," she interpreted.

"Exactly."

A man much like Nicolae, one he would respect. Destiny nodded. "All right, then. I'll stick around and see what he's like."

The action on the screen was fast-paced and intense as sinister men stalked toward the heroine's mansion. Nicolae glanced at the screen, then looked around the theater. "So this is what it is like to watch a movie from the balcony. I must confess I was never much of a movie patron." His thumb slid along the neckline of her blouse, slipped inside to caress bare skin.

A shiver of pure awareness went down her spine. "Movies are wonderful. I really admire the imaginations of the people putting together such wonderful worlds." She glanced at him. He wasn't looking at the screen but at her, his dark eyes smoky with desire, with raw sexual hunger. His hands went to the front of her blouse and her heart began to pound. "Nicolae, this really is a good movie."

"Is it?" he murmured, clearly distracted.

She was all too aware of his fingers slipping the tiny buttons open down the front of her blouse. His knuckles brushed her bare skin as the material gaped open. She tried to be shocked, but excitement set in. "Is this what you do on your movie dates?" She found it hotly erotic to be sitting in a movie theater in the dark with her blouse open and her breasts aching and swollen with need. She watched, fascinated, as his long fingers stroked her soft, creamy skin.

"Did you think I came to watch the movie?" He sounded amused.

"Well . . . yes." The breath slammed out of her lungs as his fingers began to shape her breast, his thumb lovingly brushing the nipple into a taut peak of desire.

"I wanted to watch you watch the movie. I love to watch you enjoy things. Do you object to wearing a skirt?"

"A skirt?" she echoed faintly.

"Instead of pants. A short skirt. You do not have to wear anything under it." His voice purred as his fingers stroked.

His request seemed sinfully wicked, wonderfully sexy, and as she complied in the easy way of their people, donning a short thigh-length skirt, she felt the flush of heat moving through her body. "So I'm to sit here and watch the movie while you watch me?"

"Excellent idea," he agreed. One fingernail lengthened to slit through the thin lace of her bra, freeing her full breasts from the wispy confines. "I just want you to enjoy yourself." Nicolae cupped the soft weight of one breast in his palm. The cool air teased her heated skin, tightened her nipples even more.

On the screen, the heroine was running through her large mansion as intruders finally broke in, determined to steal an important icon left to her by her father. Nicolae bent his dark head to Destiny's enticing offering. His mouth found her vulnerable throat as her head fell back. His tongue swirled, tasting her skin, the temptation of her pulse.

You move me. Every time I look at you, touch you, I know I am alive. If the strict truth were told, his insides went into total meltdown the moment he touched her body. Kissing her sent him into a heady spin. Fire raced through his veins and burned in his belly, but most of all, even greater than his tremendous physical response to her, was the intensity of his love. It shook him as nothing else ever had.

Her skin was amazingly soft. He wanted to touch every inch of her. Take his time and simply feel. Revel in his ability to do so. The contrast between a man's body and a woman's fascinated him. Her curves were lush and inviting; he wanted to sink deep into them and spend long hours enjoying every moment.

He feathered kisses down her throat, his mouth traveling to the tip of her inviting breast. The low sounds she made in her throat only served to heighten his pleasure. He wanted her needing him with the same mindless urgency he was feeling. He wanted that cool look gone from her face, her eyes cloudy with desire for him. He wanted her so distracted, she would never be able to look at a movie again without remembering this night and growing hot at the memory.

Teeth nipped and scraped gently, teasingly; his tongue lapped gently. He was pleased when her arms cradled his head, holding him to her breast. The music from the soundtrack pounded in his body, a hard, driving beat that matched the rhythm of his mouth as he took possession of her breast. She arched into him, her hips writhing in the seat, unable to stay still under the wild assault on her senses.

Destiny tangled her fist in his hair. "Wild man, let's go home. You've gone crazy on me." But she held him to her, not wanting him to stop.

He feasted on her body, teasing her breasts, first one, then the other, delighting in his ability to do so. She was his, sharing her body, allowing him free rein as he carefully explored each abundant offering. He heard the music throbbing through the theater, but time and space dropped away so he was unaware of anything but her yielding flesh.

Nicolae found the hemline of her short skirt and traced it along the top of her thighs. His hand slid between her legs and urged them apart to give him access to the treasure he knew was his. Moist heat radiated a welcome to him. Her satisfaction deepened his own desire. Destiny responded like a flower opening to him.

He stroked her thighs, found her tight curls and caressed the moist folds the small triangle guarded. His palm cupped her softness, pushed against her, was rewarded when she pushed back, seeking relief.

"I want to go home," she whispered again.

"Yes, we need to be home," he agreed, pushing his finger deep just to feel her reaction. She shivered with excitement and need. Her hips writhed on the seat.

All at once the confines of the movie theater were too restrictive. She needed to be out in the open where she could breathe. Where she could cry out with joy. Where she could have complete privacy with Nicolae. "Take me home," she said, her arms circling his neck.

Nicolae found her mouth again, sweeping her into his world of fire and pleasure, his fingers bringing her to a fever pitch. He lifted her into his arms and took her from the world of humans, back into the night. Their night. Their world.

Destiny felt tears burning behind her eyes. The night was cool on her skin. Fog slid along the ground and a soft mist instantly enveloped them. The shadows were places of beauty, not evil. She reached toward the night, embracing it. Embracing her life with Nicolae. Her mouth found his as they stood together. She belonged. Finally. Irrevocably. She belonged with this man.

She poured everything she felt into her kiss. Her needs. Her dreams. Her acceptance of him. Most of all, her complete trust in him. She forgot the scandalously short skirt she was wearing, wrapping one leg around him, pressing her body against his.

Nicolae found the bare curve of her bottom and held her tightly to him. Destiny was ravenous, matching him kiss for kiss, flame for flame. He lifted his head to the cooling mist and laughed for the sheer joy of being able to hold her in his arms. He took them to the skies, high over the city, his arms wrapped around her as they moved through the clouds.

Clothes were too much of a burden, and both shed them at nearly the exact moment. With their mouths fused together and Destiny's hands clasped at the back of his neck, she lifted her legs to wrap them firmly around his waist. The head of his erection was large, pressing tightly against her opening, seeking entrance. She knew she should wait, they were already too wild, but the temptation was far too great. She was pulsing with need, desperate for relief from the too tight, too hot feeling. Every nerve in her body cried out for his possession. Every muscle clenched with desperate urgency.

Nicolae gasped as she lowered herself onto him, right there in the air, taking him deep into her body. Her tight sheath was fiery hot, in complete contrast to the cool air surrounding them. He spun them, a dizzying drop as they flashed across the sky toward their home, making her cling tighter, her soft breasts pressed tightly against his chest.

She had intended to be perfectly still as he carried her through the sky, but the sensation of him filling her with his hard thickness was too much. The movement of flying simply added to the delicious sensations. She began to move, a slow, sexy ride, moving up and down, her hips lifting away from him, then slowly settling over his heavy erection once again.

Every muscle in his body was taut and strained. He shuddered each time she lowered her body around his, each time her sheath gripped him and stroked him with hot velvet. The friction sent flames dancing over his skin in spite of the cooling mist. It was sensuous and alluring, riding through the sky with her impaled on his hard body. Her dark cloud of hair spilled around them like a silken cape, teasing his heightened senses even more. Every movement sent her lush breasts rubbing against his chest. He could only hold her tightly, concentrate on keeping them aloft as her muscles clenched around him and she rode up and down with a leisurely rhythm.

Nicolae was nearly out of his mind by the time he took her through the levels of the mountain toward their hidden chamber. He had no time for flames or flowers; he could only think of burying himself deeper and deeper in her body. Faster and harder, he thrust, his hips surging into her. He barely had their feet on the ground before he was taking control, his hands moving over her, everywhere, shaping and exploring and arousing her further in a frenzy of need. He backed her against the nearest boulder, only remembering at the last moment to cushion her back as he thrust deep.

Destiny rained kisses on him, held him, accepted him, though she was every bit as frenzied as he was. But there it was again. Unexpected. Insidious. A snake in her garden, robbing her of paradise. This time she stayed merged with Nicolae, allowed him to see the darker shadow images slipping into her head, desperately wanting to trust him to know what to do.

Nicolae kissed her. He went from taking her body wildly to kissing her tenderly, his hands so gentle they felt like the brush of gossamer wings over her bare skin. His kiss was loving, warm, coaxing rather than taking. All the time, his body moved gently in hers. "You like to be out in the open."

"I know." She wanted to apologize, but it seemed silly when he was only making an observation, not condemning her.

He kissed her again, slowly and thoroughly, hungrily. "We are in the open. We are wherever we want to be."

Destiny closed her eyes and took the picture of the stars from his mind. Took the scent of the clean mist and held it to her while he filled her with the beauty of his hands and mouth. His body worshiped hers until her body was coming apart, soaring free with Nicolae across the sky she loved so much.

She held him to her, listening to their hearts beating together. Very slowly she opened her eyes to find them beneath the mountain in the chamber of pools. "I wanted to be wild and out of control. I'm sorry you had to be so careful with me."

Nicolae didn't point out that his body was still quite willing to take hers again. They had a few more hours before they had to seek the solace of the earth and he intended to utilize every minute together. "I do not mind being careful." His teeth bit at her neck teasingly. "I do not mind anything we do. Some day we will be wild and out of control. We have eternity together. We do not need to have everything at once." His teeth scraped along her shoulder, nibbled her breast. "One day I will have silken scarves and you will trust me enough to let me bind your hands and have my way with you and there will be no fear of intimacy between us."

"You think I'll be able to do that?" She was skeptical.

Nicolae tugged at her hand so that she followed him into the water. He turned her away from him, placing her hands on the very boulder she had forced him to hang on to. "Yes, I know you will. You will trust me completely. I intend to give you so much pleasure every time I touch you that you will only think in terms of pleasure when I am near you." His hand on her back positioned her upper body forward, so that her smooth bottom was presented to him. "Lovemaking is never about control and power. No matter what we do, it's about showing each other with our bodies what is nearly impossible to express any other way. There should never be shame, only pleasure, and I intend to give you much pleasure."

Nicolae ran his hands over her curves. "You are so beautiful, Destiny." His hands moved up her thighs, stroked caresses over her moist entrance.

"This makes me feel very vulnerable," she admitted.

He stepped close to her, reached around her to cup the fullness of her breasts in his palms. Deliberately he rubbed against her, allowing her to feel how thick and hard he was. How much his body wanted her body. "All you have to do is tell me no. That is all. We stop the moment you do not like anything we do." He pushed his finger into her, testing her readiness.

If her mind was fearful, her body wasn't. She was hot and slick, even more welcoming than before. He caught her hips and thrust deep, burying himself all the way. Her body clenched around him, then slowly opened in welcome. "Each position is just a new sensation, not a threat, Destiny," he said, waiting a heartbeat to allow her body to adjust fully to the invasion of his.

He thrust hard. Waited another heartbeat. Destiny

pushed back against him, seeking more. Her body was already hot, hotter than she had thought possible. The feeling of intense vulnerability was gone, leaving her able to participate fully. She wanted him to thrust harder, to create the firestorm all over again. Silken scarves, he had said, and her body had grown hot at the thought. She doubted she would ever trust him to that extent, but as his body took hers, she realized she was strong enough to rip through silken bonds. It was merely an image of a restraint, not the real thing.

Nicolae wanted her pleasure above his own. Destiny relaxed completely and began to move, thrusting backward into him as he surged forward, her muscles tightening and releasing, gripping and teasing. Each time his hips plunged forward, her breasts moved in the same rhythm and white-hot fire raced through her blood. She became aware of everything, even the sensation of the water lapping at her skin like tongues. His body slapped against hers, the thick length of him pistoning faster and harder until the friction threatened to set them on fire.

She didn't want him to stop and she didn't need him to be gentle. His large hands were biting into her hips, but it felt wonderful, not threatening. His body was wild, taking possession of her, obviously staking a claim, but she welcomed him, welcomed this abandoned form of lovemaking.

She went over the edge fast and unexpectedly. Destiny cried out loudly in the confines of the chamber. Her body refused to go alone, gripping and milking the seed from him so that he thrust helplessly, spilling the essence of life deep inside her.

Nicolae rested his head on her smooth back, attempting to calm his breathing. *Do you see, little one, not everything has to be perfect to be pleasurable. If there are times we can only hold one another, it will be all right. We will enjoy those times together. We will have many perfections and many near misses, and they will all be pleasurable. That is true intimacy. And that is life.*

A slow smile hovered on her lips, even though her legs were shaky and it was only sheer willpower that held her up. Nicolae reluctantly allowed his body to slide away from hers, his hands drawing her with him to the deeper center of the pool so that the water bubbled and fizzed over her breasts.

Nicolae didn't let her go; rather, he pulled her close to him, his mouth taking hers, plundering and sweet at the same time. His tongue probed and danced until she was breathless. The water fizzed in her most secret places, and then two fingers joined the sparkling water, pushing her up toward the skies again, teasing and dancing in time to his tongue while tiny bubbles burst against her nipples.

His mouth left hers to travel to her neck, teeth nipping sharply, his tongue swirling to ease the bite. Over the creamy swell of her breast, he bit deep, without preamble, so that the pleasure-pain of it seared them both. Her small muscles clenched around his fingers and he pushed deep, felt her body rock with an explosive orgasm. He fed there while she fragmented, while her feminine muscles convulsed again and again. His tongue swept the tiny pinpricks, sealing them, but leaving his mark on her so he could see the evidence of his possession. His mouth wandered lower to the tips of her breasts, catching the fizzing water to hold the bursting bubbles around her tender flesh. He was rewarded again as she climaxed, calling his name.

Her arms circled his neck and she kissed his eyes, the corner of his mouth. His body clenched in anticipation. She feathered kisses down his jaw, over his throat; her hands began to wander, slipping below the water line. Fingers danced, stroked; her palm became a tight sheath. Her tongue lapped the pulse in his throat. His heart leapt as she bit into his flesh, as her hands followed the guidance of his mind. It was his turn to share the searing ecstasy, his turn for her ministrations.

Sounds filled the cave over the next couple of hours. Soft murmurs, cries of delight, splashing water. True intimacy. Unconditional love.

Chapter Eighteen

Gregori was close. She was sure of it the moment she opened her eyes on the next rising. Destiny's heart was pounding so hard, so loud, the sound echoed through the small cavern. Her breath came in great gasps, and her lungs burned desperately for more air. She dressed hastily, her gaze darting around the small cave as if the healer might be in any corner. "I need to get out of here," she told Nicolae. "Just for a little while. I can't breathe down here." It sounded silly, like a fabricated excuse, but it was all too real.

"He is here," Nicolae announced, his hand tangling casually in the thick mass of her hair. She knew the gesture was meant to steady her.

She reached up and caught his hand, clinging unashamedly to him. Her Nicolae. Her rock. He was already dressed impeccably, elegantly, a prince of old. The man materializing deep beneath the mountain would render judgment on them. He strode toward them, a stocky man with power clinging to every inc.

of his body, lines etched into his hard features, his eyes a slashing silver.

For one moment the world wavered, turning a strange black with countless shooting stars, but Nicolae's arm wrapped around her body, drew her beneath his broad shoulder against the shelter of his strength. The spinning world righted, and she followed the steady rhythm of his breathing. Despite the weight of his opinion, this man in no way distressed Nicolae. He was unconcerned about the verdict. His gaze was hard and watchful. Behind them and a little to their right was Vikirnoff.

Destiny became aware of Vikirnoff's unblinking stare, as cold as death, watching Gregori's every move. Vikirnoff would stand solidly with his brother as always, tainted blood or no. It occurred to her that Vikirnoff had known the instant Nicolae had taken her blood and he had not merged with her in an attempt to stop him. With that awareness came the realization that Gregori had entered this small chamber beneath the earth without really knowing any of the parties within. He was truly risking his life to give them aid.

He looked big and strong and capable, a glittering menace, but the two Carpathians were ancients, every bit as well versed in battle as he. She decided Gregori was a very courageous man.

Nicolae stepped forward to greet him in the way of a warrior, gripping Gregori's forearms, his body cleverly inserted between Destiny and the stranger. "Gregori, how good of you to come so quickly. I am Nicolae, once under the command of Vladimer Dubrinsky. This is my brother, Vikirnoff." He waved toward the silent sentinel to his right.

Vikirnoff stepped forward, his cold, dead eyes meeting the glittering silver ones. "I thank you for answering the call. It is good that you are here," he said, formally clasping Gregori's forearms.

Destiny realized that the gesture made both hunters vulnerable. They were face to face, reading what they would give of their minds.

"It is good to see you. Mikhail has recently learned of the continuing existence of ancients in the world and has put out the call to return and regroup if at all possible. He will be pleased to know he has two more elders. Falcon still lives." His glittering gaze moved beyond Nicolae to rest on Destiny.

She lifted her chin at him. Let him pass his judgment. She had lived a long while without family or friends. She could do so again. Although secretly, she wasn't altogether certain that was the truth. She had begun to hope and dream in spite of her determination not to fall into that trap. Her gaze lifted to Nicolae. What if this strange man with his powerful eyes could take away her lifemate?

He cannot. Nicolae didn't send her waves of warmth and reassurance. His words were simple and calm. Completely confident. The terrible rolling in her stomach subsided.

"My lifemate, Destiny." Nicolae took her hand, drew her to him, his arm sliding around her waist possessively.

Gregori bowed low, an elegant courtly gesture she recognized from watching Nicolae. "You have had a difficult time of it. It is my privilege and honor to meet a woman so courageous." His gaze shifted around the room. "My lifemate should be here. That woman is always late." If he had tried to instill impatience into the beautiful tones of his voice, he failed utterly. He sounded so loving, Nicolae smirked and Vikirnoff raised an arrogant eyebrow.

There was a tinkle of laughter, and a small, dark-haired woman shimmered into form at Gregori's side. Nicolae knew immediately that Gregori had insisted on her safety, not allowing her to appear until he had ascertained for himself that the surroundings were perfectly safe for his lifemate. It was exactly what Nicolae would have done. He was grateful to the healer for choosing to put Destiny at ease by implying his lifemate was late.

Gregori gathered the petite woman beneath his shoulder. "My lifemate, Savannah, daughter to Prince Mikhail and his lifemate, Raven. Savannah, this is Destiny, her lifemate, Nicolae, and his brother, Vikirnoff."

Savannah wrinkled her nose. "I don't think it's necessary to give my pedigree, for heaven's sake." She rubbed her palm lovingly over Gregori's strong jaw. "It's such a pleasure to meet all of you. And such a wonderful surprise to know you're in the world with us. Our race needs every single one of us."

"Thank you for making the journey," Nicolae said. "We do not know if it is possible to remove the tainted blood from our veins, but we hope that you will try."

Gregori's face was an expressionless mask, but his voice was as gentle as a breeze. "I will confess I have never run up against exactly this problem. Aidan, one of our hunters, has a lifemate who was forced to take the blood of a vampire. The undead did not completely convert her, and the amount of blood was small as he was attempting to starve her to get her to voluntarily take his blood, but Aidan was able to cleanse her. If you have been able to fight off the effects of the blood all this time, then I have to think it is possible to remove it from your system. Your soul is intact."

Destiny's breath left her lungs in a long rush of relief. She held the healer's words close to her. Her soul was intact. Turning her face up to Nicolae she simply smiled. *I love you.*

His breath stilled in his lungs. His body went still. *Now? You are going to tell me now?*

I think it best.

We have to work on your timing. Nicolae's arm tightened possessively.

Destiny laughed aloud, the sound spilling out of her mind and heart to fill the small cave with joy. *Velda and Inez would be disappointed with me.*

He bent his dark head to hers. "I am not." He whispered the words against her lips. His kiss was loving, tender.

"Try not to notice them," Vikirnoff advised. "It is the only way. He has lost all sense and there is nothing to be done."

"I think it's great," Savannah declared, hugging Gregori closer.

"We have much to tell," Vikirnoff hissed softly at Nicolae.

Nicolae finished kissing his lifemate with leisurely unconcern for his brother. He lifted his head reluctantly, his hand sliding through her hair. "Vikirnoff is a man of few words. There is news that is important for our Prince to know."

Gregori sat on the largest of the flat boulders, drew Savannah up next to him. "We would very much like to hear, and we have information in trade."

"A trap was laid for Destiny by a vampire who goes

by the name of Pater. He not only had several lesser vampires with him, but they were well coordinated and aided each other. He even offered his blood to one of them."

Destiny watched Gregori's reaction very closely. He was a powerful, dangerous man, much like her lifemate. His mouth hardened perceptibly. "An unusual phenomenon."

Water trickled from the far cavern wall, the sound loud in the ensuing silence. "He wanted me to join with them," Destiny admitted in a little rush. "He recognized the stench of evil in my blood, and he called to me and asked me to join their movement."

Savannah made a soft sound of distress. "How awful for you, and so frightening."

"It was difficult to face the truth of his words. My blood is like a beacon drawing the vampires. When I hunt them, they are always aware of me."

Gregori held up an imperious hand. His silver eyes moved from Destiny to Nicolae. "This woman hunts the undead?"

Destiny laid her hand on Nicolae's chest, suddenly furious that he would have to defend her actions. Tiny red flames leapt in her eyes. "I don't need Nicolae to answer for me. I'm perfectly capable of speaking for myself."

Savannah's soft mouth twitched, and she coughed delicately into her hand.

Gregori shifted, a rippling of muscle. His eyes shifted back to Destiny's furious face. He bowed his head slightly. "Forgive me. In our society, women are guarded carefully as the treasures they are. We need every one of them and do not care to risk their lives. I did not mean to offend." There was a clear reprimand in his semi-conciliatory words.

Destiny met Savannah's laughing eyes. "You poor woman. Is he always like that? Vikirnoff has the same attitude."

"You get used to him." Savannah ignored Gregori's warning touch. "He's all bark, no bite. I'm doing my best to convince him I would make a great hunter, but so far he's unconvinced. Do you really hunt vampires?" There was genuine interest and admiration in her voice.

Gregori's strange silver eyes glittered with menace. "Savannah." He sounded very severe. He stirred, a menace of movement.

Savannah leaned into him but didn't subside. "How did you ever get started?" she asked Destiny.

The taunting half-smile directed in Gregori's direction froze on Destiny's face. She reached almost blindly for Nicolae's hand. He was there instantly, his fingers threading through hers. "Destiny was taken by a vampire as a small child. He forced her to take his blood and converted her. Fortunately, she is psychic and the conversion did not destroy her. She had no choice but to learn to hunt. It was the only way to gain her freedom." Nicolae gave the information easily, casually, as if he weren't telling a story of terrible atrocity and torture.

Savannah turned to her lifemate. His hand moved lovingly over her small face. He bowed again toward Destiny in a gesture of respect. "Few people could survive such a thing. It is an honor for me to attempt a healing on such a strong, courageous person. Your survival is a true testament to the beauty of a woman's spirit."

Destiny had expected to be shunned. She had steeled

herself for it. Being accepted was unsettling. She didn't know how to respond to warmth and acceptance. She gaped at the newcomers as if they had grown new heads.

Nicolae. She sounded lost. A child seeking reassurance. The sands were shifting under her feet. Everything she had believed seemed untrue. Gregori was intimidating, but certainly less so than Nicolae could be. And Savannah was completely open and friendly.

"Thank you," she managed to stammer aloud.

"Tell me more about this vampire Pater and his coalition," Gregori suggested to Nicolae.

"I have noticed the vampires have been traveling together more, banding together in small groups. They have done so at times throughout the centuries, but never in such numbers. This is the first time I have encountered one who actually tried to recruit. He spoke of the power of numbers and how they could defeat hunters by aiding one another. He spoke to others like a commander in an army. He tried hard to get Destiny. And he is smart, this one. The poisons he used are more sophisticated than any I have seen before." Nicolae raked his fingers through his hair and met Gregori's glittering eyes. "I believe the threat to our people, and in particular to our Prince, is a serious one."

There was a small silence while Gregori pondered Nicolae's remarks. "Many of the ancients use lesser or fledgling vampires as sacrificial pawns. This is not the same thing. They are actually aiding each other and sharing blood?"

"I saw Pater offer his blood to a wounded vampire," Destiny said. "He was aggressively trying to recruit me to his side. The worst of it is, he actually made sense.

They ambush their enemies and then get out fast to cut down on their losses."

Nicolae nodded. "They're using battle strategy instead of simply hitting fast and hard and emotionally. It was very unlike them." He glanced at his brother.

Vikirnoff shrugged carelessly. "Too organized. They have someone directing them; someone of power."

"A very powerful ancient. Intelligent, well versed in battle and in propaganda. He shows restraint, and the vampires he chooses to recruit and hold small bands together also show restraint," Nicolae added. "I would have to say he probably has tried this before, maybe many times over the centuries, and has learned patiently from his mistakes. He is after the death of every hunter. Then the world would be open to him."

"Patience is not something many vampires have," Gregori mused aloud. "This is unsettling news." He didn't think to question Nicolae's conclusion. Nicolae and Vikirnoff were both older and more seasoned in battle than even he.

"The poison they used was multigenerational," Nicolae said. "As the second generation mutated within the body, it was programmed to attack any healer. I have noticed for some time the use of poison as a method for capturing and defeating hunters. I know that those humans hunting all of us have used such methods, and it is my belief that this coalition of vampires uses those humans for experimenting with chemical ways to defeat us."

Gregori sighed. "Very sophisticated chemicals, it seems. I have seen vampires use the human society of hunters to further their own cause. It is not difficult for one to infiltrate their ranks."

"Pater mentioned spies, Carpathians perhaps, working with him," Destiny said. "At least he implied it."

"No Carpathian would do such a thing." Savannah sounded shocked at the idea. "They would have had to turn vampire."

"Well, you'd smell a vampire a mile away," Destiny said.

"Not necessarily," Gregori said. "Many are able to shadow themselves, projecting an image even to those of us who know them. Every Carpathian has power in varying degrees. What one does, perhaps another cannot. It is so with vampires."

"I can always smell a vampire," Destiny asserted. "And they can always scent me. Blood calls to blood." She ran her hand down Nicolae's arm. "I was so upset when Nicolae took my blood and infected himself. As a hunter, he will no longer be able to surprise them. They will know he is coming for them."

Gregori's silver eyes turned thoughtful. "You are saying that no matter what the circumstances, no matter how powerful the vampire, you *always* know when one is close by? You do not need the sudden surge of power or the blank void they often leave behind in their wake to detect their presence?"

Destiny thought back over her vampire hunting. "I use the surge of power and also the blank spots as a guide. I use everything I can to find them, and once in a while I find a vampire that is elusive to me, but most of the time I know them simply by the stench of their blood."

"The elusive vampire is more powerful than the others?"

Destiny shook her head. "Not necessarily. Sometimes

he is a fledgling and other times a master. It is rare for my blood not to recognize theirs."

Above her head, Nicolae and Gregori exchanged a long, thoughtful look.

"No." Vikirnoff said the word softly, explosively. "What you are thinking is an abomination of all we believe in. Our women must be protected at all times. Both of you have lifemates. You have seen what thc tainted blood does. Destiny has been in agony, suffering tremendous pain, both physical and psychological. All of our women are needed for a higher purpose than war. They must bring children into the world."

Savannah caught Gregori's arm. "You wouldn't dare. Not even for the life of my father would I allow such a thing."

"Certainly not a woman, and, no, Nicolae, I know what you are thinking, but Vikirnoff is right, we cannot risk a mated pair. Mikhail must hear of this firsthand. I must return to our homeland as soon as your healing is complete."

"There is more." Nicolae produced the photograph of the mysterious woman. "A vampire entered the office of a human friend of ours, MaryAnn Delaney, who helps battered women. He was searching for this woman in the photograph. He buried a compulsion in MaryAnn's mind to call him if she spotted the woman. There are a couple of interesting facts. MaryAnn herself is psychic. She is able to be converted should she have a lifemate among us, yet this vampire didn't attempt to seize her for himself. I have always assumed vampires searched for women with psychic abilities in the hope of finding a mate to return their soul to them. It is evidently not the case in this instance. They must be looking for something we have yet to figure out, or why would they ignore the psychic women in this area? With the exception of this one woman."

Gregori continued to study Nicolae's dark features before he took the photograph. His restless gaze noted the way Vikirnoff seemed riveted to the picture. "I have not seen this woman, have you, Savannah?"

She studied the face carefully. "No, but her eyes are so haunted. We must find her, Gregori. She can't be left to the vampires."

"Vikirnoff has agreed to look for her," Nicolae assured them. "This is the business card and number the vampire gave to MaryAnn." He passed the small card to Gregori. "She has no memory of his appearance, so I do not know if he is familiar to me or not."

"It wasn't Pater," Destiny said. "The stench was there, but not his."

"Morrison Center for Psychic Research," Gregori read aloud.

"Yet he had no interest in MaryAnn's ability. And there is another in the neighborhood, an older woman who also exhibits talent. I could not detect any interest in her by any of the vampires."

"I have heard the name Morrison on more than one occasion," Gregori said heavily. "The first time was in northern California. Coincidentally, it was also a time I was injected with a poison developed to defeat us. At that time I learned this Morrison mingled with human society, was adept at raising funds and mixed in the scientific world. I nearly met him again in New Orleans."

Savannah twisted around to look up at her lifemate. "You didn't tell me that."

"It was unnecessary. The name was attached to the laboratory where the human hunters were attempting to interrogate an innocent human woman. It is where I met Gary, Savannah. This name came up again just recently. Dayan's lifemate was married to a young man of talent who went to this agency, Morrison Center for Psychic Research, to be tested. He was murdered, and an attempt was made to acquire Dayan's lifemate, who was quite ill. We have just come from her bedside where she gave birth to a female child of extraordinary talent."

"Perhaps we should send word to guard the child," Savannah said, frowning. "If Destiny was taken, it is possible this vampire thinks to strike at children."

"Guarding the child would be a good idea, although I think this Morrison is looking for a particular talent. This is no child," Nicolae said, waving the photograph in the air. "She is a woman who is strong and knows she is being pursued."

Vikirnoff reached out and rescued the photograph from his brother, slipping it inside his shirt almost protectively.

Nicolae ignored the gesture. "There are three women with psychic talent in this area. There is also a priest who has knowledge of our people."

Gregori's breath hissed between his teeth. "Tell me of this man."

"Some years ago, a priest in Romania—"

"Father Hummer." Gregori snapped the name, his strong white teeth coming together in a bite. "Mikhail's friend. He was captured by vampire hunters and later killed by a vampire. Mikhail was the target."

"He evidently corresponded with a cardinal, asking theological questions, seeking aid in his search. The cardinal burned his letters with the exception of one. Father Mulligan found the letter upon the cardinal's death. He has since burned it, recognizing the danger to our species, but he retains the knowledge."

Gregori rubbed his dark eyebrows. "I fear trouble is brewing for our people. We must get to our homeland." He looked directly at Vikirnoff as if measuring him. "If this woman is important enough for a vampire to risk revealing himself, it is just as important to our people to find her. I will put out the word, but I will tell our Prince it is in your hands."

Vikirnoff bowed slightly. "I will find her. I give you my word of honor I will not choose the dawn until I see to her safety."

"It could take years."

"I have Nicolae and Destiny to guide me through dark times. They share their laughter with me, and their hope. I will survive."

Gregori inclined his head. "So it will be. We must think about this tainted blood of yours, Destiny. You said you would have recognized the stench of Pater's blood. You are able to detect a difference in each vampire's blood?"

Destiny nodded. "Yes. If I've met them before, I always recognize them and I know they recognize me. That makes it more difficult if I miss the first time when I'm hunting. But it gives me some advantage if they don't know I'm a hunter, because they identify me as one of the undead."

"This would be a great tool," Gregori mused aloud, "but dangerous for anyone without an anchor. And far too dangerous for anyone with a lifemate."

"You don't even know if you can rid our blood of the

infections," Nicolae pointed out. "Perhaps you will know more once you have looked. It is much like an acid and contaminates everything it touches. In one wholly evil, it apparently has no harmful effects, but to one of the light, it is painful and dangerous."

Destiny looked at him quickly, anxiously. "You're beginning to feel the effects, aren't you? Please heal him first if you can, Gregori. I'm used to the feeling, and it doesn't really bother me. Nicolae should never have done such a thing."

"I would have done exactly the same thing," Gregori said.

Destiny studied his face. "No, you wouldn't have."

Savannah laughed softly. "Oh, yes, he would."

"If Savannah were infected, I would never hesitate. We are bound, two halves of the same whole. I would not have thought twice," Gregori said decisively. "Are you feeling the effects, Nicolae?"

Nicolae nodded. "I have examined my internal body, and the lesions are already forming in great numbers. The toxins are multiplying at a far faster rate than in Destiny's body. I carry a seed of darkness, even with Destiny as my anchor, and the toxins sense it and feed as if in a frenzy."

Destiny turned on him, her expression fiercely protective. "There is no darkness in you. You're so silly, Nicolae. You don't know yourself at all. I've seen darkness, I've seen monsters. You do *not* carry even a tiny germ of such evil."

His arms immediately surrounded her, held her trembling body safe. "We are not all made up of one trait, little one," he soothed softly. "I know it is hard to think I could have more than one side, but darkness can be many things, including strength. It does not have to be used for evil. One's very flaws can be utilized for good."

"This is quite interesting. Aidan's lifemate, Alexandria, endured a particularly difficult conversion, but he did not report lesions and these things you speak of. We may as well get started," Gregori decided. "I want to know what I am dealing with. I expect this will take much time and energy, so I will heal Nicolae first."

"Absolutely not." Nicolae was resolute.

"Hear me out," Gregori suggested mildly. "Your instinct is to ensure Destiny's health first, but that is not the wisest choice. She has carried the vampire's blood, and indeed was converted by it. Her healing will be much more difficult. I will need much blood to accomplish such a feat. There are only Vikirnoff and Savannah to supply me as my energy wanes. I will have need of you. The surges of power will certainly tip off every vampire in the area to our exact location. There is only Vikirnoff to hold them off. This will be no small struggle, and I will need your strength."

Destiny curled her fingers through Nicolae's, brought his hand to her mouth. Her teeth nibbled nervously on his knuckles. She had spent so little time with other people. Her instincts told her Gregori was powerful. There was a slight chance he could heal them. Deep inside, where it counted, where she would admit things she couldn't face, she knew Nicolae spoke the truth about the darkness in him. She recognized it. It was very strong in Vikirnoff, and it was strong in Gregori. She had learned, from her experience with Nicolae, to discern the difference between the hunters carrying the darkness and the actual taint of the vampire's blood.

But it was there. It was present. She was surrounded

by it, and it made her nervous. It also called to the darkness in her blood. She was hot and restless, having to work at controlling her body's temperature. Only her love for Nicolae kept her in the small confines of the cave. If she went along with this, she would be totally vulnerable. Nicolae would be under a stranger's control.

I am an ancient, Destiny. Vikirnoff remains to see to our safety, even though he feels a need to begin his hunt. There is little that can be done to harm me without my knowledge. I will be able to break away from Gregori should there be need. But it is up to you. If you do not want to do this thing, we will not.

She heard the utter sincerity in his voice. It was that simple for him. If she were uncomfortable and chose not to allow the healer to perform, he would calmly go along with her decision.

"You're crazy, you know that?" She gave an exaggerated sigh as she shoved him toward Gregori. Her heart was pounding like crazy, but she would not allow him to suffer because she was a coward.

"In case you are wondering what that meant," Nicolae explained to the others, "Destiny is showing me her affection and complete devotion."

"It sounds familiar to me," Savannah laughed. "Don't worry, Destiny, he's in good hands. Gregori goes around looking intimidating and mean because in the old country the mothers scared their children by telling them stories of the dark one. He liked the image and cultivated it."

Gregori flexed his broad shoulders, and muscles rippled impressively across his body. His expression didn't change. "It always helps when I wish to intimidate Savannah's father."

"The Prince?" Destiny asked.

"Why are you listening to him?" Savannah demanded. "As if my father would ever be intimidated by him. They're best friends, Destiny. He's teasing you."

Destiny looked skeptical. Gregori didn't intimidate her nearly as much as Vikirnoff, but only because of Savannah. The way Gregori looked at the petite woman negated every vestige of menace in his eyes. Vikirnoff was without emotion, simply watching all of them with his flat, cold stare. It was only his intense loyalty to Nicolae that kept him there, that allowed him to take Destiny under his protection.

Vikirnoff is no different from me before I found you. He must hold on until he finds his lifemate.

Just hurry and do this, Nicolae, before you find out I'm not nearly as courageous as you think I am.

Nicolae framed her face with his hands, ignoring the others. "Stay right here while Gregori is working on me."

She looked into his dark, intense eyes. "I wouldn't want to be anywhere else. Someone has to watch over you."

He closed the scant inches between them, claiming her mouth, storming his way straight to her heart. She kissed him back hungrily, a little desperately, afraid for him. Nicolae held her close while her heart beat frantically against his.

"Hurry, Nicolae, before I change my mind." It was a soft whispered plea.

Gregori opened the earth, searching for a bed of deep soil. Nicolae seated himself in the lush richness, drawing Destiny down beside him, his hand firmly enveloping hers. She found herself clinging to his strength, her mind remaining firmly merged with his. Her body was trembling. There was so much riding on this—their entire future.

No, there is not, Destiny. Our future is secure together whether Gregori succeeds or not. The difference is whether we will be able to bring children into the world.

Children? There you go again, bringing up that subject out of the blue. In all the times we were making love, you never once mentioned children.

I thought it best not to.

Her Nicolae. Understanding her. Going along with her teasing because he knew she joked when she was afraid.

And then she felt him. A power like no other she'd ever experienced. Gregori. The dark one. Healer of the Carpathian people. His spirit was immensely strong, a hot white light moving through Nicolae without preamble. She felt Nicolae's insides burning hot, but not painfully so. The healer examined him thoroughly. She knew Gregori was aware of her presence, but he paid strict attention to Nicolae's body.

Destiny had no idea of time passing. She too was studying the effects of the vampire blood on Nicolae. His body had the blood of the ancients and it was fighting valiantly, but she could see the damage that had already been done. She didn't make the mistake of gasping with her physical body, but she was appalled at the destruction.

Nicolae had calmly endured it. And he meant to continue to do so should Gregori be unable to rid his body of the hideous toxins. Her respect and love for him grew to new proportions. She emerged at the same time as the healer withdrew.

Gregori let his breath out slowly. "Nasty stuff, vampire blood."

Savannah rubbed his neck soothingly. "It moved away from you."

"Yes, I suspect it has some knowledge I have come to remove it. The fear is a good thing. If it is afraid and moving from my presence, I should be able to find a way to remove it from Nicolae's body."

"Can you help him?" Destiny asked anxiously.

Nicolae noted immediately that she hadn't said "us." He tightened his fingers around hers. "I cannot turn vampire, Destiny," he assured her quietly. "I have you as my anchor."

Gregori shook his head. "It is puzzling how such a minute amount of vampire blood could infect you so quickly. You have lesions everywhere; they are spreading across every organ. Alexandria did not have such a thing or Aidan would have told me. He described to me his healing of her in detail but there was none of this."

"Destiny has whole colonies of them," Nicolae said.

Gregori frowned. "Savannah, we will need candles, and the bag we brought with us from New Orleans. We did not need it for Dayan's lifemate, but I fear we will need all of it here."

Savannah nodded. "It's lucky we didn't use it." She produced a large satchel and tossed it to her lifemate.

Nicolae inhaled the contents of the satchel deeply. Vikirnoff followed suit. Destiny was startled by their reaction. She took an exploratory sniff. The scent was of earth. Clean, fresh dirt. It smelled different from any she had ever encountered. She looked at Nicolae. There was something close to rapture on his face.

"What is it?" she asked curiously.

"Soil from our homeland," Nicolae answered, awe in

his voice. "How did you come to have such a gift?" he asked Savannah.

"Julian Savage, one of our people, had it brought many years ago to New Orleans. He stored it in a hidden chamber and left it for us when we became lifemates," she explained. "It was a shocking but very welcome surprise."

Destiny could sense Nicolae's eagerness to put to use the treasure the healer had brought.

"We took some of the soil with us, thinking we might need it to aid Dayan and his lifemate when she was so ill, but it was not needed. We kept it for just such an emergency as this." Gregori smiled down at his lifemate. "It was Savannah's suggestion that we bring it along."

Destiny looked into the dark bag, saw the deep richness and felt her palms itch. Nicolae plunged his hands into the soil and closed his eyes.

Vikirnoff. You must feel this. I feel it all the way to my bones. A welcoming such as I have not had in centuries. Our homeland is in this small bag.

Vikirnoff reached into the bag slowly. His hands tunneled deep into the rich soil. *I am sharing your mind, Nicolae. This will sustain me as nothing else could. I feel a sense of peace for the first time in so long. Thank you for allowing me this experience.*

Destiny was sharing it with the two brothers. She sensed the intensity of Nicolae's feelings for his brother and realized that the only way Vikirnoff could feel that love was through Nicolae's emotions.

Emotions you returned to him, Vikirnoff reminded them.

Returned to us, Nicolae corrected.

Chapter Nineteen

There was silence in the cave. Destiny looked around her at the candles burning in every conceivable space. Hundreds of them, tiny pinpoints of light releasing a soothing aroma of spice and the scents of healing. Essential oils were warming in small, nearly flat receptacles heated by the flames. These candles were meticulously crafted by the Carpathian people to be used in difficult healing sessions.

Gregori looked even more impressive as he seated himself beside Nicolae, his dark hair gleaming in the flickering light, his eyes liquid silver. Nicolae lay in a shallow depression of earth beside Gregori, his head in Destiny's lap. She stroked strands of long, silky hair from his face with gentle fingers. His dark gaze was firmly locked on hers.

Breathe, little one. You look so frightened. You will give me no choice but to kiss that look from your face. Gregori is a great man. He has not condemned us as you feared. Rather, he and his lifemate have welcomed

*you, welcomed us and agreed to aid us with this heal-
ing. You must trust him.*

Destiny took a deep breath, took the healing scents
deep into her lungs. *I trust only you, Nicolae, no other.
I almost wish they had condemned us. This woman is
the Prince's daughter, yet she welcomes me with open
arms. She has no idea what lies hidden inside me. I feel
guilty every time I look at her, as if I'm hiding some
terrible secret.*

*What Gregori knows, his lifemate knows. Savannah
is Carpathian and typical of our people. None would
condemn you. All will welcome you and would seek to
aid you. Do not fear belonging, Destiny.*

She tunneled her fingers in his hair, gripping with her
fists as if she might hold him to her. Her tongue moist-
ened her suddenly dry lips and she lifted her chin,
meeting the strange, glittering eyes of the healer. She
met his merciless gaze without flinching, trying to convey with a look what she felt. She didn't dare say it
aloud, not with Nicolae so certain this man would aid
them. She hoped the healer could read that she didn't
fear death. She didn't fear anything this man could do
to her. But if he harmed Nicolae in any way, she would
cut out his heart and incinerate it before welcoming her
own death.

Gregori's eyebrows lifted as if he were reading her
mind and he glanced briefly at his lifemate. *I do not
think my considerable charm has worked on her.*

Savannah looked at him lovingly, her fingers sliding
through his hair. "I know you can do this, Gregori." She
spoke aloud to encourage Destiny. Gregori didn't need
her encouragement. *You forgot to smile,* she told him.
I have mentioned on more than one occasion that

smiling is considered important in public relations. I fear I'll never manage to get that through your head.

If it were possible, his dark eyebrows rose higher, his silver eyes warming with love and suppressed laughter before he turned, completely sober, back to Nicolae.

Destiny watched the man as he simply shed his body and withdrew from them. He became light, energy in its purest, most selfless form. He entered Nicolae's body and began waging the most difficult battle he had ever fought. The tainted blood separated from ancient blood, rushing away from him, straight toward Nicolae's heart, as if attacking its host.

Destiny, merged deeply with Nicolae, watched in horror as the hideous brew raced for his heart. *Sleep!* Without preamble, using their strong blood bond, she shut down Nicolae's heart and lungs instantly, trapping the blood in his veins, preventing the sludge from reaching its objective. She stayed hovering there, watching the nearly blinding light moving through Nicolae's body, aware of the intense heat. There was no feeling of censure from the healer, nor did Gregori hesitate or become distracted by her interference.

The blood congealed into a thick, pulsating mass. Destiny could see pinpoints of hemorrhage and masses of lesions. Internal organs were slightly misshapen, and colonies of toxins were scattered throughout Nicolae's system. She realized the tainted blood was willing to fight for possession of the host body.

The healer was undaunted, moving unerringly toward the thick clots of infestation. To Destiny's horror, something thin and black moved within the pulsating mass. Tiny creatures, living parasites. She wanted to scream and scream. The need was so strong, she pressed her hand to her mouth to keep from diverting the healer from his task. Those hideous creatures lived inside her, she knew, and she had infected Nicolae. The idea was repulsive. Disgusting. She had lived with the creatures for years, never fully realizing how abnormal they were until she saw them infesting Nicolae's body.

Nicolae stirred. His heart beat once, twice. The horrible wriggling creatures massed as if eagerly awaiting the movement of blood.

Your distress is calling to him. Calm yourself. Gregori connected through the mind merge Destiny had with her lifemate. *He can do no other than come to you if you need him. You are Carpathian, woman, not vampire. Do not allow him to awaken.*

The voice, more than anything else, calmed her. She forced air through her lungs, beat away despair and horror, soothing Nicolae back to the Carpathian sleep. Her fingers bunched in his hair, her only lifeline to sanity. She couldn't think about what lived and squirmed inside her. What she had passed to Nicolae. Unclean. She was unclean.

Focus! The voice was firm. *I need your help with this.*

Destiny would do anything to rid Nicolae of the tainted blood. She pushed her revulsion and emotions as far from her as she could and concentrated on the bright light. Gregori was moving steadily toward the series of thick clots. The ugly masses erupted with swarming tiny black wormlike parasites. Several attacked, throwing their wriggling bodies at the light as if they might consume it. The hideous things hit an invisible barrier and were instantly destroyed.

Pandemonium broke out. Light exploded, a laser show of bright white, obliterating everything in its path. Time passed as the healer meticulously began to hunt the parasites and destroy them, herding them inevitably toward the ancient blood lying dormant in the veins. As he chased them, Gregori obliterated colony after colony.

Destiny couldn't believe how long he worked, examining every inch of Nicolae to ferret out the infestation. The healer had to examine every artery, every vein, networks of blood vessels.

It was then Destiny became aware of the chanting of familiar words. Savannah and Vikirnoff lifted their voices in the age-old healing ritual. The light was fading, blurring around the edges and turning almost transparent.

Gregori's spirit emerged from Nicolae's body. The healer was swaying with weariness, so pale he was nearly gray. Destiny bit her lower lip as she watched Vikirnoff offer his wrist to the healer. She knew Nicolae's brother was offering his life. He had no lifemate to anchor him to the world. Giving Gregori his blood would create a bond between them. Gregori could easily track him should there be need. It was a selfless act, and one that unexpectedly tugged at her heartstrings.

She sat quietly, rocking back and forth, stroking Nicolae's hair, not wanting to look at Gregori or his lifemate. Destiny hadn't known the ugly truth about her blood. Nicolae had been infected only a couple of risings. She had been infected for long years. She had never realized that the parasites had been passed to her from the vampire who had taken her as a child. She hadn't known what was normal and what wasn't.

The healer was not finished with Nicolae, and yet he was already swaying with weariness, his great strength drained. It seemed an impossibility that he could heal her after so many years of being infected.

Gregori took a great deal of blood, leaving Vikirnoff weak. Destiny saw the ancient warrior stagger as he turned away.

"You must feed well. Nicolae will need your blood," Gregori instructed.

"I will go quickly, but perhaps you should wait for my return before going in again," Vikirnoff suggested. "I do not want to leave you and the women vulnerable to an attack."

"I do not think I have time to wait if I am to do this thing. His brain and every organ must be cleansed." Gregori sprinkled the rich Carpathian soil over Nicolae, opened his palms and placed some in his hands. "Return as quickly as you can," he urged.

"Is it possible to do this?" Destiny asked. "Did you know those things were there? Have you ever encountered them before?" She didn't want it to be just her, that she was the only one tainted. "If Nicolae's body is so infected, what must mine be like?"

Gregori's peculiar eyes moved over her face, leaving behind a strange, warming calm. "No, I had no idea they were there. Certainly Alexandria had no such creatures in her blood when Aidan performed the healing ritual. This is far different, but I have no idea why. I will heal Nicolae, Destiny, and I will heal you. The vampire will not claim a victory here." He spoke with complete confidence. Destiny couldn't tell whether he believed his statement or not, but his words gave her a semblance of hope.

Without further hesitation, Gregori once more shed his physical body to become the healing light of his kind.

Destiny was aware on one level of Vikirnoff leaving the chamber, but she concentrated on watching Gregori's meticulous assault on the vampire's blood. The organs were harboring a few tiny, immature parasites. They seemed capable of tremendous damage, tunneling into the organs, burning as they did so.

The healer dispatched them wherever he found them, cleansing the organs and carefully reshaping them. Destiny watched with awe, respect for the man growing as he worked. She was aware of the difficulties, the amount of strength it took to be outside one's body. She began to understand that the form of energy he was utilizing to heal was nearly impossible to maintain for any length of time. She was witnessing a miracle.

She was so engrossed in what he was doing, she nearly failed to notice the sudden stirring of the remaining creatures in Nicolae's blood. They leapt, almost with excitement, wriggling like frenzied maggots. A dark shadow slipped across her soul.

The vampires are here, in this place with us, she told Gregori. She could not reach Vikirnoff without Nicolae. Her lifemate lay as still as death, and even if she awakened him, he would be drained of all strength, helpless. Gregori was in his brain, continuing his careful, meticulous healing.

I dare not stop; he would not survive.

I can hold them off. She spoke with complete confidence. *You keep my lifemate safe and I will keep yours safe.* It was a threat as well as a promise. If Gregori pulled out before he finished, Nicolae would die of a brain hemorrhage.

Gregori's instincts were to save his lifemate from the vampires first, yet he would give Destiny an opportunity to protect them all. He had been immersed in Nicolae's mind, read his many battles, his brilliant strategies, and knew he had passed his skills on to Destiny. Gregori could just as easily read the battles Destiny had fought. He was determined to give her the chance to save her lifemate by keeping his Savannah safe. If Savannah were in imminent danger, he could do no other than act in her behalf, but he was willing to allow Destiny to do what she did best, destroy the vampire.

Destiny understood that reasoning and accepted it, just as he accepted her own determination to save Nicolae.

Savannah was already moving to place her small body between the danger and her lifemate and his patient.

Destiny leapt upon her, one arm circling her throat, claws emerging to press tightly into her delicate skin. "Trust me." She mouthed the words against Savannah's neck, praying the healer would realize she was buying them time. Vikirnoff would be in the city now, taking much-needed blood. He would return with all haste.

"Brethren!" a vampire called. "Come to me in haste. I have the daughter of the Prince as a gift to buy my way into the alliance. Hurry before the other hunter returns and this one regains his strength. He is stuck in the body of the other. Our blood is strong and holds him there."

Savannah struggled, looking as helpless as she could. Destiny dragged Savannah's arm behind her back and placed a dagger in her palm, their bodies concealing the weapon between them.

The first intruder erupted from the ground, spewing dirt in a dark cloud as he rose. A second scaled the cavern wall, much like a human lizard, clinging to the rock above their heads. Destiny watched them, her mind assimilating the threat, choosing quickly which of the two was the more experienced and more dangerous.

"Take her," Destiny invited, thrusting Savannah toward the lesser vampire. "I'll kill the healer." She did a back-flip, raced up the wall toward the creature overhead, trusting Savannah to make the kill.

Savannah had never hunted the undead. Gregori had been adamant that she not ever place her life in danger, but she had been in his head enough to know what to do. She acted at once, without hesitation, stumbling forward as if unable to control her momentum. The vampire's fetid breath scorched her face. She felt his hands on her shoulders, reaching to yank her to him. And she went, the dagger concealed along her wrist. At the last possible second she plunged the razor-sharp instrument deep into his chest, straight into his heart.

Blackened blood poured over her hand, burning abominably. The vampire screamed, stumbling backward, his hands going to the dagger. Savannah leapt away from him, careful to keep her body between her lifemate and the undead.

Destiny reached the other vampire as he paused to witness the capture of such a prize as the Prince's daughter. He saw her coming too late to move, or shapeshift, relying on attack instead. They came together in a furious assault, bodies slamming together.

They fell to the cavern floor, only inches from the wounded vampire, both scrambling to regain their footing. Destiny threw herself into a scissors lock, weaving her legs through the vampire's and twisting as they both came down again, dropping him to the ground and pinning him there. She drove her fist deep, needing victory fast. She could see the wounded vampire pulling the knife from his chest. Worse, she felt the presence of another one, the ancient one. Pater had arrived.

"Get out, Savannah," Destiny instructed harshly.

Savannah leapt over the writhing vampire, trying to avoid the spewing blood, kicking him hard in the head so that he dropped backward like a stone. Her tactic gave Destiny the precious time she needed to extract the heart from the chest of the undead she had pinned. She threw the withered organ a distance from her and was already on the wounded one, straddling him, holding him down to take his heart.

Savannah built the necessary energy to incinerate the first heart, successfully completing the kill. As she turned back, she saw a black shadow loom above Destiny, one hand drawn back, the discarded and bloody dagger in his hand.

"Look out!" She had been about to direct the orange ball of flame at the body of the vampire, but turned it toward the shadow instead.

Destiny had managed to close her fingers around the heart of the wounded vampire, jerking hard as he thrashed and raked and battered her, fighting tooth and nail for his life. At Savannah's warning, she flinched sideways, still drawing the heart toward her, recognizing the danger but needing to finish off the vampire before he could regenerate or get away.

Pater plunged the dagger downward just as Destiny shifted, and the ball of energy, flaming red and white-hot, seared his shoulder, ruining his aim. The blade missed her back completely, slicing through her arm up high so that the heart fell from her suddenly nerveless fingers. It rolled away from her almost to the feet of the ancient undead.

Pater stared at the obscene organ; then his eyes went to Destiny's pale face. He hissed, a deadly promise of retribution, and instantly was gone.

Destiny clamped her hand over the gushing wound and looked at Savannah. "Destroy the heart and the vampire. I'm going after him. Vikirnoff will be here any minute or Pater probably wouldn't have left. Be certain to cleanse your hands or you'll blister and burn. You don't want to take the chance of getting any of that blood into your system."

Before Savannah could reply, Destiny had shifted shape, streaking through the network of caves to follow Pater. She knew where he would go. She knew what he had in mind. Nothing could stop her, not even the echo of Nicolae's cry of protest in her mind. Destiny had weaknesses the vampire could exploit, and every one of them was in the city. He would go after the people she had befriended.

She made no effort to hide her pursuit, hoping Pater would double back on her and attempt an ambush. At least that would keep her friends safe. It was three in the morning and most people would be asleep in bed, thinking themselves safe.

Destiny, return to me at once.

Nicolae was extremely weak. Gregori could not provide for him. Destiny was uncertain whether Gregori had managed to complete the healing ritual. In any case, she could not leave unsuspecting humans to a vampire.

Nicolae knew it and sighed. *Vikirnoff is replenishing us. You will have aid soon enough. Do not be careless.*

Before she could answer, she heard the call. A summoning. The power in the voice was awesome. Pater was an ancient, a powerful vampire, and his voice was thrown out over the neighborhood, calling sweetly to her friends. The compulsion in his voice slid down her spine like a shiver of fear.

Destiny forced calm into her mind. Where was the echo of his call, his scent? She scanned the skies for a blankness in an attempt to pinpoint his exact position. Frustrated by his skill, by his ability to hide, she went first to MaryAnn's house. The door to MaryAnn's home was open and Destiny could see her walking along the sidewalk dressed in her robe. As she passed the rectory, Father Mulligan emerged, dressed in sweats, without his glasses perched on his nose.

Destiny swooped down on them, taking her human shape as she hit the sidewalk running. She caught each of them by an arm and dragged them to the church. It took strength when they both tried vainly to reach the golden voice calling to them. As she unlocked the doors, MaryAnn escaped and had to be retrieved. Destiny thrust them both firmly into the safety of the church.

At once the sound of the vampire's melodic tones changed to a growling, spitting evil. Father Mulligan blinked and looked around him, astonished to find himself in the church. "I was having a dream."

MaryAnn sat in the nearest pew and glared at Destiny. "Not again. I'm in my bathrobe, for heaven's sake."

"Stay here. Don't you dare leave this church," Destiny ordered. She didn't stop to explain, closing the double doors behind her.

Destiny ran down the block to turn on the street where The Tavern was located. The priest and MaryAnn had both been heading in that direction. To her horror, she saw Tim and Martin shuffling down the back fire escape toward the street. She hurried toward them, racing up the street in the direction of the home of Inez and Velda. They weren't out yet, but she was certain they would be on the street momentarily.

Tim dropped from the ladder to the sidewalk, nearly in front of her. Without looking at her, or looking back at Martin, he began to walk down the block. Martin dropped to the sidewalk and hurried after his departing friend.

Spinning black clouds gathered swiftly overhead. Veins of lightning arced from cloud to cloud. Warily, Destiny glanced toward the sky. The wind rushed along the street, knocking Tim and Martin to the ground, releasing them from their enthrallment. The full force hit Destiny like a punch, lifting her off her feet, sending her flying backward to land a distance from the two human men.

Pay attention to the battle. You cannot help them if you are dead! Nicolae's voice was calm, but she knew him all too well now. He was on the move and he was angry. The storm generating over her head held a particular controlled fury she recognized.

Destiny rolled, dissolved to vapor, felt the brush of claws against her wounded shoulder. Droplets of red scattered across the ground, giving away her position in the gathering fog. She shifted course on the run, drawing the vampire away from the humans, taking several leaps to add distance before landing in a crouch, preparing herself for the attack she knew was coming.

The vampire rose up in front of her, a hideous sight with jagged teeth and flaming eyes. His breath was putrid, reeking of rot and decay. She had only time for one heartbeat of recognition. This was not Pater. Once again the wily ancient had sent in a lesser vampire to occupy her while he wreaked his vengeance.

She heard Tim scream in fear, as if at a distance, the thick fog muffling the sound. Martin was eerily silent. She had no time to get to them. She felt the impact as the vampire struck, tearing through muscle and tissue. She was staring straight into those blood-red eyes. Her fist had driven deep. They stared at one another. She watched his face contort, felt the power moving through her, and knew Nicolae was using her to destroy her enemy. The vampire began to gasp for air. The claw tearing through her body weakened, fell away from her.

Destiny staggered, forced strength into her arm where it was buried deep in the chest of the vampire. She dragged the heart from the body and managed to toss it a distance from her. Stumbling, she pushed her rubbery legs into action, searching for the two men.

A hand came out of the fog, gripped the front of her shirt and carelessly threw her through the air. She didn't see the vampire, only his hand coming out of the vapor with blurring speed. She hit the wall of Velda and Inez's house, slid down to the sidewalk, the air slamming out of her lungs. He was alarmingly strong.

Now would be a good time for you to rescue me. Destiny couldn't get her legs under her. She could only remain slumped against the wall.

He came out of the fog. Pater. His face was a mask of hatred. Of cold rage.

Focus on him. Nicolae was even closer than before.

Destiny couldn't keep her gaze steady on the vampire. His image continually blurred, so that it was impossible for Nicolae to lock onto him through her.

Move, Destiny. Get away from him. There was an edge to Nicolae's voice.

She couldn't move. She could only watch the creature grow in power and stature as he advanced on her. His body was fuzzy, replicating itself over and over as he loomed over her. He was hissing his hatred, a cross between the growl of a predator and the cold, reptilian hiss of a snake. Destiny felt the force of his hatred hit her hard before he reached her.

"You ruined everything, and in the end you will die as you should have long ago when you betrayed your blood," he snarled as he reached for her. One hand was extended, going for her throat, the nails long and razor-sharp.

Destiny simply watched the claw as it stretched out abnormally and waited for him to crush her. Before Pater reached her, a body inserted itself between the vampire and his prey. The woman was small with pink-tipped hair and matching tennis shoes. She looked frail but she stood her ground resolutely. "You will not touch her."

Destiny's heart nearly stopped. She couldn't watch this courageous woman, well into her seventies, die to give her a few more precious minutes of life. "Velda," she whispered softly in protest.

Velda faced the vampire unflinchingly. "You will not touch her," she said again. She managed to look and sound dignified and regal, even authoritative, dressed in baggy sweatpants and a sweatshirt with glittery hearts strewn across it, matching her neon pink tennis shoes.

Destiny blinked back tears of admiration and struggled to get to her feet, desperate to save Velda from her courageous folly.

To Destiny's astonishment, Pater froze, clearly shocked,

stiffening, every muscle tense. His face paled visibly, and for one moment, emotion stirred on the frightful mask of his face. Something crept into his expression— guilt, regret, sorrow. Destiny couldn't identify it.

Wind rushed through the street. Lightning flashed across the sky. Thunder crashed overhead, booming so loud it shook the houses. The lightning illuminated the face of the vampire, once handsome and sensual, now ravaged by evil. A gaunt parody of a man with blood-stained teeth and a withered, blackened heart. His expression changed from one of fleeting sorrow to cunning craftiness.

Pater let out his breath in a long, slow hiss of fury. "Do not try to trick me, old woman. Leave this place or I will kill you."

"This place is my home and you no longer belong here. Go and leave this girl." Velda sounded very firm and continued to look unflinchingly into his flaming gaze. His hypnotic voice clearly didn't work on her. The compulsion buried in his command failed to get results.

Pater stepped close to the old woman and bent his head toward her neck, his incisors prominently displayed. Instead of recoiling as expected, Velda moved to meet the tall, thin vampire as if to embrace him. She laid one withered hand on his chest, so that he paused, his mouth against her skin. "I waited for you. There was no other in my life. There could be no other. I will grieve for you and hope that God has mercy on your soul." She whipped up her other hand, concealed in the folds of her too large sweat pants, and attempted to drive the stake she held through Pater's chest.

He threw back his head and howled, his hand clamping around Velda's fragile wrist like a vise. Destiny used every ounce of remaining strength, drew on Nicolae for aid and leapt to her feet, shoving Velda's arm hard, driving the stake deep into Pater's heart. Destiny dragged the other woman backward, away from the flailing vampire. Pater screamed curses, spewing vile threats at the two women.

Velda's small body was shaking. She pressed her hand to her mouth, took a step toward the vampire, her hand out, obviously wanting to comfort him. "I'm sorry, I'm so sorry. You gave me no other choice."

"The only way to aid him is by giving him death," Destiny said, trying to comfort Velda even as she protectively thrust the older woman behind her.

Pater whirled away from them, only to find Gregori standing behind him. He turned back to the women to find Nicolae blocking his way. Vikirnoff was to his right.

Destiny slipped her arm around Velda. "We have to go, right now." She staggered as she tried to urge Velda back into the comparative safety of her home. "You don't want to see this."

Velda steadied Destiny, turned for one last look. Pater's gaze locked with hers. Velda's lips trembled. Destiny tugged at her, regaining the older woman's attention. "Please, Velda, let them do their job."

Velda burst into tears, a low cry of pain as she firmly closed the door, blocking out the wind and fog and death. "I felt him close by. He was meant for me. He was, Destiny. All these years I've been alone, waiting for him to come. And he is evil."

Destiny sank into a chair, her legs no longer able to hold herself up. "I'm sorry, Velda, so sorry. He wasn't always evil. There was a time in his life when he was a great man. I'm certain of it."

Velda hung her head. "Why didn't he find me?"

"I don't know. I have no answer for you."

"I could see the evil in him, as if he had rotted from the inside out. He embraced evil. Rejoiced in it. I looked for his heart and it was black. I looked for his soul and it was gone." Velda pressed a trembling hand to her mouth. "All these years alone, and it was for him. One moment I saw it in his eyes, an awareness of what could have been, and he rejected it. I saw him reject it."

"I'm so sorry, Velda." Destiny didn't know how to comfort her. "But thank you for having the courage to save my life."

"I would have saved him had he let me." Velda covered her face with her hands and sobbed as if her heart were broken.

"It was too late," Destiny said softly. "He gave in a long time ago."

Inez came out of the bedroom, frowning as she pulled at the cotton balls stuffed in her ears. "Whatever is going on? Velda. Dearest sister. You cannot cry like this. You'll make yourself ill." She slipped her arm around Velda's shoulders and turned her attention to Destiny. "You need an ambulance. You're soaked in blood."

Nicolae came through the door without knocking. Destiny's hungry gaze went to his face. Nicolae. Her sanity. Her white knight. Sorrow for Velda rose up to overwhelm her. *We cannot leave her this way.*

I will help her. Your strength is gone, and you're severely injured.

She looked down at the blood soaking her shirt. Revulsion made her shudder. She was rotting from the inside out, just as Velda had said Pater had done.

No, you are nothing like Pater. You have fought every

inch of the way for your honor and your integrity and for the welfare of others. Blood does not make up who you are, Destiny.

I can't bear to have vampire blood running through my veins. Destiny ducked her head, ashamed for thinking of her own discomfort as she heard Velda's soft weeping and the murmur of Inez trying to console her. Velda had lost everything, and Destiny still had Nicolae. Would always have him. *Please help her, Nicolae.*

Nicolae waved his hand toward the older woman, respect and admiration in his expression. "I thank you for saving my lifemate at such a cost to yourself. I give you the only gift I have, distance from the one who would have belonged to you." He bowed low, a courtly salute of honor. His spell wouldn't take away the terrible sorrow—Velda would grieve for her lifemate—but he dimmed the emotion enough to make it more bearable.

He gathered Destiny into his arms. *It is over. Even wounded, he was a powerful enemy. Seeing Velda face to face shook him. I hope there will be a semblance of peace for Velda with what I have wrought.*

"Put her to bed, Inez," Nicolae said aloud. "Velda, you will sleep and heal."

Nicolae carried Destiny out into the cool of the night. The breeze had taken the stench of the vampire and carried it out to sea. The air was clean and fresh with promise. Nicolae soared through the darkened sky, taking her back to the cave. Anger smoldered deep in the pit of his belly, mixed with fear and relief. "You took a terrible risk, Destiny." He buried his face in her hair.

"Was Gregori able to heal you completely? Is he certain?"

"He did, at great cost to his strength. He is anxious to get started on healing you."

She brushed her hand over his face, lingering along the seam of his lips, pressed tightly together in a frown. "He doesn't think he will be able to heal me, does he?" Her voice wobbled alarmingly.

"He will heal you. It will take time. Maybe more than one session, but he will do it." Nicolae tenderly stroked the hair from her face with gentle fingers as he settled into the darkened cavern. He waved his hand to light the waiting candles.

"Poor Velda. She recognized Pater as her true life-mate. What a terrible tragedy. A waste for them both. And for a moment, he recognized her. I saw it in his eyes. He felt something. With her speaking to him, looking at him, he felt something."

His fingers wiped the tears from her face. "She showed tremendous courage. He would have killed you." He brought her hands to the warmth of his mouth, kissing her knuckles lovingly. "When a Carpathian male turns, the tragedy of it is that there might be a woman waiting somewhere, or in some other time. Pater should have held on to his honor. Velda is an extraordinary woman. In the end, she did her best to free him."

"He would have killed her," Destiny said sadly.

"He would have had no choice. The undead cannot see themselves: their reflection in a mirror provides too much of the truth; the eyes of a lifemate reveal an unbearable reality."

Gregori and Savannah joined them. "Your friends are safe in their homes and have no memories of what transpired. The lifemate of the vampire will know, of course, and I did not remove the memories of the priest or MaryAnn Delaney. MaryAnn has psychic ability and should be persuaded to visit the Carpathian Mountains as the guest of our Prince. I hope that you will invite her when it is convenient."

She knew Gregori was concerned that there might be a Carpathian male who could be saved. Destiny clutched at Nicolae, unashamed that she did so. She was tired and shaky and feeling terribly vulnerable. The idea of her tainted blood was repulsive to her. "Can you get rid of the vampire's blood?"

"I am certain that I will be able to do so, but I ask that you donate blood first to allow us to examine it. It might be useful to us. The colonies seem to spawn the infestation. Who knows what can be done once we understand what is going on?"

"Feel free, take as much as you like," Destiny offered. "I'm tired and want to sleep." It was the only safe thing to do. The thought of those hideous creatures living inside her sickened her as nothing else could. She felt unclean, and nothing Nicolae or Gregori said would ever make a difference. "If you can't heal me, Gregori, don't let me live. I don't think I could bear it, knowing what's inside me."

"A Carpathian endures," Gregori said softly. "As your lifemate endured all those centuries of darkness. You will endure."

Destiny reached for Nicolae, framed his face with her hands. "You gave me hope and dreams and everything good I've ever known. Thank you for that."

Nicolae kissed her, his mouth so tender it brought tears to her eyes. They glittered on her lashes as he sent her to sleep.

Chapter Twenty

She woke to the knowledge that she was whole and clean and her blood was free of the vampire, but the scars remained in her heart and mind. She woke to find she was deeply in love and she was at peace. There was no pain on awakening. There was no agony, only a sense of hope and the looking forward to her life. She lay very still and let the sounds and scents of her world fill her with joy.

Destiny knew exactly where she was. Home. And home lay beside her, his body curved protectively around hers. Her bottom fit snugly into the cradle of his hips, and she could feel him, already awake, already aware, his body hard and aggressive, even as he lay so quietly. His hand cupped her breast possessively, yet he was still, savoring just waking up and holding her. Nicolae. Her everything.

He moved then. His mouth on her shoulder, his lips soft as he feathered kisses over her skin. *I thought you would never wake up.*

The voice of an angel. Her angel. Nicolae. Destiny smiled as the silk of his hair brushed her bare arm and fanned across her breast. *You should have called to me.* Deliberately she used their private telepathic ability. She loved the intimacy of speaking with him mind to mind. She loved the feel of his hands on her body. At his urging she turned onto her back. Above her head the stars spread across the cave ceiling, sparkling like gems.

She laughed softly. First roses and now stars. He knew she loved the open night sky and had provided her with a blanket of stars, even deep beneath the earth.

"I love the sound of your laughter." His hands moved over her body possessively, caressing every inch of her. His mouth followed, feathering kisses and teasing nips and lapping at her with a hot, erotic tongue.

His lovemaking was slow and thorough, wickedly designed to bring her to climax over and over. He made love to her as if they had all the time in the world. He took care to inspect every secret place that might bring her more pleasure.

Destiny returned the favor, losing herself in the beauty of his masculine body. Her hands and mouth wandered everywhere, telling him without words what he meant to her. When he entered her, she cried, so that he leaned forward to find out what tears of joy tasted like.

For the first time she wasn't afraid of exchanging blood and initiated the ritual, driving him into a heated frenzy of desire. They ended up exploding, imploding, flying so high and then free-falling until they could only lie for a long time together, hearts beating wildly, struggling for breath, sated and happy.

Destiny pushed a shaky hand through her hair. "You can do that anytime, Nicolae. You're very good at it."

He propped himself up on one elbow. "I am most grateful you think so."

"Don't go fishing for compliments, because you aren't going to get any. How long was I in the ground? I know time has passed. I don't sense the presence of any of the others close to us."

"Gregori wanted to start back to our homeland as soon as possible. He felt it important to give the Prince the news of vampires forming some sort of organization. He also thought the blood was an important find. No one has ever analyzed vampire blood. We all knew it was toxic, but no one imagined it created an environment to spawn a separate life-form. Of course, we still do not know for certain. The vampire that took you as a child might have somehow been infected by something else. Or the infection could have been a result of the poison injected into you. Gregori feels it is important to find out. In any case, we know for a fact it is completely different from what was found in Alexandria's body. Gregori contacted Aidan, who said there was no such damage. Gregori wants to find out the significance of the difference."

She ducked her head. The thought of the tainted blood still repulsed her. "I'm glad it's over. I hope they get rid of that blood; it sickens me to think of it inside me . . . inside you. I had no idea. I saw the lesions and felt the pain of it, but I never once suspected something living." She shuddered. "They reminded me of maggots."

"Most were microscopic." He didn't share with her the condition in which the healer had found her body, and it was significant to him that she didn't look at his memories. It had taken the healer two risings to ferret out every trace of the tenacious blood and reshape her organs and tissue. They had nearly lost her on two occasions.

It had been Gregori's tenacity and Nicolae's sheer will that had saved Destiny's life. Gregori had worked a miracle, and Nicolae was forever in his debt. Savannah had lent her considerable strength and blood along with Vikirnoff and Nicolae. Carpathian soil had been packed around Destiny and she had been left in the ground for nearly a week in the hope of renewing her strength and vitality. In the end, both Nicolae and Gregori were in awe of Destiny's ability to live and function with her body in such condition.

"Where's Vikirnoff?" Destiny didn't want to ever think about vampire blood again. She felt as if she'd been granted a miracle. It was enough for her.

"We thought it best that he start his search for the poor woman being hunted by the vampire organization. It took years for me to find you. We are hoping he finds her before the undead does."

Destiny sighed. "I wish him the best of luck. Are you worried for him?" She tunneled her fingers in his luxurious hair. "He's well able to care for himself."

Nicolae turned his head to kiss her fingers. "I know he is. Often when a hunter close to turning is given a job such as this, it allows him more breathing space. He does not have to kill, and the call of the darkness is not so loud." He stood up, donning clothes. "Come on, the sky is beautiful tonight."

Destiny followed him, grateful for the ability to fly. It was her favorite pastime. She laughed aloud. It *had* been her favorite pastime.

Nicolae caught her thought, and there in the air, as they burst from the cave, he pulled her to him and kissed her until the world spun out of control and they were forced to break apart. The wind blew in their faces and scattered the stars as they made their way to the neighborhood Destiny loved so much.

They stood together in front of the church. Destiny gazed at the building for a long while. It had been a refuge to her; now it was an old friend. "I love this place, Nicolae. And the people. I know you would like to go back to your homeland, and I'll go with you . . . I will . . . but this will always be my favorite place to live. And the people here will always be in my heart."

"We do not have to live in my homeland, Destiny. In truth, it has been many centuries since I have walked in my mountains. A visit will be enough for me. Perhaps, when you are ready, we can go for a short vacation."

Her face lit up. "Then you would be willing to make this place our main residence?" She had dreaded leaving the people who had become so dear to her.

"I find myself very fond of this neighborhood, and in particular, a certain chamber filled with various pools. We will have to find a suitable house and establish a home so we can blend in."

"That would be perfect, Nicolae. And I will go to the Carpathian Mountains with you. Gregori and Savannah were wonderful and very accepting of me. I can hardly be a coward and refuse to visit the Prince. We owe them both so much."

"No one would ever call you a coward, Destiny," he said decisively.

She stretched, raising her arms toward the moon and sparkling stars. "I think we should visit Velda. And it would be good to know how the doctor's death affected our friends after all the problems he caused them." She liked the term "friends." She had never thought to have any, and she cherished each of them.

With her dark hair blowing in the wind, enfolding her body like a living cape of silk, he thought she looked like a mysterious, ethereal witch worshiping nature. She turned her head to look at him, and at once he was drowning in her blue-green eyes.

"I worship you," she said softly. "I shouldn't and I don't want you to let it go to your head, but for this one moment in time, I do."

A slow smile curved his sculpted lips. "I do not think there is much of a chance of anything going to my head." Nicolae held out his hand to her.

Destiny shook her head. "I was so absolutely certain the culprit had to be a vampire. For so long I had it in my head that what I had become was a monster and humans were good unless something evil such as drugs took hold."

His hand curled around the nape of her neck, his fingers beginning a slow massage. "Monsters come in all shapes and sizes and species. Not all Carpathians turn into vampires. They are just people attempting to survive. As all humans are simply people struggling to live the best life they can. You were robbed of your childhood, Destiny, but you are a survivor, and you managed to carve out a life for yourself."

She leaned into him. "You were always there for me, Nicolae. I always had you." She turned up her face, blatantly inviting his kiss.

He bent his dark head to hers and took possession of her mouth. The earth beneath their feet shifted. His arms wrapped her up, strong and tight, and drew her against the hard length of him.

"I'm afraid you can't do that sort of thing here," Father Mulligan pointed out as he came out of the church and regarded them with a twinkling eye.

"Don't you ever go to bed?" Destiny asked him as Nicolae reluctantly broke their kiss. "Isn't there a priest curfew or something?"

Father Mulligan's eyebrow nearly shot up into his scalp. "My dear child. A priest is like an angel without wings, one who may be called upon at any time of the day or night."

Destiny burst out laughing. Nicolae felt his heart turn over. There was no sound as beautiful as her laughter. "You are terrible, Father. Would you like to come to Velda's house with us? We'd like to make certain she's all right."

"Of course I'll come. I've been visiting daily. Velda took to her bed, and no one seems to know how to help her."

"Maybe I'll be able to help," Destiny said.

They followed him in silence down the block to turn onto Velda's street. "You look much happier, my dear," Father Mulligan said. "It's good to see."

Destiny slipped her hand into Nicolae's. It wasn't all that long ago she had come to the church, ashamed of what she was, thinking herself a monster, and the priest had left the doors unlocked for her. "It's good to feel happy." And at peace. She would never be rid of the trauma she had suffered, but she could accept those memories as a small price to pay. She had a life. She had a home and friends. And she had Nicolae.

Inez opened the door to them with a small, falsely

cheery smile. "Velda is still not receiving visitors," she greeted. "Come into the kitchen and sit down. I'll see if I can get her to come out of her room."

"Let me go in," Destiny said. "I think I can help her."

Inez hesitated, then nodded, leading the way through the small but neat house. Velda was sitting in an armchair, staring out the window with blank, empty eyes. She didn't look up when Destiny entered and closed the door behind her.

"Velda. Please look at me." Destiny knelt in front of the chair, took the weathered hand in hers. "You are not alone. You will never be alone. You have Inez and Nicolae. And you have me. I can barely remember my mother. My childhood was hell. Most of it was violent and frightening. I have no social skills. No trust. I don't know how to express my feelings to anybody. You accepted me and gave me hope when I couldn't accept myself. Don't go away from me so soon. I need you here with me." She stated the facts sincerely. "I do, Velda. I need you."

Velda blinked back tears and pulled her gaze from the empty future stretching before her. She looked at Destiny's face. "Child, you're such a wonder to me. I look at your aura and it is light and beauty. You have no need of a burned-out, empty old woman. Your life is all ahead of you, and mine is behind me."

"You're a woman of courage and compassion and most of all, wisdom. I have a great need of you, and so does this community. Please, Velda. Allow Nicolae to help you separate more. It won't take away the pain, but it will lessen it so that you can bear it. Stay with me now when I need you so much."

Velda studied her face for a long time before sighing

softly. She patted Destiny's cheek. "Take me to this miracle worker, dear. If I am to survive, he will have to work some kind of magic. I feel empty and lost."

Nicolae? Are you listening? Help her now, while she consents. She knows it is manipulation but she can't bear the pain.

There was a small silence. *It is done. She will remember, but the pain will be even less. Her love for you is great enough to sustain her.*

Destiny felt her love for Nicolae so strongly, she couldn't contain it. It spilled from her mind and into his so that, sitting in the kitchen, he was shaken by the force of it. He wanted her, wanted to be alone with her. Wanted time with her.

He held out his hand to her when she entered the room with Velda, standing as he did so out of respect for the older woman. He bent to kiss Velda's cheek. "It is wonderful to see you, Velda. I hope you are better?"

She nodded, managing a smile. "Thank you. I appreciate your help."

Father Mulligan had risen too. "I did call MaryAnn," he told Destiny, indicating that her friend had arrived. "Nicolae said you wouldn't mind."

MaryAnn hugged Velda and Destiny. "He said it was a town meeting."

They sat around the table and talked long into the night. Nicolae and Destiny listened quietly to the story of the doctor's unexpected confession and suicide. Blythe was already home with Harry, although she was very withdrawn and refused counseling. MaryAnn was hoping eventually she would come to her. Helena and John Paul were once more together and seemed happy. Tim and Martin said little about what had happened, but Father Mulligan was keeping a close eye on them.

Destiny looked around the small, comfortable kitchen, listened to the murmur of voices, inhaled the scent of tea as Inez served the others. She studied Nicolae's dark, sensual features. *Have I told you lately that I love you? Because I do, very, very much.*

Her heart was so full, she was afraid it might burst. She had never dared to dream she would have a home and a family. She had never conceived of having friends. Life might never be perfect, but she had Nicolae, and he would always understand those terrible moments when the memories crept out from behind the doors in her mind. He would be there to hold her and help her. *You are my everything, Nicolae.*

Have I told you that, although I enjoy all these wonderful people, I have had enough of visiting and I want to go home and spend the rest of the night making love to you?

A very good idea. Destiny was in complete agreement. *There's this one thing that you do . . .*

They stood as if by mutual consent, hands linked, murmuring a hasty goodbye, and hurried out. When Father Mulligan looked out the window, all he saw was a comet streaking low across the night sky.